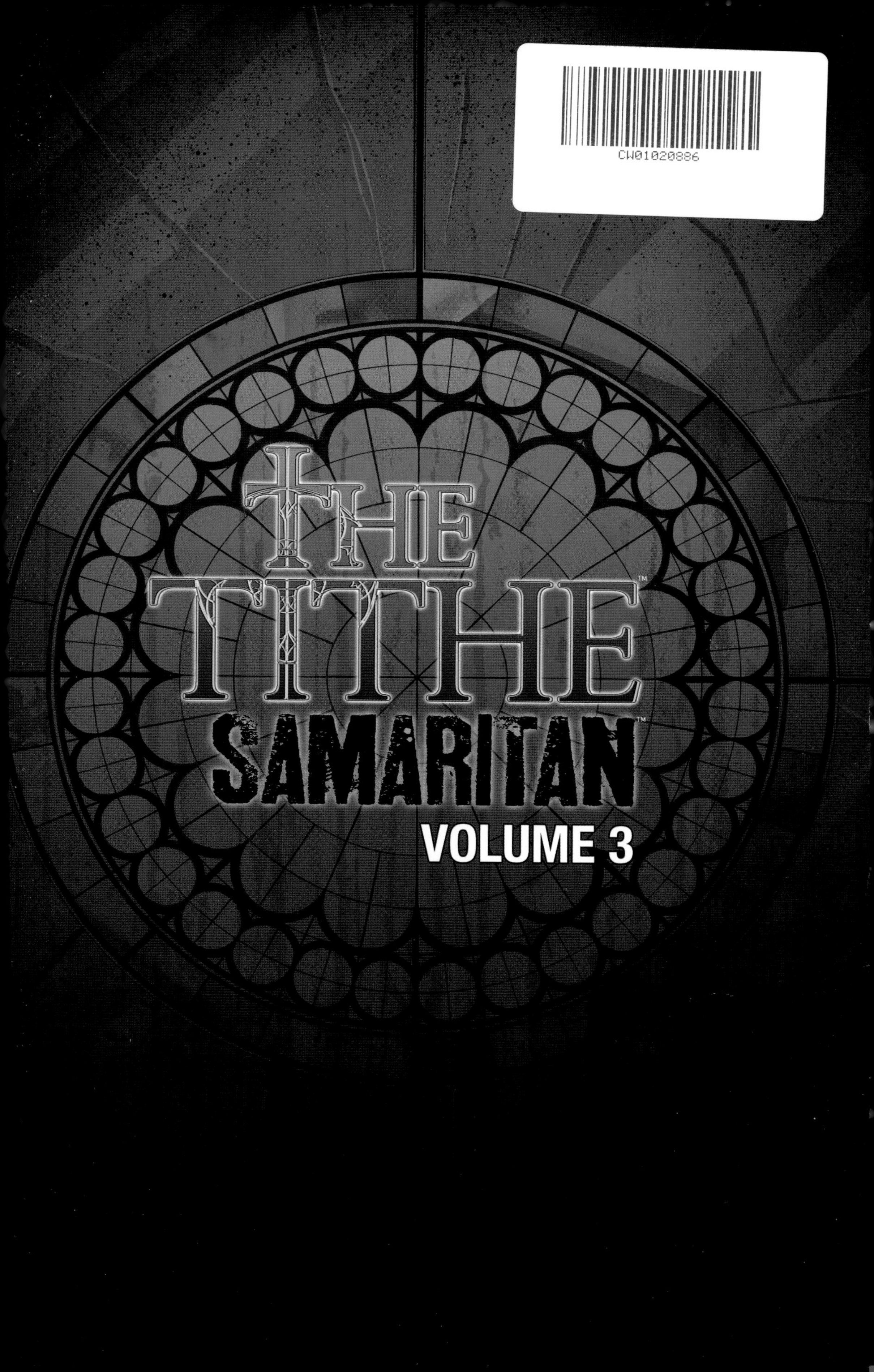
THE TITHE™
SAMARITAN™
VOLUME 3

SAMARITAN
VERITAS

CREATED BY
Matt Hawkins & Rahsan Ekedal

WRITER
Matt Hawkins

ARTIST & COLOR
Atilio Rojo

LETTERER
Troy Peteri

EDITORS
Elena Salcedo & Bryan Hill

PRODUCTION
Carey Hall

COVER ART
Atilio Rojo

To find the comic
shop nearest you, call:
1-888-COMICBOOK

Want more info? Check out:
www.topcow.com
for news & exclusive Top Cow merchandise!

For Top Cow Productions, Inc.
For Top Cow Productions, Inc.
Marc Silvestri - CEO
Matt Hawkins - President & COO
Elena Salcedo - Vice President of Operations
Henry Barajas - Director of Operations
Vincent Valentine - Production Manager
Dylan Gray - Marketing Director

IMAGE COMICS, INC.
Robert Kirkman—Chief Operating Officer
Erik Larsen—Chief Financial Officer
Todd McFarlane—President
Marc Silvestri—Chief Executive Officer
Jim Valentine—Vice President

Eric Stephenson—Publisher
Corey Murphy—Director of Sales
Jeff Boison—Director of Publishing Planning & Book Trade Sales
Chris Ross—Director of Digital Sales
Jeff Stang—Director of Specialty Sales
Kat Salazar—Director of PR & Marketing
Branwyn Bigglestone—Controller
Kali Dugan—Senior Accounting Manager
Sue Korpela—Accounting & HR Manager
Drew Gill—Art Director
Heather Doornink—Production Director
Leigh Thomas—Print Manager
Tricia Ramos—Traffic Manager
Briah Skelly—Publicist
Aly Hoffman—Events & Conventions Coordinator
Sasha Head—Sales & Marketing Production Designer
David Brothers—Branding Manager
Melissa Gifford—Content Manager
Drew Fitzgerald—Publicity Assistant
Vincent Kukua—Production Artist
Erika Schnatz—Production Artist
Ryan Brewer—Production Artist
Shanna Matuszak—Production Artist
Carey Hall—Production Artist
Esther Kim—Direct Market Sales Representative
Emilio Bautista—Digital Sales Representative
Leanna Caunter—Accounting Analyst
Chloe Ramos-Peterson—Library Market Sales Representative
Maria Eizik—Administrative Assistant
IMAGECOMICS.COM

THE TITHE: SAMARITAN, VOLUME 3. First printing. September 2017. Published by Image Comics, Inc. Office of publication: 2701 NW Vaughn St., Suite 780, Portland, OR 97210. Copyright © 2017 Top Cow Productions, Inc. All rights reserved. Contains material originally published in single magazine form as SAMARITAN VERITAS #1–3 and EDEN'S FALL #1–3. "THE TITHE," "SAMARITAN VERITAS," "EDEN'S FALL," its logos, and the likenesses of all characters herein are trademarks of Matt Hawkins, Rahsan Ekedal & Top Cow Productions, Inc., unless otherwise noted. "Image" and the Image Comics logos are registered trademarks of Image Comics, Inc. No part of this publication may be reproduced or transmitted, in any form or by any means (except for short excerpts for journalistic or review purposes), without the express written permission of Matt Hawkins, Rahsan Ekedal & Top Cow Productions, Inc., or Image Comics, Inc. All names, characters, events, and locales in this publication are entirely fictional. Any resemblance to actual persons (living or dead), events, or places, without satiric intent, is coincidental. Printed in the USA. For information regarding the CPSIA on this printed material call: 203-595-3636 and provide reference #RICH–762722. ISBN: 978-1-5343-0379-9.

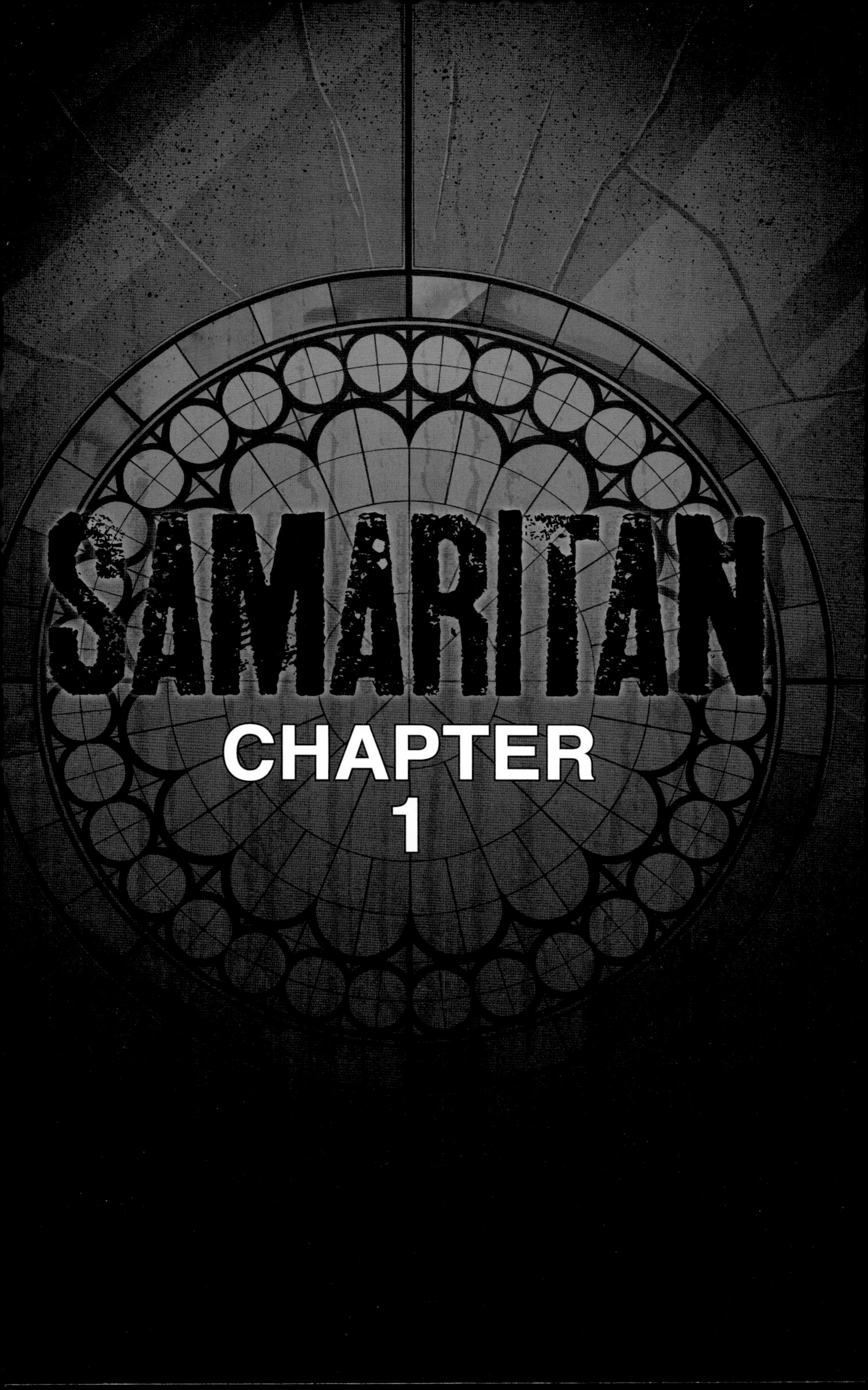

SAMARITAN

CHAPTER 1

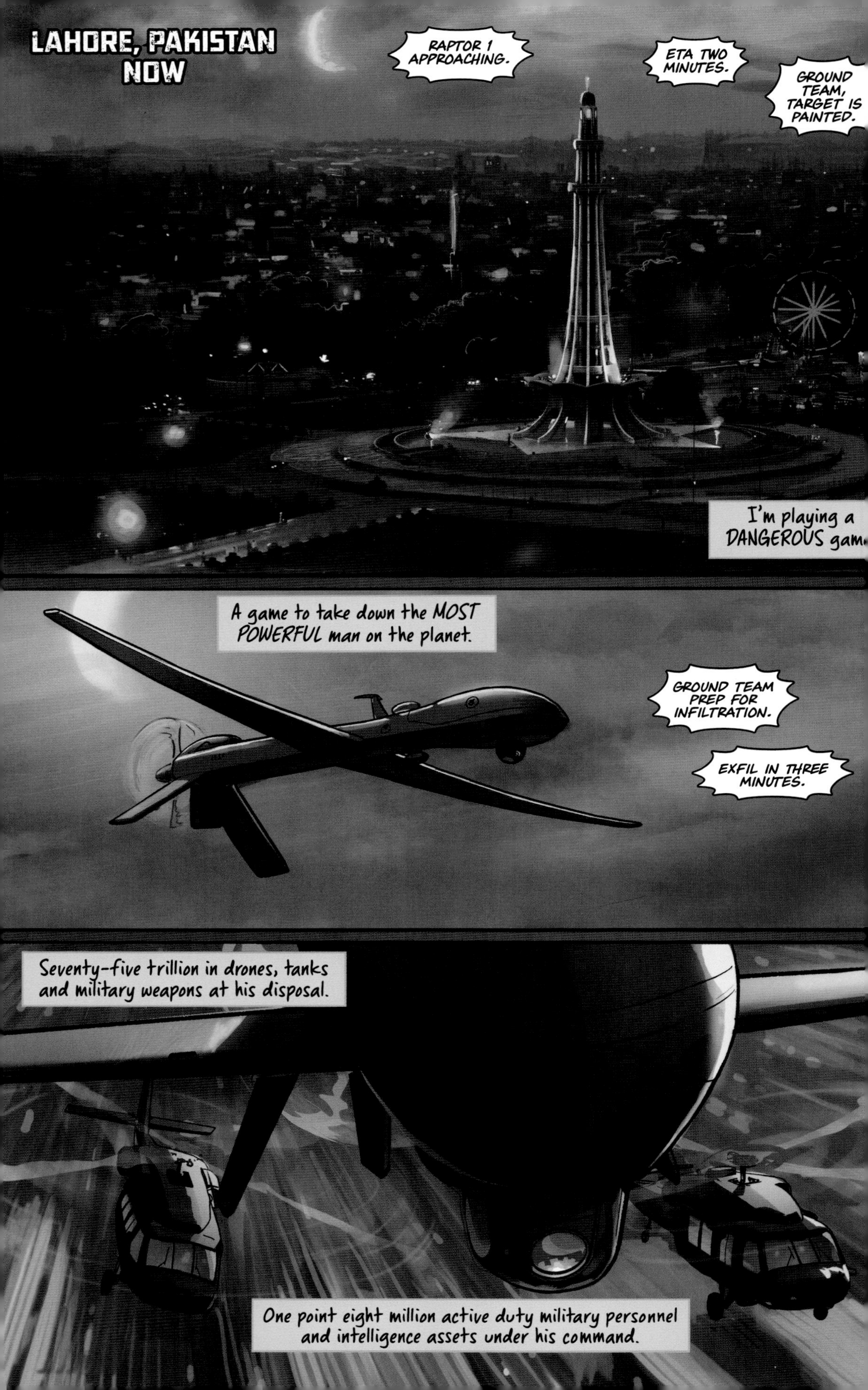

LAHORE, PAKISTAN NOW
RAPTOR 1 APPROACHING.
ETA TWO MINUTES.
GROUND TEAM, TARGET IS PAINTED.
I'm playing a DANGEROUS gam
A game to take down the MOST POWERFUL man on the planet.
GROUND TEAM PREP FOR INFILTRATION.
EXFIL IN THREE MINUTES.
Seventy-five trillion in drones, tanks and military weapons at his disposal.
One point eight million active duty military personnel and intelligence assets under his command.

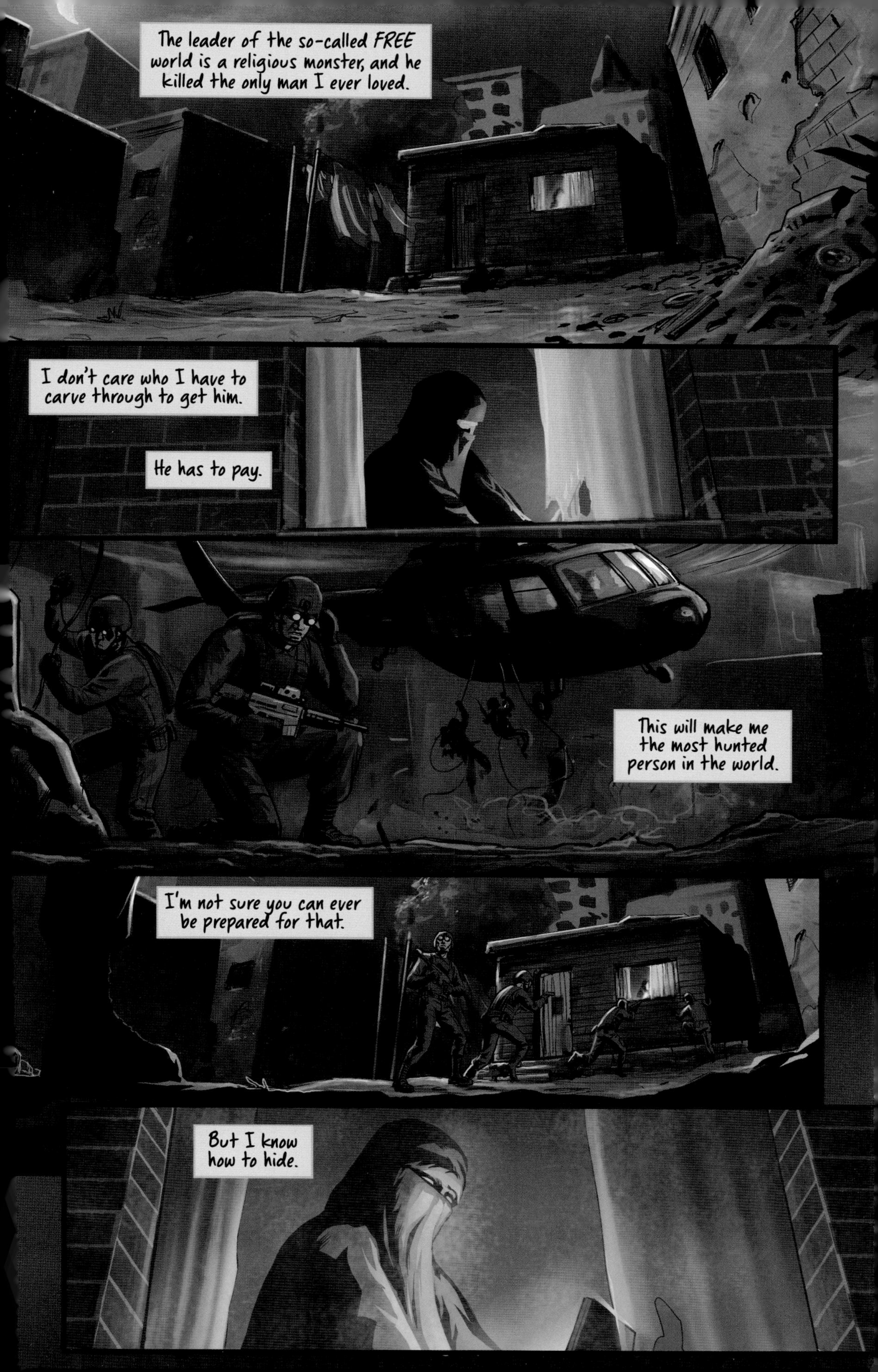
The leader of the so-called FREE world is a religious monster, and he killed the only man I ever loved.
I don't care who I have to carve through to get him.
He has to pay.
This will make me the most hunted person in the world.
I'm not sure you can ever be prepared for that.
But I know how to hide.

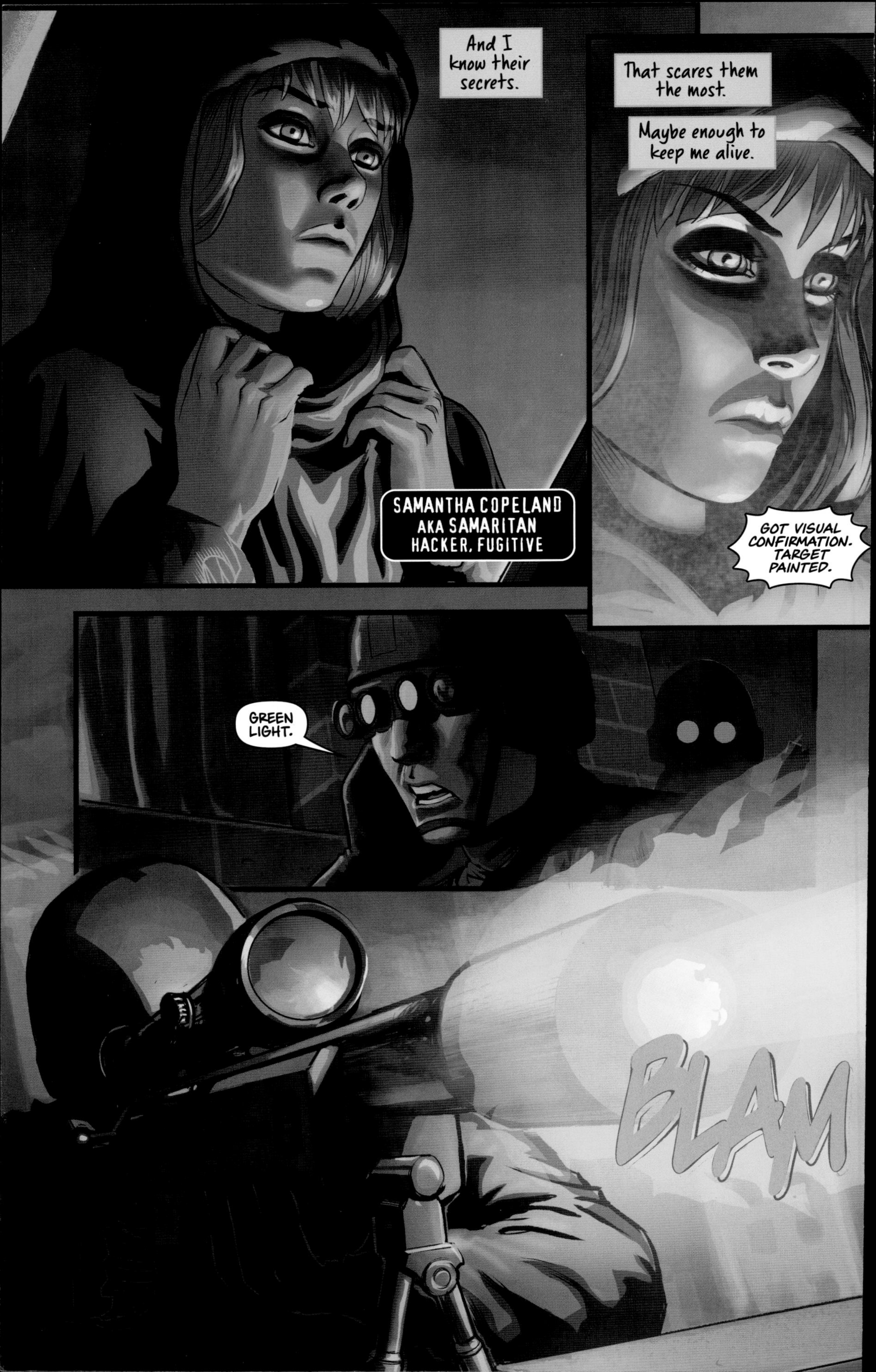
And I know their secrets.
SAMANTHA COPELAND AKA SAMARITAN HACKER, FUGITIVE
That scares them the most.
Maybe enough to keep me alive.
GOT VISUAL CONFIRMATION. TARGET PAINTED.
GREEN LIGHT.
BLAM

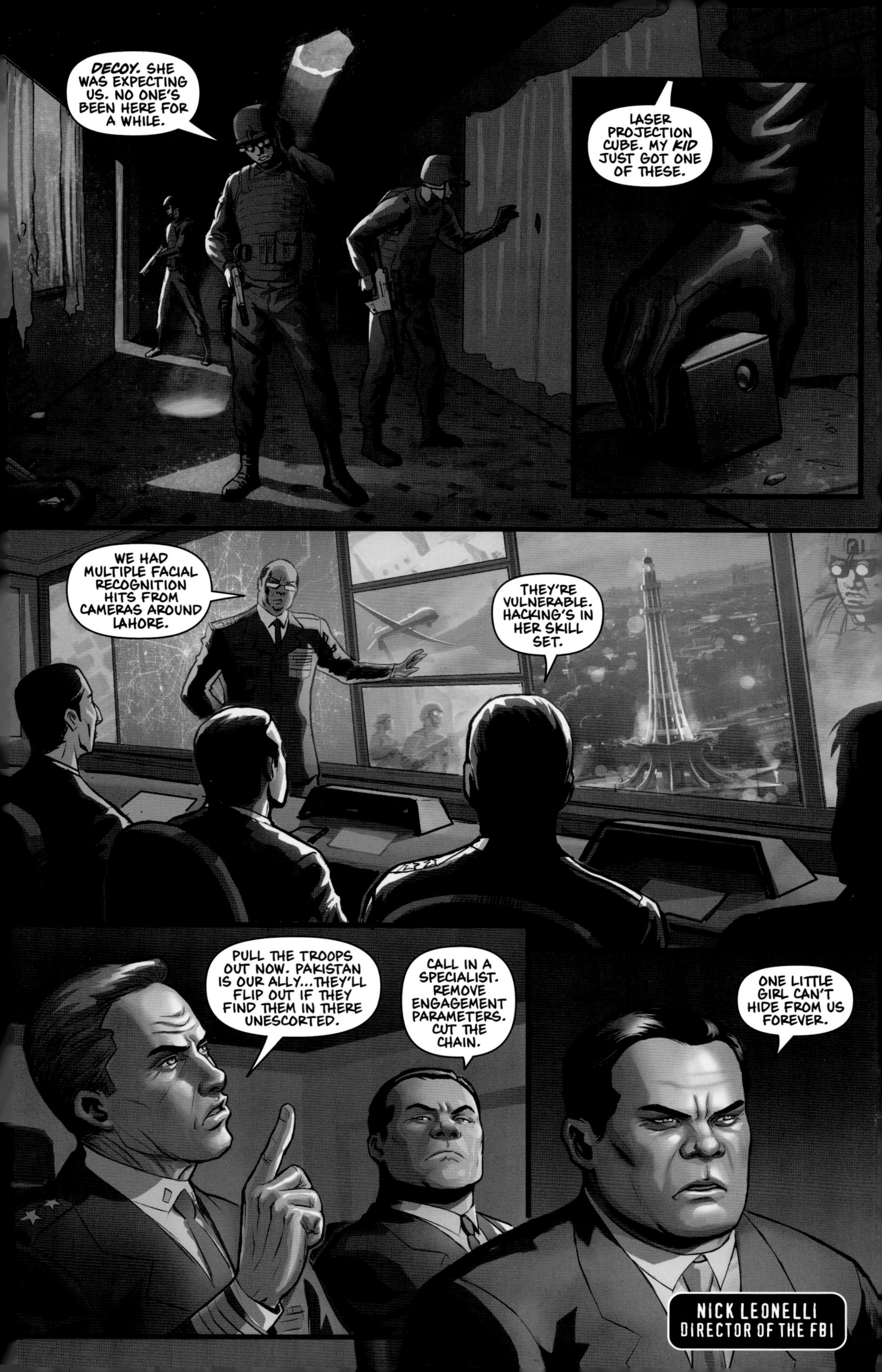
DECOY. SHE WAS EXPECTING US. NO ONE'S BEEN HERE FOR A WHILE.
LASER PROJECTION CUBE. MY KID JUST GOT ONE OF THESE.
WE HAD MULTIPLE FACIAL RECOGNITION HITS FROM CAMERAS AROUND LAHORE.
THEY'RE VULNERABLE. HACKING'S IN HER SKILL SET.
PULL THE TROOPS OUT NOW. PAKISTAN IS OUR ALLY...THEY'LL FLIP OUT IF THEY FIND THEM IN THERE UNESCORTED.
CALL IN A SPECIALIST. REMOVE ENGAGEMENT PARAMETERS. CUT THE CHAIN.
ONE LITTLE GIRL CAN'T HIDE FROM US FOREVER.
NICK LEONELLI
DIRECTOR OF THE FBI

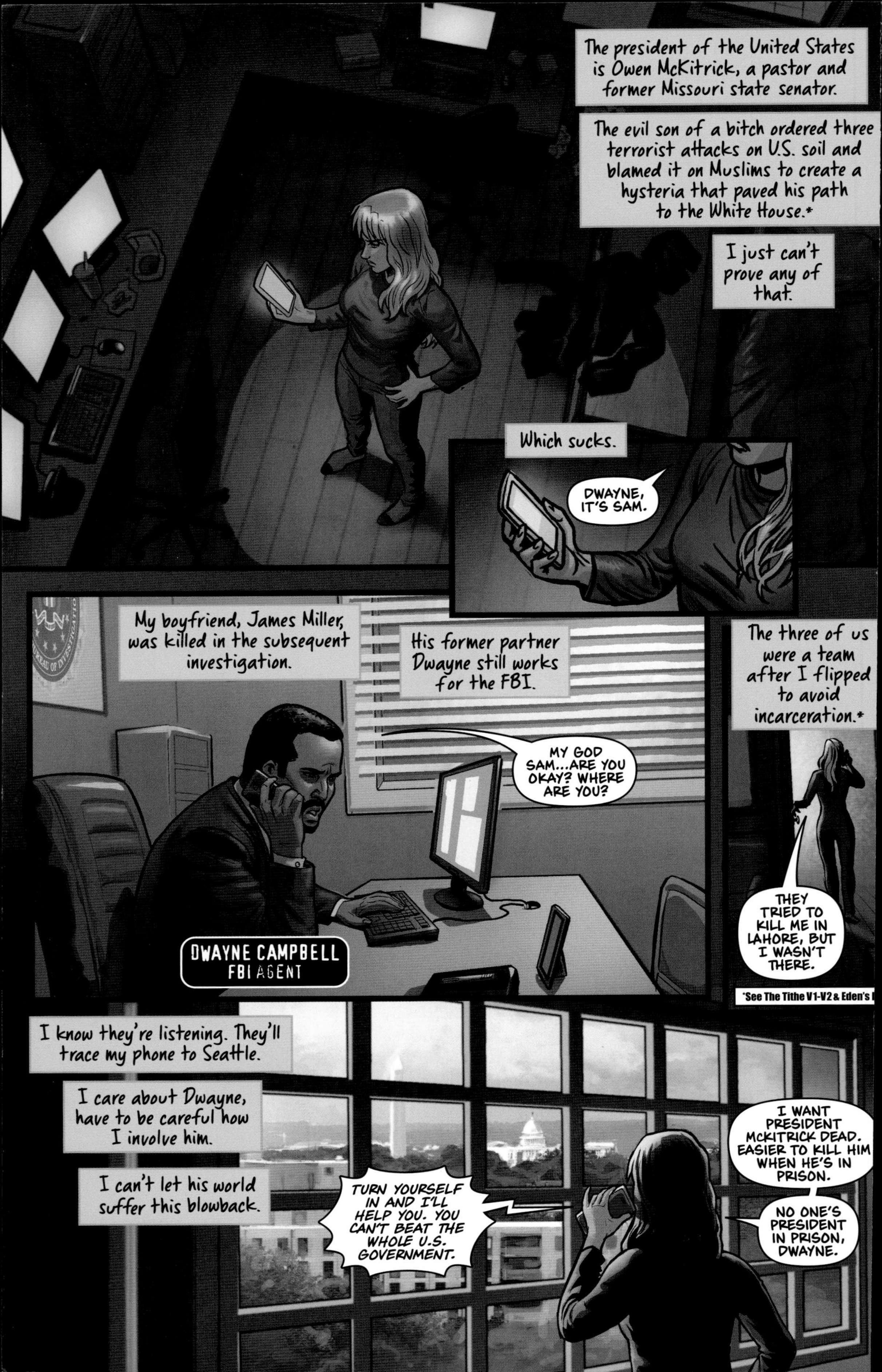
The president of the United States is Owen McKitrick, a pastor and former Missouri state senator.
The evil son of a bitch ordered three terrorist attacks on U.S. soil and blamed it on Muslims to create a hysteria that paved his path to the White House.*
I just can't prove any of that.
Which sucks.
DWAYNE, IT'S SAM.
My boyfriend, James Miller, was killed in the subsequent investigation.
His former partner Dwayne still works for the FBI.
MY GOD SAM...ARE YOU OKAY? WHERE ARE YOU?
DWAYNE CAMPBELL
FBI AGENT
The three of us were a team after I flipped to avoid incarceration.*
THEY TRIED TO KILL ME IN LAHORE, BUT I WASN'T THERE.
*See The Tithe V1-V2 & Eden's
I know they're listening. They'll trace my phone to Seattle.
I care about Dwayne, have to be careful how I involve him.
I can't let his world suffer this blowback.
TURN YOURSELF IN AND I'LL HELP YOU. YOU CAN'T BEAT THE WHOLE U.S. GOVERNMENT.
I WANT PRESIDENT McKITRICK DEAD. EASIER TO KILL HIM WHEN HE'S IN PRISON.
NO ONE'S PRESIDENT IN PRISON, DWAYNE.

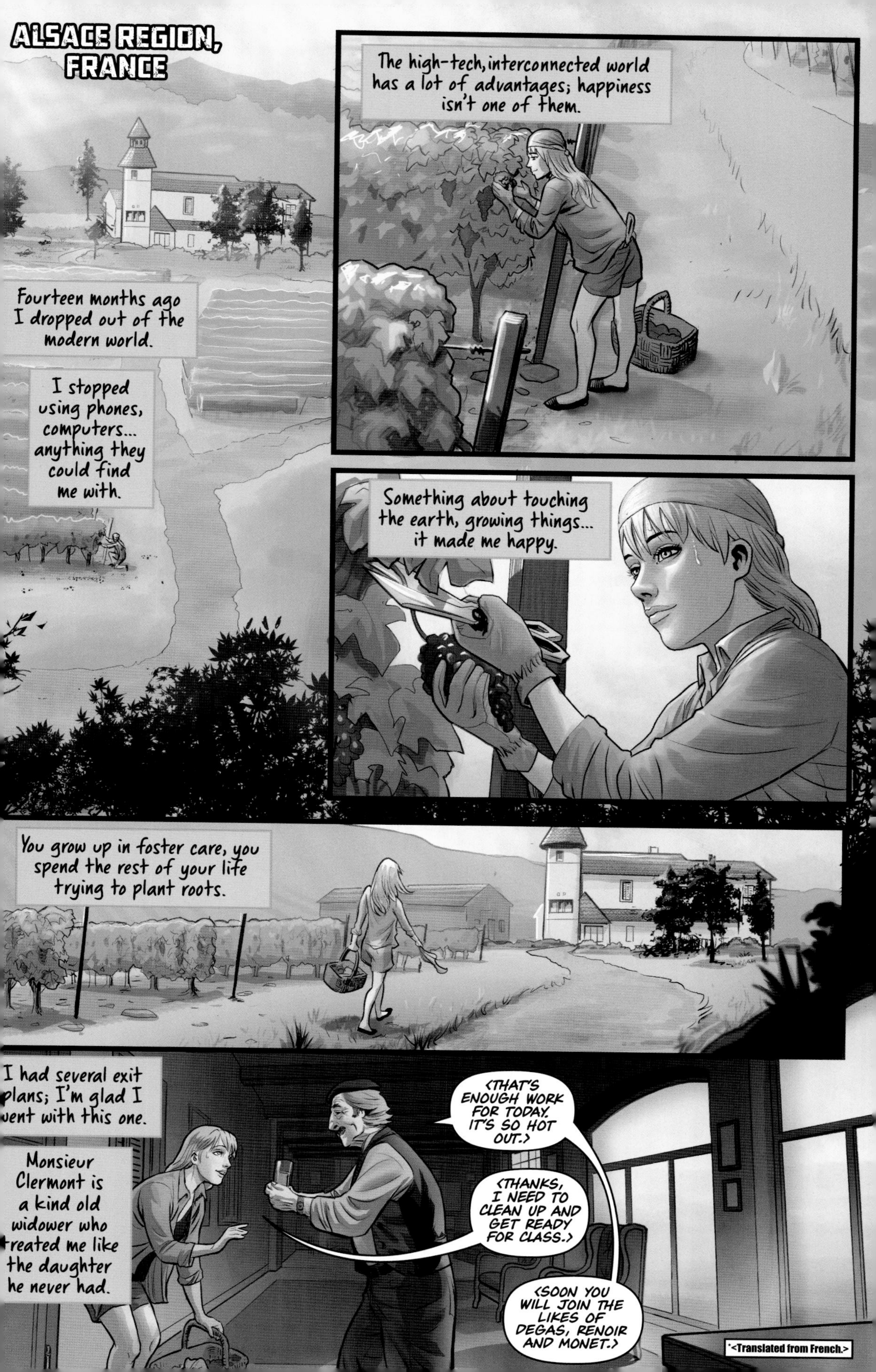
ALSACE REGION, FRANCE
Fourteen months ago I dropped out of the modern world.
I stopped using phones, computers... anything they could find me with.
The high-tech, interconnected world has a lot of advantages; happiness isn't one of them.
Something about touching the earth, growing things... it made me happy.
You grow up in foster care, you spend the rest of your life trying to plant roots.
I had several exit plans; I'm glad I went with this one.
Monsieur Clermont is a kind old widower who treated me like the daughter he never had.
<THAT'S ENOUGH WORK FOR TODAY. IT'S SO HOT OUT.>
<THANKS, I NEED TO CLEAN UP AND GET READY FOR CLASS.>
<SOON YOU WILL JOIN THE LIKES OF DEGAS, RENOIR AND MONET.>
*<Translated from French.>

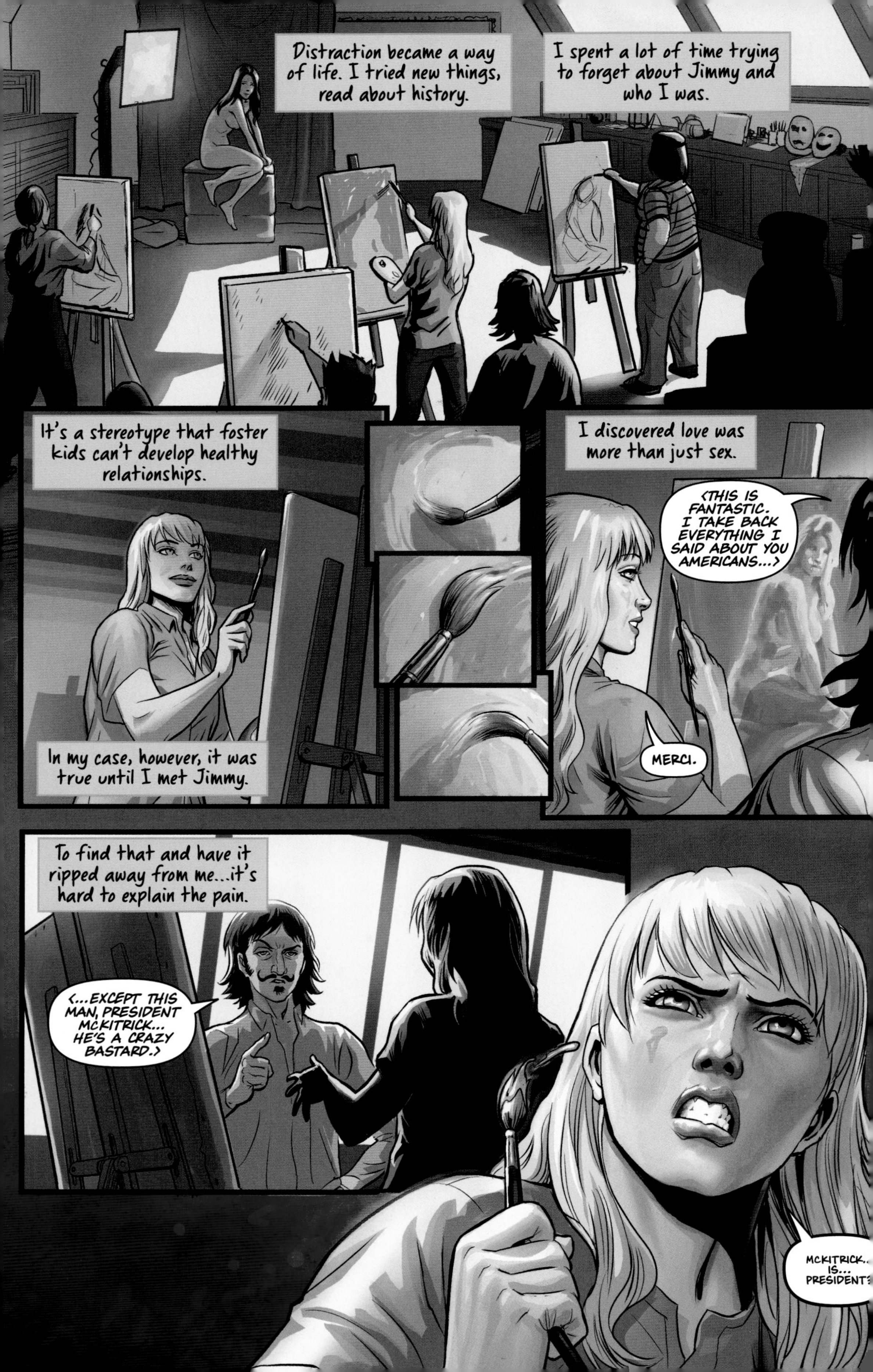
Distraction became a way of life. I tried new things, read about history.
I spent a lot of time trying to forget about Jimmy and who I was.
It's a stereotype that foster kids can't develop healthy relationships.
In my case, however, it was true until I met Jimmy.
I discovered love was more than just sex.
<THIS IS FANTASTIC. I TAKE BACK EVERYTHING I SAID ABOUT YOU AMERICANS...>
MERCI.
To find that and have it ripped away from me...it's hard to explain the pain.
<...EXCEPT THIS MAN, PRESIDENT MCKITRICK... HE'S A CRAZY BASTARD.>
MCKITRICK... IS... PRESIDENT?

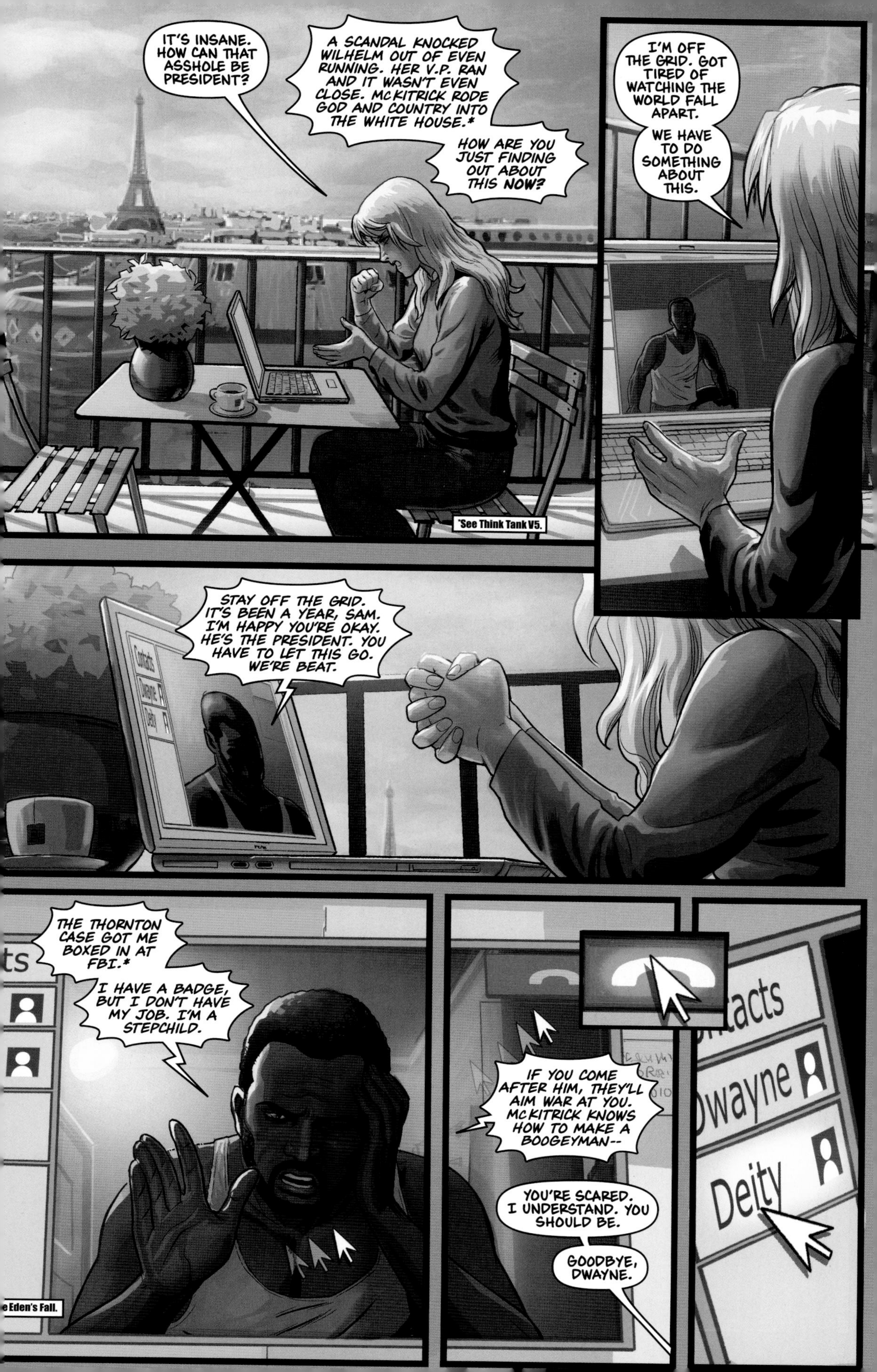
IT'S INSANE. HOW CAN THAT ASSHOLE BE PRESIDENT?
A SCANDAL KNOCKED WILHELM OUT OF EVEN RUNNING. HER V.P. RAN AND IT WASN'T EVEN CLOSE. MCKITRICK RODE GOD AND COUNTRY INTO THE WHITE HOUSE.*
HOW ARE YOU JUST FINDING OUT ABOUT THIS NOW?
*See Think Tank V5.
I'M OFF THE GRID. GOT TIRED OF WATCHING THE WORLD FALL APART.
WE HAVE TO DO SOMETHING ABOUT THIS.
STAY OFF THE GRID. IT'S BEEN A YEAR, SAM. I'M HAPPY YOU'RE OKAY. HE'S THE PRESIDENT. YOU HAVE TO LET THIS GO. WE'RE BEAT.
Contacts
Dwayne
Deity
THE THORNTON CASE GOT ME BOXED IN AT FBI.*
I HAVE A BADGE, BUT I DON'T HAVE MY JOB. I'M A STEPCHILD.
e Eden's Fall.
IF YOU COME AFTER HIM, THEY'LL AIM WAR AT YOU. MCKITRICK KNOWS HOW TO MAKE A BOOGEYMAN--
YOU'RE SCARED. I UNDERSTAND. YOU SHOULD BE.
GOODBYE, DWAYNE.
Dwayne
Deity

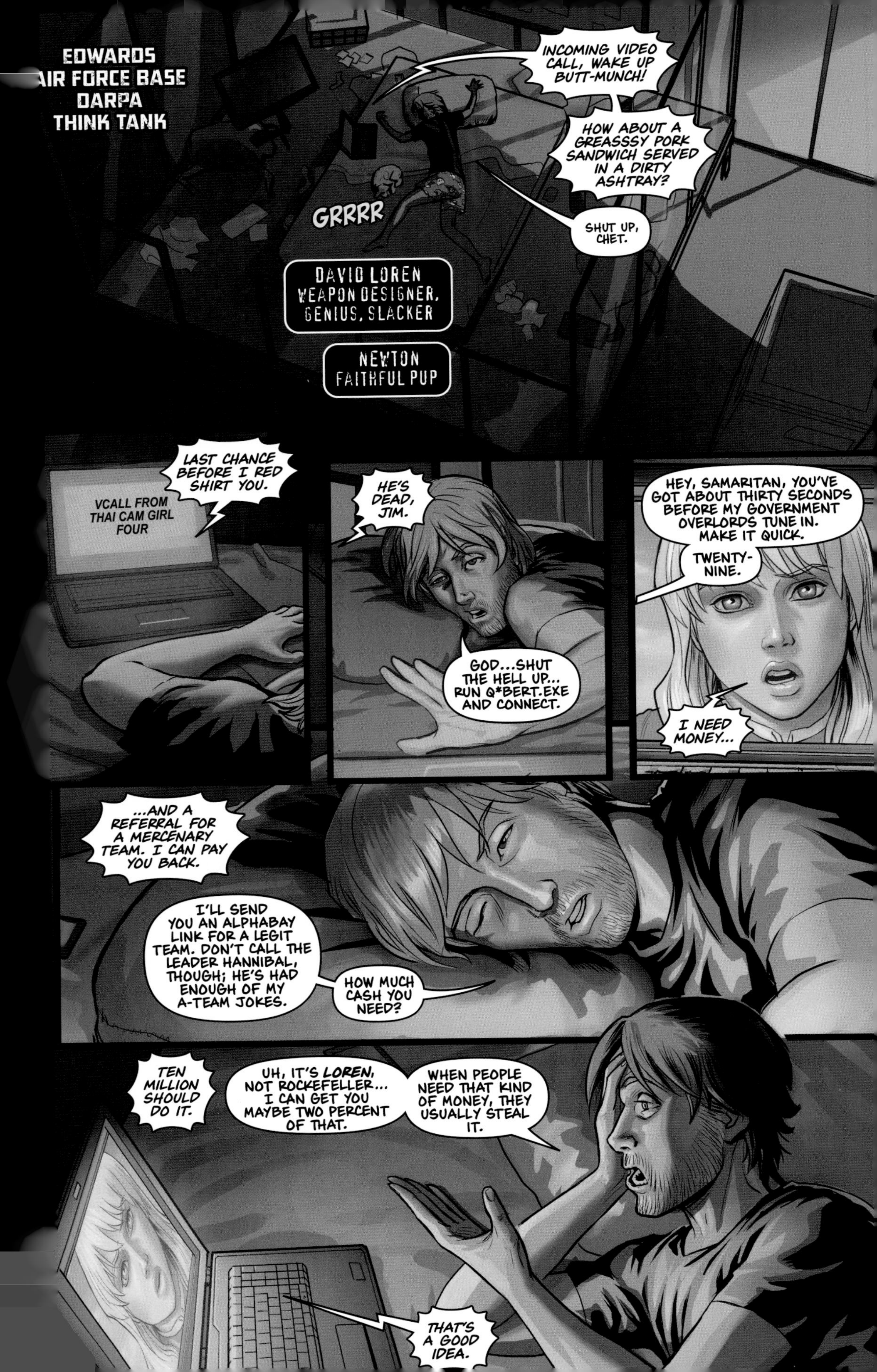
EDWARDS AIR FORCE BASE DARPA THINK TANK
INCOMING VIDEO CALL, WAKE UP BUTT-MUNCH!
HOW ABOUT A GREASSSY PORK SANDWICH SERVED IN A DIRTY ASHTRAY?
GRRRR
SHUT UP, CHET.
DAVID LOREN WEAPON DESIGNER, GENIUS, SLACKER
NEWTON FAITHFUL PUP
LAST CHANCE BEFORE I RED SHIRT YOU.
VCALL FROM THAI CAM GIRL FOUR
HE'S DEAD, JIM.
GOD...SHUT THE HELL UP... RUN Q*BERT.EXE AND CONNECT.
HEY, SAMARITAN, YOU'VE GOT ABOUT THIRTY SECONDS BEFORE MY GOVERNMENT OVERLORDS TUNE IN. MAKE IT QUICK.
TWENTY-NINE.
I NEED MONEY...
...AND A REFERRAL FOR A MERCENARY TEAM. I CAN PAY YOU BACK.
I'LL SEND YOU AN ALPHABAY LINK FOR A LEGIT TEAM. DON'T CALL THE LEADER HANNIBAL, THOUGH; HE'S HAD ENOUGH OF MY A-TEAM JOKES.
HOW MUCH CASH YOU NEED?
TEN MILLION SHOULD DO IT.
UH, IT'S LOREN, NOT ROCKEFELLER... I CAN GET YOU MAYBE TWO PERCENT OF THAT.
WHEN PEOPLE NEED THAT KIND OF MONEY, THEY USUALLY STEAL IT.
THAT'S A GOOD IDEA.

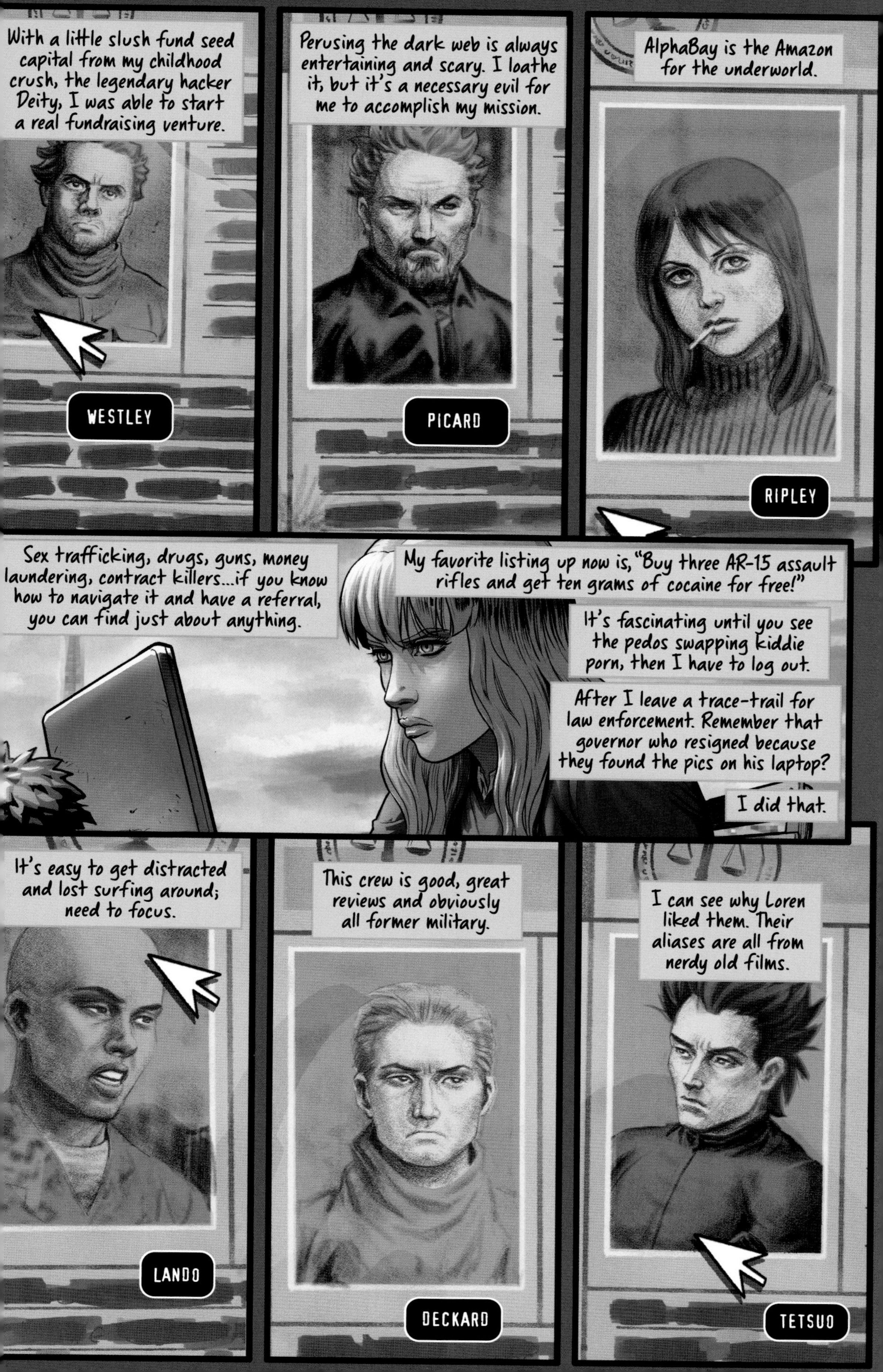
With a little slush fund seed capital from my childhood crush, the legendary hacker Deity, I was able to start a real fundraising venture.
WESTLEY
Perusing the dark web is always entertaining and scary. I loathe it, but it's a necessary evil for me to accomplish my mission.
PICARD
AlphaBay is the Amazon for the underworld.
RIPLEY
Sex trafficking, drugs, guns, money laundering, contract killers...if you know how to navigate it and have a referral, you can find just about anything.
My favorite listing up now is, "Buy three AR-15 assault rifles and get ten grams of cocaine for free!"
It's fascinating until you see the pedos swapping kiddie porn, then I have to log out.
After I leave a trace-trail for law enforcement. Remember that governor who resigned because they found the pics on his laptop?
I did that.
It's easy to get distracted and lost surfing around; need to focus.
LANDO
This crew is good, great reviews and obviously all former military.
DECKARD
I can see why Loren liked them. Their aliases are all from nerdy old films.
TETSUO

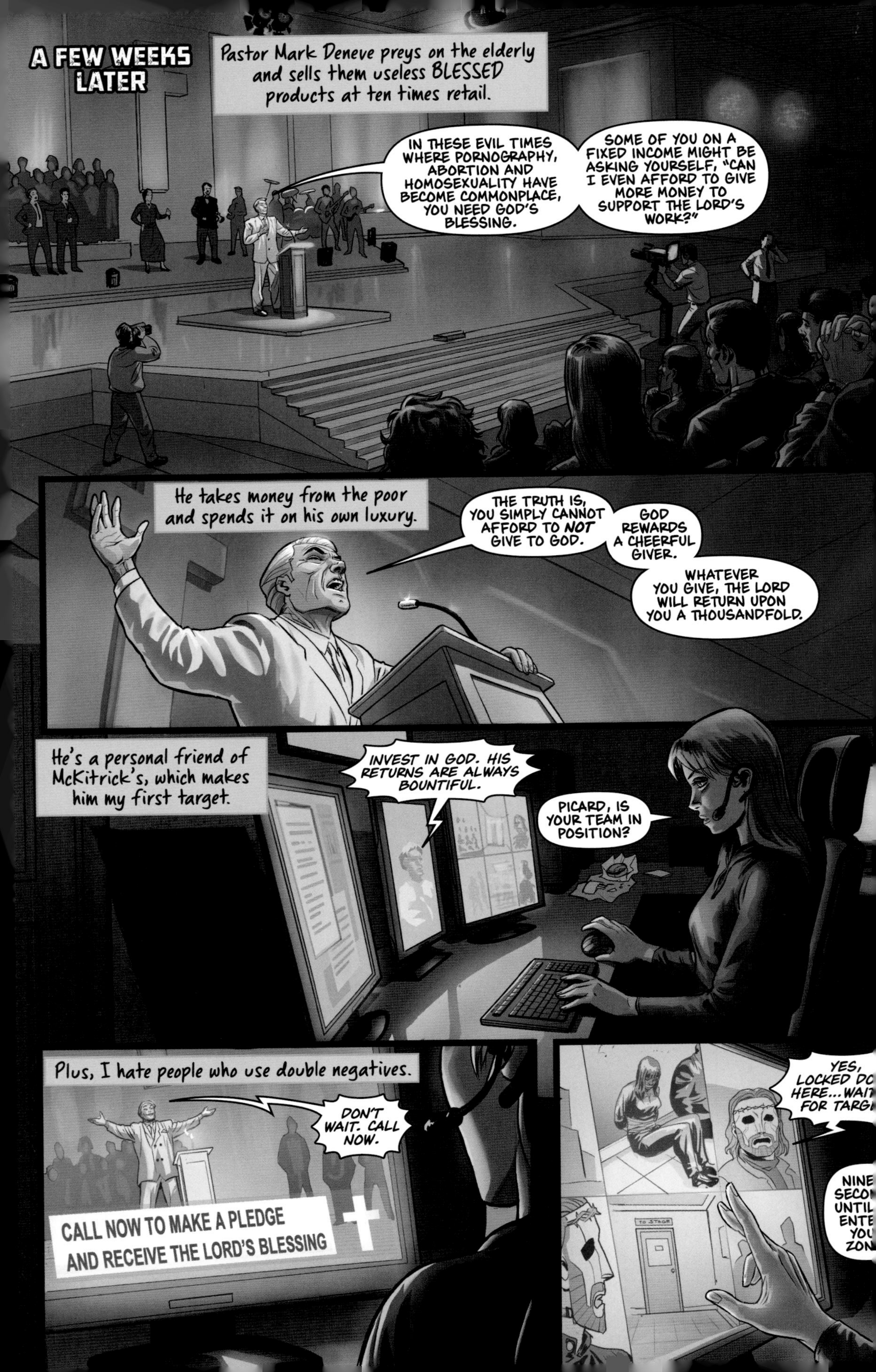
A FEW WEEKS LATER
Pastor Mark Deneve preys on the elderly and sells them useless BLESSED products at ten times retail.
IN THESE EVIL TIMES WHERE PORNOGRAPHY, ABORTION AND HOMOSEXUALITY HAVE BECOME COMMONPLACE, YOU NEED GOD'S BLESSING.
SOME OF YOU ON A FIXED INCOME MIGHT BE ASKING YOURSELF, "CAN I EVEN AFFORD TO GIVE MORE MONEY TO SUPPORT THE LORD'S WORK?"
He takes money from the poor and spends it on his own luxury.
THE TRUTH IS, YOU SIMPLY CANNOT AFFORD TO NOT GIVE TO GOD.
GOD REWARDS A CHEERFUL GIVER.
WHATEVER YOU GIVE, THE LORD WILL RETURN UPON YOU A THOUSANDFOLD.
He's a personal friend of McKitrick's, which makes him my first target.
INVEST IN GOD. HIS RETURNS ARE ALWAYS BOUNTIFUL.
PICARD, IS YOUR TEAM IN POSITION?
Plus, I hate people who use double negatives.
DON'T WAIT. CALL NOW.
CALL NOW TO MAKE A PLEDGE AND RECEIVE THE LORD'S BLESSING
TO STAGE

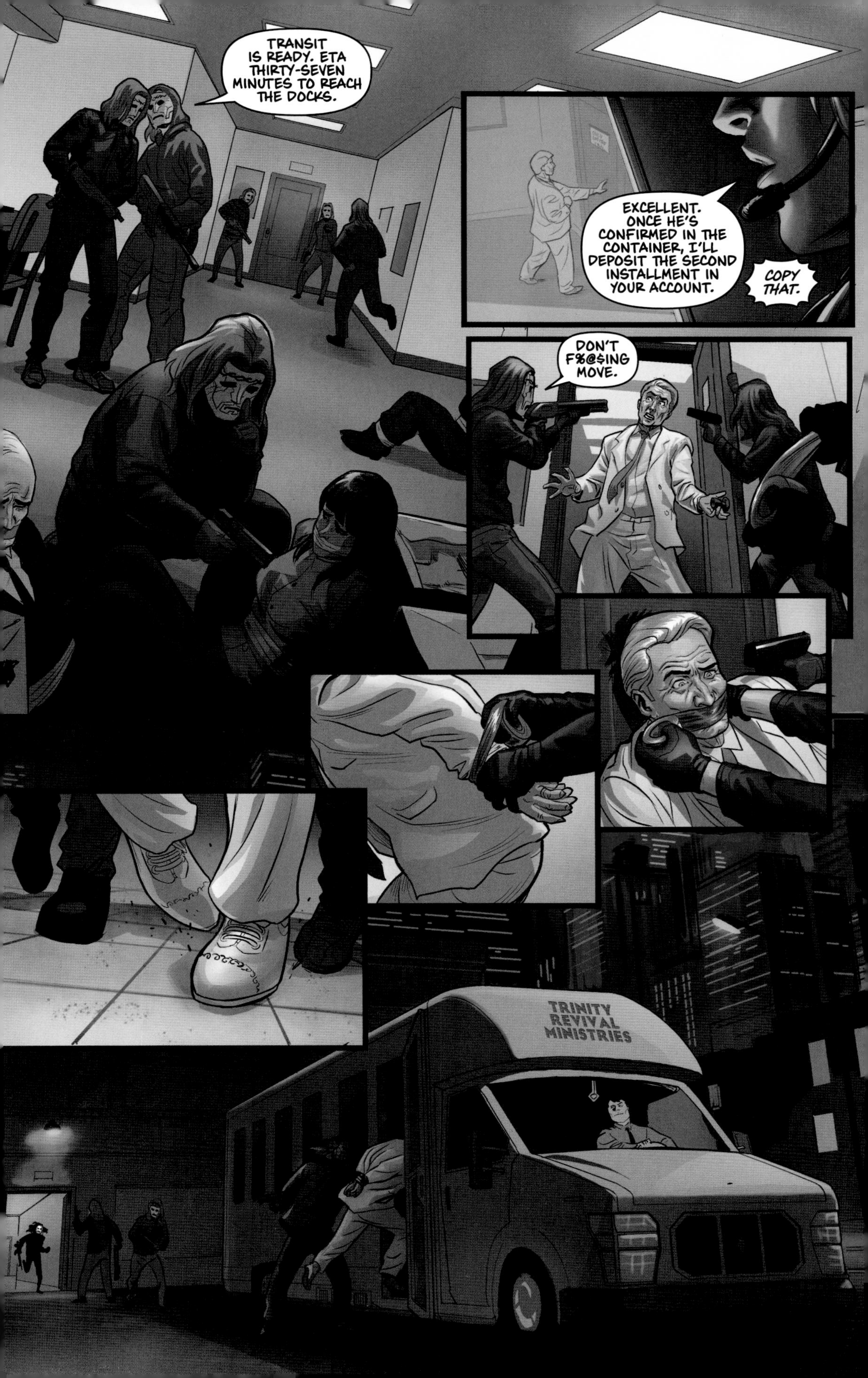
TRANSIT IS READY. ETA THIRTY-SEVEN MINUTES TO REACH THE DOCKS.
EXCELLENT. ONCE HE'S CONFIRMED IN THE CONTAINER, I'LL DEPOSIT THE SECOND INSTALLMENT IN YOUR ACCOUNT.
COPY THAT.
DON'T F%@$ING MOVE.
TRINITY REVIVAL MINISTRIES

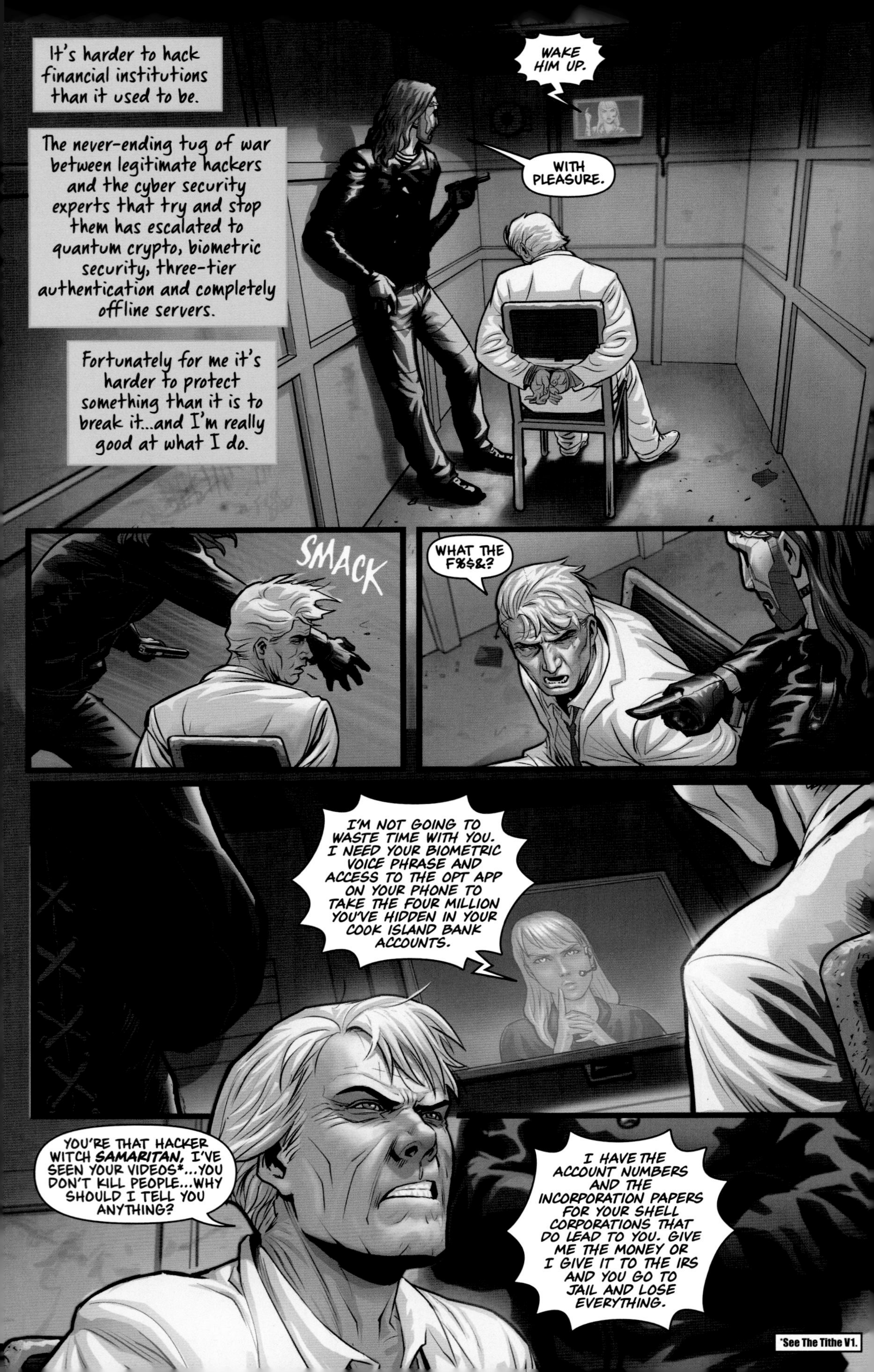
It's harder to hack financial institutions than it used to be.
The never-ending tug of war between legitimate hackers and the cyber security experts that try and stop them has escalated to quantum crypto, biometric security, three-tier authentication and completely offline servers.
Fortunately for me it's harder to protect something than it is to break it...and I'm really good at what I do.
WAKE HIM UP.
WITH PLEASURE.
SMACK
WHAT THE F%$&?
I'M NOT GOING TO WASTE TIME WITH YOU. I NEED YOUR BIOMETRIC VOICE PHRASE AND ACCESS TO THE OPT APP ON YOUR PHONE TO TAKE THE FOUR MILLION YOU'VE HIDDEN IN YOUR COOK ISLAND BANK ACCOUNTS.
YOU'RE THAT HACKER WITCH SAMARITAN, I'VE SEEN YOUR VIDEOS*...YOU DON'T KILL PEOPLE...WHY SHOULD I TELL YOU ANYTHING?
I HAVE THE ACCOUNT NUMBERS AND THE INCORPORATION PAPERS FOR YOUR SHELL CORPORATIONS THAT DO LEAD TO YOU. GIVE ME THE MONEY OR I GIVE IT TO THE IRS AND YOU GO TO JAIL AND LOSE EVERYTHING.
*See The Tithe V1.

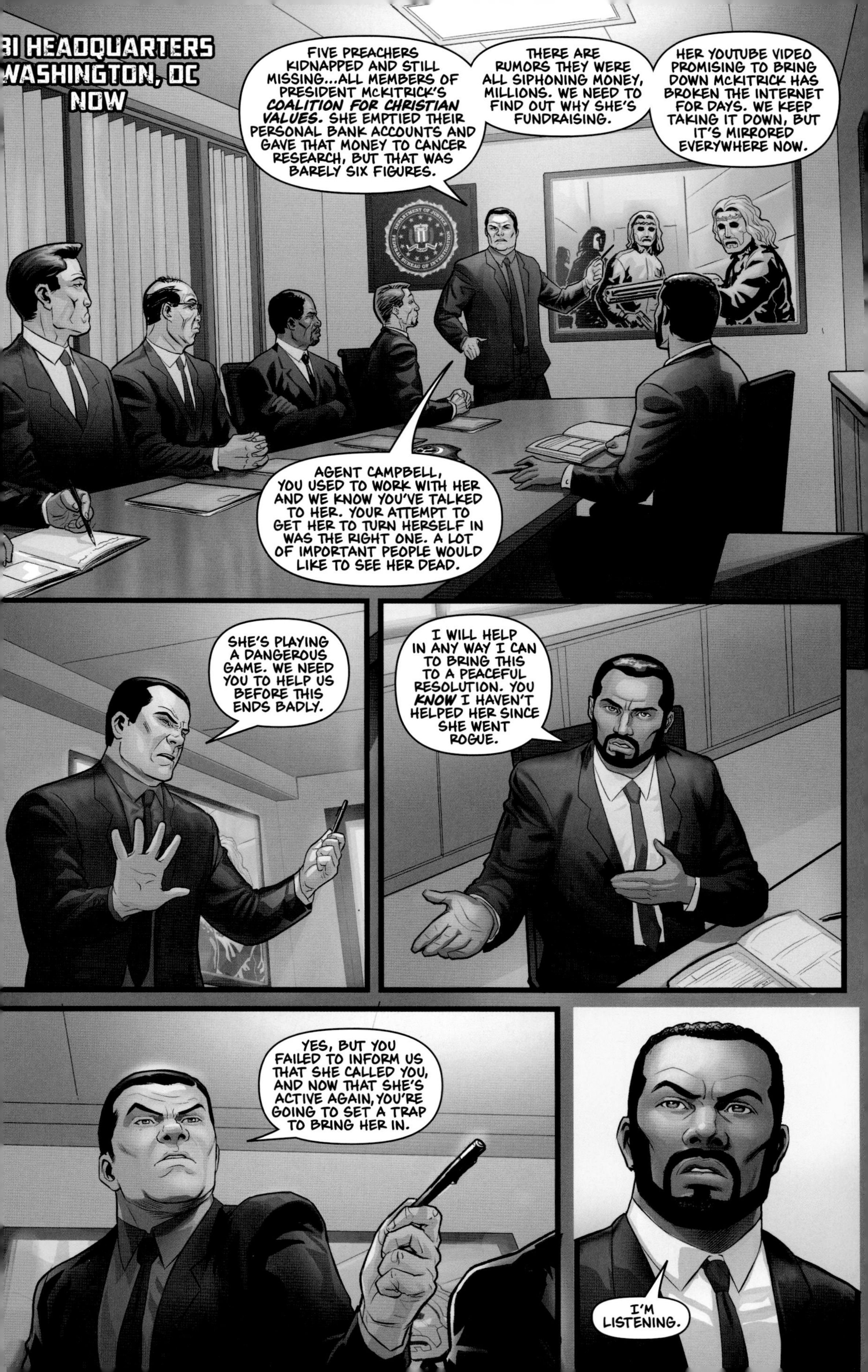

BI HEADQUARTERS WASHINGTON, DC NOW
FIVE PREACHERS KIDNAPPED AND STILL MISSING...ALL MEMBERS OF PRESIDENT McKITRICK'S COALITION FOR CHRISTIAN VALUES. SHE EMPTIED THEIR PERSONAL BANK ACCOUNTS AND GAVE THAT MONEY TO CANCER RESEARCH, BUT THAT WAS BARELY SIX FIGURES.
THERE ARE RUMORS THEY WERE ALL SIPHONING MONEY, MILLIONS. WE NEED TO FIND OUT WHY SHE'S FUNDRAISING.
HER YOUTUBE VIDEO PROMISING TO BRING DOWN McKITRICK HAS BROKEN THE INTERNET FOR DAYS. WE KEEP TAKING IT DOWN, BUT IT'S MIRRORED EVERYWHERE NOW.
AGENT CAMPBELL, YOU USED TO WORK WITH HER AND WE KNOW YOU'VE TALKED TO HER. YOUR ATTEMPT TO GET HER TO TURN HERSELF IN WAS THE RIGHT ONE. A LOT OF IMPORTANT PEOPLE WOULD LIKE TO SEE HER DEAD.
SHE'S PLAYING A DANGEROUS GAME. WE NEED YOU TO HELP US BEFORE THIS ENDS BADLY.
I WILL HELP IN ANY WAY I CAN TO BRING THIS TO A PEACEFUL RESOLUTION. YOU KNOW I HAVEN'T HELPED HER SINCE SHE WENT ROGUE.
YES, BUT YOU FAILED TO INFORM US THAT SHE CALLED YOU, AND NOW THAT SHE'S ACTIVE AGAIN, YOU'RE GOING TO SET A TRAP TO BRING HER IN.
I'M LISTENING.

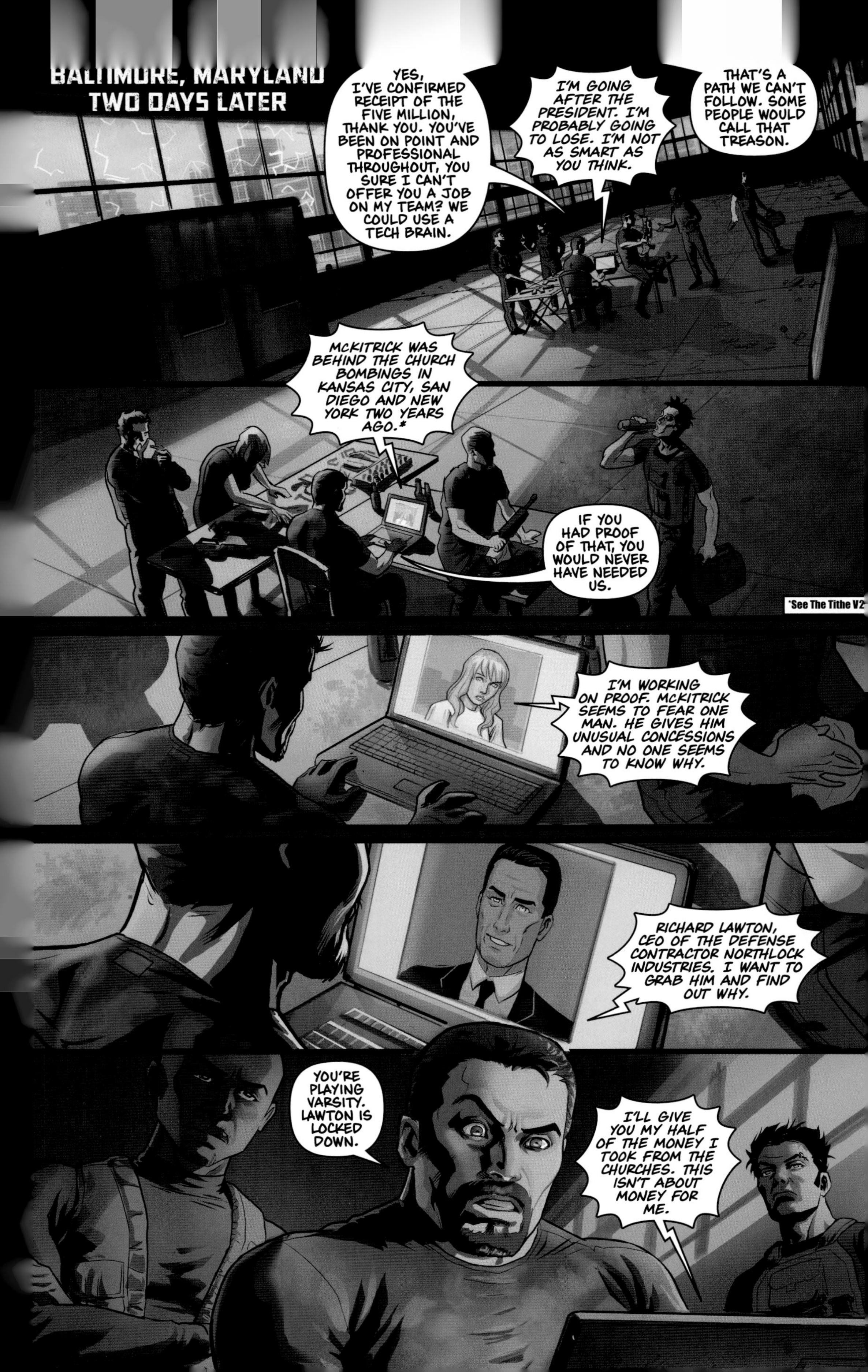
BALTIMORE, MARYLAND
TWO DAYS LATER
YES, I'VE CONFIRMED RECEIPT OF THE FIVE MILLION, THANK YOU. YOU'VE BEEN ON POINT AND PROFESSIONAL THROUGHOUT, YOU SURE I CAN'T OFFER YOU A JOB ON MY TEAM? WE COULD USE A TECH BRAIN.
I'M GOING AFTER THE PRESIDENT. I'M PROBABLY GOING TO LOSE. I'M NOT AS SMART AS YOU THINK.
THAT'S A PATH WE CAN'T FOLLOW. SOME PEOPLE WOULD CALL THAT TREASON.
McKITRICK WAS BEHIND THE CHURCH BOMBINGS IN KANSAS CITY, SAN DIEGO AND NEW YORK TWO YEARS AGO.*
IF YOU HAD PROOF OF THAT, YOU WOULD NEVER HAVE NEEDED US.
*See The Tithe V2
I'M WORKING ON PROOF. McKITRICK SEEMS TO FEAR ONE MAN. HE GIVES HIM UNUSUAL CONCESSIONS AND NO ONE SEEMS TO KNOW WHY.
RICHARD LAWTON, CEO OF THE DEFENSE CONTRACTOR NORTHLOCK INDUSTRIES. I WANT TO GRAB HIM AND FIND OUT WHY.
YOU'RE PLAYING VARSITY. LAWTON IS LOCKED DOWN.
I'LL GIVE YOU MY HALF OF THE MONEY I TOOK FROM THE CHURCHES. THIS ISN'T ABOUT MONEY FOR ME.

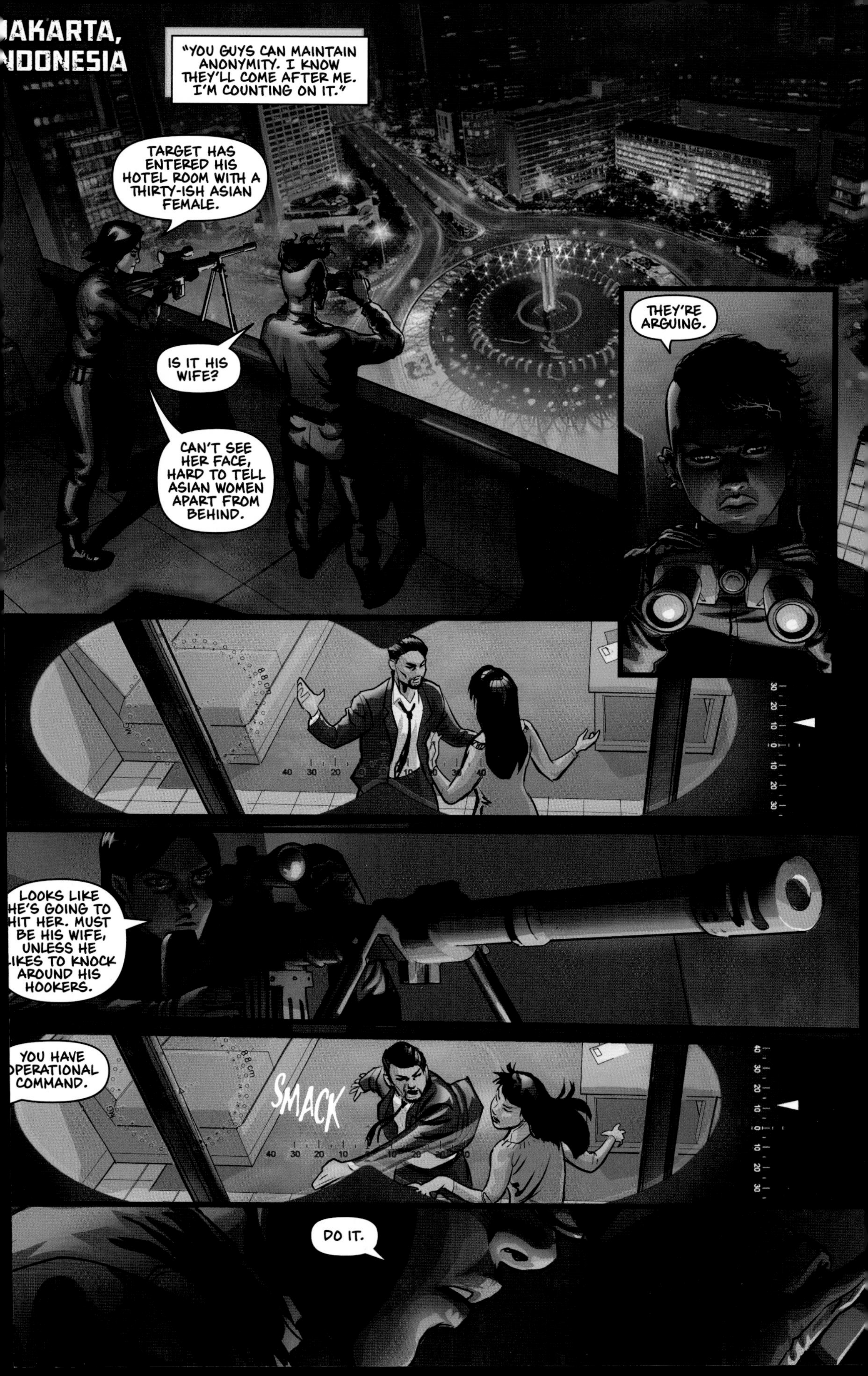
JAKARTA, INDONESIA
"YOU GUYS CAN MAINTAIN ANONYMITY. I KNOW THEY'LL COME AFTER ME. I'M COUNTING ON IT."
TARGET HAS ENTERED HIS HOTEL ROOM WITH A THIRTY-ISH ASIAN FEMALE.
IS IT HIS WIFE?
CAN'T SEE HER FACE, HARD TO TELL ASIAN WOMEN APART FROM BEHIND.
THEY'RE ARGUING.
LOOKS LIKE HE'S GOING TO HIT HER. MUST BE HIS WIFE, UNLESS HE LIKES TO KNOCK AROUND HIS HOOKERS.
YOU HAVE OPERATIONAL COMMAND.
SMACK
DO IT.

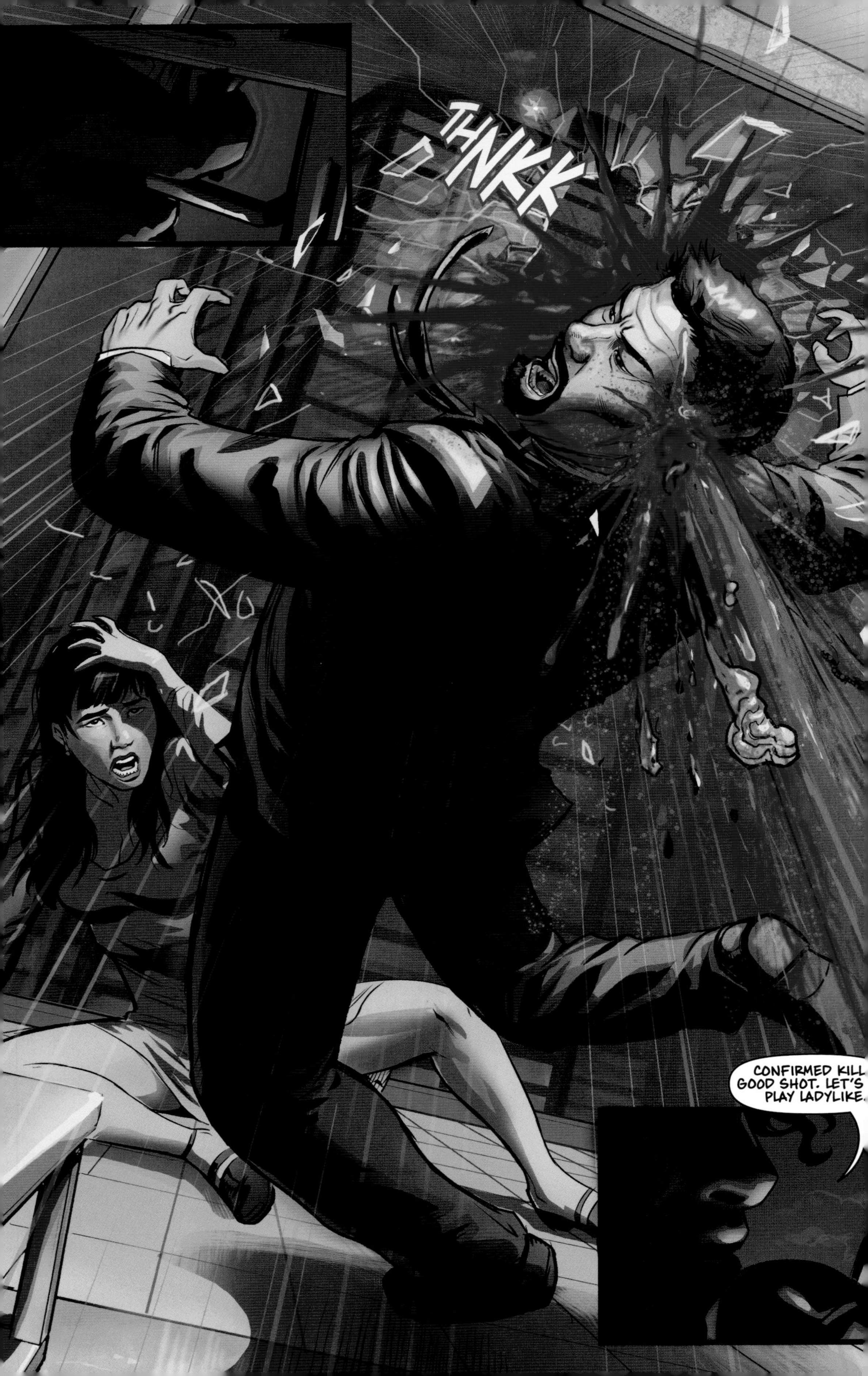
THNKK
CONFIRMED KILL. GOOD SHOT. LET'S PLAY LADYLIKE.

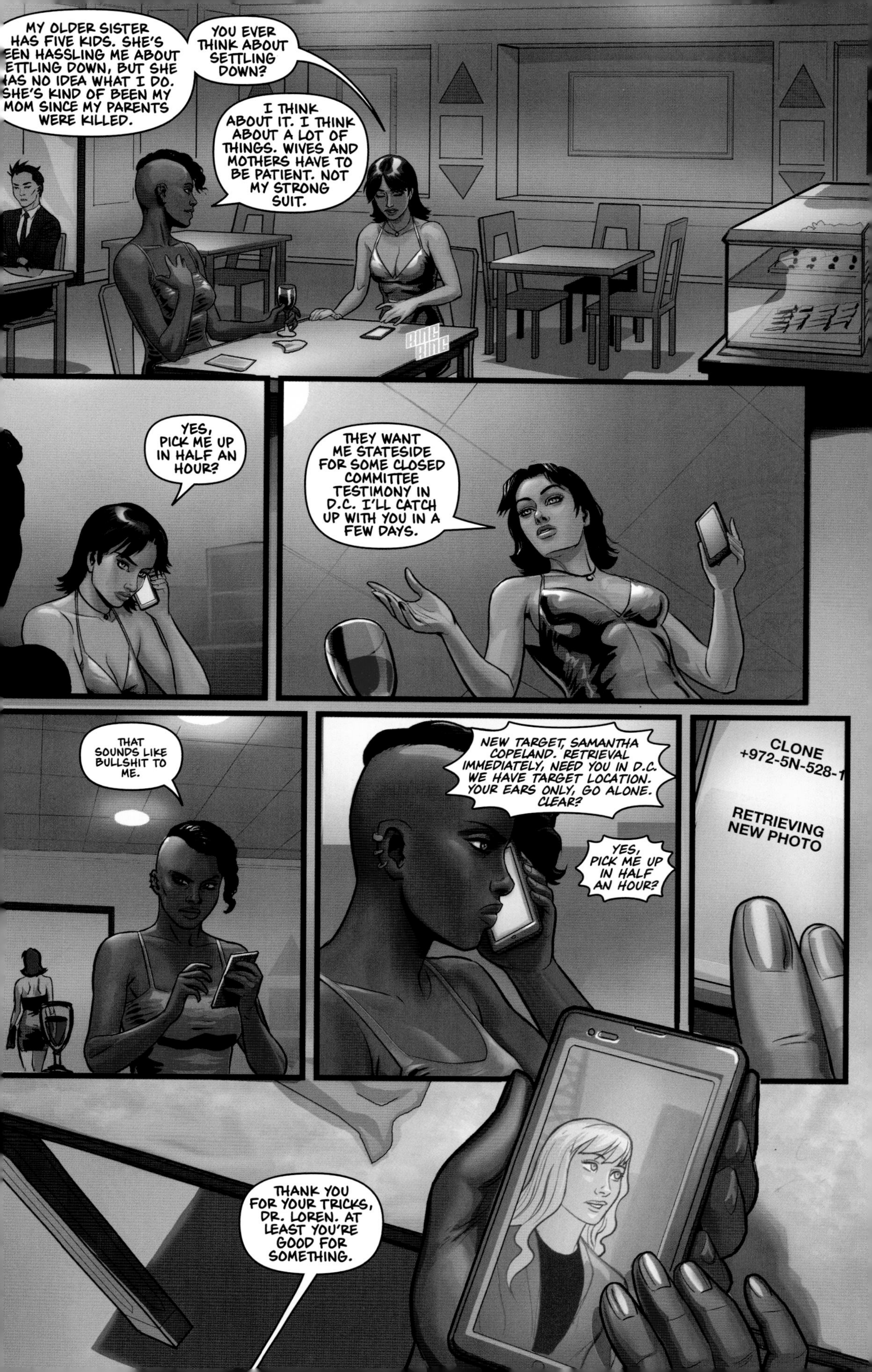
MY OLDER SISTER HAS FIVE KIDS. SHE'S EEN HASSLING ME ABOUT ETTLING DOWN, BUT SHE AS NO IDEA WHAT I DO. SHE'S KIND OF BEEN MY MOM SINCE MY PARENTS WERE KILLED.
YOU EVER THINK ABOUT SETTLING DOWN?
I THINK ABOUT IT. I THINK ABOUT A LOT OF THINGS. WIVES AND MOTHERS HAVE TO BE PATIENT. NOT MY STRONG SUIT.
RING RING
YES, PICK ME UP IN HALF AN HOUR?
THEY WANT ME STATESIDE FOR SOME CLOSED COMMITTEE TESTIMONY IN D.C. I'LL CATCH UP WITH YOU IN A FEW DAYS.
THAT SOUNDS LIKE BULLSHIT TO ME.
NEW TARGET, SAMANTHA COPELAND. RETRIEVAL IMMEDIATELY, NEED YOU IN D.C. WE HAVE TARGET LOCATION. YOUR EARS ONLY, GO ALONE. CLEAR?
YES, PICK ME UP IN HALF AN HOUR?
CLONE +972-5N-528-1
RETRIEVING NEW PHOTO
THANK YOU FOR YOUR TRICKS, DR. LOREN. AT LEAST YOU'RE GOOD FOR SOMETHING.

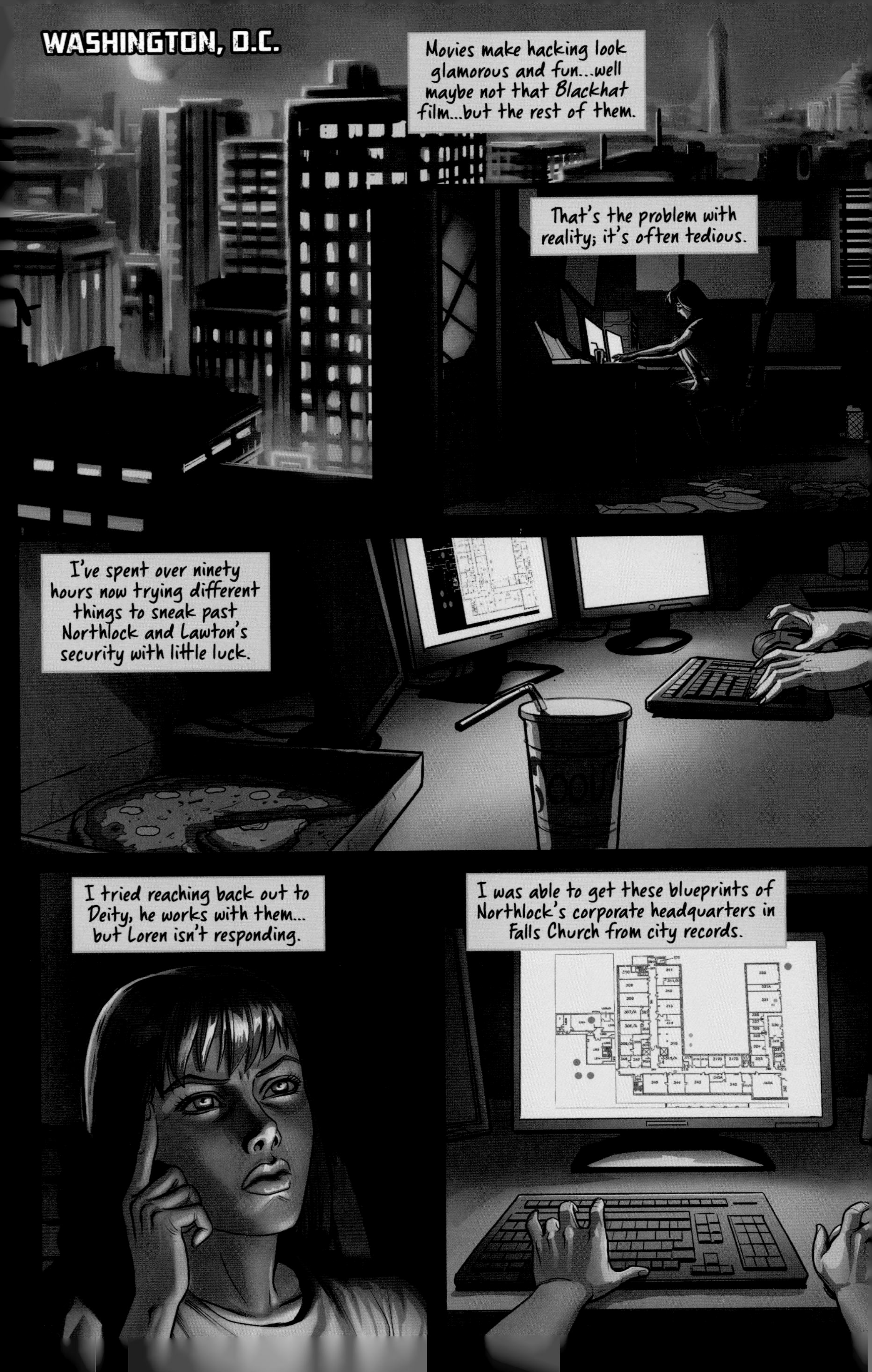
WASHINGTON, D.C.
Movies make hacking look glamorous and fun...well maybe not that Blackhat film...but the rest of them.
That's the problem with reality; it's often tedious.
I've spent over ninety hours now trying different things to sneak past Northlock and Lawton's security with little luck.
I tried reaching back out to Deity, he works with them... but Loren isn't responding.
I was able to get these blueprints of Northlock's corporate headquarters in Falls Church from city records.

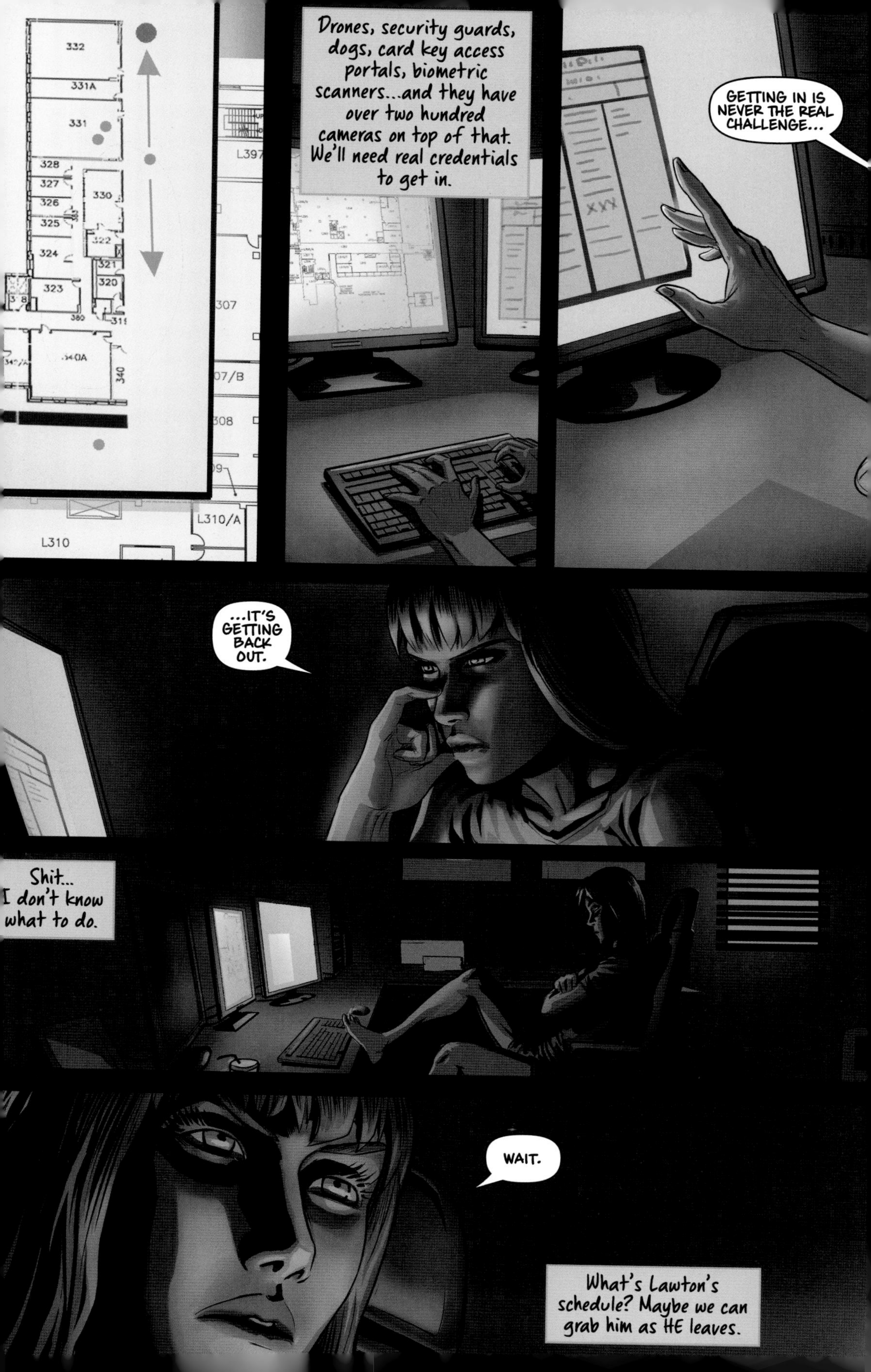
332
331A
331
328
327
326
325
324
323
330
322
321
320
340A
340
L397
307
307/B
308
L310/A
L310
Drones, security guards, dogs, card key access portals, biometric scanners...and they have over two hundred cameras on top of that. We'll need real credentials to get in.
GETTING IN IS NEVER THE REAL CHALLENGE...
...IT'S GETTING BACK OUT.
Shit... I don't know what to do.
WAIT.
What's Lawton's schedule? Maybe we can grab him as HE leaves.

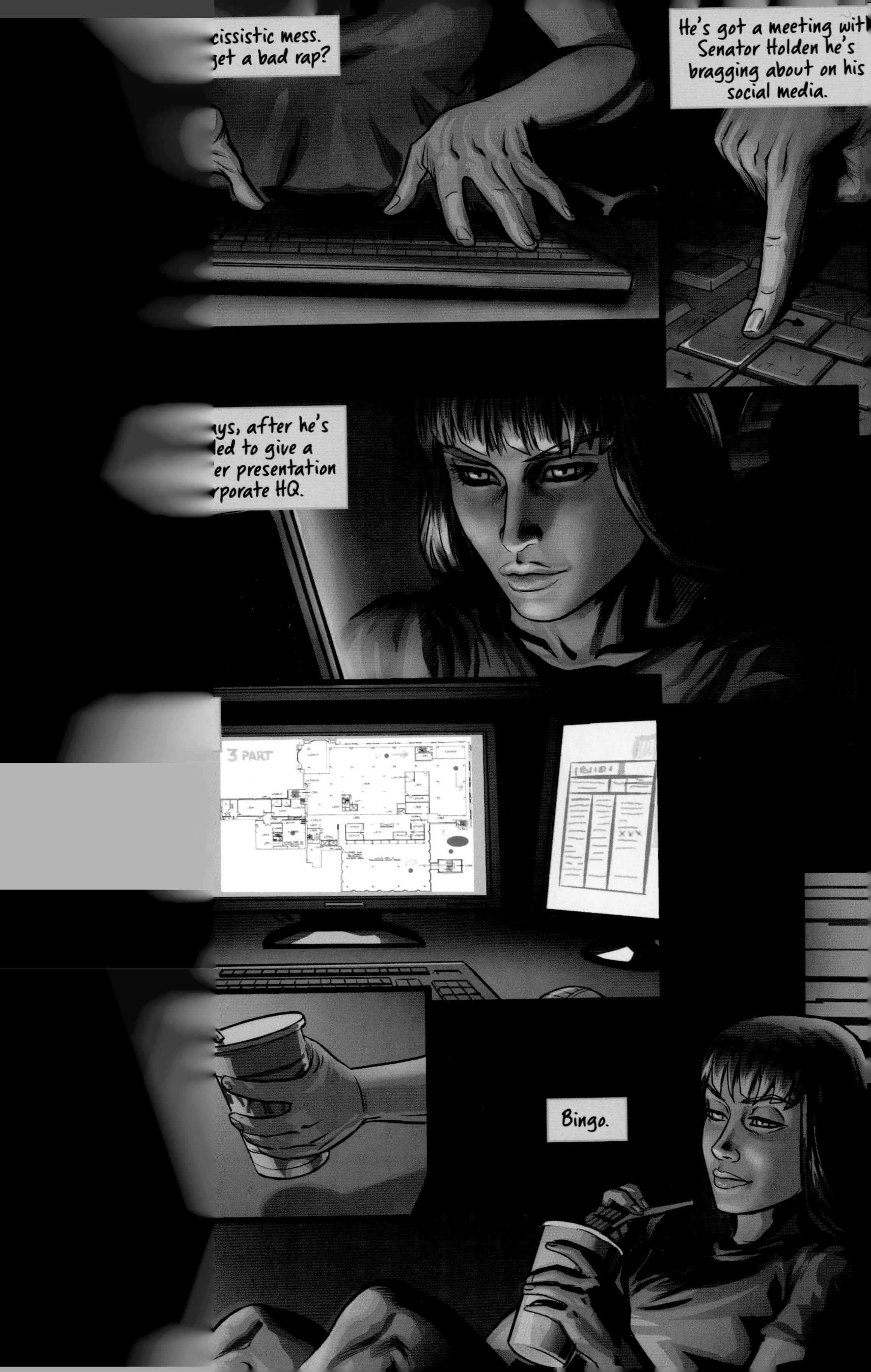
cissistic mess.
get a bad rap?
He's got a meeting with Senator Holden he's bragging about on his social media.
ys, after he's
led to give a
er presentation
rporate HQ.
3 PART
Bingo.

SAMANTHA COPELAND IS THE MARK. SHE'S WORKING WITH A PROFESSIONAL TEAM, WE ASSUME ONE OF THE EX-MILITARY MERCENARY GROUPS THAT WE SOMETIMES USE, BUT WE DON'T KNOW WHICH ONE SO WE CAN'T SQUEEZE THEM.

WHO DO YOU WANT ME TO IMPLICATE IN HER MURDER?

AN FBI AGENT SHE USED TO WORK WITH.

IT'S ALL IN THE FILE ALONG WITH HER LOCATION.

SHE'S HOLED UP IN AN APARTMENT NOT TOO FAR FROM GEORGETOWN.

CONSIDER IT DONE.

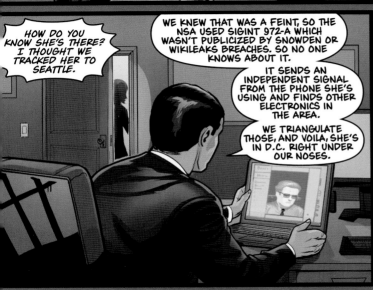

HOW DO YOU KNOW SHE'S THERE? I THOUGHT WE TRACKED HER TO SEATTLE.

WE KNEW THAT WAS A FEINT, SO THE NSA USED SIGINT 972-A WHICH WASN'T PUBLICIZED BY SNOWDEN OR WIKILEAKS BREACHES. SO NO ONE KNOWS ABOUT IT.

IT SENDS AN INDEPENDENT SIGNAL FROM THE PHONE SHE'S USING AND FINDS OTHER ELECTRONICS IN THE AREA.

WE TRIANGULATE THOSE, AND VOILA, SHE'S IN D.C. RIGHT UNDER OUR NOSES.

I WANT THIS BITCH DEAD.

YES, MR. PRESIDENT.

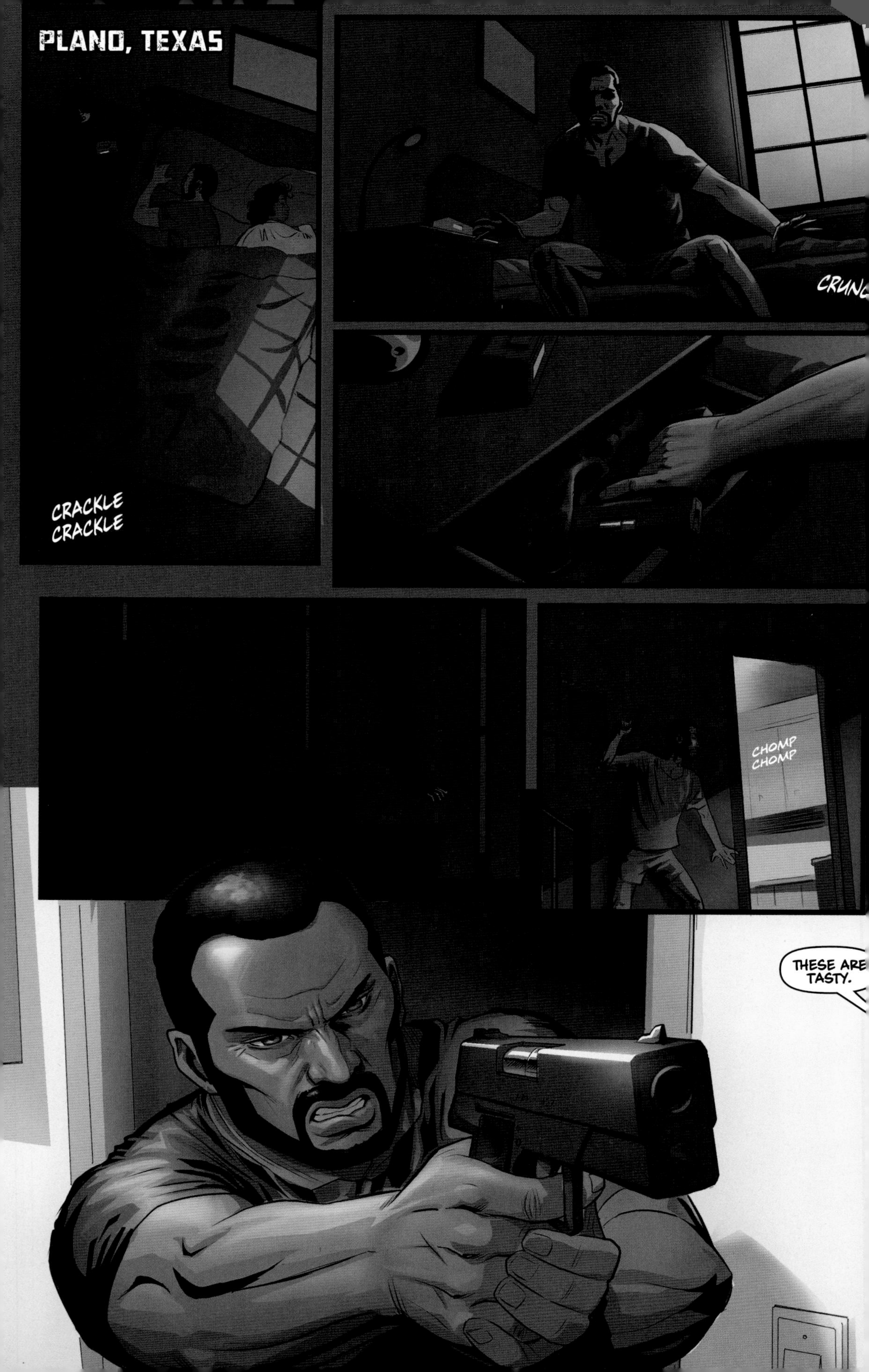
PLANO, TEXAS
CRACKLE CRACKLE
CHOMP CHOMP
THESE ARE TASTY.

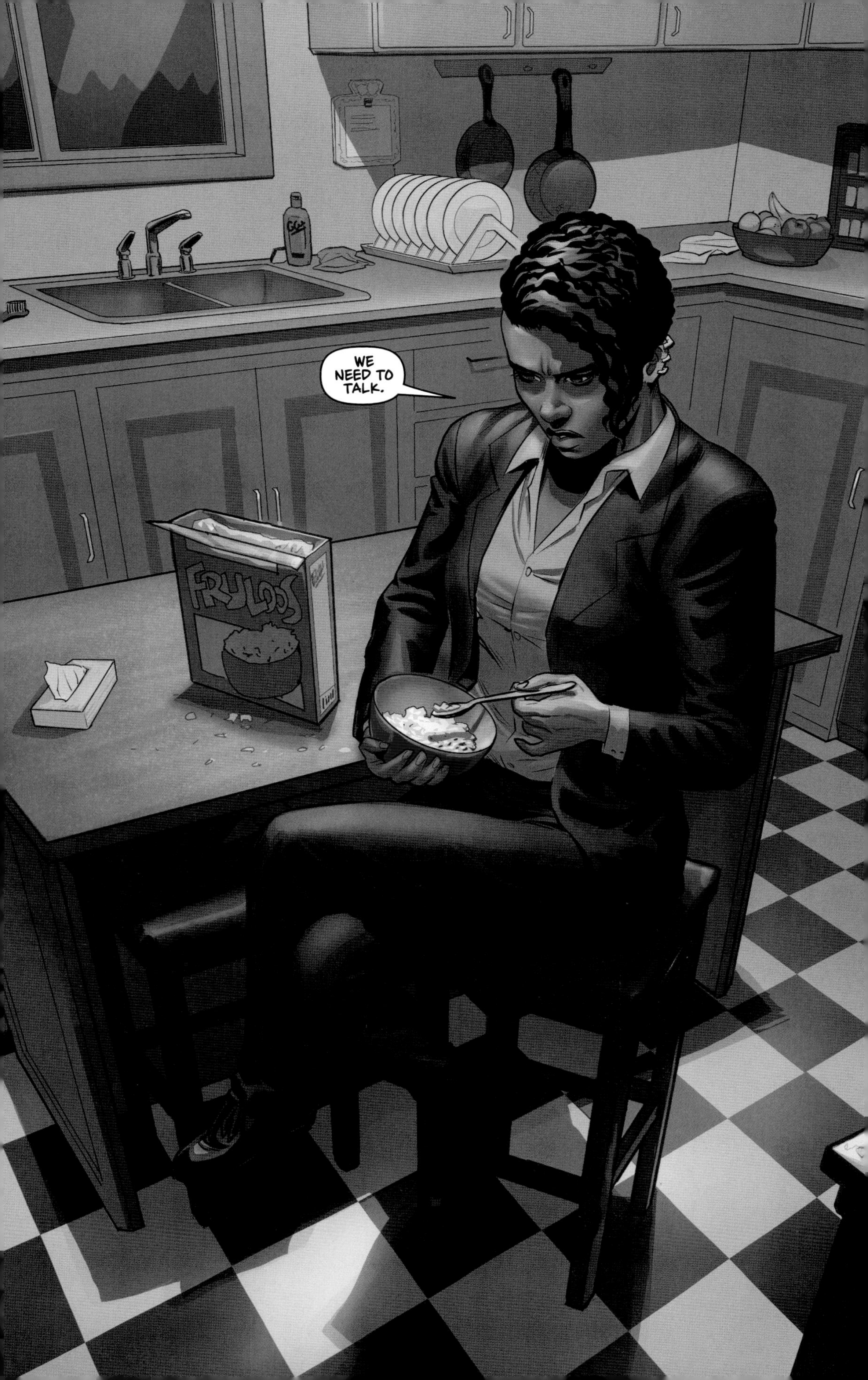
WE NEED TO TALK.
FRULOOS

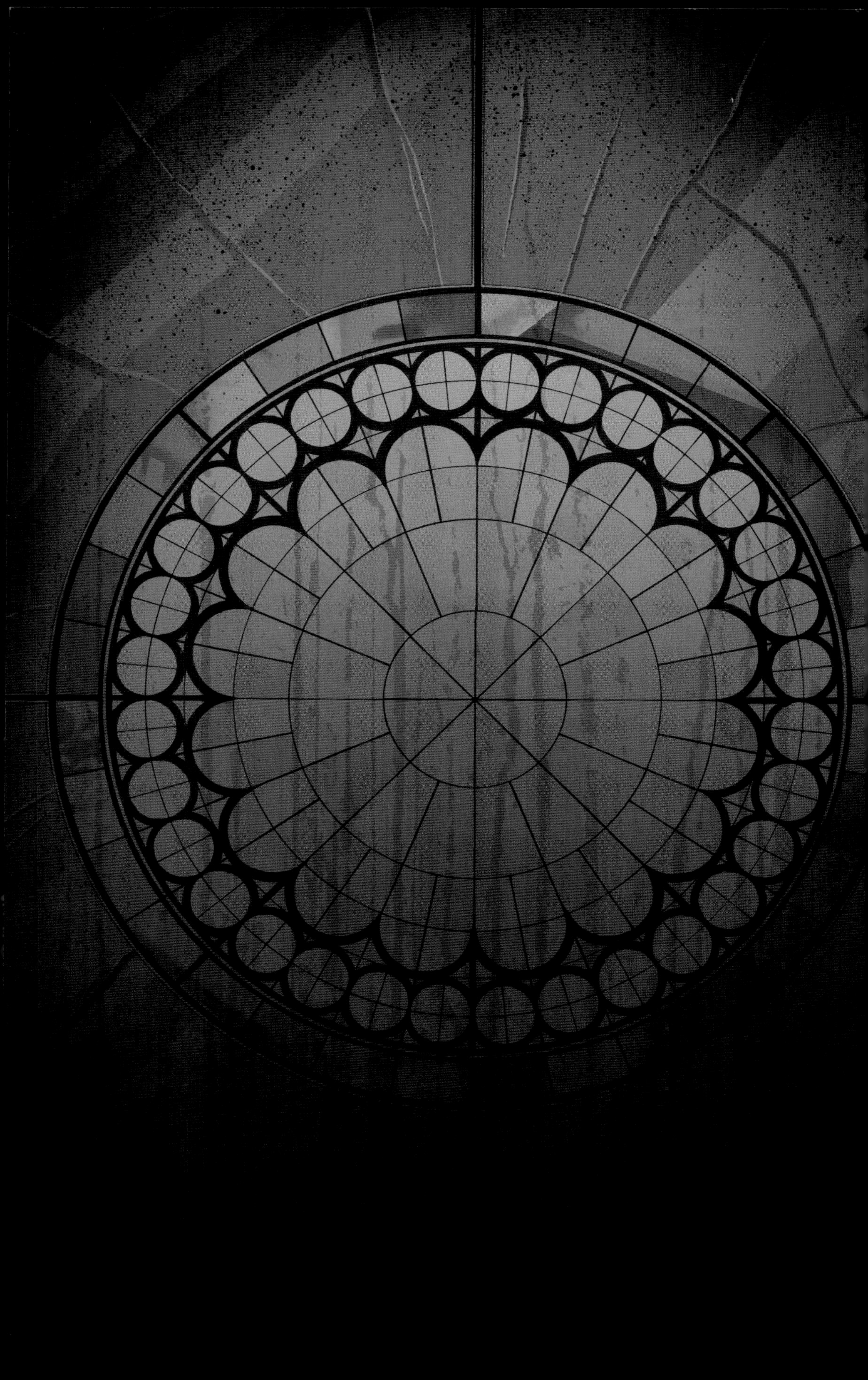

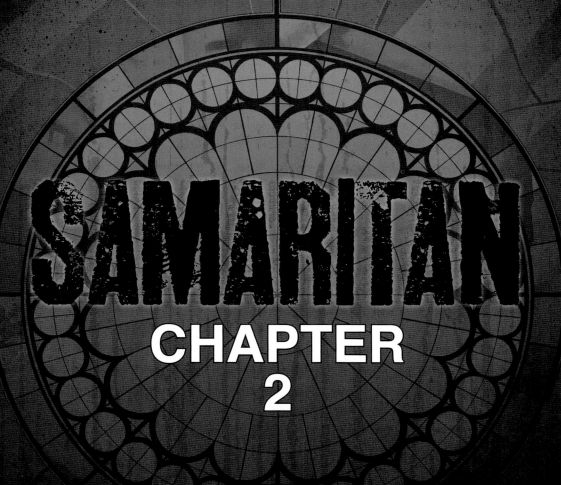

SAMARITAN

CHAPTER
2

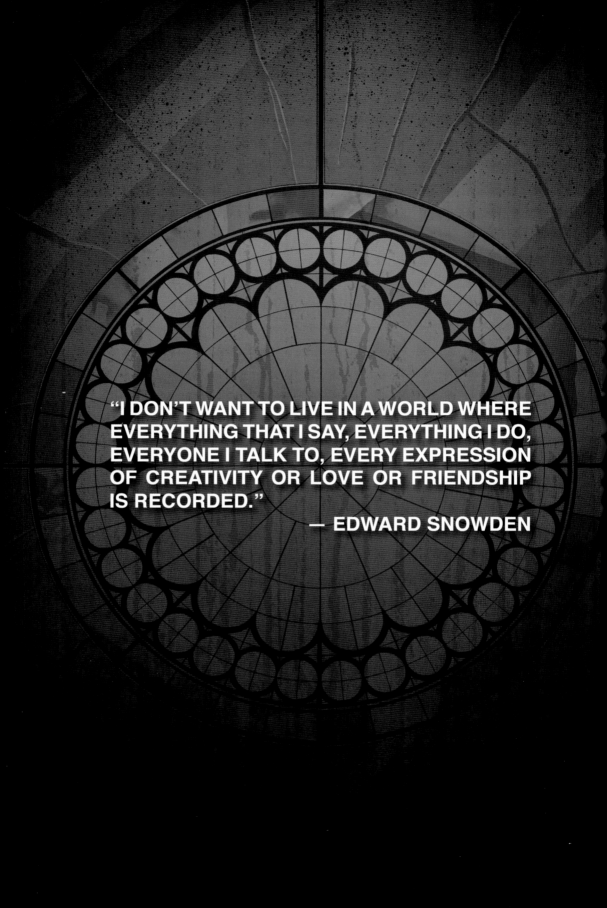

"I DON'T WANT TO LIVE IN A WORLD WHERE EVERYTHING THAT I SAY, EVERYTHING I DO, EVERYONE I TALK TO, EVERY EXPRESSION OF CREATIVITY OR LOVE OR FRIENDSHIP IS RECORDED."

— EDWARD SNOWDEN

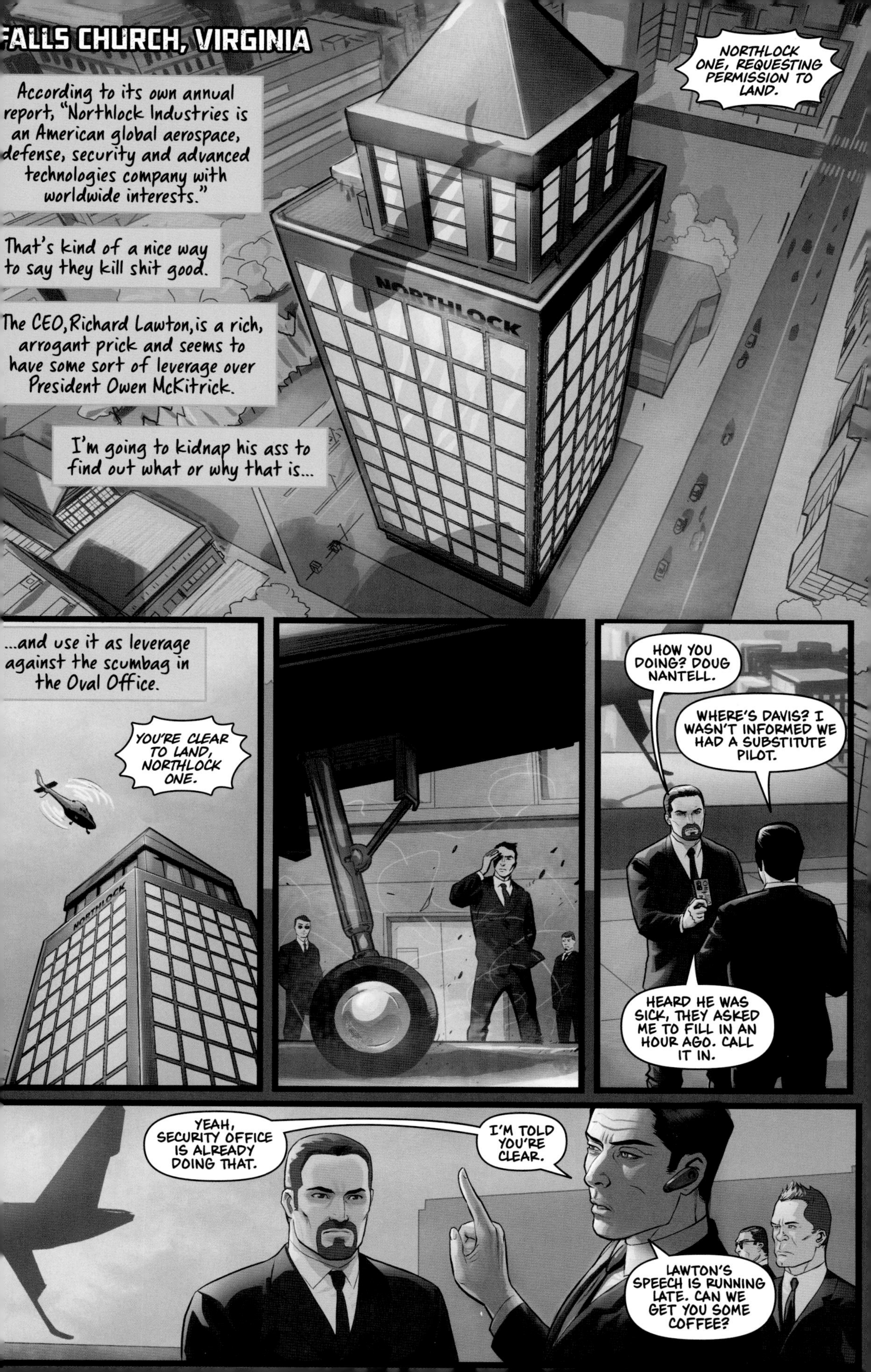
FALLS CHURCH, VIRGINIA
According to its own annual report, "Northlock Industries is an American global aerospace, defense, security and advanced technologies company with worldwide interests."
NORTHLOCK ONE, REQUESTING PERMISSION TO LAND.
That's kind of a nice way to say they kill shit good.
NORTHLOCK
The CEO, Richard Lawton, is a rich, arrogant prick and seems to have some sort of leverage over President Owen McKitrick.
I'm going to kidnap his ass to find out what or why that is...
...and use it as leverage against the scumbag in the Oval Office.
YOU'RE CLEAR TO LAND, NORTHLOCK ONE.
NORTHLOCK
HOW YOU DOING? DOUG NANTELL.
WHERE'S DAVIS? I WASN'T INFORMED WE HAD A SUBSTITUTE PILOT.
HEARD HE WAS SICK, THEY ASKED ME TO FILL IN AN HOUR AGO. CALL IT IN.
YEAH, SECURITY OFFICE IS ALREADY DOING THAT.
I'M TOLD YOU'RE CLEAR.
LAWTON'S SPEECH IS RUNNING LATE. CAN WE GET YOU SOME COFFEE?

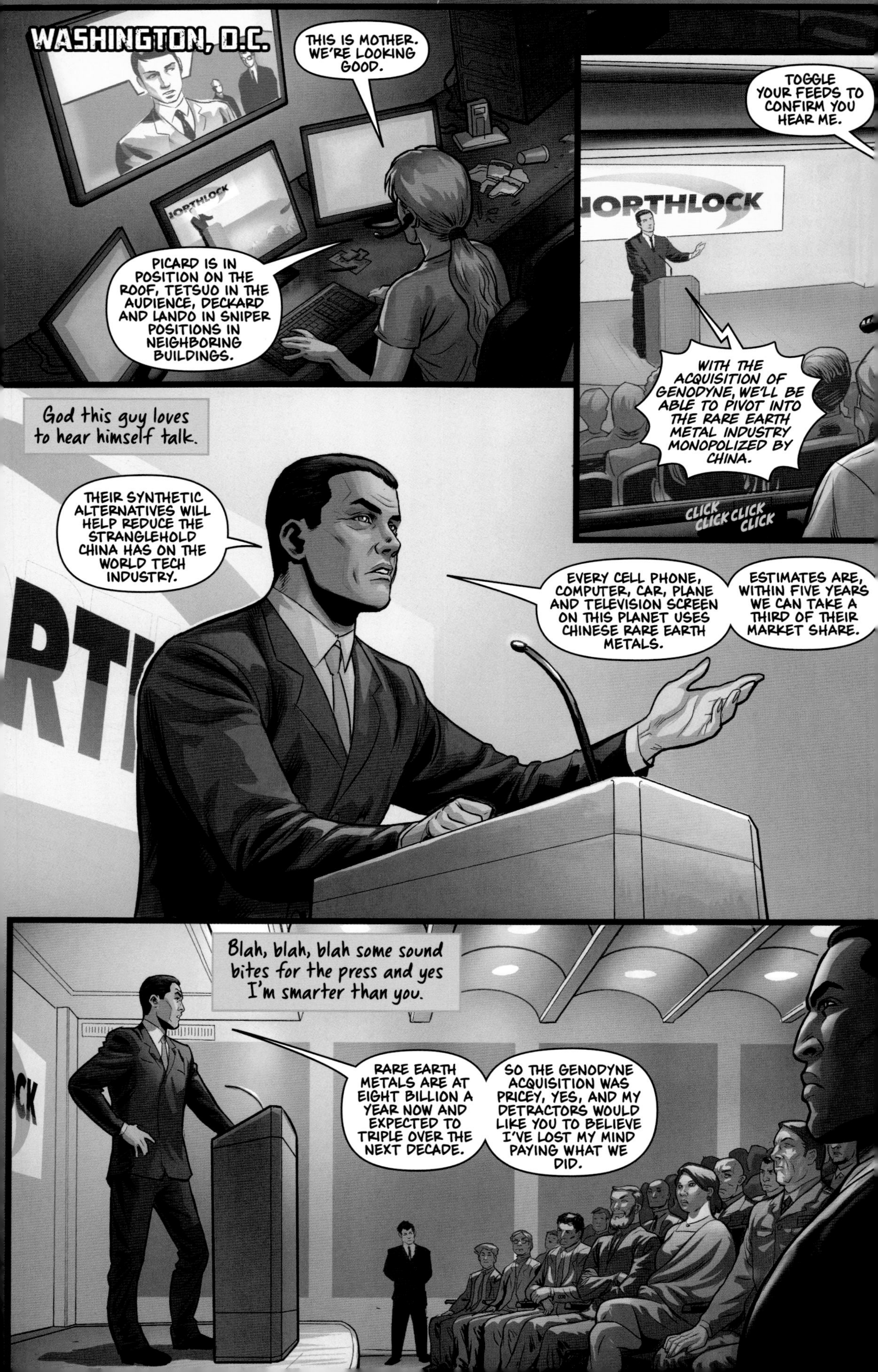
WASHINGTON, D.C.
THIS IS MOTHER. WE'RE LOOKING GOOD.
PICARD IS IN POSITION ON THE ROOF, TETSUO IN THE AUDIENCE, DECKARD AND LANDO IN SNIPER POSITIONS IN NEIGHBORING BUILDINGS.
NORTHLOCK
TOGGLE YOUR FEEDS TO CONFIRM YOU HEAR ME.
NORTHLOCK
WITH THE ACQUISITION OF GENODYNE, WE'LL BE ABLE TO PIVOT INTO THE RARE EARTH METAL INDUSTRY MONOPOLIZED BY CHINA.
CLICK CLICK CLICK CLICK
God this guy loves to hear himself talk.
THEIR SYNTHETIC ALTERNATIVES WILL HELP REDUCE THE STRANGLEHOLD CHINA HAS ON THE WORLD TECH INDUSTRY.
EVERY CELL PHONE, COMPUTER, CAR, PLANE AND TELEVISION SCREEN ON THIS PLANET USES CHINESE RARE EARTH METALS.
ESTIMATES ARE, WITHIN FIVE YEARS WE CAN TAKE A THIRD OF THEIR MARKET SHARE.
Blah, blah, blah some sound bites for the press and yes I'm smarter than you.
RARE EARTH METALS ARE AT EIGHT BILLION A YEAR NOW AND EXPECTED TO TRIPLE OVER THE NEXT DECADE.
SO THE GENODYNE ACQUISITION WAS PRICEY, YES, AND MY DETRACTORS WOULD LIKE YOU TO BELIEVE I'VE LOST MY MIND PAYING WHAT WE DID.

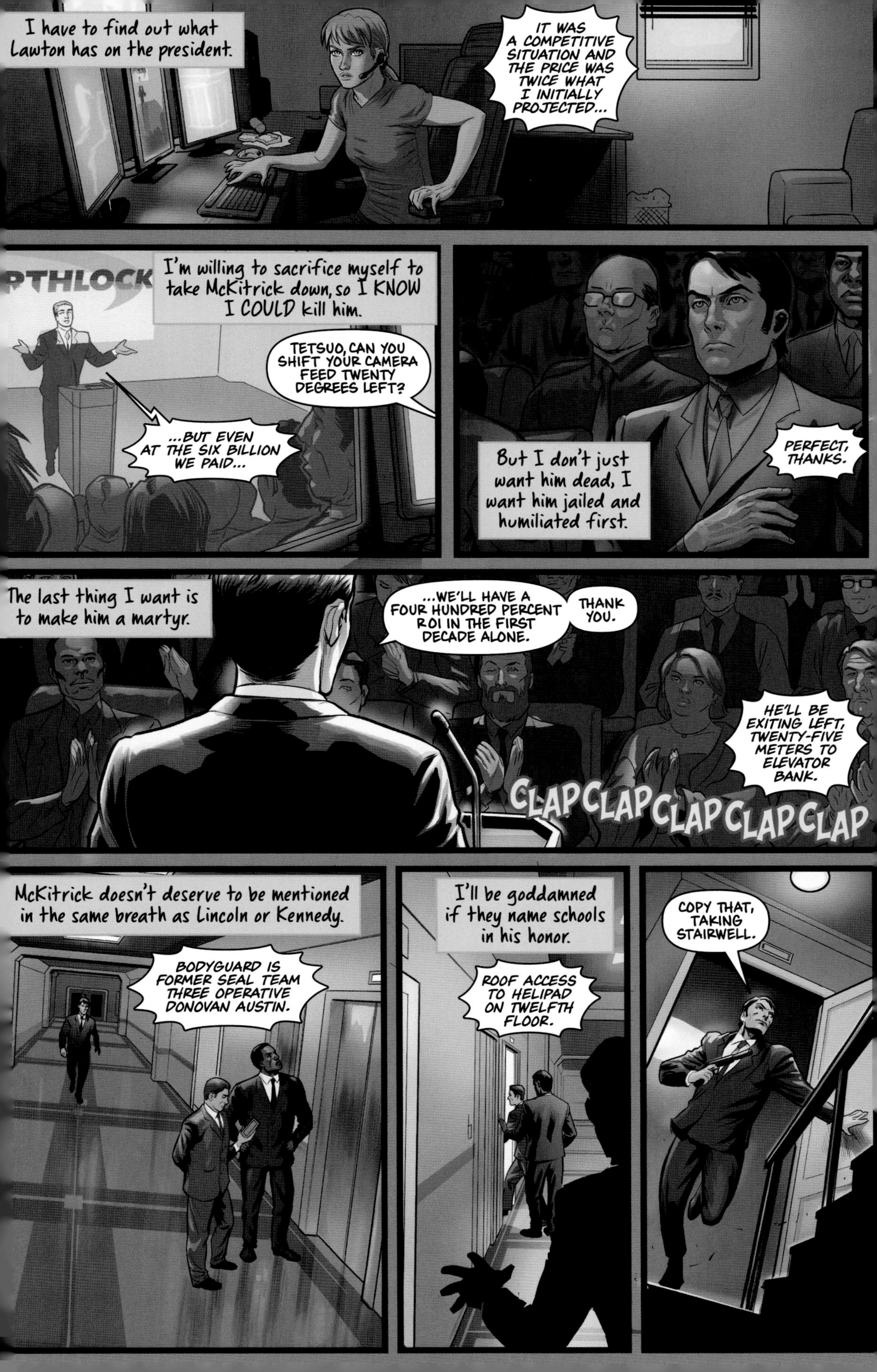

I have to find out what Lawton has on the president.
IT WAS A COMPETITIVE SITUATION AND THE PRICE WAS TWICE WHAT I INITIALLY PROJECTED...
RTHLOCK
I'm willing to sacrifice myself to take McKitrick down, so I KNOW I COULD kill him.
TETSUO, CAN YOU SHIFT YOUR CAMERA FEED TWENTY DEGREES LEFT?
...BUT EVEN AT THE SIX BILLION WE PAID...
But I don't just want him dead, I want him jailed and humiliated first.
PERFECT, THANKS.
The last thing I want is to make him a martyr.
...WE'LL HAVE A FOUR HUNDRED PERCENT ROI IN THE FIRST DECADE ALONE.
THANK YOU.
HE'LL BE EXITING LEFT, TWENTY-FIVE METERS TO ELEVATOR BANK.
CLAP CLAP CLAP CLAP CLAP
McKitrick doesn't deserve to be mentioned in the same breath as Lincoln or Kennedy.
BODYGUARD IS FORMER SEAL TEAM THREE OPERATIVE DONOVAN AUSTIN.
I'll be goddamned if they name schools in his honor.
ROOF ACCESS TO HELIPAD ON TWELFTH FLOOR.
COPY THAT, TAKING STAIRWELL.

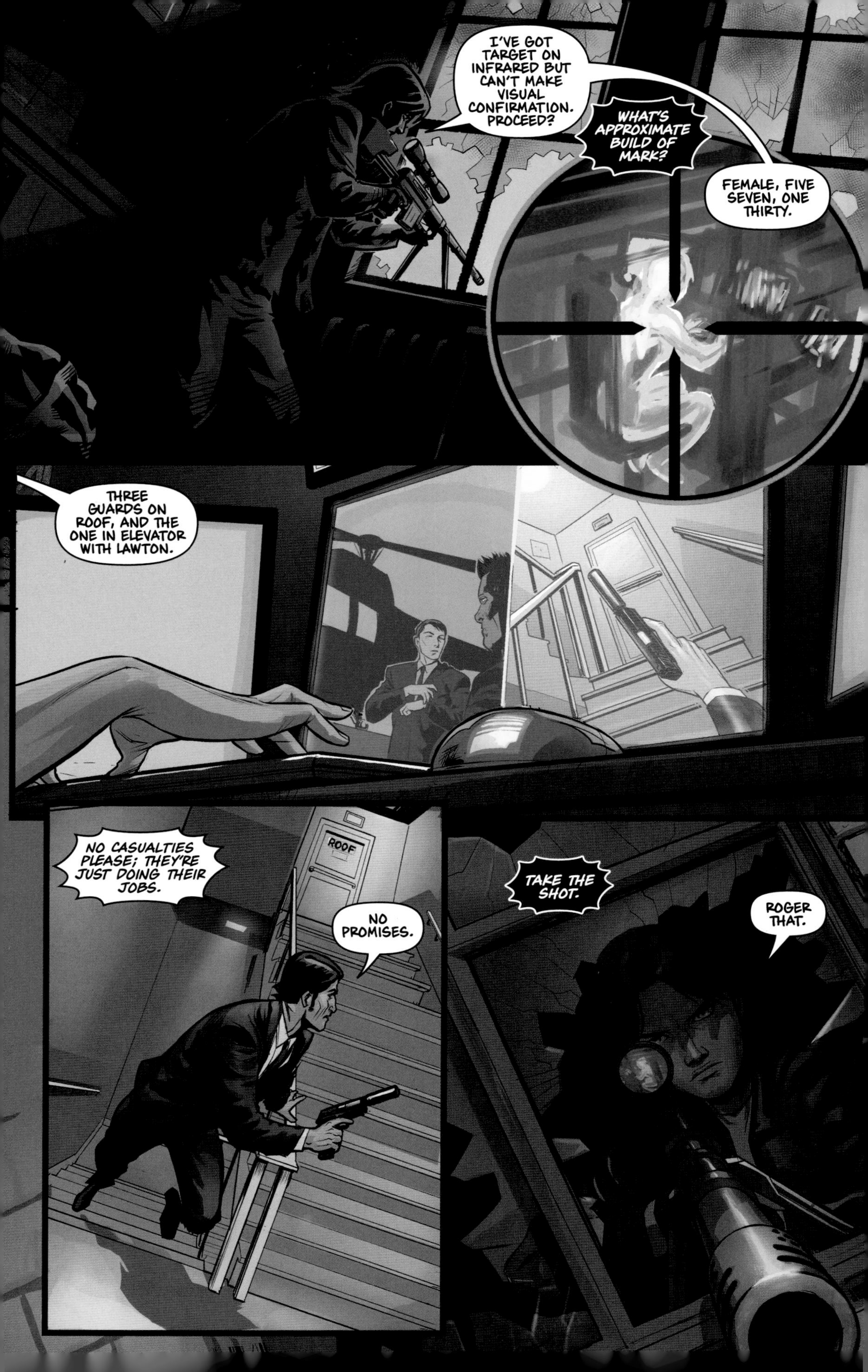
I'VE GOT TARGET ON INFRARED BUT CAN'T MAKE VISUAL CONFIRMATION. PROCEED?
WHAT'S APPROXIMATE BUILD OF MARK?
FEMALE, FIVE SEVEN, ONE THIRTY.
THREE GUARDS ON ROOF, AND THE ONE IN ELEVATOR WITH LAWTON.
ROOF
NO CASUALTIES PLEASE; THEY'RE JUST DOING THEIR JOBS.
NO PROMISES.
TAKE THE SHOT.
ROGER THAT.

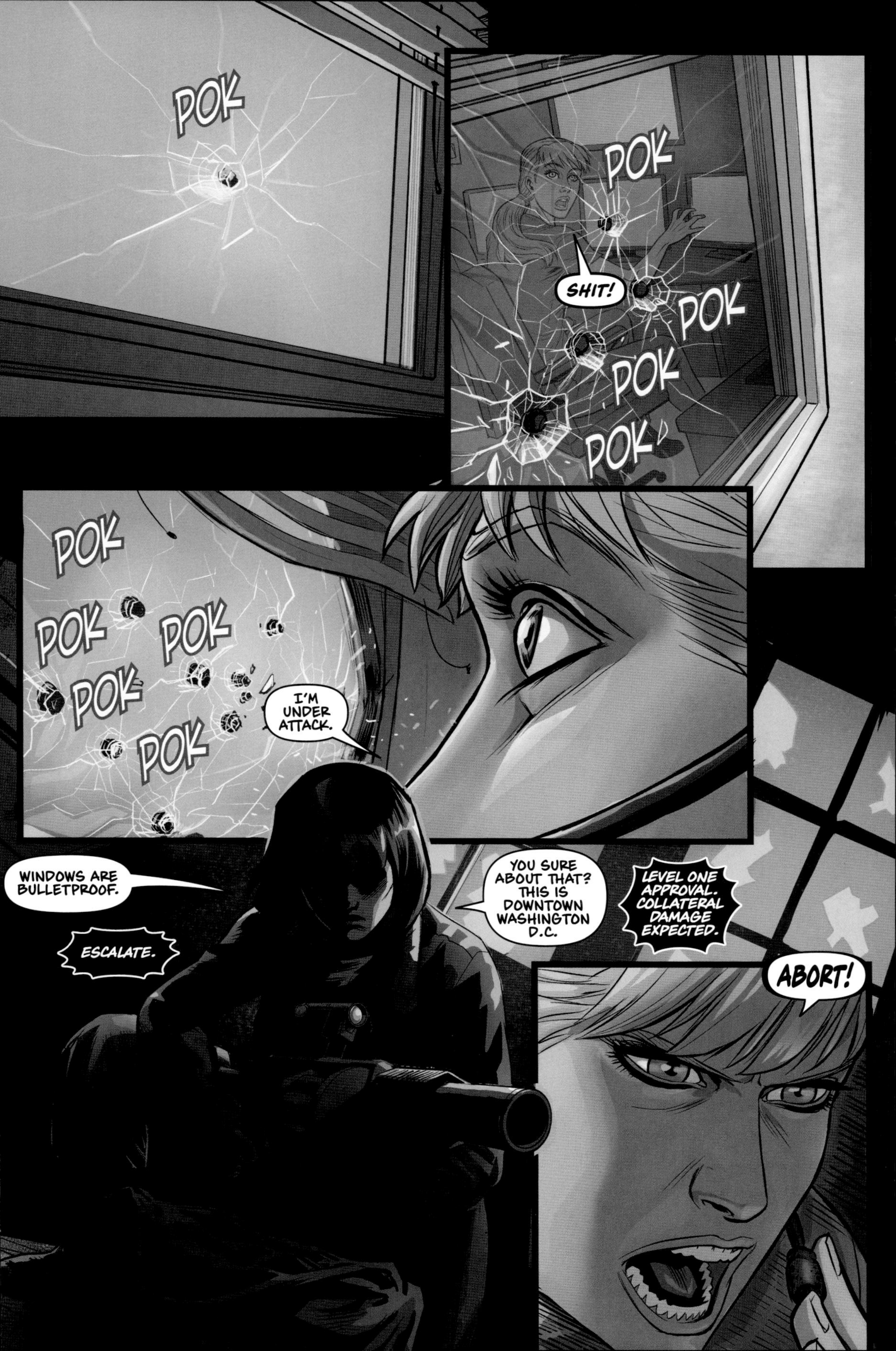
POK
POK
SHIT!
POK
POK
POK
POK
POK
POK
POK
POK
I'M UNDER ATTACK.
WINDOWS ARE BULLETPROOF.
ESCALATE.
YOU SURE ABOUT THAT? THIS IS DOWNTOWN WASHINGTON D.C.
LEVEL ONE APPROVAL. COLLATERAL DAMAGE EXPECTED.
ABORT!

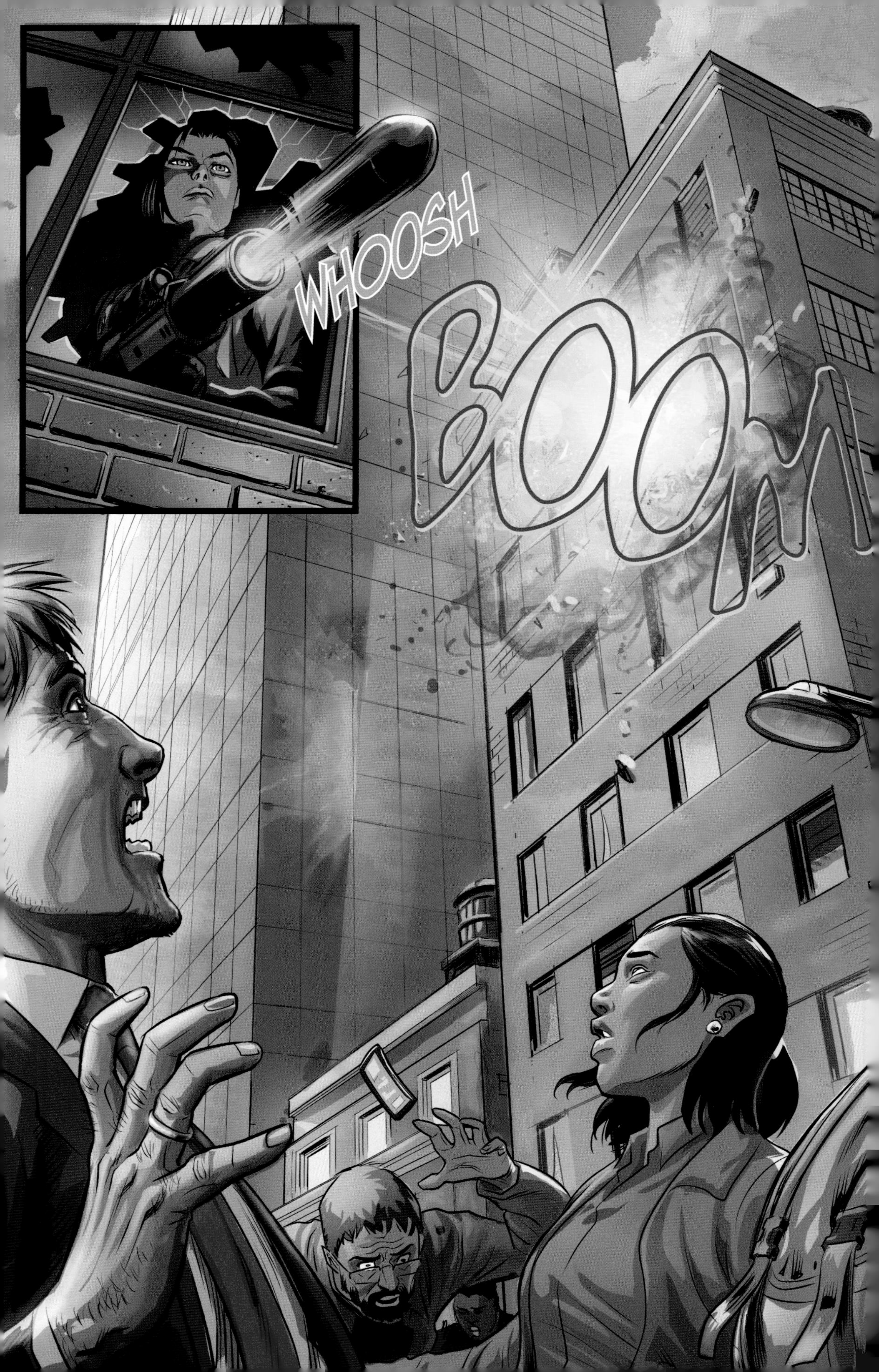
WHOOSH
BOOM

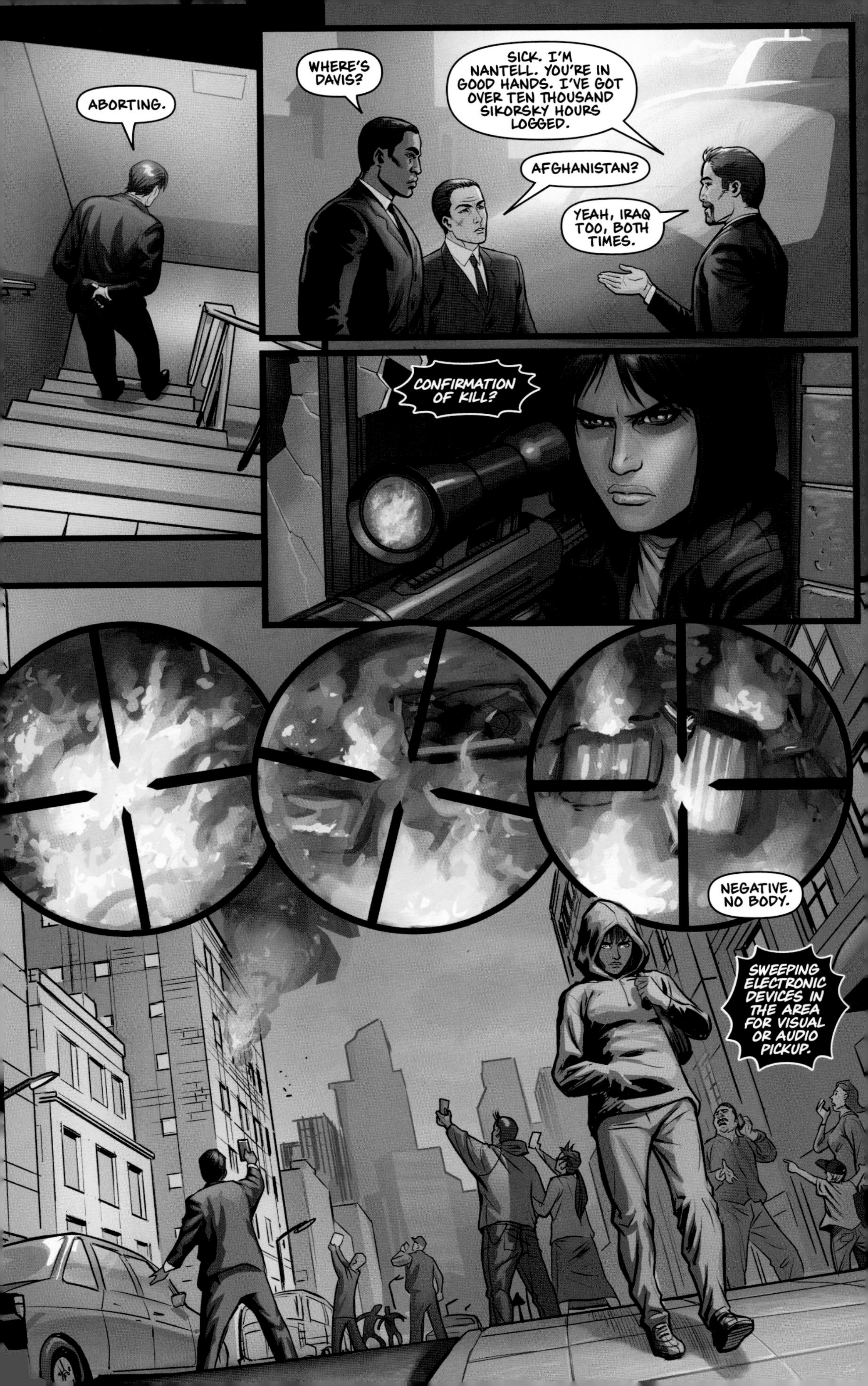
ABORTING.
WHERE'S DAVIS?
SICK. I'M NANTELL. YOU'RE IN GOOD HANDS. I'VE GOT OVER TEN THOUSAND SIKORSKY HOURS LOGGED.
AFGHANISTAN?
YEAH, IRAQ TOO, BOTH TIMES.
CONFIRMATION OF KILL?
NEGATIVE. NO BODY.
SWEEPING ELECTRONIC DEVICES IN THE AREA FOR VISUAL OR AUDIO PICKUP.

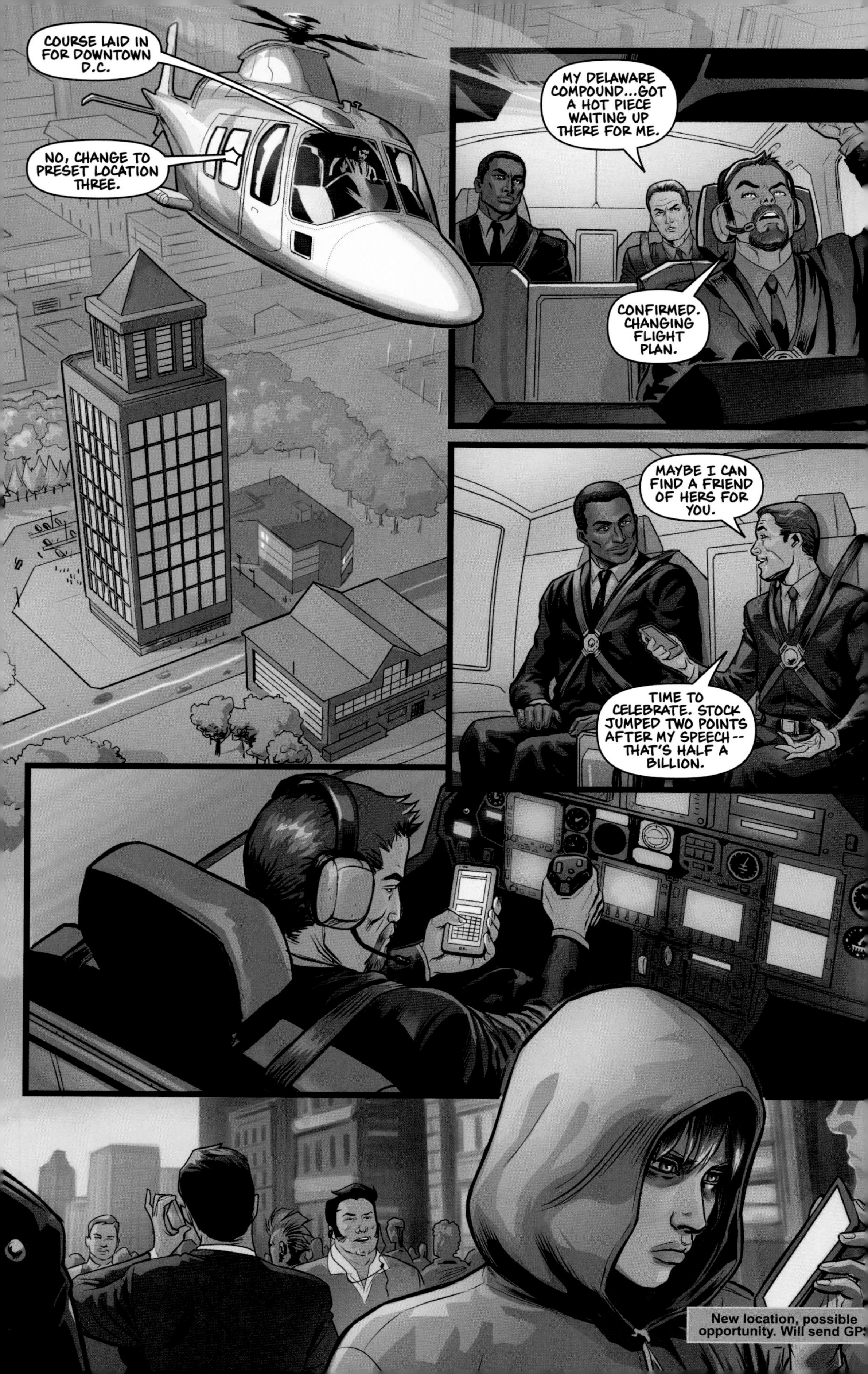
COURSE LAID IN FOR DOWNTOWN D.C.
NO, CHANGE TO PRESET LOCATION THREE.
MY DELAWARE COMPOUND...GOT A HOT PIECE WAITING UP THERE FOR ME.
CONFIRMED. CHANGING FLIGHT PLAN.
MAYBE I CAN FIND A FRIEND OF HERS FOR YOU.
TIME TO CELEBRATE. STOCK JUMPED TWO POINTS AFTER MY SPEECH -- THAT'S HALF A BILLION.
New location, possible opportunity. Will send GP

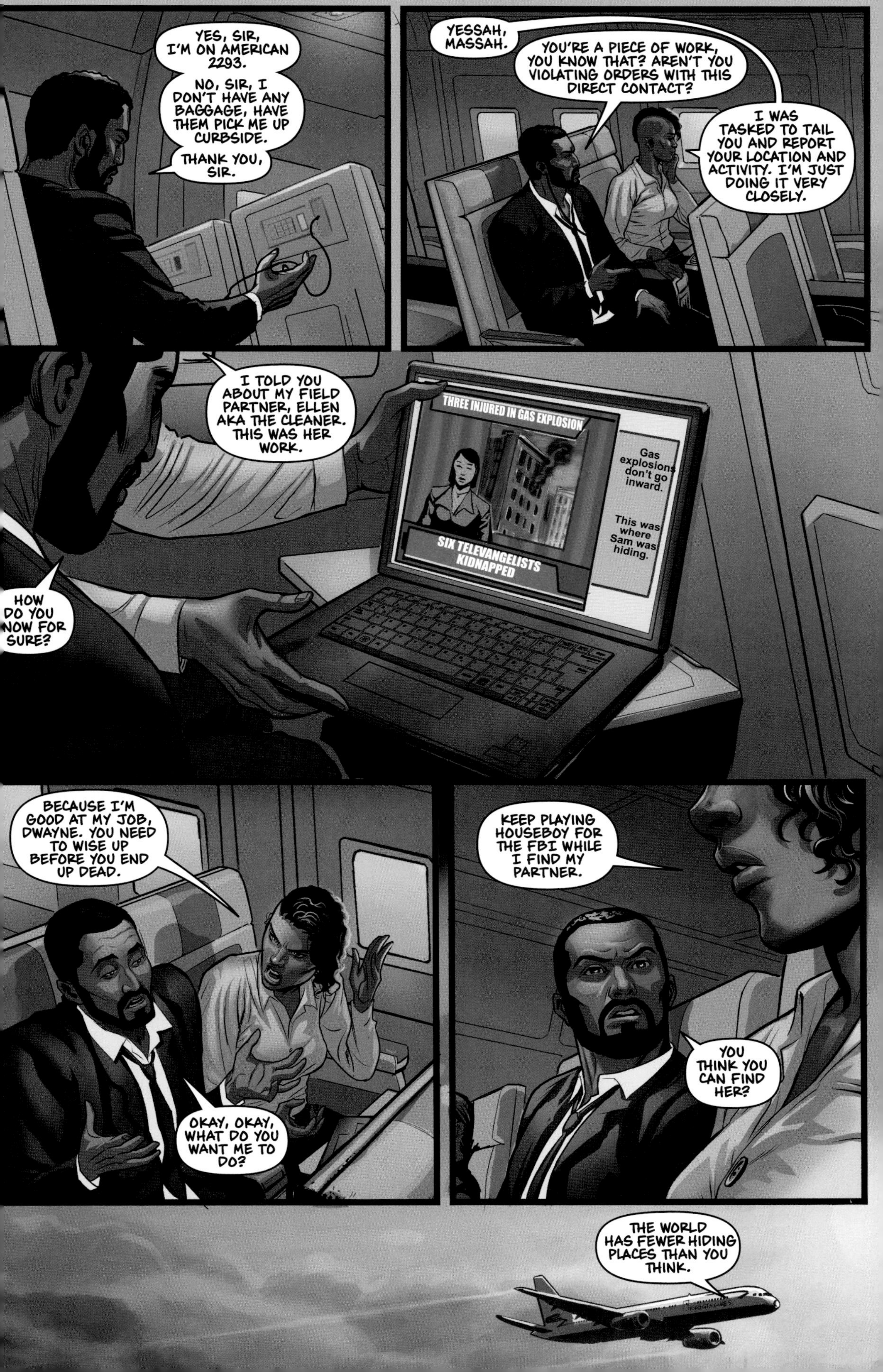
YES, SIR, I'M ON AMERICAN 2293.
NO, SIR, I DON'T HAVE ANY BAGGAGE, HAVE THEM PICK ME UP CURBSIDE.
THANK YOU, SIR.
YESSAH, MASSAH.
YOU'RE A PIECE OF WORK, YOU KNOW THAT? AREN'T YOU VIOLATING ORDERS WITH THIS DIRECT CONTACT?
I WAS TASKED TO TAIL YOU AND REPORT YOUR LOCATION AND ACTIVITY. I'M JUST DOING IT VERY CLOSELY.
I TOLD YOU ABOUT MY FIELD PARTNER, ELLEN AKA THE CLEANER. THIS WAS HER WORK.
THREE INJURED IN GAS EXPLOSION
SIX TELEVANGELISTS KIDNAPPED
Gas explosions don't go inward.
This was where Sam was hiding.
HOW DO YOU NOW FOR SURE?
BECAUSE I'M GOOD AT MY JOB, DWAYNE. YOU NEED TO WISE UP BEFORE YOU END UP DEAD.
OKAY, OKAY, WHAT DO YOU WANT ME TO DO?
KEEP PLAYING HOUSEBOY FOR THE FBI WHILE I FIND MY PARTNER.
YOU THINK YOU CAN FIND HER?
THE WORLD HAS FEWER HIDING PLACES THAN YOU THINK.

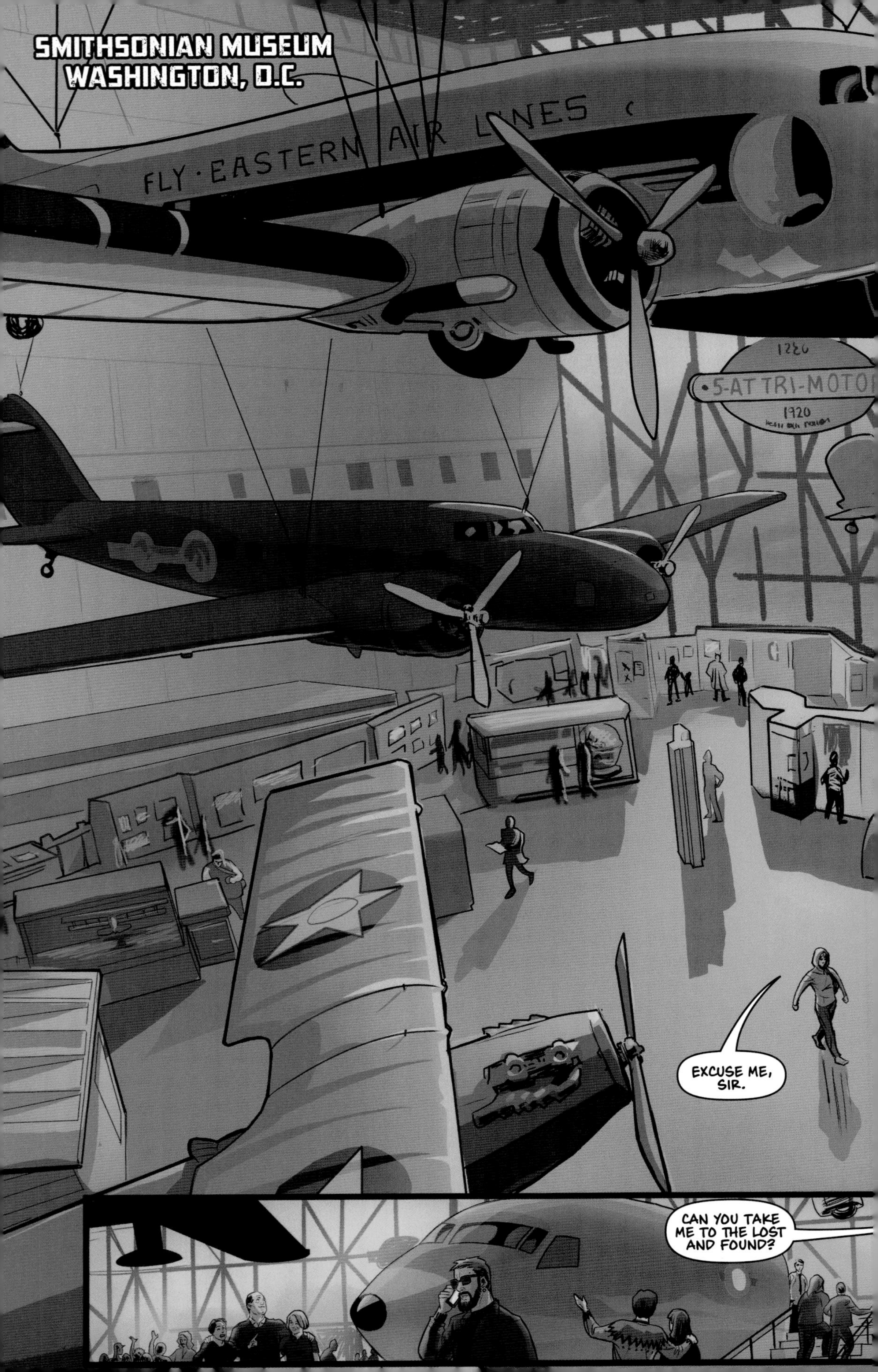
SMITHSONIAN MUSEUM
WASHINGTON, D.C.
FLY·EASTERN AIR LINES
5-AT TRI-MOTOR
EXCUSE ME, SIR.
CAN YOU TAKE ME TO THE LOST AND FOUND?

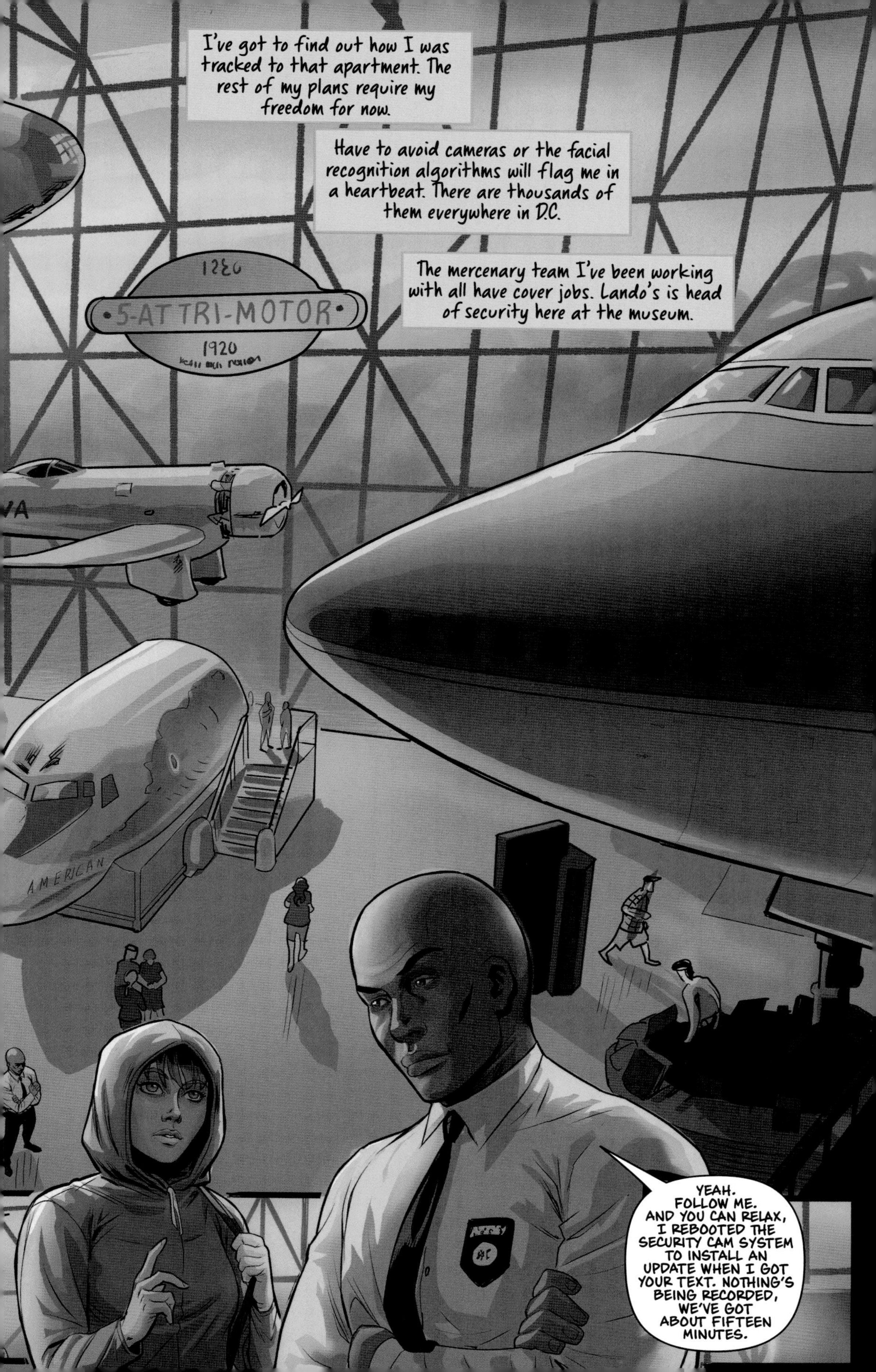
I've got to find out how I was tracked to that apartment. The rest of my plans require my freedom for now.
Have to avoid cameras or the facial recognition algorithms will flag me in a heartbeat. There are thousands of them everywhere in D.C.
The mercenary team I've been working with all have cover jobs. Lando's is head of security here at the museum.
1260
5-AT TRI-MOTOR
1920
AMERICAN
YEAH. FOLLOW ME. AND YOU CAN RELAX, I REBOOTED THE SECURITY CAM SYSTEM TO INSTALL AN UPDATE WHEN I GOT YOUR TEXT. NOTHING'S BEING RECORDED, WE'VE GOT ABOUT FIFTEEN MINUTES.

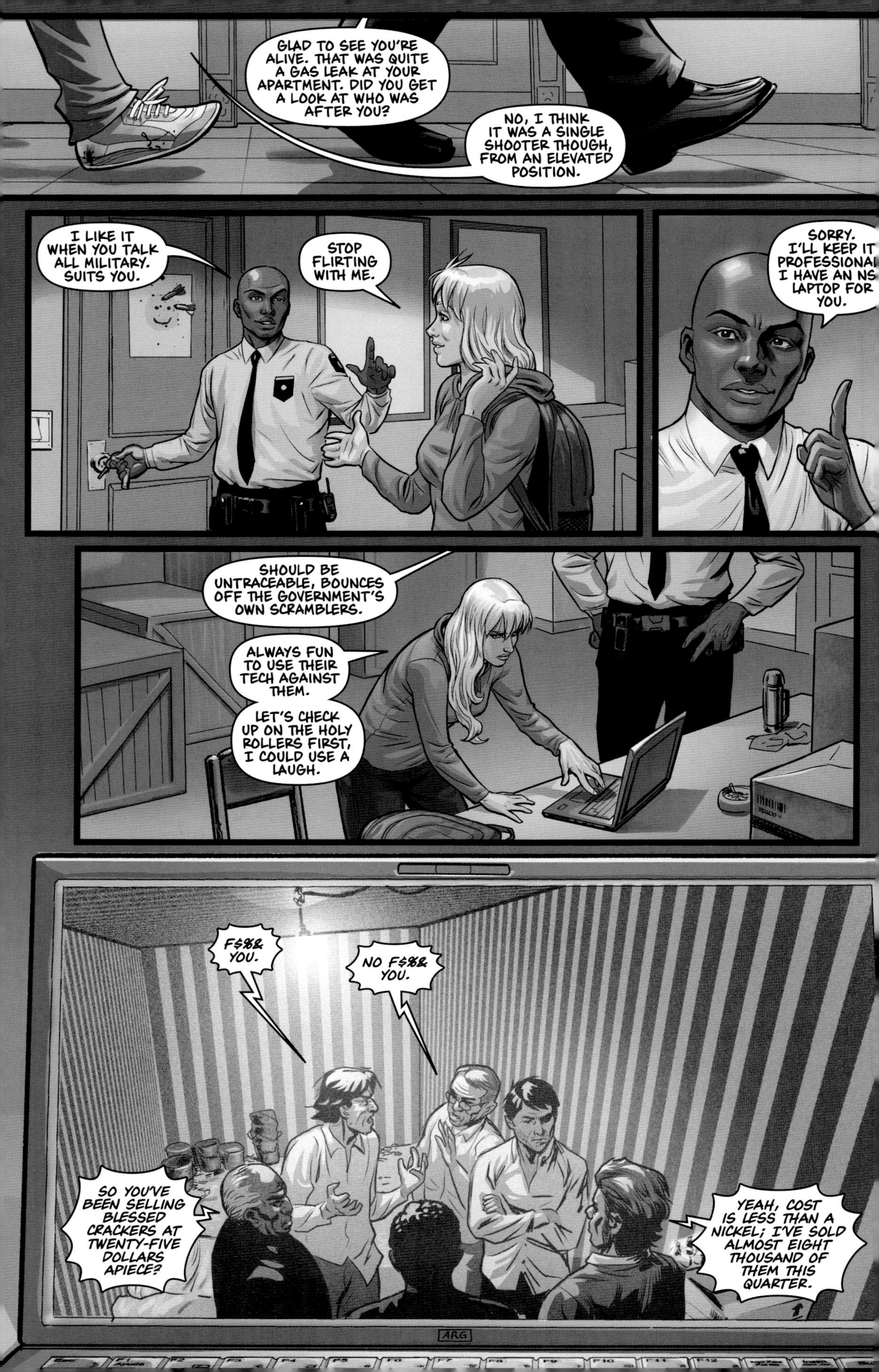
GLAD TO SEE YOU'RE ALIVE. THAT WAS QUITE A GAS LEAK AT YOUR APARTMENT. DID YOU GET A LOOK AT WHO WAS AFTER YOU?
NO, I THINK IT WAS A SINGLE SHOOTER THOUGH, FROM AN ELEVATED POSITION.
I LIKE IT WHEN YOU TALK ALL MILITARY. SUITS YOU.
STOP FLIRTING WITH ME.
SORRY. I'LL KEEP IT PROFESSIONA I HAVE AN NS LAPTOP FOR YOU.
SHOULD BE UNTRACEABLE, BOUNCES OFF THE GOVERNMENT'S OWN SCRAMBLERS.
ALWAYS FUN TO USE THEIR TECH AGAINST THEM.
LET'S CHECK UP ON THE HOLY ROLLERS FIRST, I COULD USE A LAUGH.
F$%& YOU.
NO F$%& YOU.
SO YOU'VE BEEN SELLING BLESSED CRACKERS AT TWENTY-FIVE DOLLARS APIECE?
YEAH, COST IS LESS THAN A NICKEL; I'VE SOLD ALMOST EIGHT THOUSAND OF THEM THIS QUARTER.
ARG

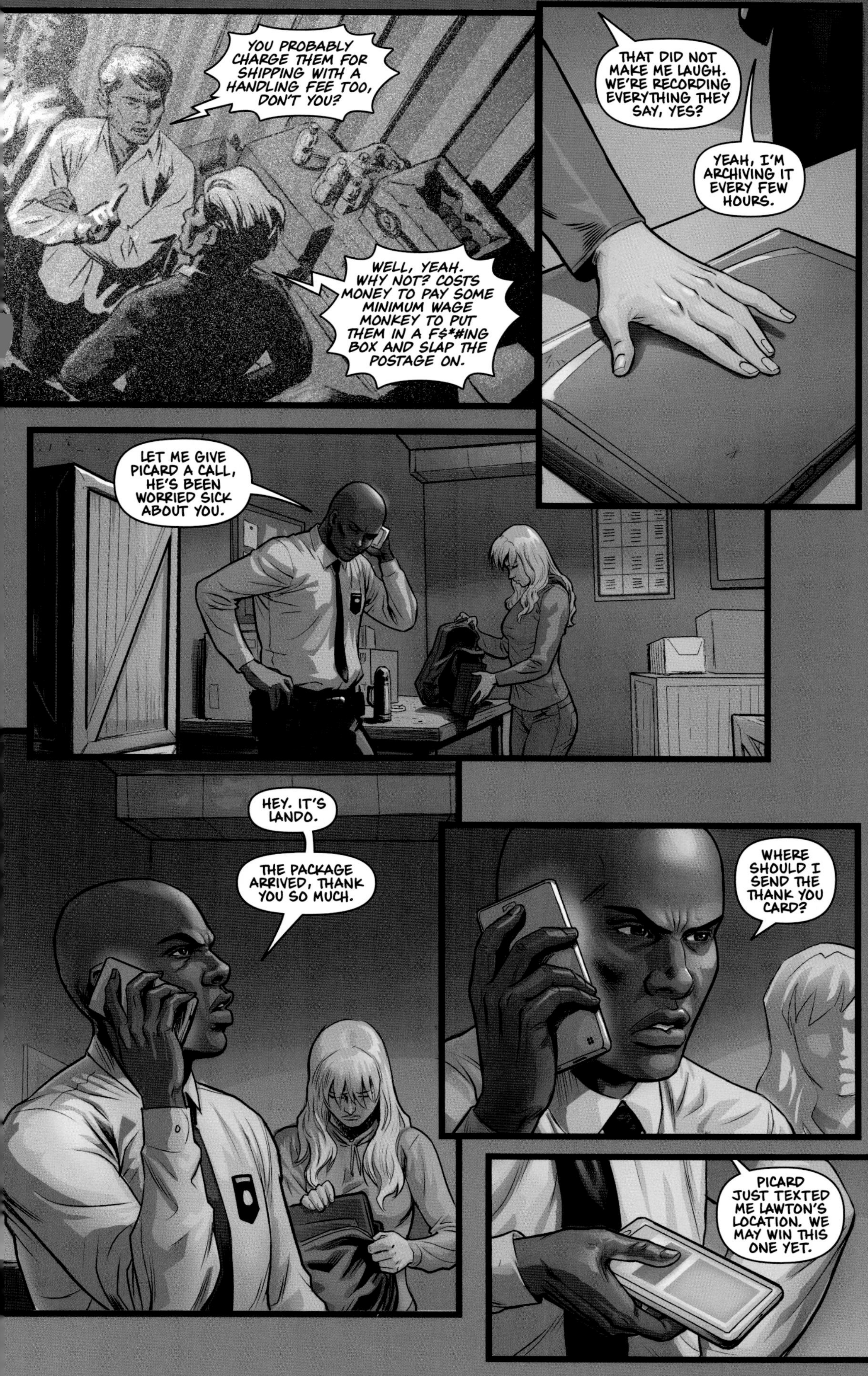
YOU PROBABLY CHARGE THEM FOR SHIPPING WITH A HANDLING FEE TOO, DON'T YOU?
WELL, YEAH. WHY NOT? COSTS MONEY TO PAY SOME MINIMUM WAGE MONKEY TO PUT THEM IN A F$*#ING BOX AND SLAP THE POSTAGE ON.
THAT DID NOT MAKE ME LAUGH. WE'RE RECORDING EVERYTHING THEY SAY, YES?
YEAH, I'M ARCHIVING IT EVERY FEW HOURS.
LET ME GIVE PICARD A CALL, HE'S BEEN WORRIED SICK ABOUT YOU.
HEY. IT'S LANDO.
THE PACKAGE ARRIVED, THANK YOU SO MUCH.
WHERE SHOULD I SEND THE THANK YOU CARD?
PICARD JUST TEXTED ME LAWTON'S LOCATION. WE MAY WIN THIS ONE YET.

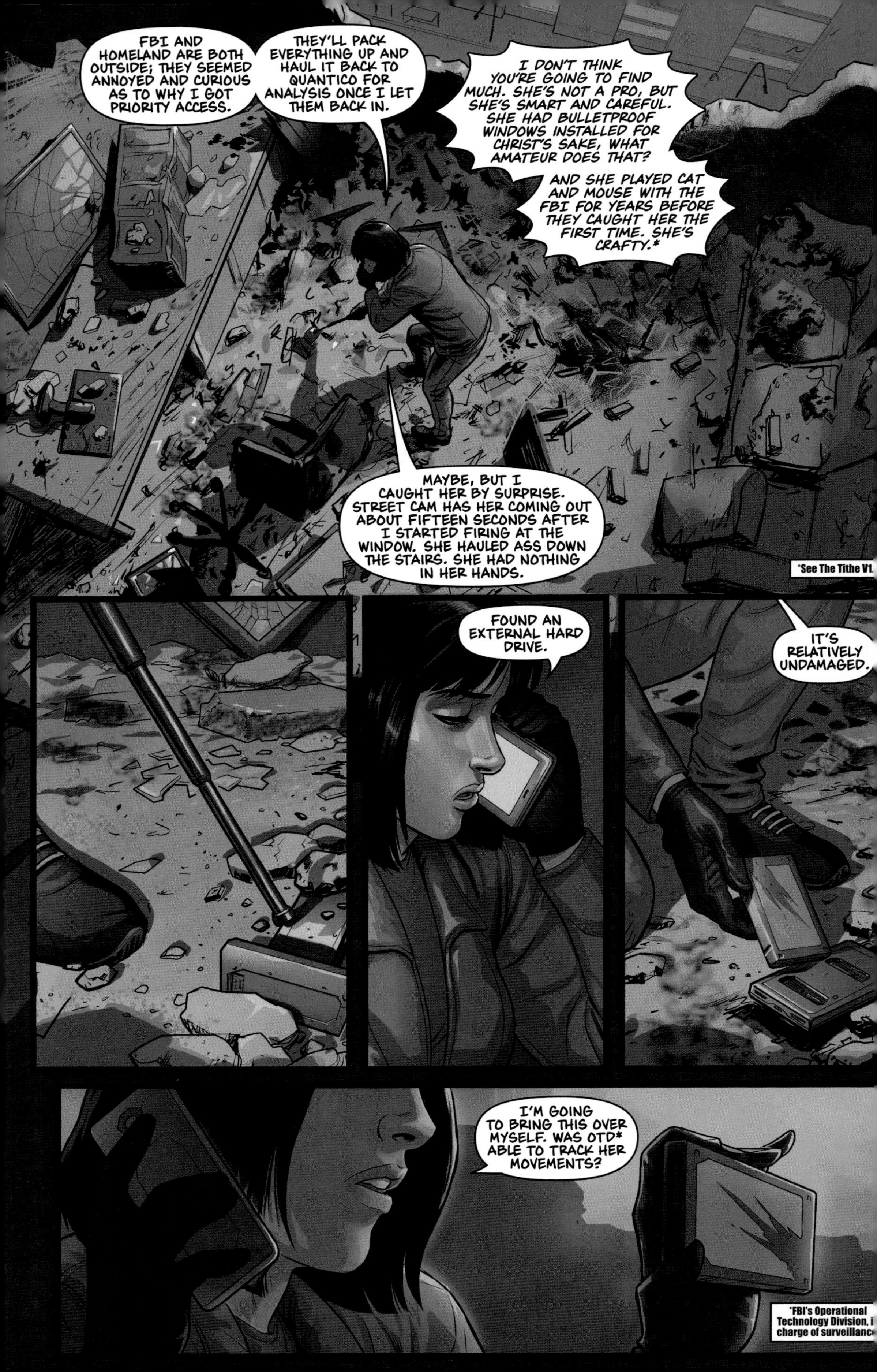
FBI AND HOMELAND ARE BOTH OUTSIDE; THEY SEEMED ANNOYED AND CURIOUS AS TO WHY I GOT PRIORITY ACCESS.
THEY'LL PACK EVERYTHING UP AND HAUL IT BACK TO QUANTICO FOR ANALYSIS ONCE I LET THEM BACK IN.
I DON'T THINK YOU'RE GOING TO FIND MUCH. SHE'S NOT A PRO, BUT SHE'S SMART AND CAREFUL. SHE HAD BULLETPROOF WINDOWS INSTALLED FOR CHRIST'S SAKE, WHAT AMATEUR DOES THAT?
AND SHE PLAYED CAT AND MOUSE WITH THE FBI FOR YEARS BEFORE THEY CAUGHT HER THE FIRST TIME. SHE'S CRAFTY.*
MAYBE, BUT I CAUGHT HER BY SURPRISE. STREET CAM HAS HER COMING OUT ABOUT FIFTEEN SECONDS AFTER I STARTED FIRING AT THE WINDOW. SHE HAULED ASS DOWN THE STAIRS. SHE HAD NOTHING IN HER HANDS.
*See The Tithe V1
FOUND AN EXTERNAL HARD DRIVE.
IT'S RELATIVELY UNDAMAGED.
I'M GOING TO BRING THIS OVER MYSELF. WAS OTD* ABLE TO TRACK HER MOVEMENTS?
*FBI's Operational Technology Division, i charge of surveillanc

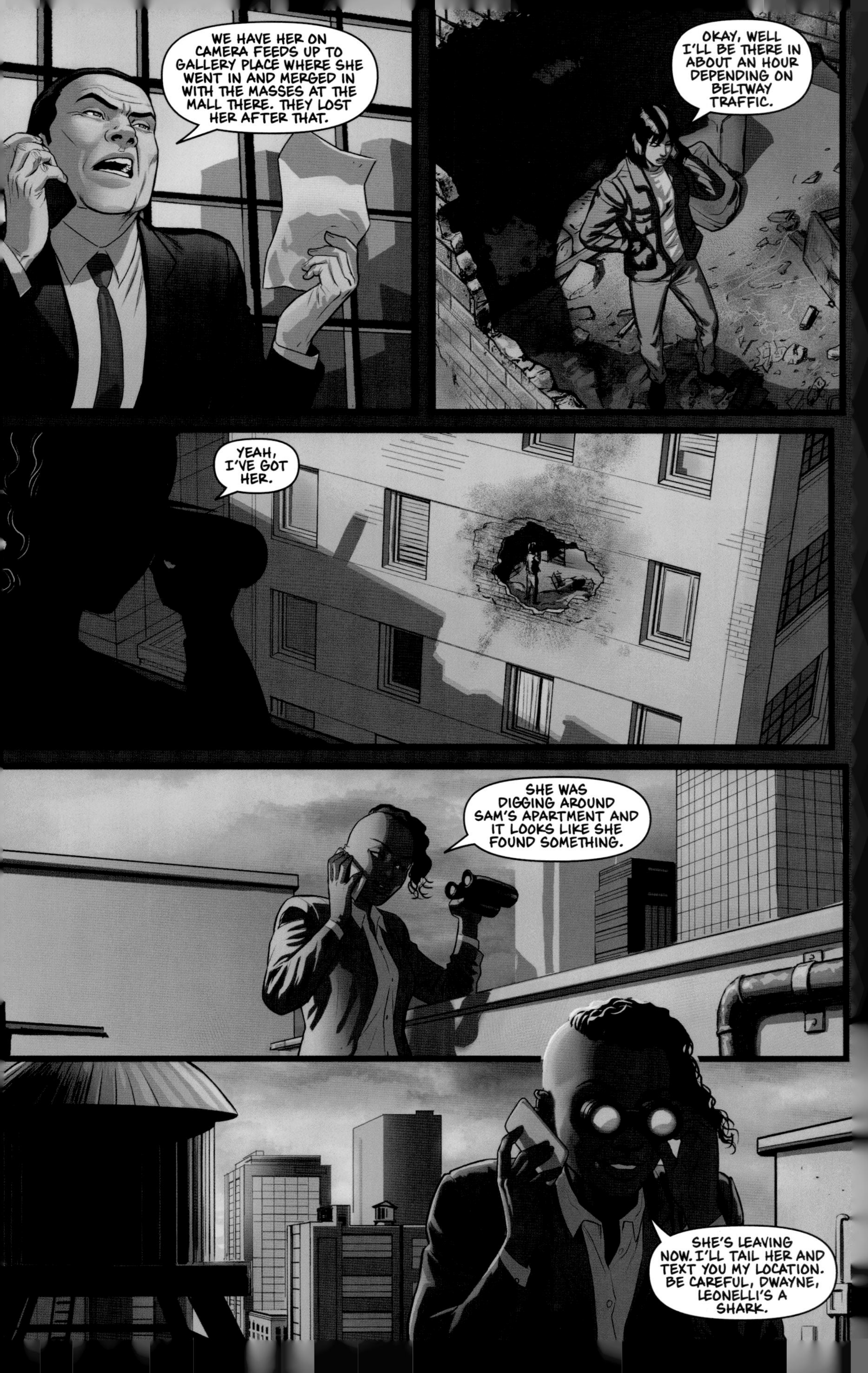
WE HAVE HER ON CAMERA FEEDS UP TO GALLERY PLACE WHERE SHE WENT IN AND MERGED IN WITH THE MASSES AT THE MALL THERE. THEY LOST HER AFTER THAT.
OKAY, WELL I'LL BE THERE IN ABOUT AN HOUR DEPENDING ON BELTWAY TRAFFIC.
YEAH, I'VE GOT HER.
SHE WAS DIGGING AROUND SAM'S APARTMENT AND IT LOOKS LIKE SHE FOUND SOMETHING.
SHE'S LEAVING NOW. I'LL TAIL HER AND TEXT YOU MY LOCATION. BE CAREFUL, DWAYNE, LEONELLI'S A SHARK.

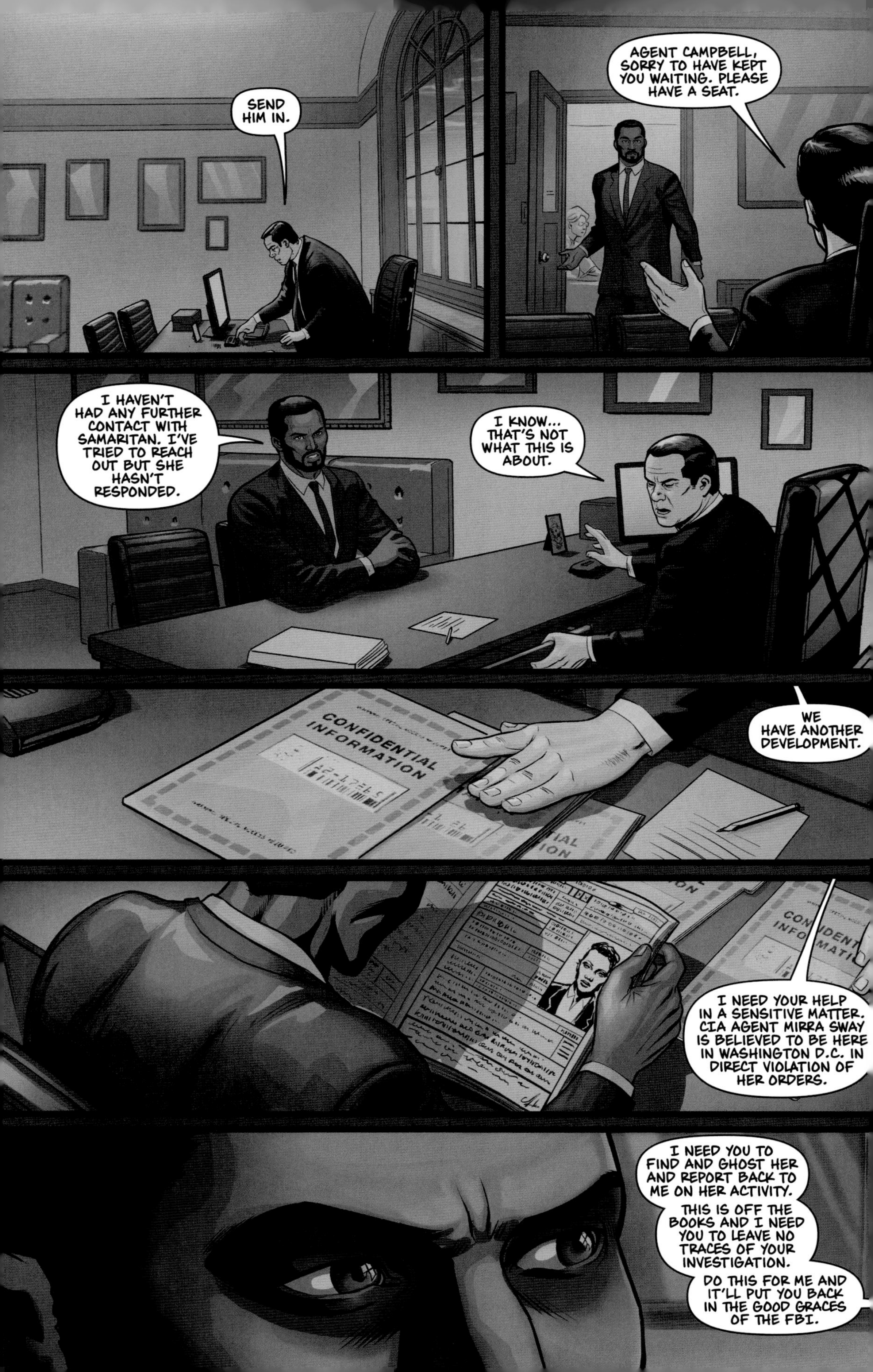
SEND HIM IN.
AGENT CAMPBELL, SORRY TO HAVE KEPT YOU WAITING. PLEASE HAVE A SEAT.
I HAVEN'T HAD ANY FURTHER CONTACT WITH SAMARITAN. I'VE TRIED TO REACH OUT BUT SHE HASN'T RESPONDED.
I KNOW... THAT'S NOT WHAT THIS IS ABOUT.
CONFIDENTIAL INFORMATION
WE HAVE ANOTHER DEVELOPMENT.
I NEED YOUR HELP IN A SENSITIVE MATTER. CIA AGENT MIRRA SWAY IS BELIEVED TO BE HERE IN WASHINGTON D.C. IN DIRECT VIOLATION OF HER ORDERS.
I NEED YOU TO FIND AND GHOST HER AND REPORT BACK TO ME ON HER ACTIVITY.
THIS IS OFF THE BOOKS AND I NEED YOU TO LEAVE NO TRACES OF YOUR INVESTIGATION.
DO THIS FOR ME AND IT'LL PUT YOU BACK IN THE GOOD GRACES OF THE FBI.

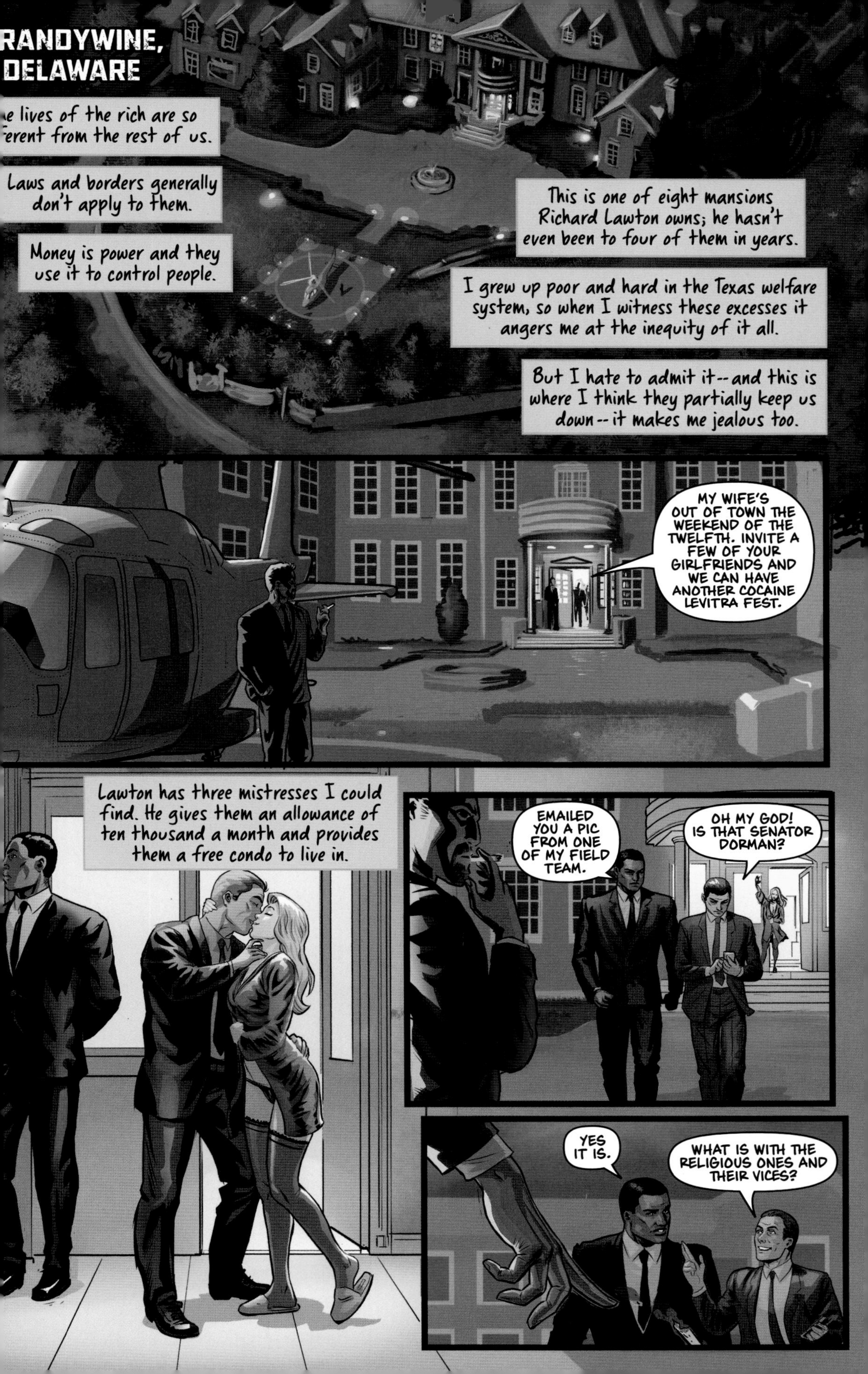
RANDYWINE, DELAWARE
e lives of the rich are so ferent from the rest of us.
Laws and borders generally don't apply to them.
Money is power and they use it to control people.
This is one of eight mansions Richard Lawton owns; he hasn't even been to four of them in years.
I grew up poor and hard in the Texas welfare system, so when I witness these excesses it angers me at the inequity of it all.
But I hate to admit it--and this is where I think they partially keep us down--it makes me jealous too.
MY WIFE'S OUT OF TOWN THE WEEKEND OF THE TWELFTH. INVITE A FEW OF YOUR GIRLFRIENDS AND WE CAN HAVE ANOTHER COCAINE LEVITRA FEST.
Lawton has three mistresses I could find. He gives them an allowance of ten thousand a month and provides them a free condo to live in.
EMAILED YOU A PIC FROM ONE OF MY FIELD TEAM.
OH MY GOD! IS THAT SENATOR DORMAN?
YES IT IS.
WHAT IS WITH THE RELIGIOUS ONES AND THEIR VICES?

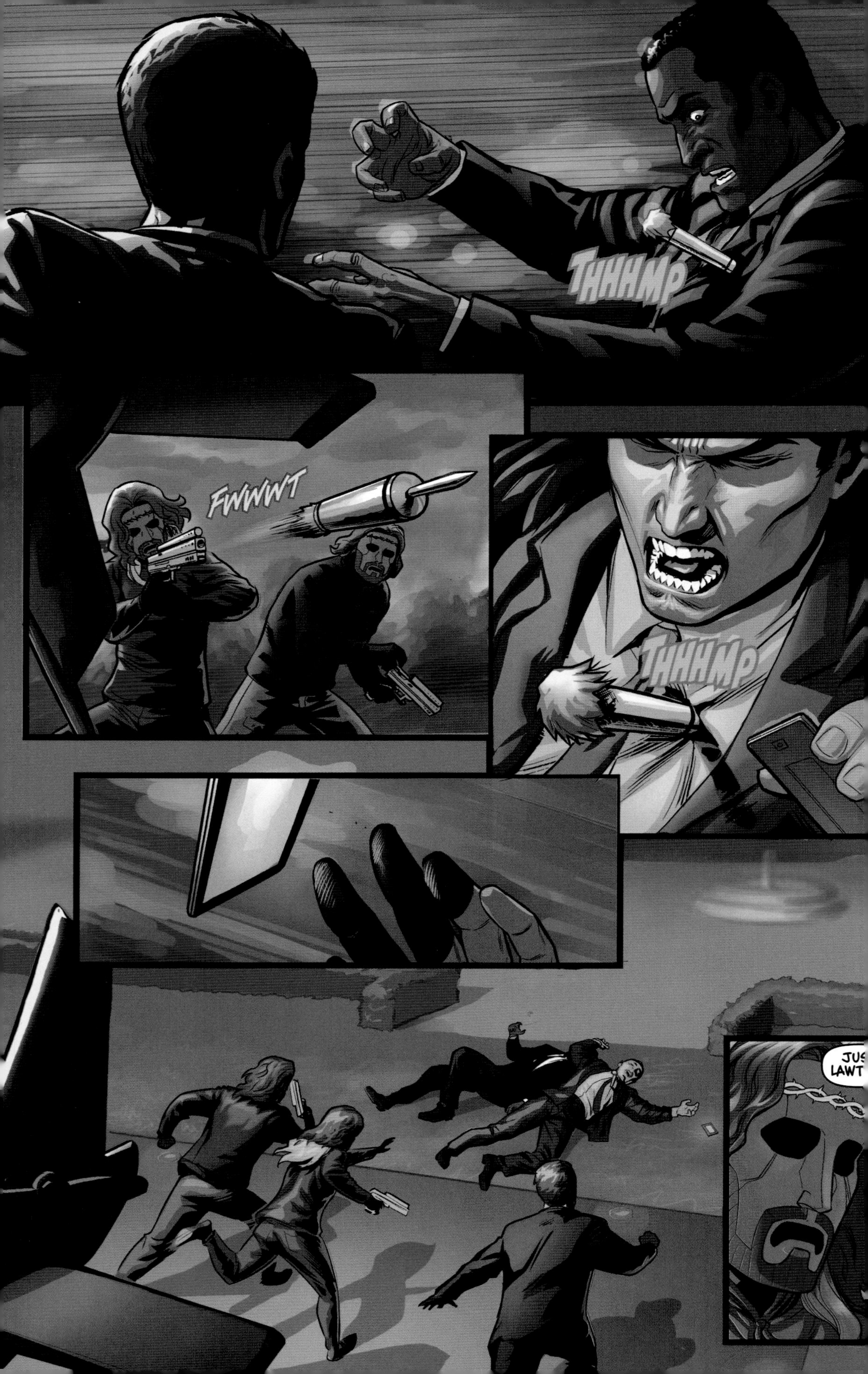
THHHMP
FWWWT
THHHMP

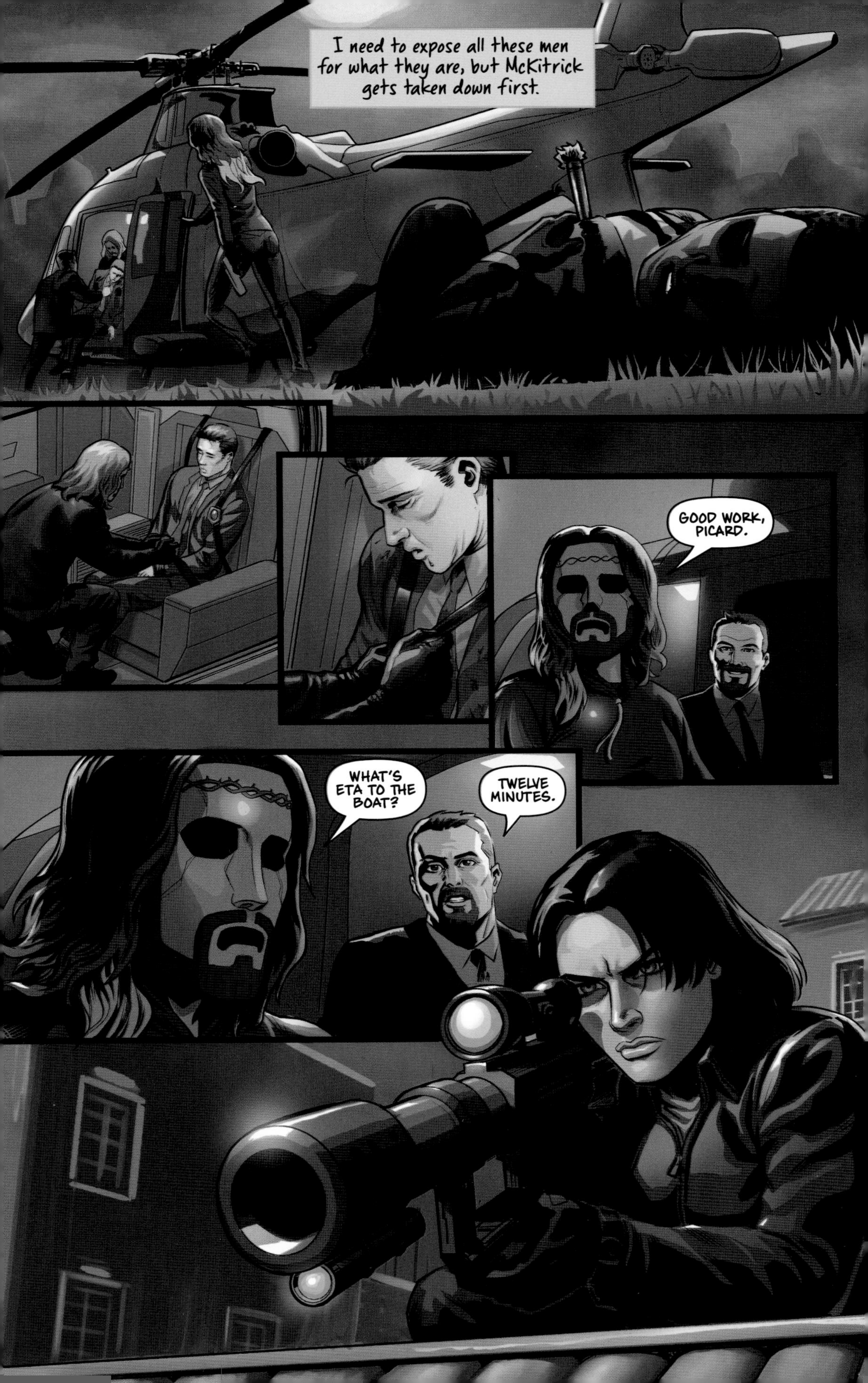
I need to expose all these men for what they are, but McKitrick gets taken down first.
GOOD WORK, PICARD.
WHAT'S ETA TO THE BOAT?
TWELVE MINUTES.

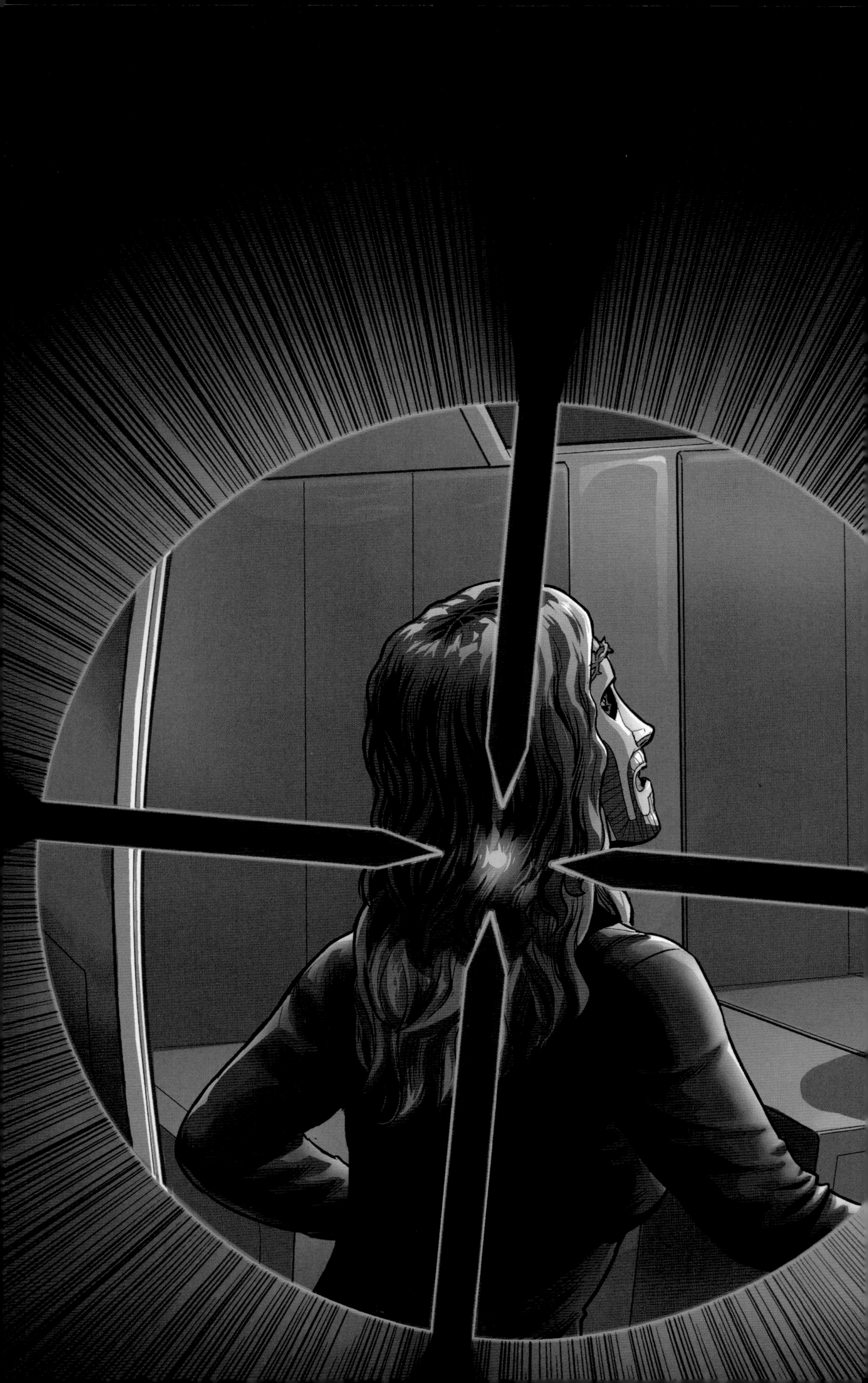

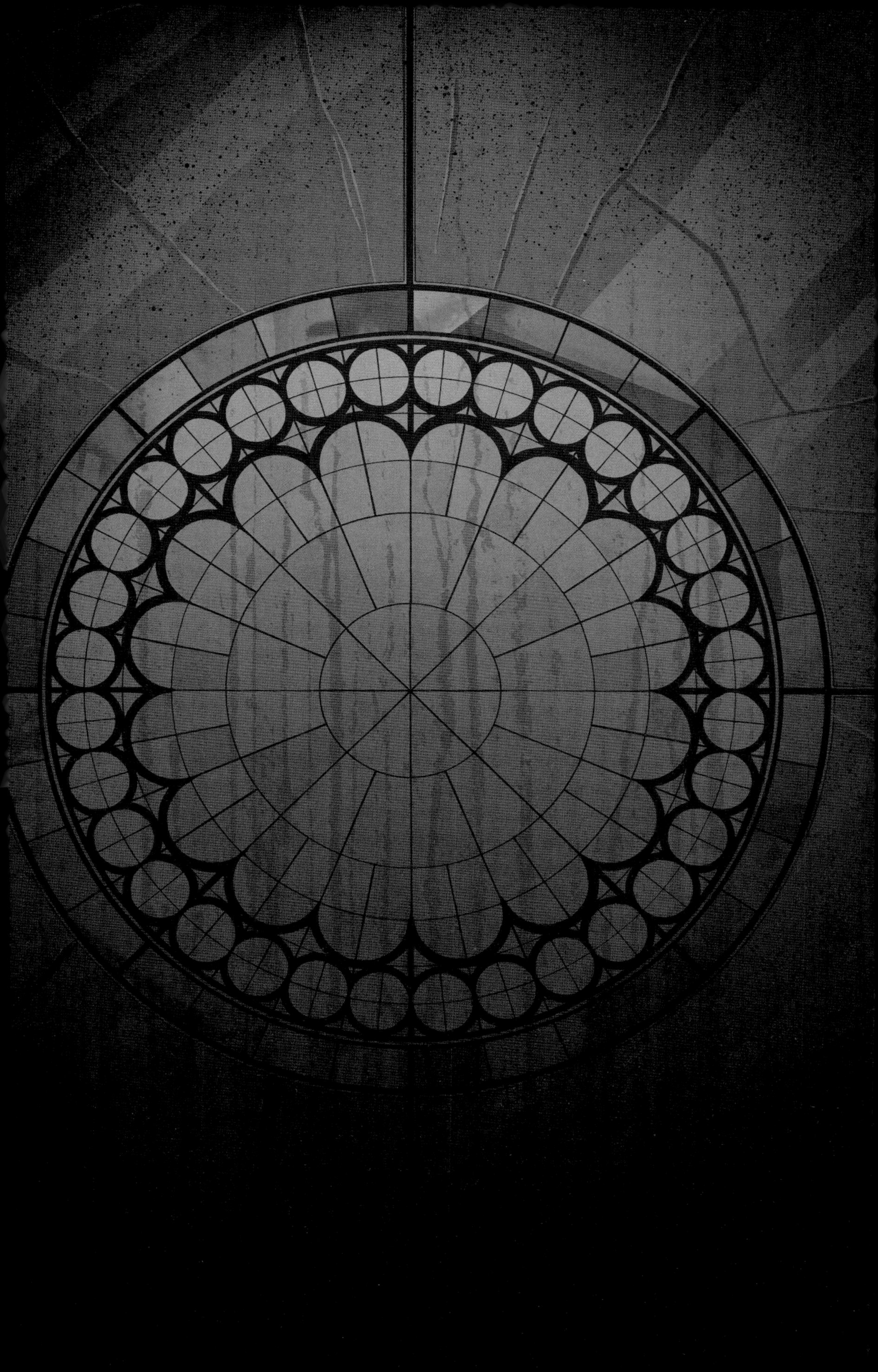

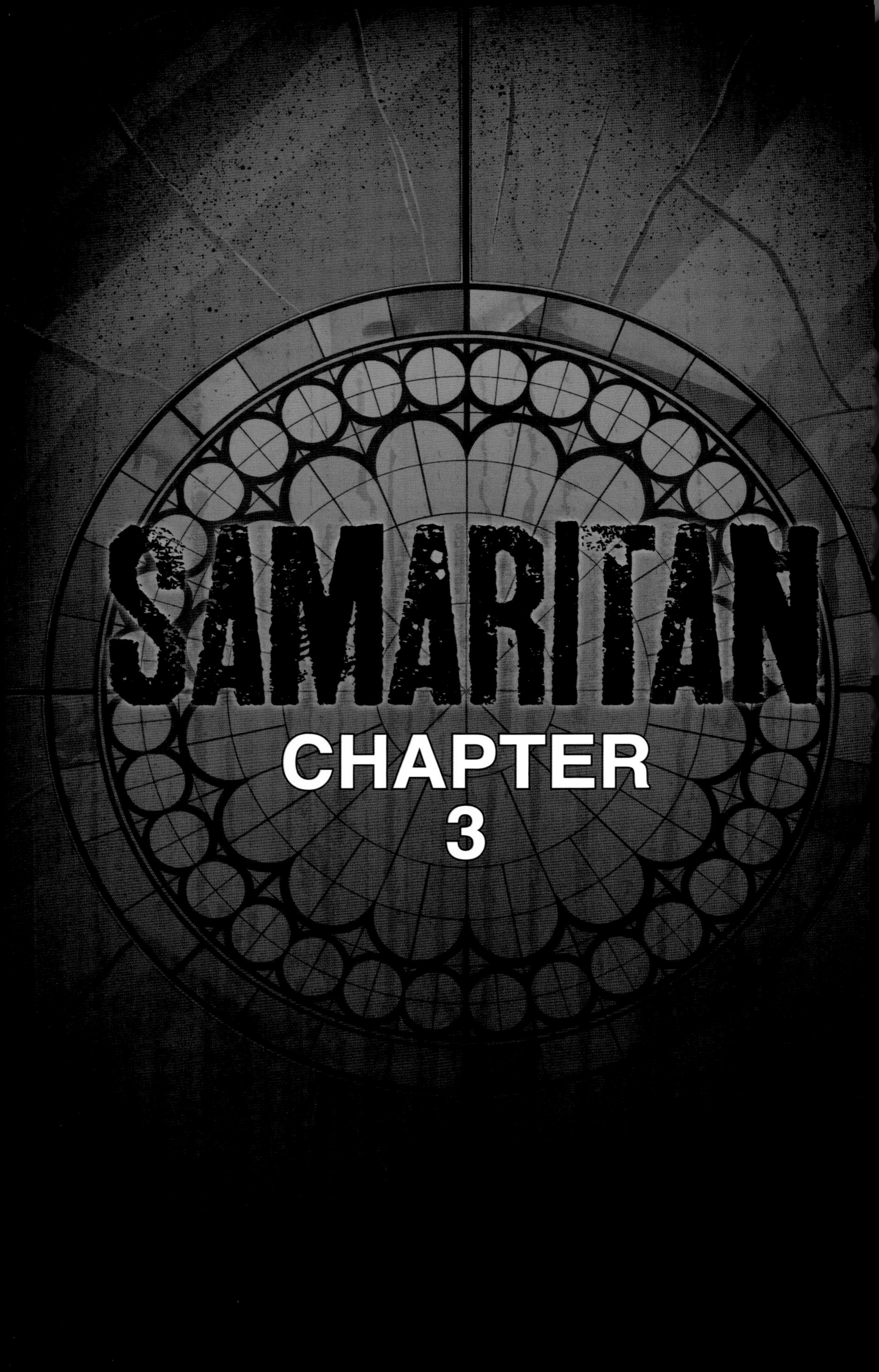
SAMARITAN
CHAPTER
3

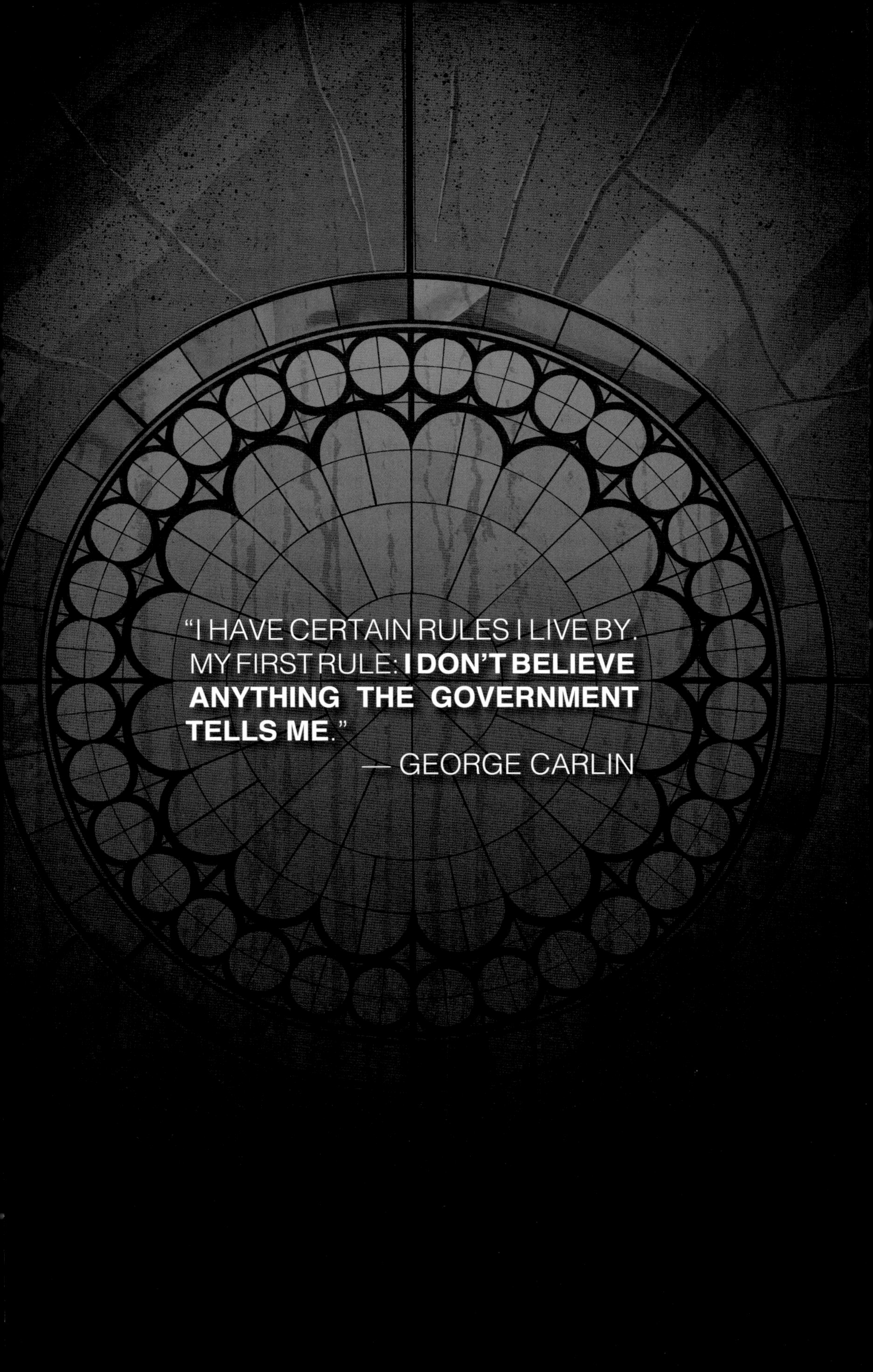

"I HAVE CERTAIN RULES I LIVE BY. MY FIRST RULE: **I DON'T BELIEVE ANYTHING THE GOVERNMENT TELLS ME**."

— GEORGE CARLIN

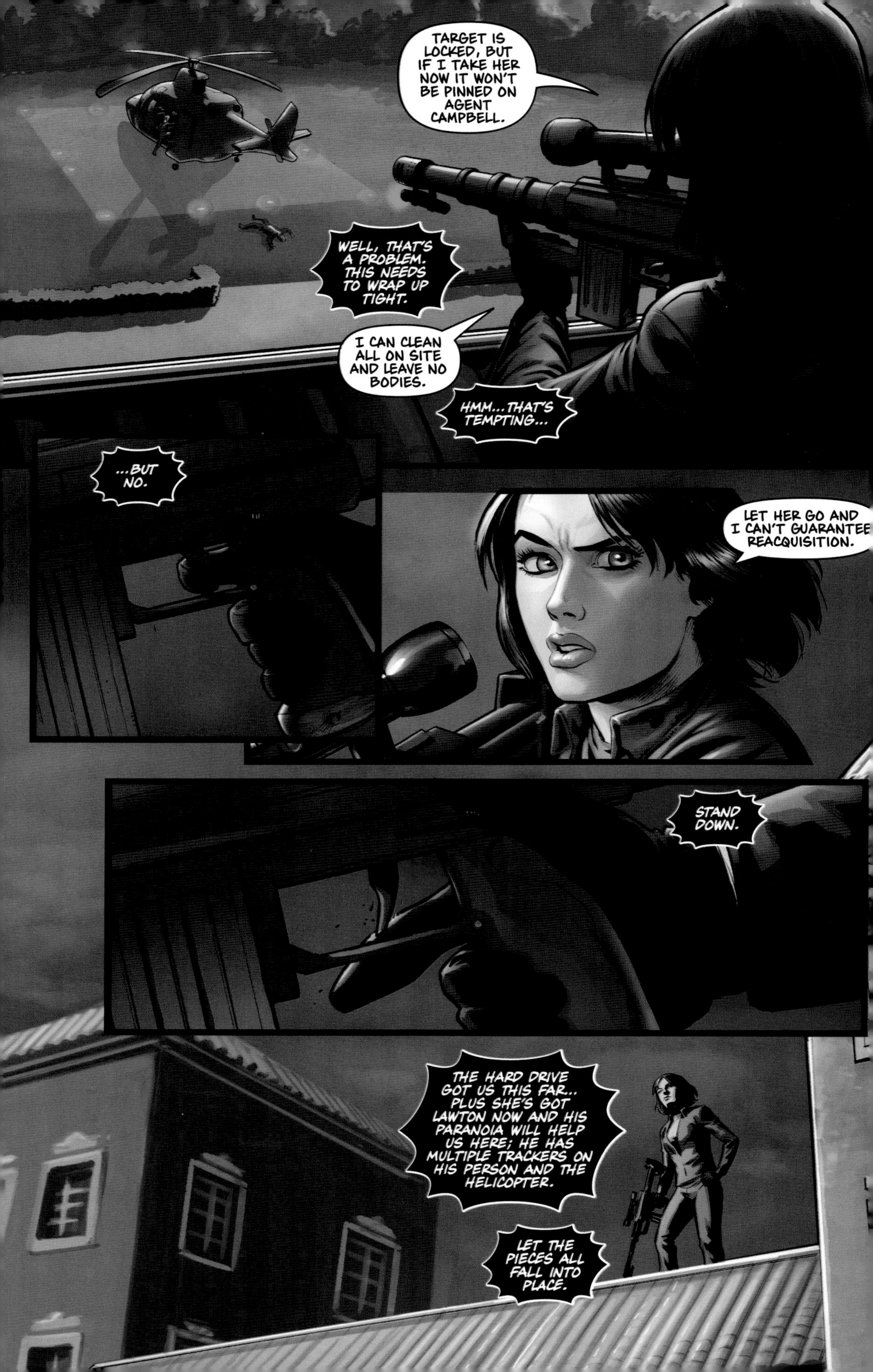
TARGET IS LOCKED, BUT IF I TAKE HER NOW IT WON'T BE PINNED ON AGENT CAMPBELL.
WELL, THAT'S A PROBLEM. THIS NEEDS TO WRAP UP TIGHT.
I CAN CLEAN ALL ON SITE AND LEAVE NO BODIES.
HMM... THAT'S TEMPTING...
...BUT NO.
LET HER GO AND I CAN'T GUARANTEE REACQUISITION.
STAND DOWN.
THE HARD DRIVE GOT US THIS FAR... PLUS SHE'S GOT LAWTON NOW AND HIS PARANOIA WILL HELP US HERE; HE HAS MULTIPLE TRACKERS ON HIS PERSON AND THE HELICOPTER.
LET THE PIECES ALL FALL INTO PLACE.

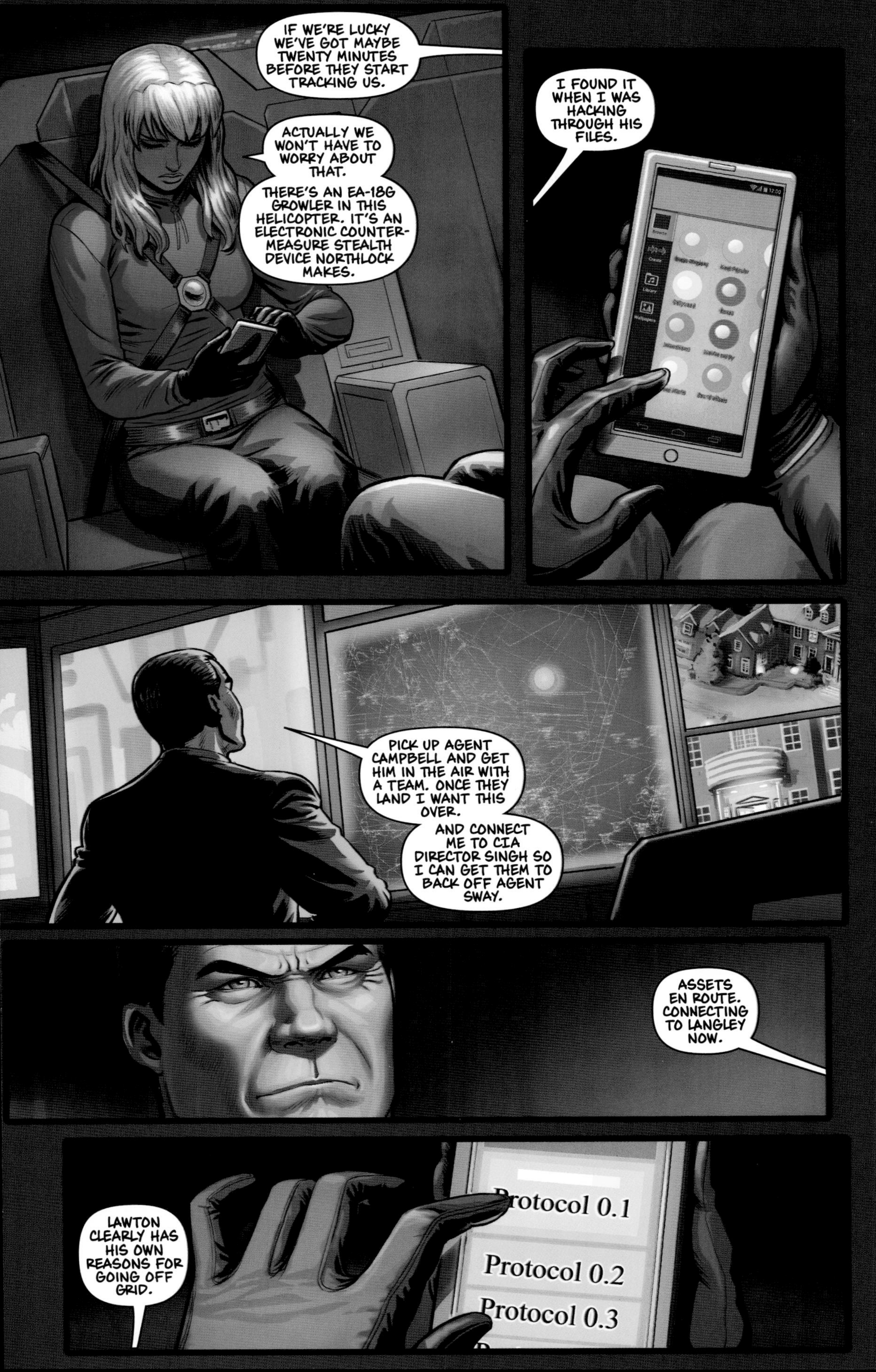
IF WE'RE LUCKY WE'VE GOT MAYBE TWENTY MINUTES BEFORE THEY START TRACKING US.
ACTUALLY WE WON'T HAVE TO WORRY ABOUT THAT.
THERE'S AN EA-18G GROWLER IN THIS HELICOPTER. IT'S AN ELECTRONIC COUNTER-MEASURE STEALTH DEVICE NORTHLOCK MAKES.
I FOUND IT WHEN I WAS HACKING THROUGH HIS FILES.
PICK UP AGENT CAMPBELL AND GET HIM IN THE AIR WITH A TEAM. ONCE THEY LAND I WANT THIS OVER.
AND CONNECT ME TO CIA DIRECTOR SINGH SO I CAN GET THEM TO BACK OFF AGENT SWAY.
ASSETS EN ROUTE. CONNECTING TO LANGLEY NOW.
LAWTON CLEARLY HAS HIS OWN REASONS FOR GOING OFF GRID.
Protocol 0.1
Protocol 0.2
Protocol 0.3

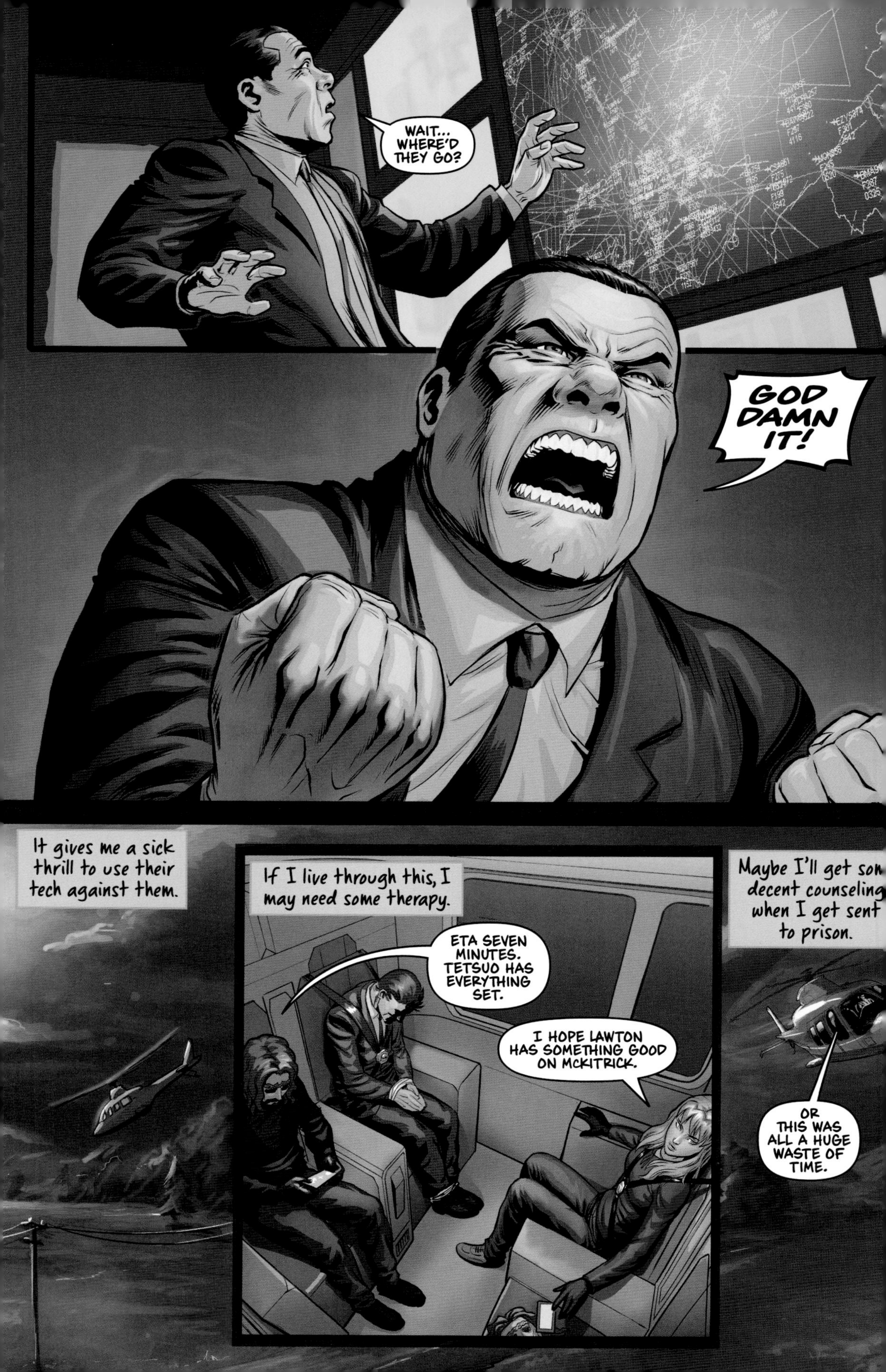
WAIT... WHERE'D THEY GO?
GOD DAMN IT!
It gives me a sick thrill to use their tech against them.
If I live through this, I may need some therapy.
Maybe I'll get son decent counseling when I get sent to prison.
ETA SEVEN MINUTES. TETSUO HAS EVERYTHING SET.
I HOPE LAWTON HAS SOMETHING GOOD ON MCKITRICK.
OR THIS WAS ALL A HUGE WASTE OF TIME.

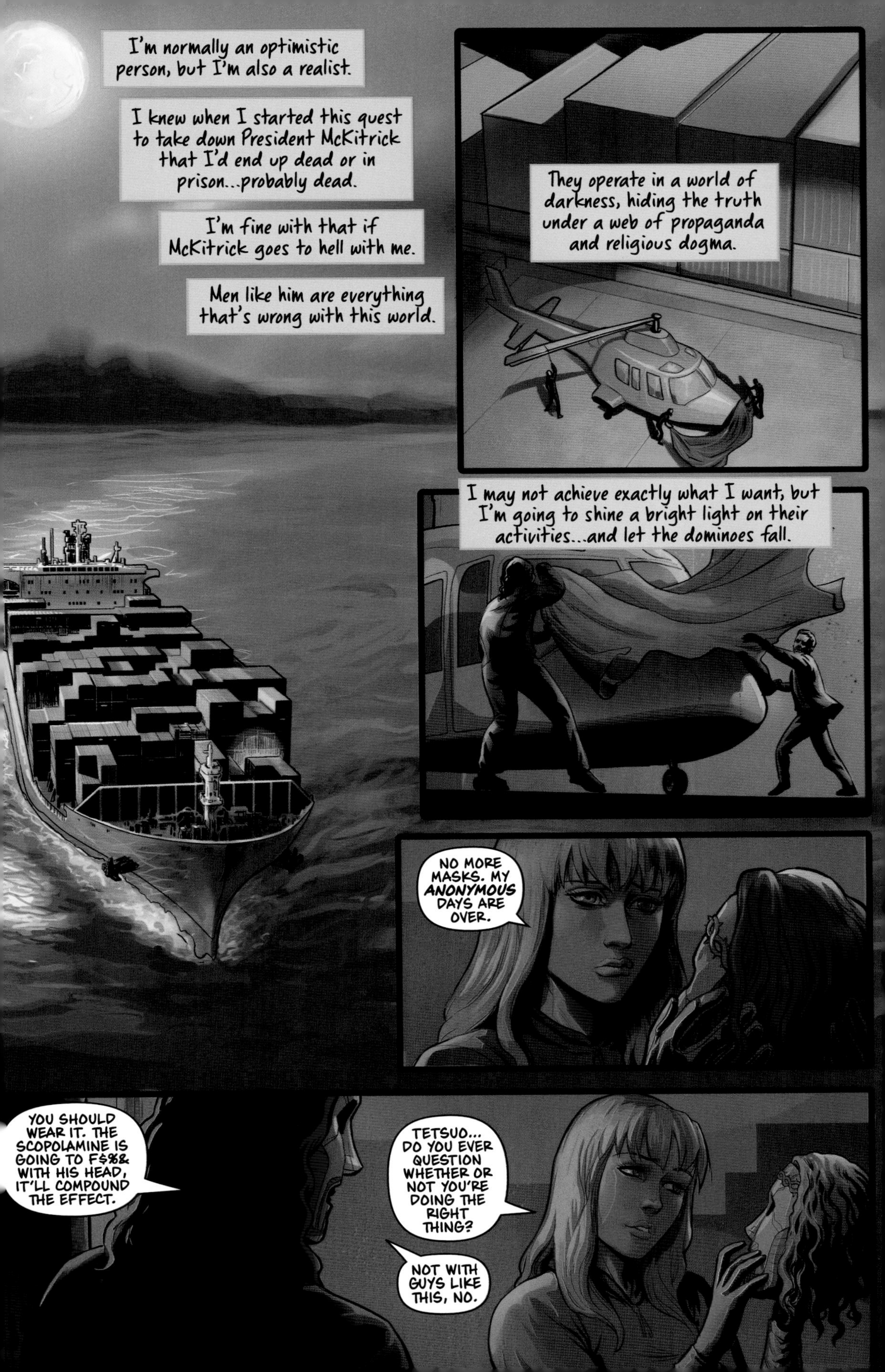
I'm normally an optimistic person, but I'm also a realist.
I knew when I started this quest to take down President McKitrick that I'd end up dead or in prison...probably dead.
I'm fine with that if McKitrick goes to hell with me.
Men like him are everything that's wrong with this world.
They operate in a world of darkness, hiding the truth under a web of propaganda and religious dogma.
I may not achieve exactly what I want, but I'm going to shine a bright light on their activities...and let the dominoes fall.
NO MORE MASKS. MY ANONYMOUS DAYS ARE OVER.
YOU SHOULD WEAR IT. THE SCOPOLAMINE IS GOING TO F$%& WITH HIS HEAD, IT'LL COMPOUND THE EFFECT.
TETSUO... DO YOU EVER QUESTION WHETHER OR NOT YOU'RE DOING THE RIGHT THING?
NOT WITH GUYS LIKE THIS, NO.

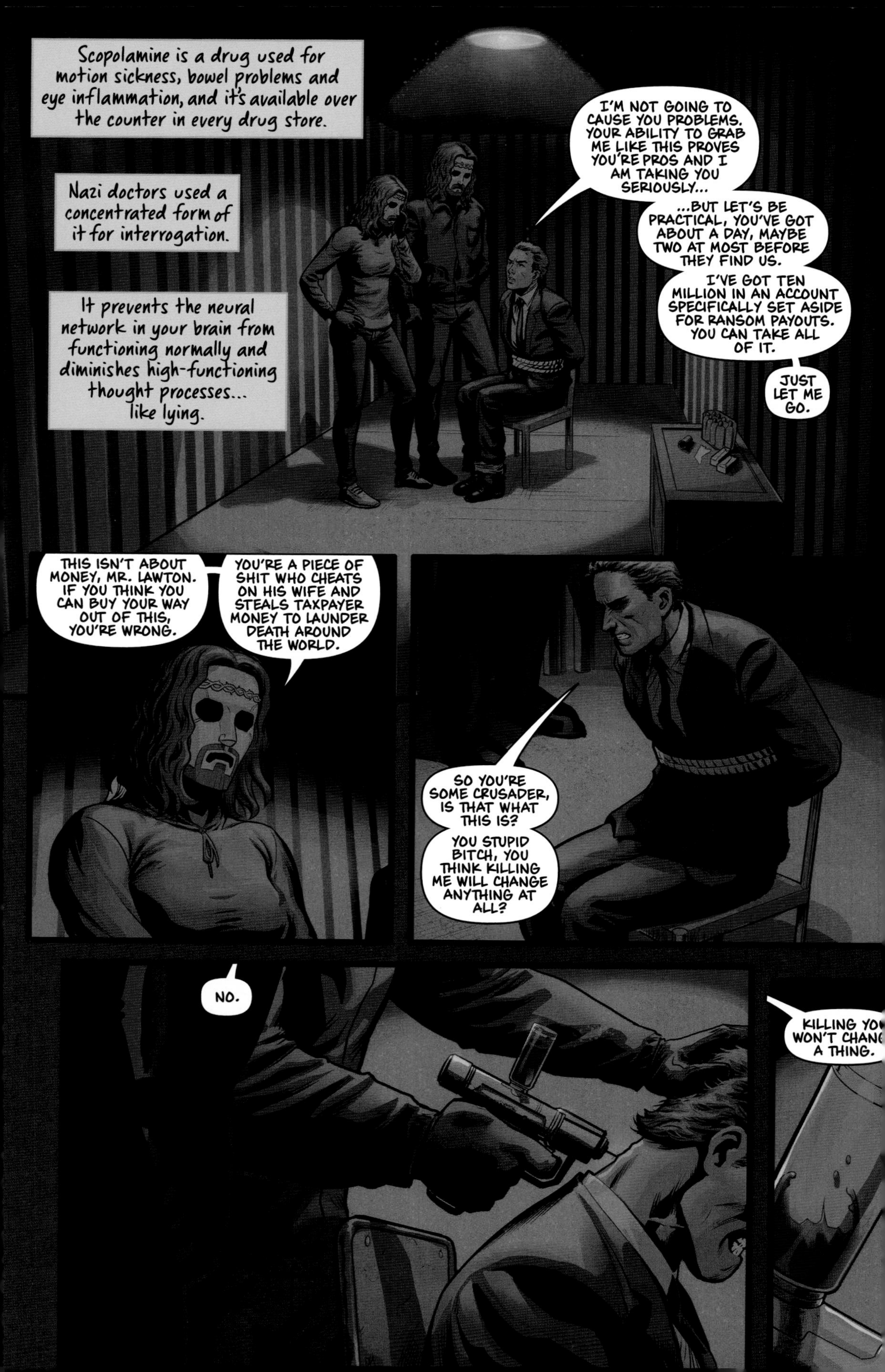
Scopolamine is a drug used for motion sickness, bowel problems and eye inflammation, and it's available over the counter in every drug store.
Nazi doctors used a concentrated form of it for interrogation.
It prevents the neural network in your brain from functioning normally and diminishes high-functioning thought processes... like lying.
I'M NOT GOING TO CAUSE YOU PROBLEMS. YOUR ABILITY TO GRAB ME LIKE THIS PROVES YOU'RE PROS AND I AM TAKING YOU SERIOUSLY...
...BUT LET'S BE PRACTICAL, YOU'VE GOT ABOUT A DAY, MAYBE TWO AT MOST BEFORE THEY FIND US.
I'VE GOT TEN MILLION IN AN ACCOUNT SPECIFICALLY SET ASIDE FOR RANSOM PAYOUTS. YOU CAN TAKE ALL OF IT.
JUST LET ME GO.
THIS ISN'T ABOUT MONEY, MR. LAWTON. IF YOU THINK YOU CAN BUY YOUR WAY OUT OF THIS, YOU'RE WRONG.
YOU'RE A PIECE OF SHIT WHO CHEATS ON HIS WIFE AND STEALS TAXPAYER MONEY TO LAUNDER DEATH AROUND THE WORLD.
SO YOU'RE SOME CRUSADER, IS THAT WHAT THIS IS?
YOU STUPID BITCH, YOU THINK KILLING ME WILL CHANGE ANYTHING AT ALL?
NO.
KILLING YO WON'T CHANG A THING.

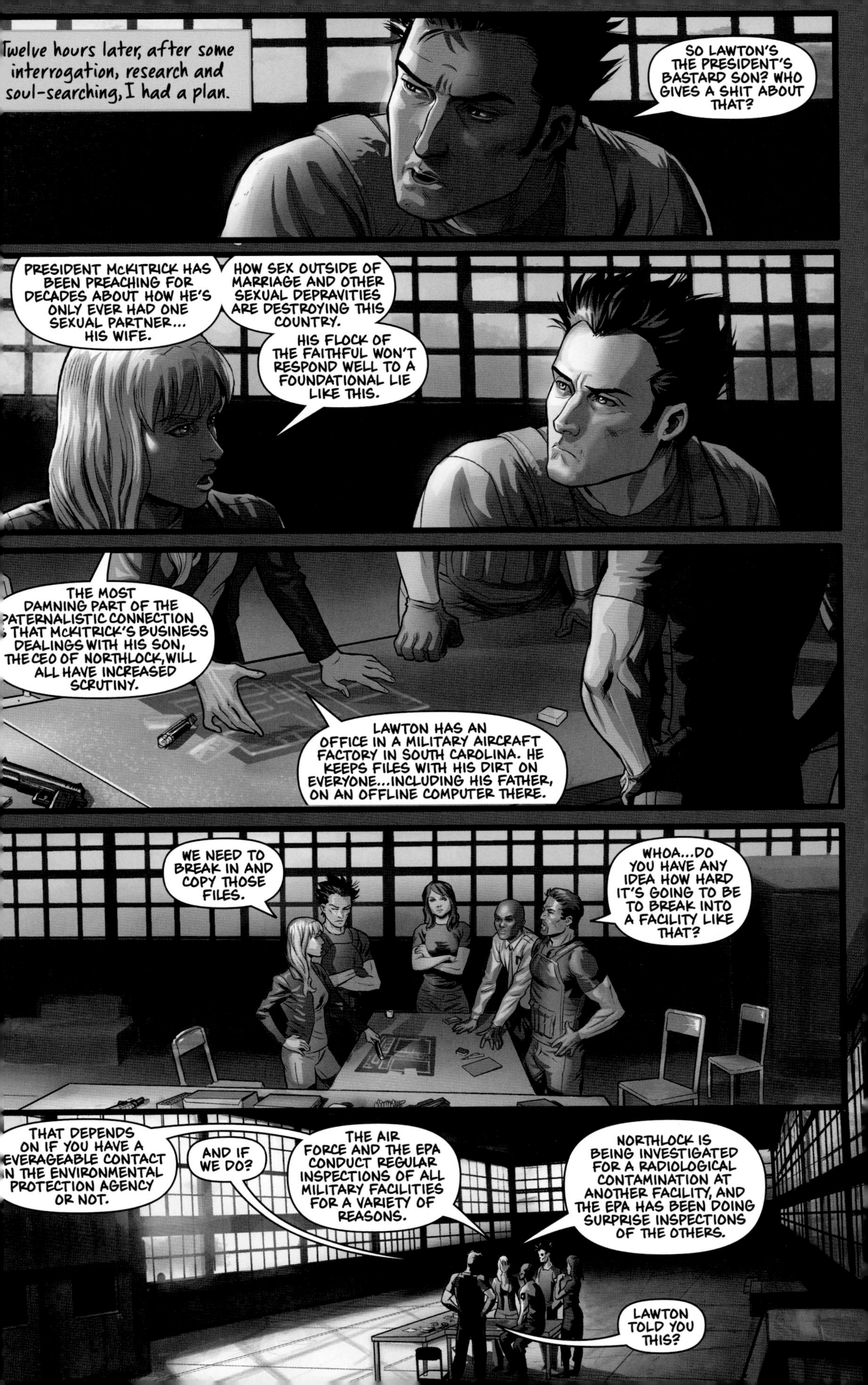
Twelve hours later, after some interrogation, research and soul-searching, I had a plan.
SO LAWTON'S THE PRESIDENT'S BASTARD SON? WHO GIVES A SHIT ABOUT THAT?
PRESIDENT McKITRICK HAS BEEN PREACHING FOR DECADES ABOUT HOW HE'S ONLY EVER HAD ONE SEXUAL PARTNER... HIS WIFE.
HOW SEX OUTSIDE OF MARRIAGE AND OTHER SEXUAL DEPRAVITIES ARE DESTROYING THIS COUNTRY.
HIS FLOCK OF THE FAITHFUL WON'T RESPOND WELL TO A FOUNDATIONAL LIE LIKE THIS.
THE MOST DAMNING PART OF THE PATERNALISTIC CONNECTION IS THAT McKITRICK'S BUSINESS DEALINGS WITH HIS SON, THE CEO OF NORTHLOCK, WILL ALL HAVE INCREASED SCRUTINY.
LAWTON HAS AN OFFICE IN A MILITARY AIRCRAFT FACTORY IN SOUTH CAROLINA. HE KEEPS FILES WITH HIS DIRT ON EVERYONE...INCLUDING HIS FATHER, ON AN OFFLINE COMPUTER THERE.
WE NEED TO BREAK IN AND COPY THOSE FILES.
WHOA...DO YOU HAVE ANY IDEA HOW HARD IT'S GOING TO BE TO BREAK INTO A FACILITY LIKE THAT?
THAT DEPENDS ON IF YOU HAVE A LEVERAGEABLE CONTACT IN THE ENVIRONMENTAL PROTECTION AGENCY OR NOT.
AND IF WE DO?
THE AIR FORCE AND THE EPA CONDUCT REGULAR INSPECTIONS OF ALL MILITARY FACILITIES FOR A VARIETY OF REASONS.
NORTHLOCK IS BEING INVESTIGATED FOR A RADIOLOGICAL CONTAMINATION AT ANOTHER FACILITY, AND THE EPA HAS BEEN DOING SURPRISE INSPECTIONS OF THE OTHERS.
LAWTON TOLD YOU THIS?

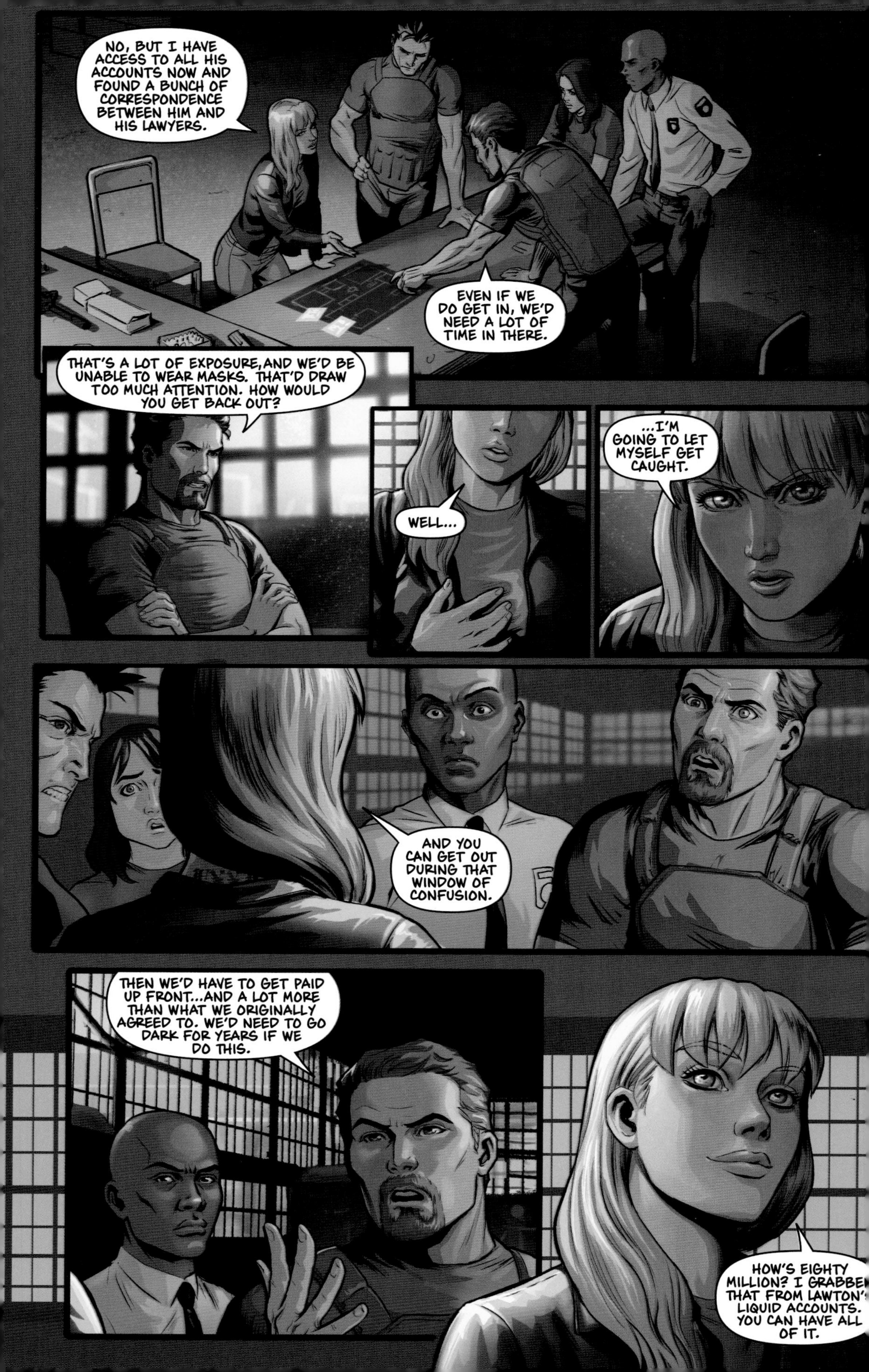
NO, BUT I HAVE ACCESS TO ALL HIS ACCOUNTS NOW AND FOUND A BUNCH OF CORRESPONDENCE BETWEEN HIM AND HIS LAWYERS.
EVEN IF WE DO GET IN, WE'D NEED A LOT OF TIME IN THERE.
THAT'S A LOT OF EXPOSURE, AND WE'D BE UNABLE TO WEAR MASKS. THAT'D DRAW TOO MUCH ATTENTION. HOW WOULD YOU GET BACK OUT?
WELL...
...I'M GOING TO LET MYSELF GET CAUGHT.
AND YOU CAN GET OUT DURING THAT WINDOW OF CONFUSION.
THEN WE'D HAVE TO GET PAID UP FRONT...AND A LOT MORE THAN WHAT WE ORIGINALLY AGREED TO. WE'D NEED TO GO DARK FOR YEARS IF WE DO THIS.
HOW'S EIGHTY MILLION? I GRABBE THAT FROM LAWTON' LIQUID ACCOUNTS. YOU CAN HAVE ALL OF IT.

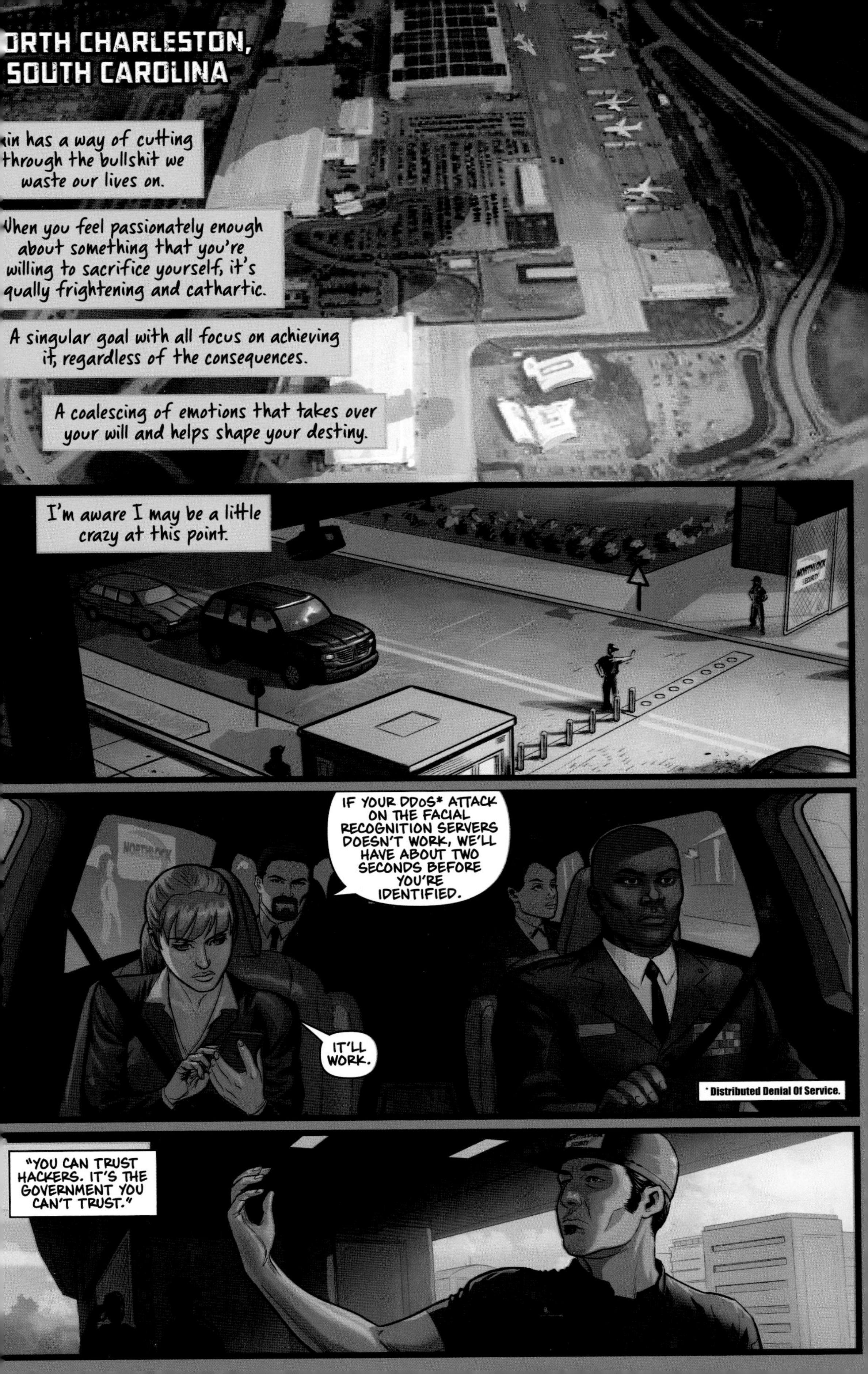
ORTH CHARLESTON, SOUTH CAROLINA
in has a way of cutting through the bullshit we waste our lives on.
Vhen you feel passionately enough about something that you're willing to sacrifice yourself, it's qually frightening and cathartic.
A singular goal with all focus on achieving it, regardless of the consequences.
A coalescing of emotions that takes over your will and helps shape your destiny.
I'm aware I may be a little crazy at this point.
IF YOUR DDOS* ATTACK ON THE FACIAL RECOGNITION SERVERS DOESN'T WORK, WE'LL HAVE ABOUT TWO SECONDS BEFORE YOU'RE IDENTIFIED.
IT'LL WORK.
* Distributed Denial Of Service.
"YOU CAN TRUST HACKERS. IT'S THE GOVERNMENT YOU CAN'T TRUST."

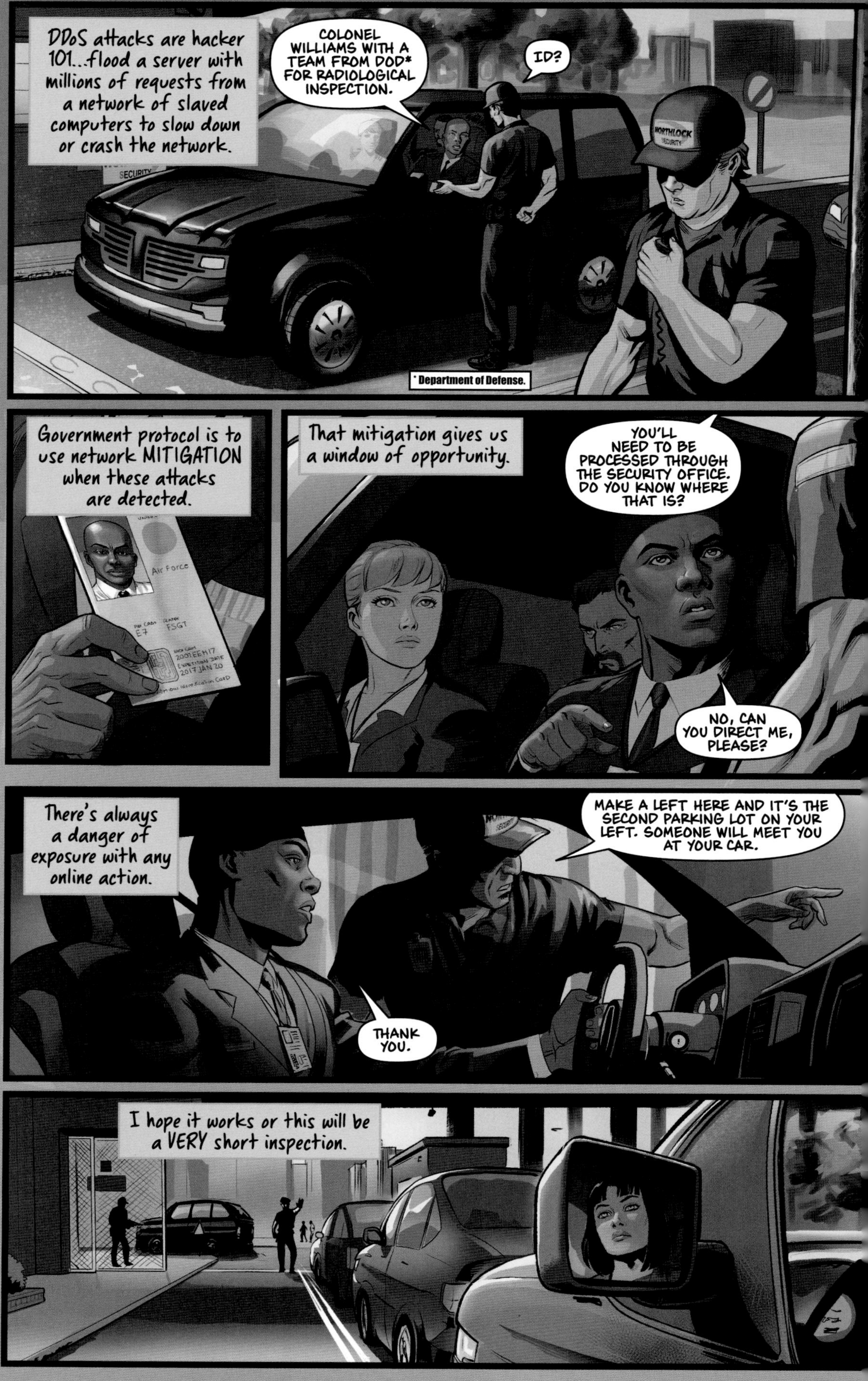
DDoS attacks are hacker 101...flood a server with millions of requests from a network of slaved computers to slow down or crash the network.
COLONEL WILLIAMS WITH A TEAM FROM DOD* FOR RADIOLOGICAL INSPECTION.
ID?
NORTHLOCK SECURITY
* Department of Defense.
Government protocol is to use network MITIGATION when these attacks are detected.
Air Force
That mitigation gives us a window of opportunity.
YOU'LL NEED TO BE PROCESSED THROUGH THE SECURITY OFFICE. DO YOU KNOW WHERE THAT IS?
NO, CAN YOU DIRECT ME, PLEASE?
There's always a danger of exposure with any online action.
MAKE A LEFT HERE AND IT'S THE SECOND PARKING LOT ON YOUR LEFT. SOMEONE WILL MEET YOU AT YOUR CAR.
THANK YOU.
I hope it works or this will be a VERY short inspection.

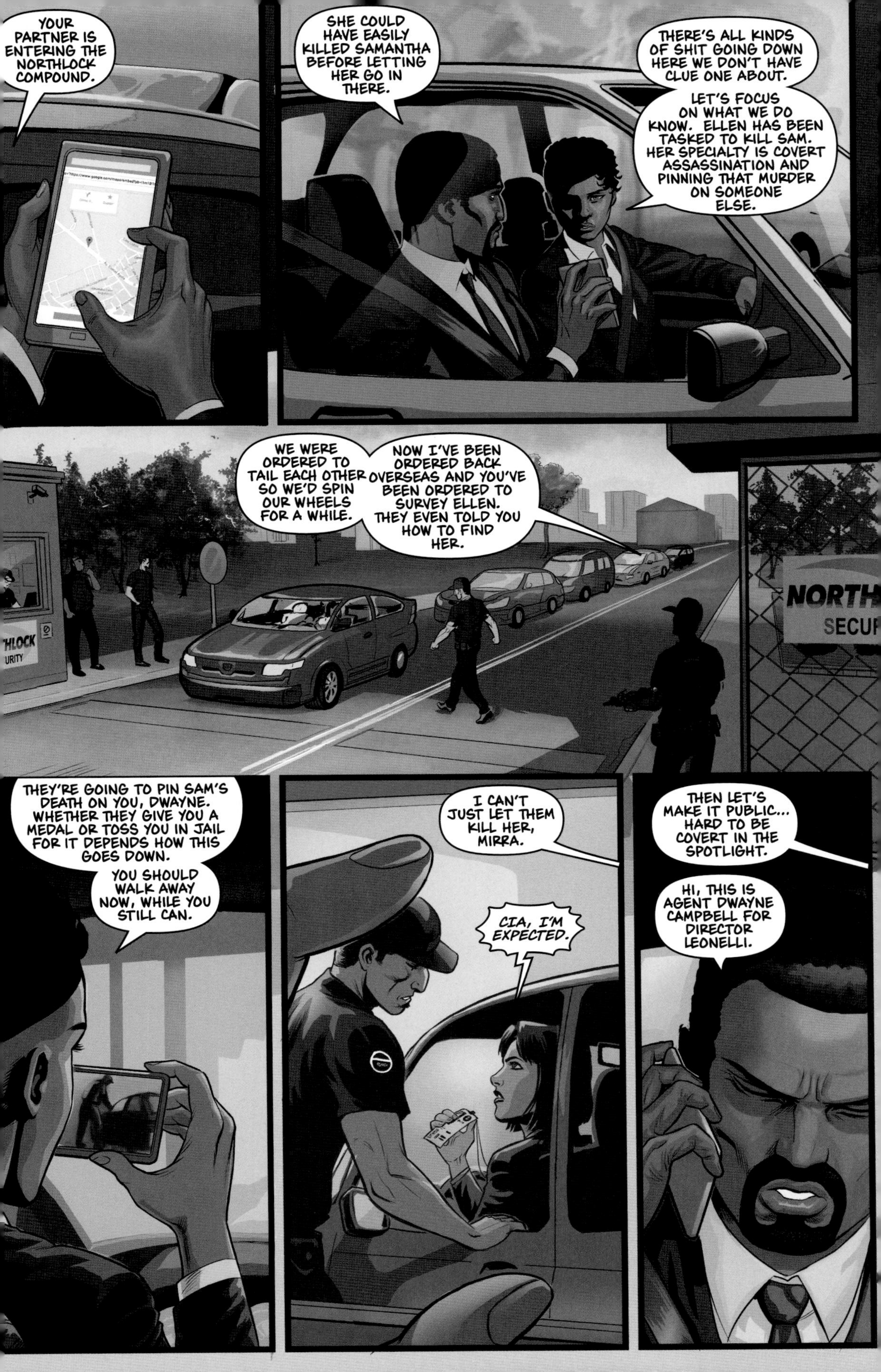
YOUR PARTNER IS ENTERING THE NORTHLOCK COMPOUND.
SHE COULD HAVE EASILY KILLED SAMANTHA BEFORE LETTING HER GO IN THERE.
THERE'S ALL KINDS OF SHIT GOING DOWN HERE WE DON'T HAVE CLUE ONE ABOUT.
LET'S FOCUS ON WHAT WE DO KNOW. ELLEN HAS BEEN TASKED TO KILL SAM. HER SPECIALTY IS COVERT ASSASSINATION AND PINNING THAT MURDER ON SOMEONE ELSE.
WE WERE ORDERED TO TAIL EACH OTHER SO WE'D SPIN OUR WHEELS FOR A WHILE.
NOW I'VE BEEN ORDERED BACK OVERSEAS AND YOU'VE BEEN ORDERED TO SURVEY ELLEN. THEY EVEN TOLD YOU HOW TO FIND HER.
NORTH
SECU
'HLOCK
URITY
THEY'RE GOING TO PIN SAM'S DEATH ON YOU, DWAYNE. WHETHER THEY GIVE YOU A MEDAL OR TOSS YOU IN JAIL FOR IT DEPENDS HOW THIS GOES DOWN.
YOU SHOULD WALK AWAY NOW, WHILE YOU STILL CAN.
I CAN'T JUST LET THEM KILL HER, MIRRA.
CIA, I'M EXPECTED.
THEN LET'S MAKE IT PUBLIC... HARD TO BE COVERT IN THE SPOTLIGHT.
HI, THIS IS AGENT DWAYNE CAMPBELL FOR DIRECTOR LEONELLI.

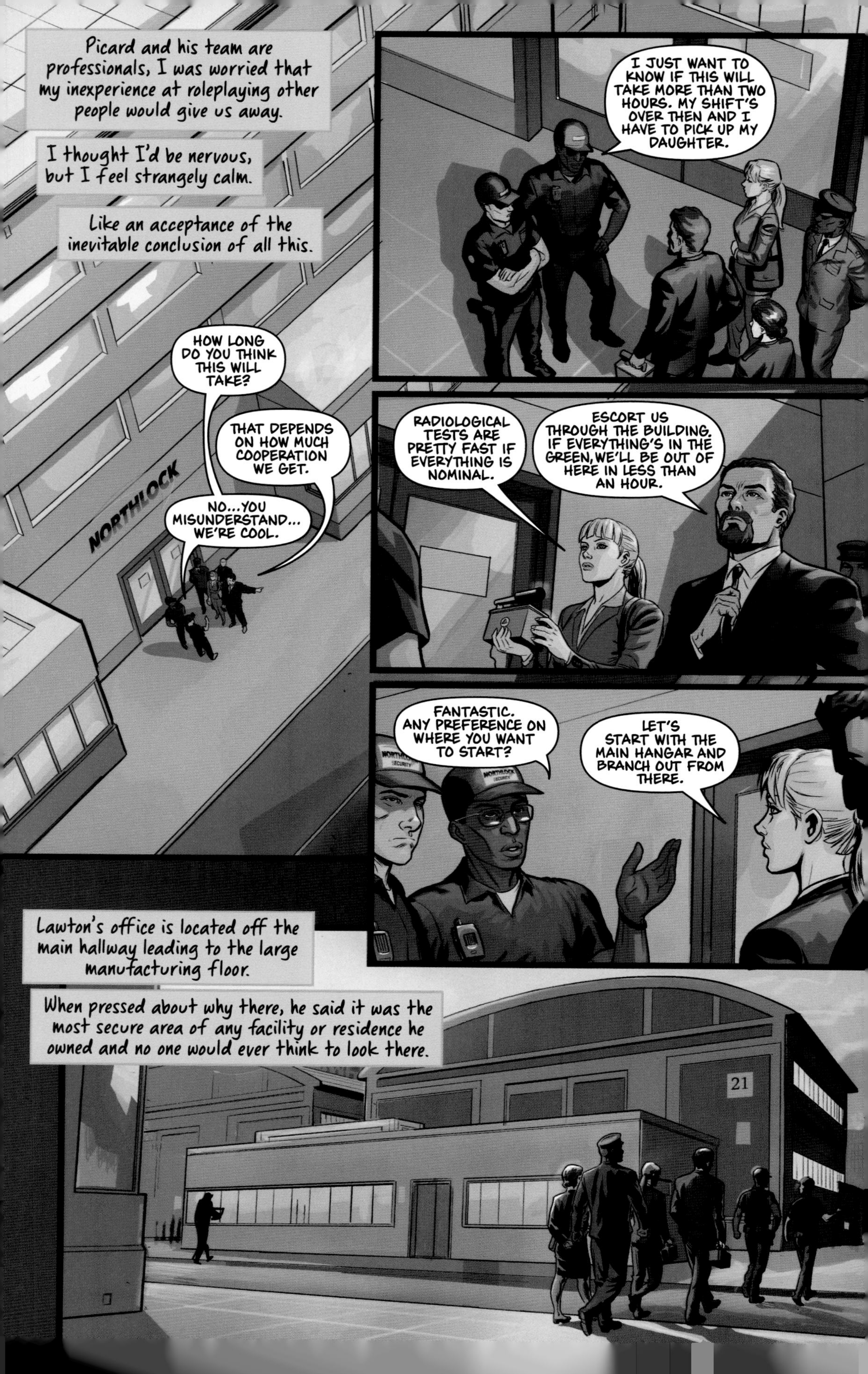

Picard and his team are professionals, I was worried that my inexperience at roleplaying other people would give us away.
I thought I'd be nervous, but I feel strangely calm.
Like an acceptance of the inevitable conclusion of all this.
HOW LONG DO YOU THINK THIS WILL TAKE?
THAT DEPENDS ON HOW MUCH COOPERATION WE GET.
NO...YOU MISUNDERSTAND... WE'RE COOL.
NORTHLOCK
I JUST WANT TO KNOW IF THIS WILL TAKE MORE THAN TWO HOURS. MY SHIFT'S OVER THEN AND I HAVE TO PICK UP MY DAUGHTER.
RADIOLOGICAL TESTS ARE PRETTY FAST IF EVERYTHING IS NOMINAL.
ESCORT US THROUGH THE BUILDING. IF EVERYTHING'S IN THE GREEN, WE'LL BE OUT OF HERE IN LESS THAN AN HOUR.
FANTASTIC. ANY PREFERENCE ON WHERE YOU WANT TO START?
LET'S START WITH THE MAIN HANGAR AND BRANCH OUT FROM THERE.
Lawton's office is located off the main hallway leading to the large manufacturing floor.
When pressed about why there, he said it was the most secure area of any facility or residence he owned and no one would ever think to look there.
21

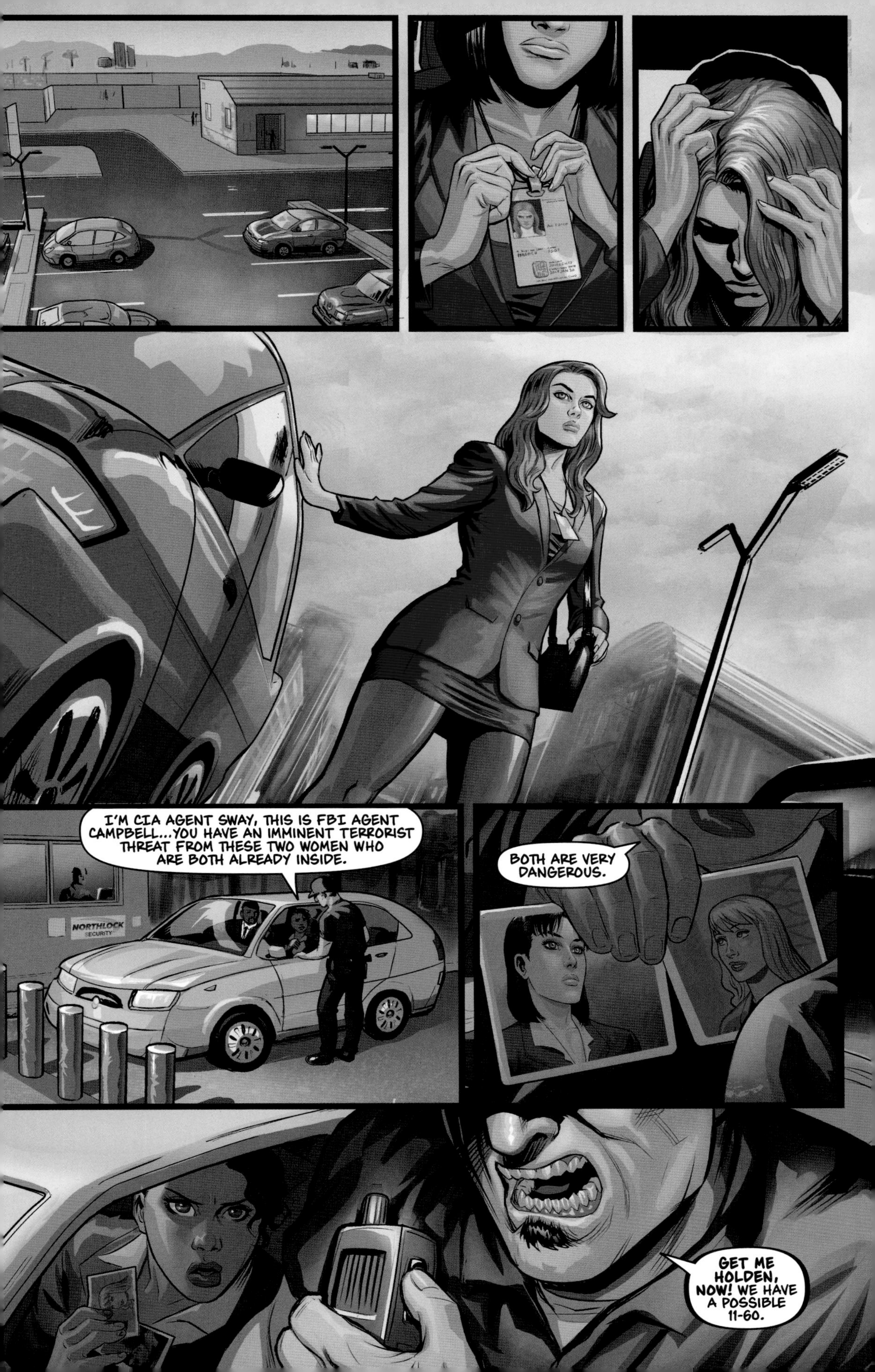
I'M CIA AGENT SWAY, THIS IS FBI AGENT CAMPBELL...YOU HAVE AN IMMINENT TERRORIST THREAT FROM THESE TWO WOMEN WHO ARE BOTH ALREADY INSIDE.
NORTHLOCK SECURITY
BOTH ARE VERY DANGEROUS.
GET ME HOLDEN, NOW! WE HAVE A POSSIBLE 11-60.

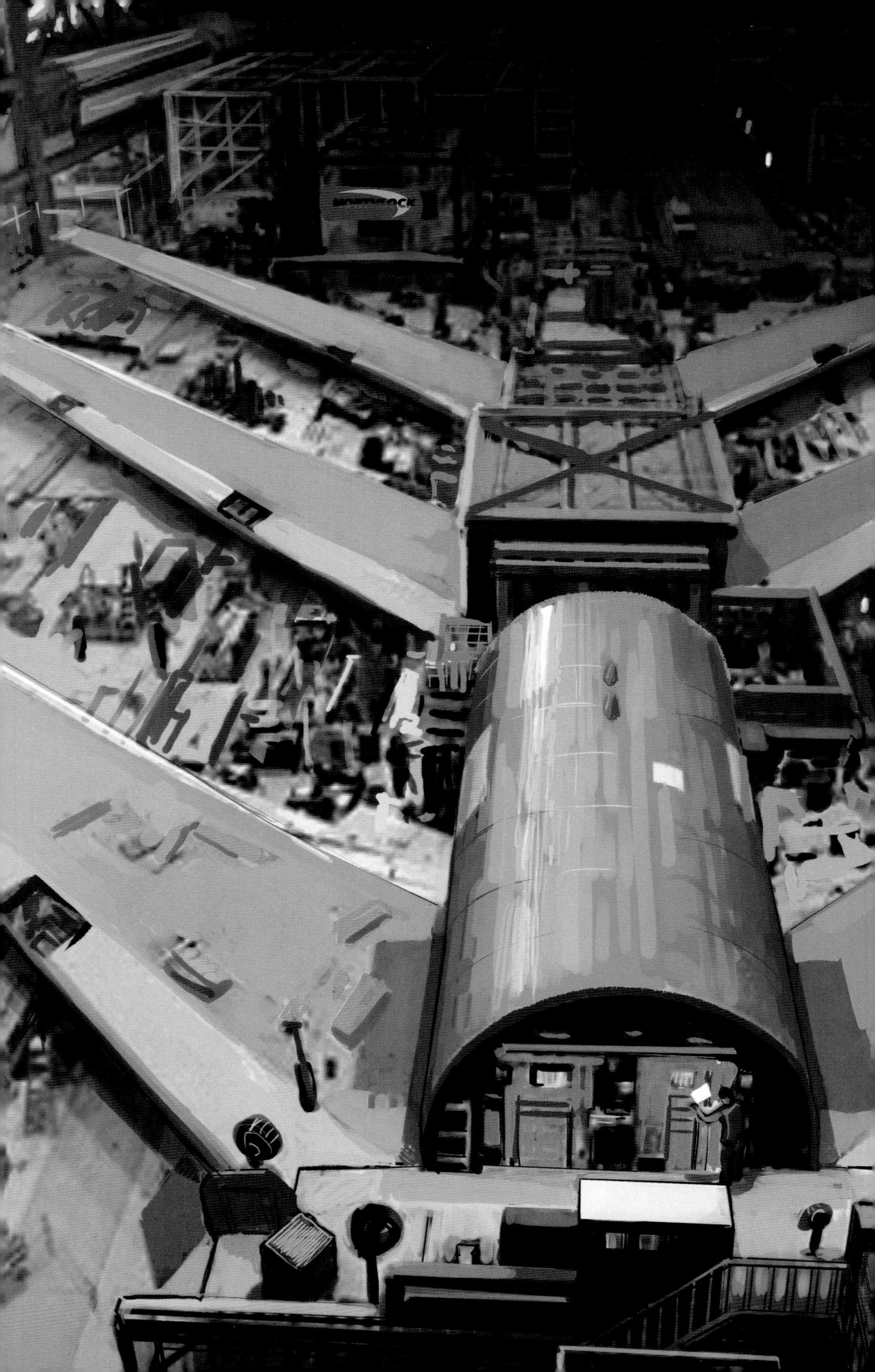

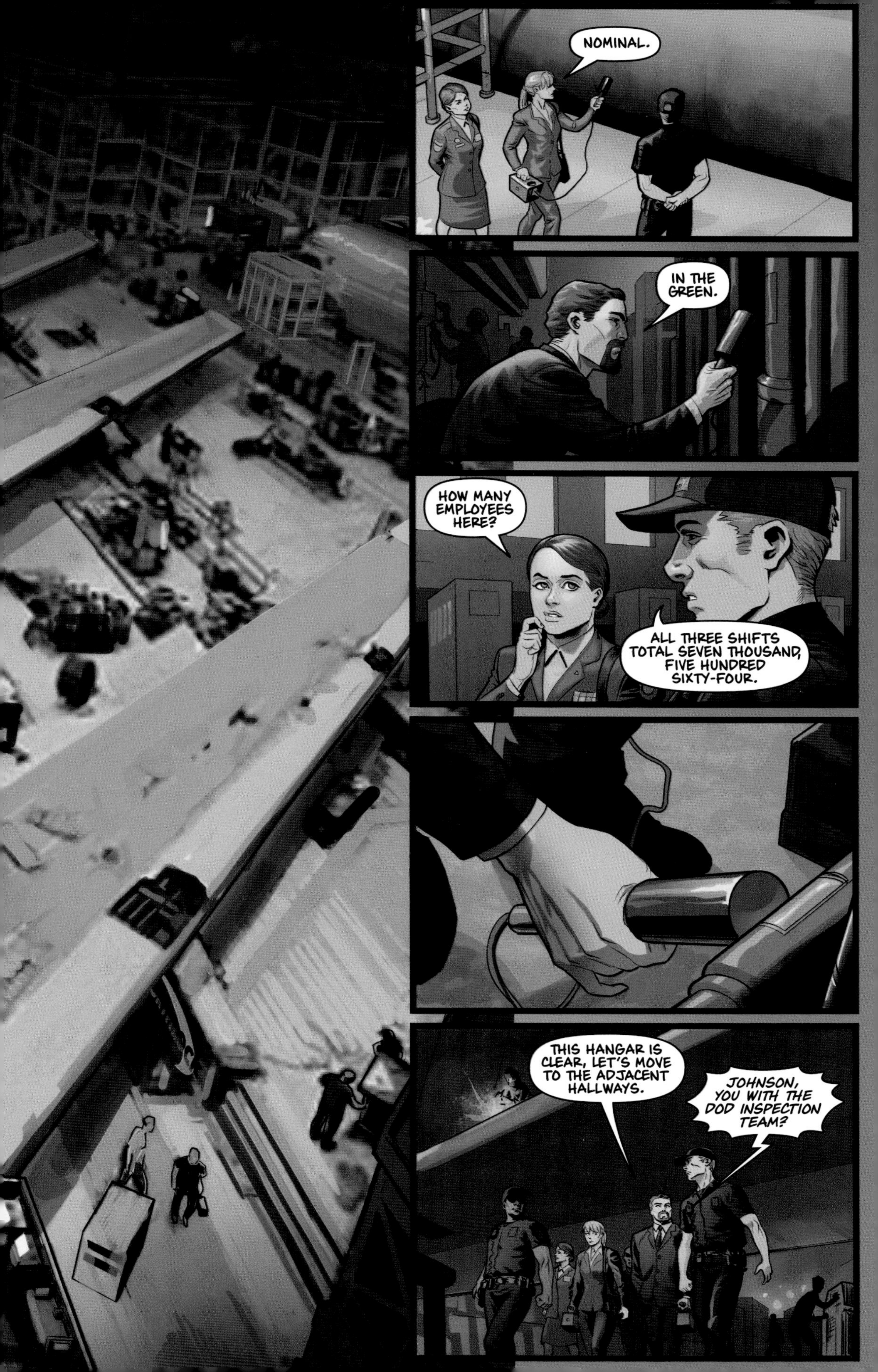
NOMINAL.
IN THE GREEN.
HOW MANY EMPLOYEES HERE?
ALL THREE SHIFTS TOTAL SEVEN THOUSAND, FIVE HUNDRED SIXTY-FOUR.
THIS HANGAR IS CLEAR, LET'S MOVE TO THE ADJACENT HALLWAYS.
JOHNSON, YOU WITH THE DOD INSPECTION TEAM?

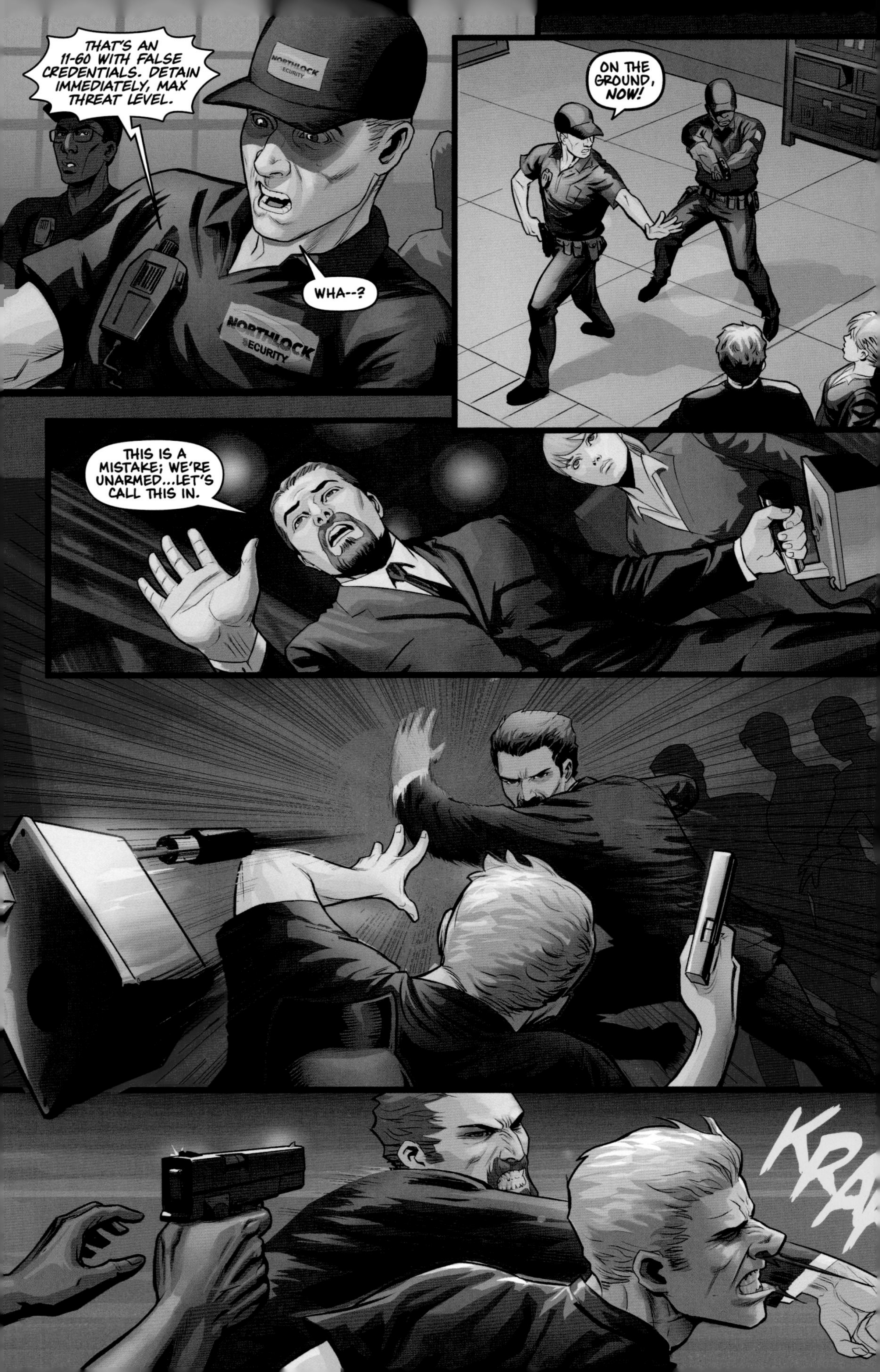
THAT'S AN 11-60 WITH FALSE CREDENTIALS. DETAIN IMMEDIATELY, MAX THREAT LEVEL.
NORTHLOCK SECURITY
WHA--?
NORTHLOCK SECURITY
ON THE GROUND, NOW!
THIS IS A MISTAKE; WE'RE UNARMED...LET'S CALL THIS IN.
KRA

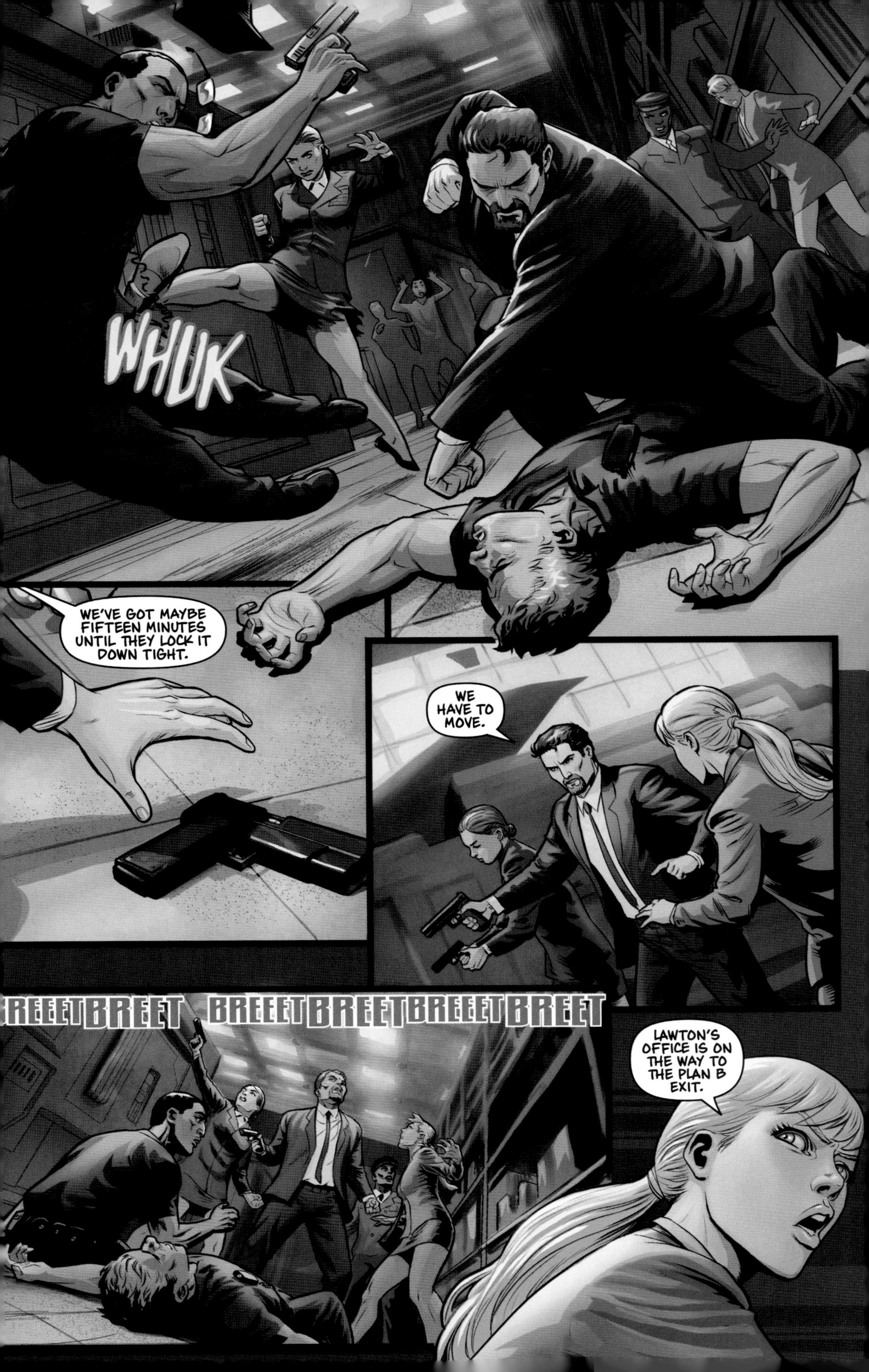
WHUK
WE'VE GOT MAYBE FIFTEEN MINUTES UNTIL THEY LOCK IT DOWN TIGHT.
WE HAVE TO MOVE.
BREEET BREET BREEET BREEET BREEET BREET
LAWTON'S OFFICE IS ON THE WAY TO THE PLAN B EXIT.

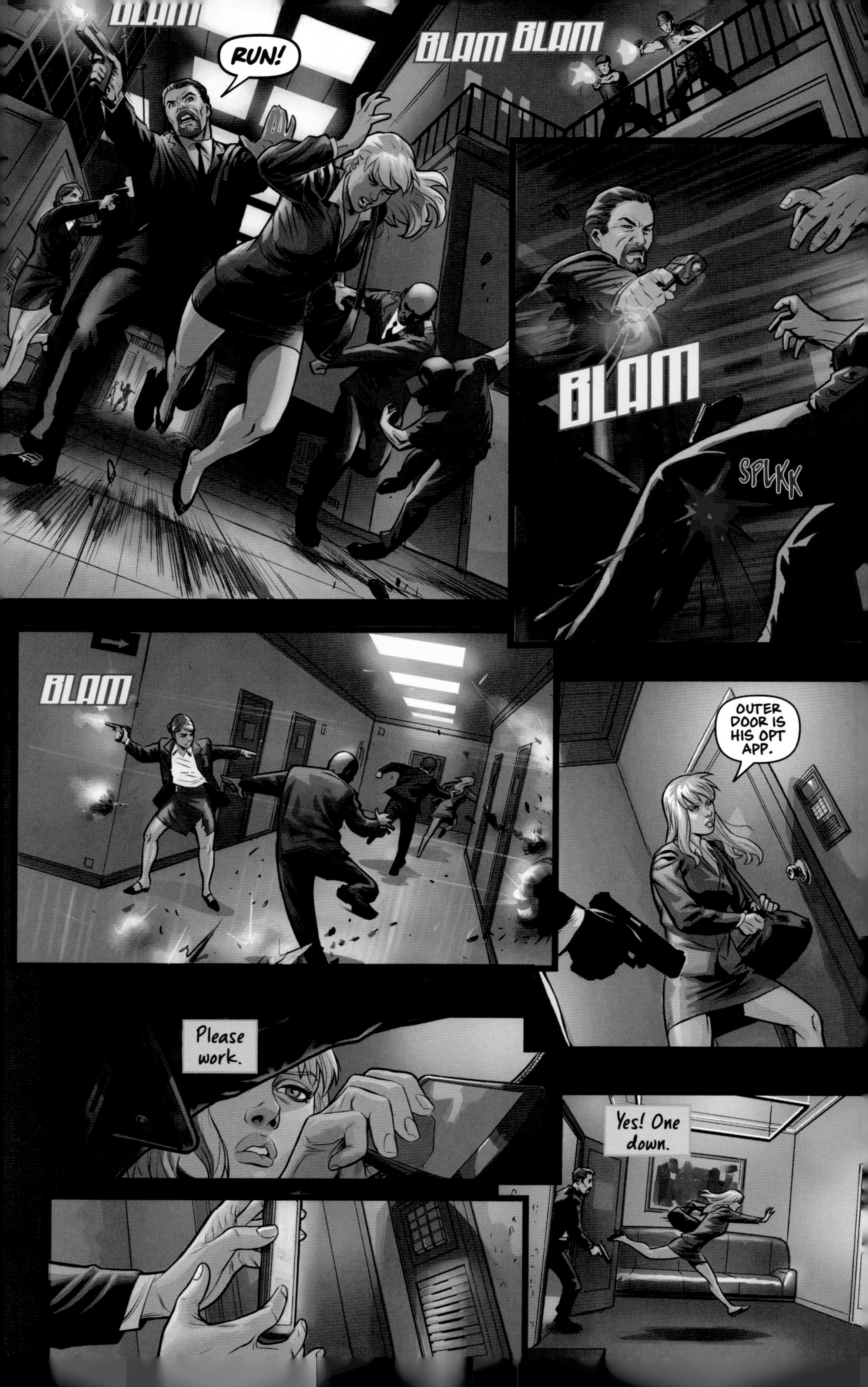
BLAM
RUN!
BLAM BLAM
BLAM
SPLKK
BLAM
OUTER DOOR IS HIS OPT APP.
Please work.
Yes! One down.

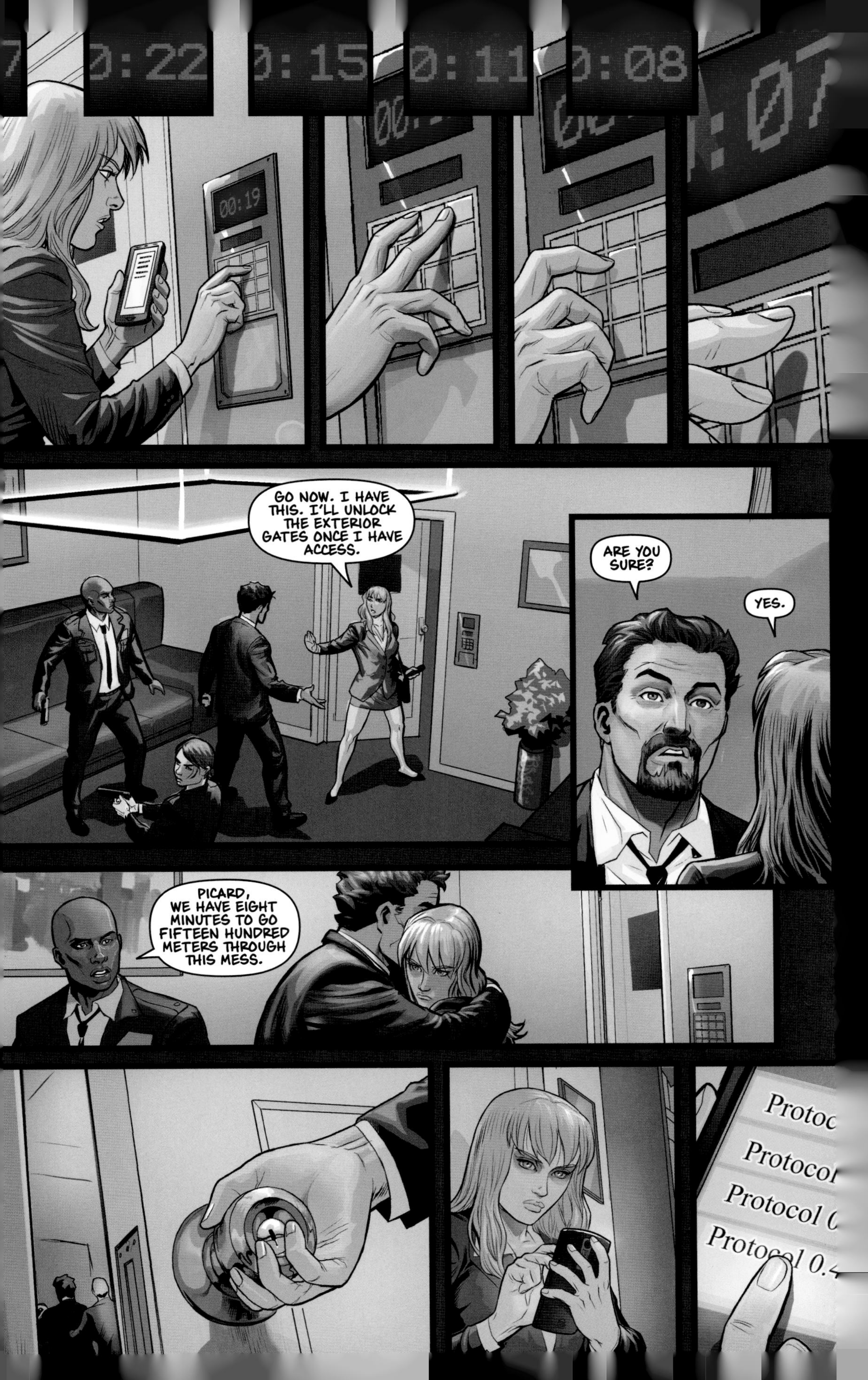
0:22
0:15
0:11
0:08
00:19
GO NOW. I HAVE THIS. I'LL UNLOCK THE EXTERIOR GATES ONCE I HAVE ACCESS.
ARE YOU SURE?
YES.
PICARD, WE HAVE EIGHT MINUTES TO GO FIFTEEN HUNDRED METERS THROUGH THIS MESS.

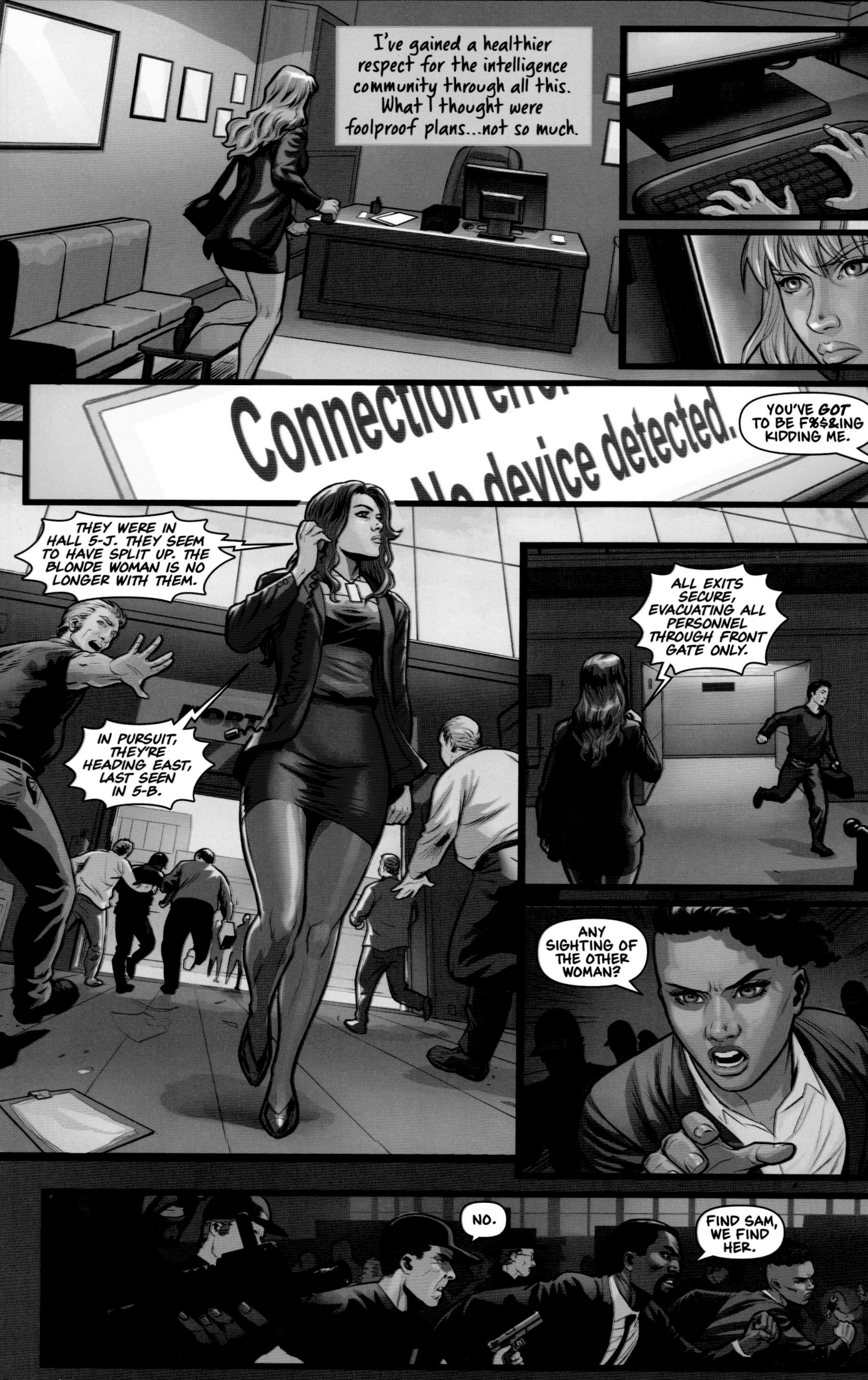
I've gained a healthier respect for the intelligence community through all this. What I thought were foolproof plans...not so much.
Connection error
No device detected.
YOU'VE GOT TO BE F%$&ING KIDDING ME.
THEY WERE IN HALL 5-J. THEY SEEM TO HAVE SPLIT UP. THE BLONDE WOMAN IS NO LONGER WITH THEM.
IN PURSUIT, THEY'RE HEADING EAST, LAST SEEN IN 5-B.
ALL EXITS SECURE, EVACUATING ALL PERSONNEL THROUGH FRONT GATE ONLY.
ANY SIGHTING OF THE OTHER WOMAN?
NO.
FIND SAM, WE FIND HER.

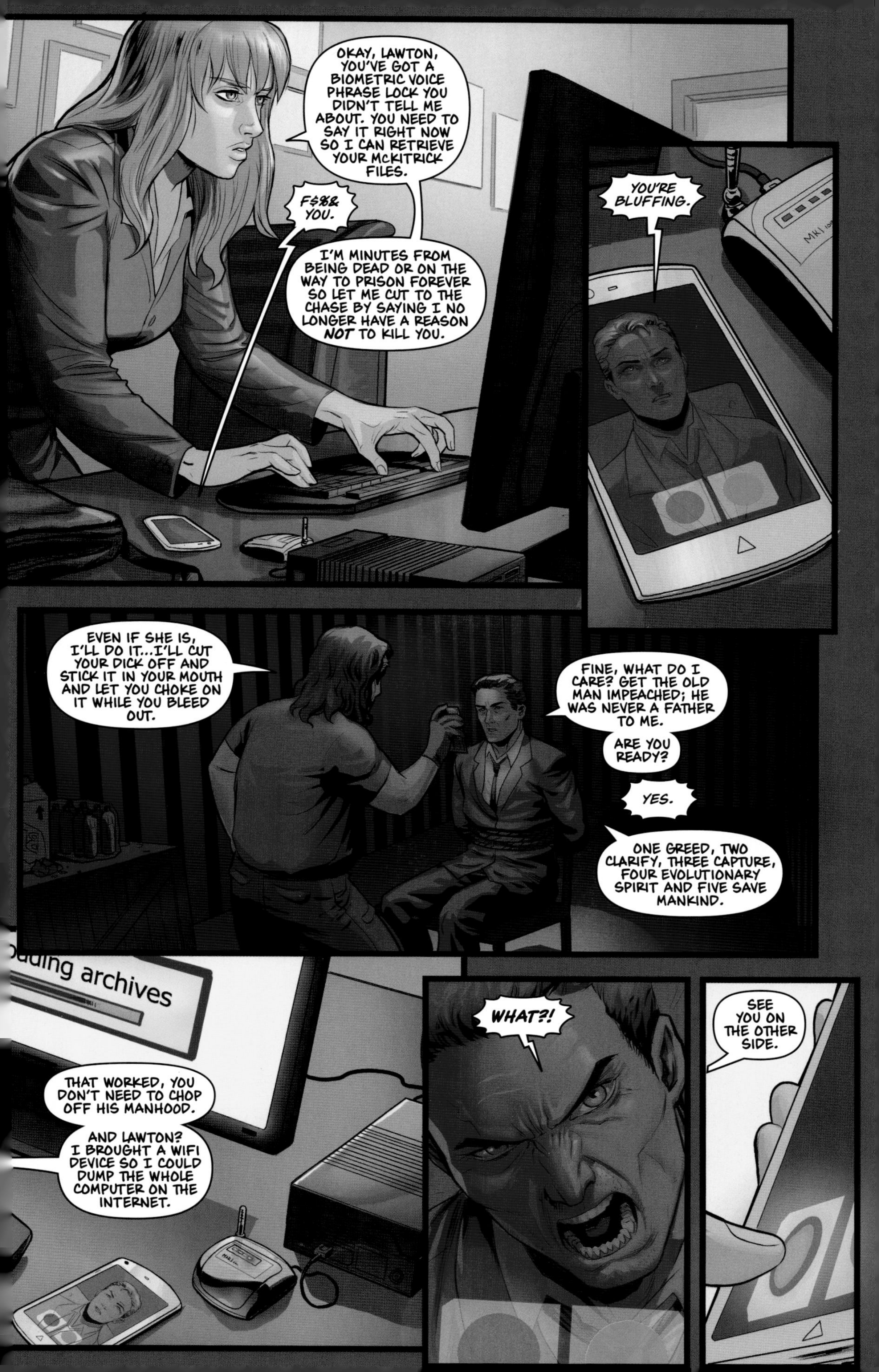
OKAY, LAWTON, YOU'VE GOT A BIOMETRIC VOICE PHRASE LOCK YOU DIDN'T TELL ME ABOUT. YOU NEED TO SAY IT RIGHT NOW SO I CAN RETRIEVE YOUR McKITRICK FILES.
F$%& YOU.
I'M MINUTES FROM BEING DEAD OR ON THE WAY TO PRISON FOREVER SO LET ME CUT TO THE CHASE BY SAYING I NO LONGER HAVE A REASON NOT TO KILL YOU.
YOU'RE BLUFFING.
EVEN IF SHE IS, I'LL DO IT...I'LL CUT YOUR DICK OFF AND STICK IT IN YOUR MOUTH AND LET YOU CHOKE ON IT WHILE YOU BLEED OUT.
FINE, WHAT DO I CARE? GET THE OLD MAN IMPEACHED; HE WAS NEVER A FATHER TO ME.
ARE YOU READY?
YES.
ONE GREED, TWO CLARIFY, THREE CAPTURE, FOUR EVOLUTIONARY SPIRIT AND FIVE SAVE MANKIND.
ading archives
THAT WORKED, YOU DON'T NEED TO CHOP OFF HIS MANHOOD.
AND LAWTON? I BROUGHT A WIFI DEVICE SO I COULD DUMP THE WHOLE COMPUTER ON THE INTERNET.
WHAT?!
SEE YOU ON THE OTHER SIDE.

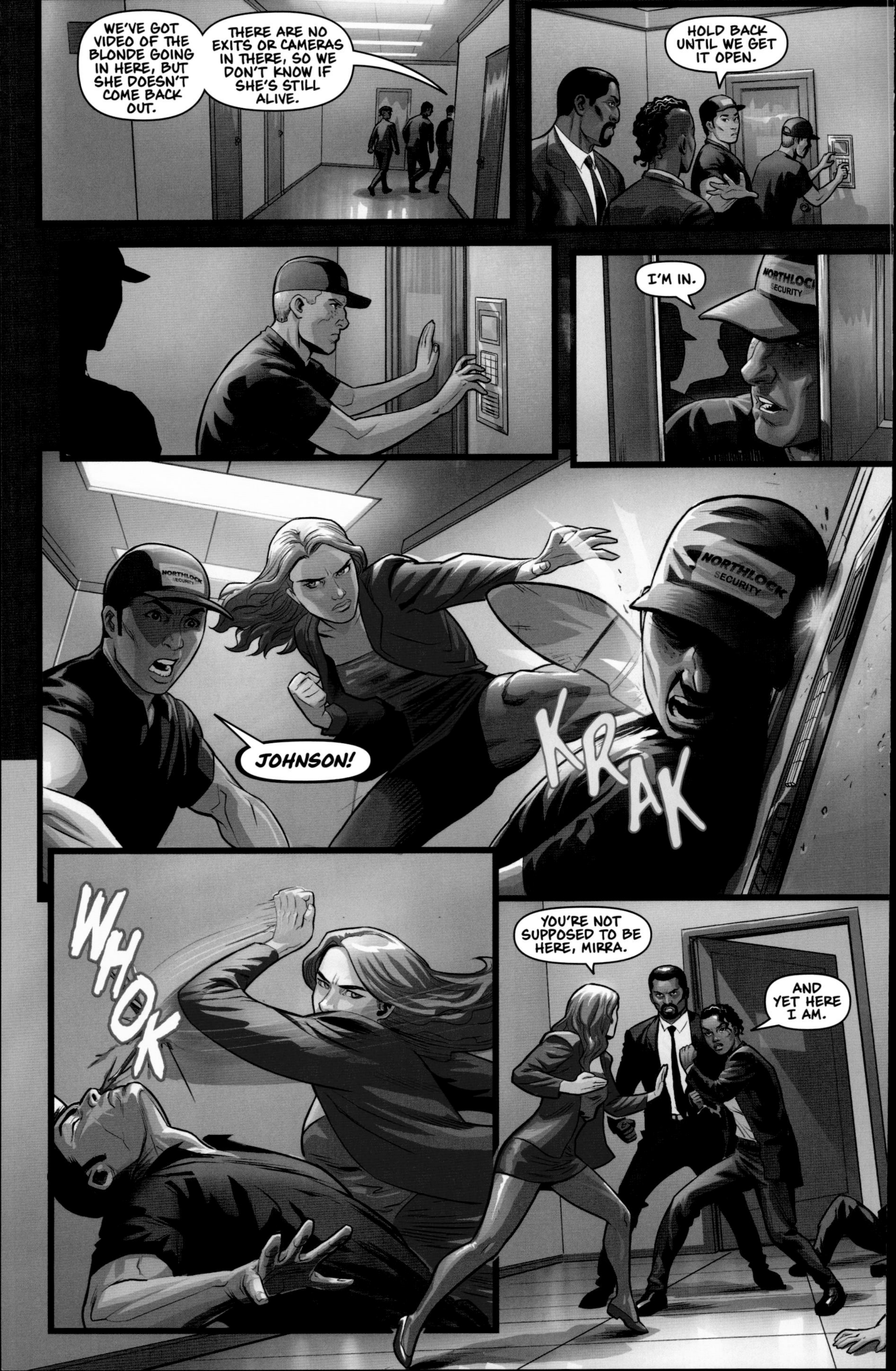
WE'VE GOT VIDEO OF THE BLONDE GOING IN HERE, BUT SHE DOESN'T COME BACK OUT.
THERE ARE NO EXITS OR CAMERAS IN THERE, SO WE DON'T KNOW IF SHE'S STILL ALIVE.
HOLD BACK UNTIL WE GET IT OPEN.
I'M IN.
NORTHLOCK SECURITY
NORTHLOCK SECURITY
NORTHLOCK SECURITY
JOHNSON!
KRAK
WHOK
YOU'RE NOT SUPPOSED TO BE HERE, MIRRA.
AND YET HERE I AM.

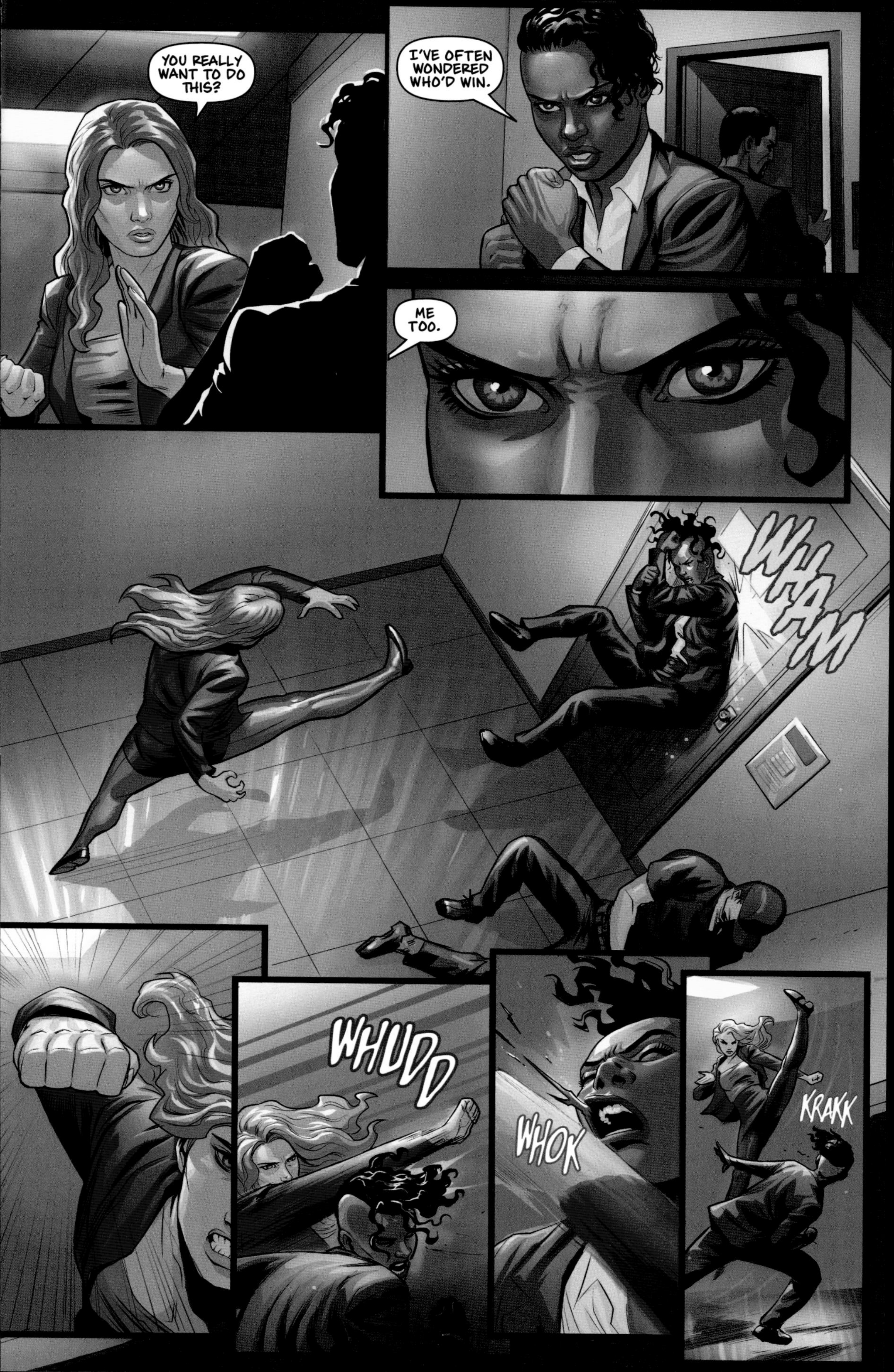
YOU REALLY WANT TO DO THIS?
I'VE OFTEN WONDERED WHO'D WIN.
ME TOO.
WHAM
WHUDD
WHOK
KRAKK

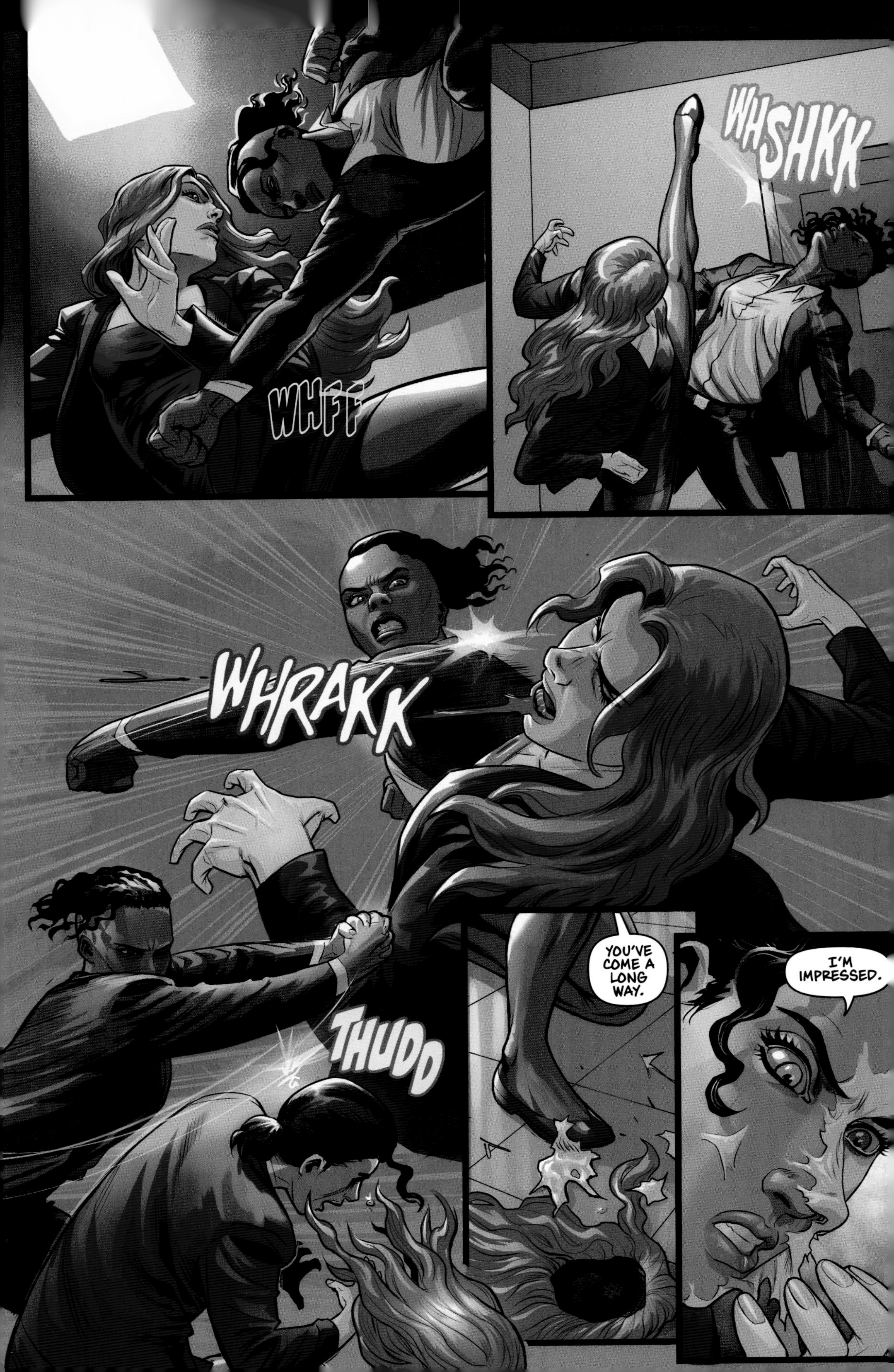
WHFF
WHSHKK
WHRAKK
THUDD
YOU'VE COME A LONG WAY.
I'M IMPRESSED.

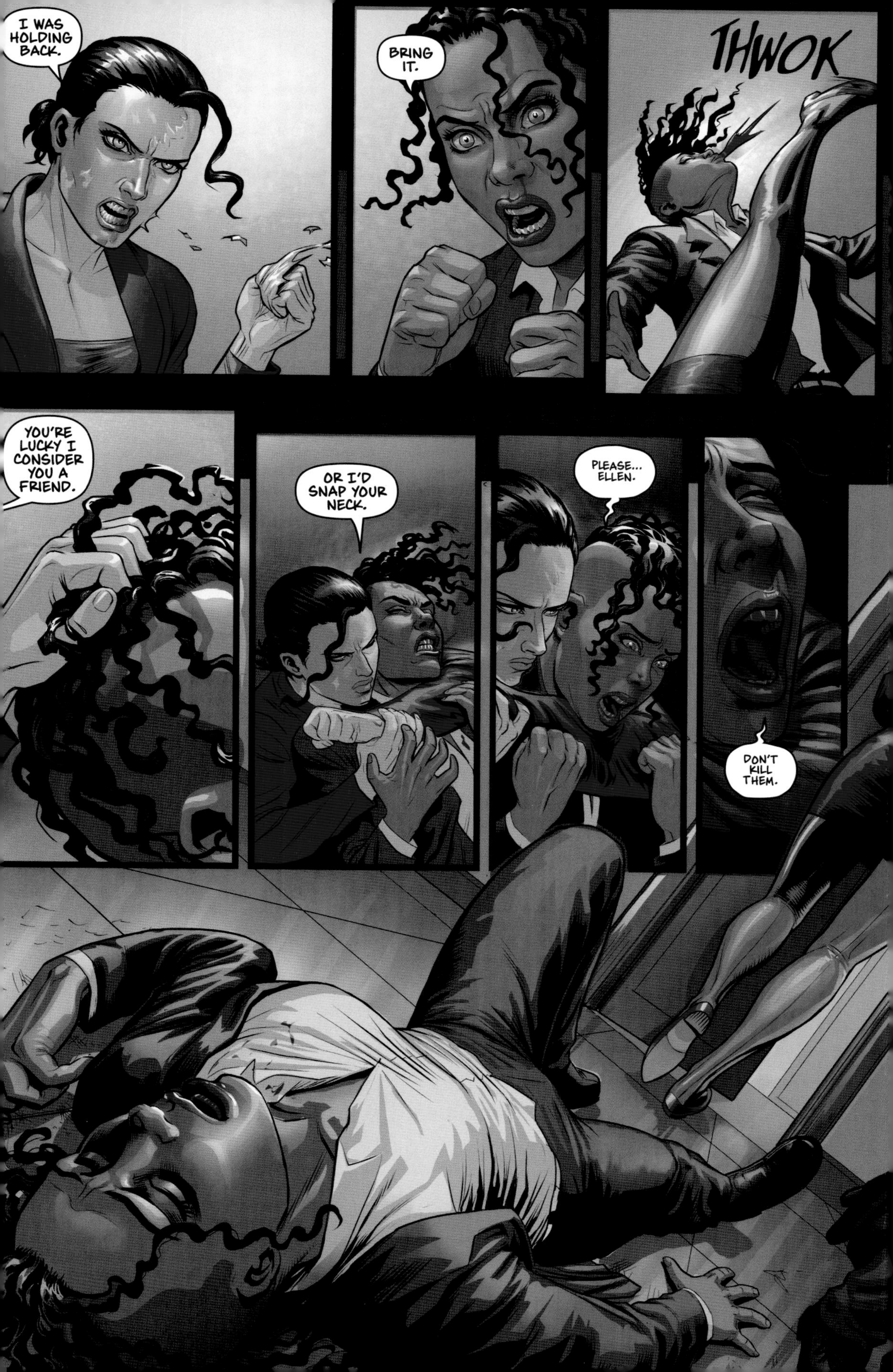
I WAS HOLDING BACK.
BRING IT.
THWOK
YOU'RE LUCKY I CONSIDER YOU A FRIEND.
OR I'D SNAP YOUR NECK.
PLEASE... ELLEN.
DON'T KILL THEM.

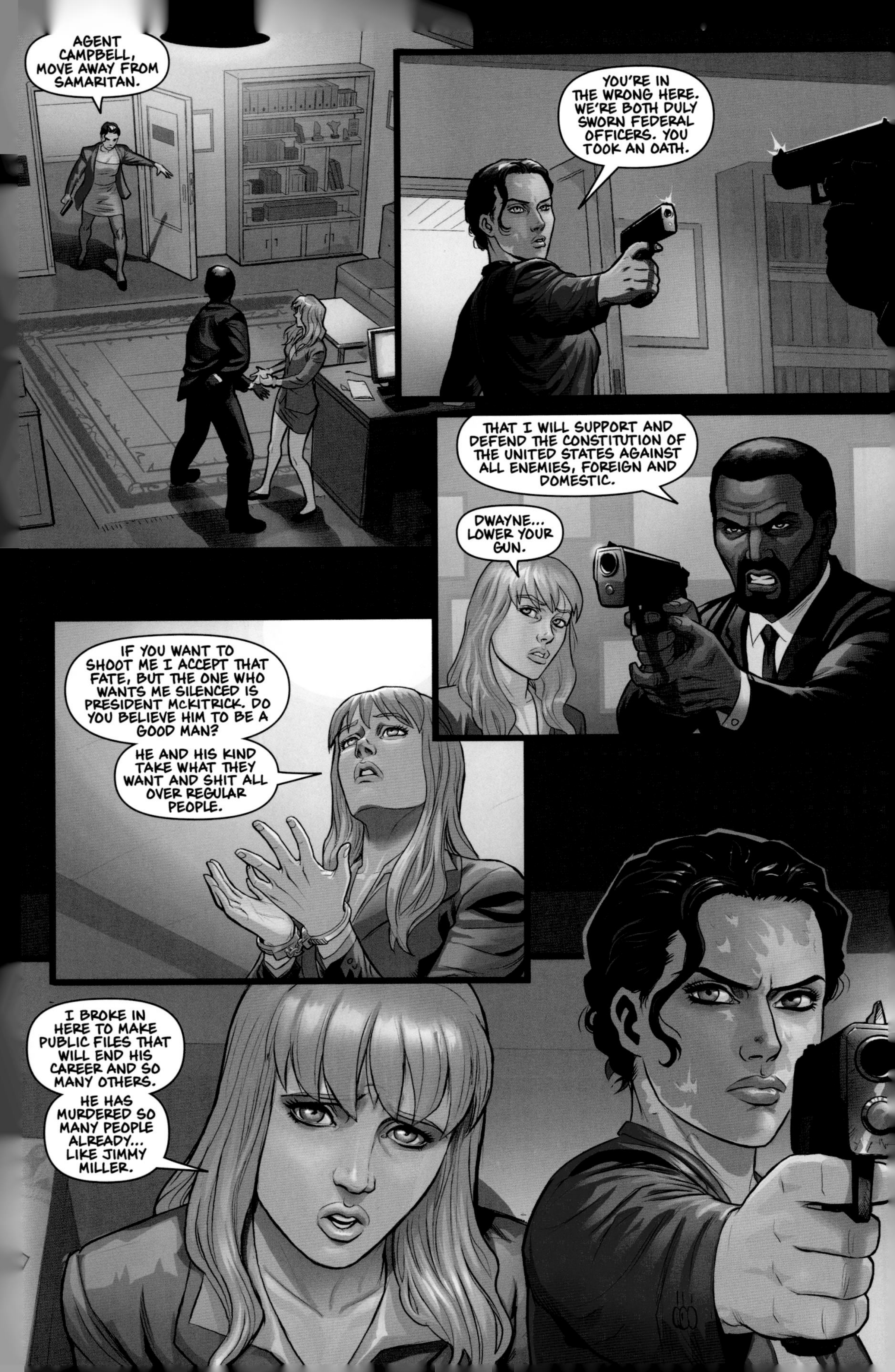
AGENT CAMPBELL, MOVE AWAY FROM SAMARITAN.
YOU'RE IN THE WRONG HERE. WE'RE BOTH DULY SWORN FEDERAL OFFICERS. YOU TOOK AN OATH.
THAT I WILL SUPPORT AND DEFEND THE CONSTITUTION OF THE UNITED STATES AGAINST ALL ENEMIES, FOREIGN AND DOMESTIC.
DWAYNE... LOWER YOUR GUN.
IF YOU WANT TO SHOOT ME I ACCEPT THAT FATE, BUT THE ONE WHO WANTS ME SILENCED IS PRESIDENT McKITRICK. DO YOU BELIEVE HIM TO BE A GOOD MAN?
HE AND HIS KIND TAKE WHAT THEY WANT AND SHIT ALL OVER REGULAR PEOPLE.
I BROKE IN HERE TO MAKE PUBLIC FILES THAT WILL END HIS CAREER AND SO MANY OTHERS.
HE HAS MURDERED SO MANY PEOPLE ALREADY... LIKE JIMMY MILLER.

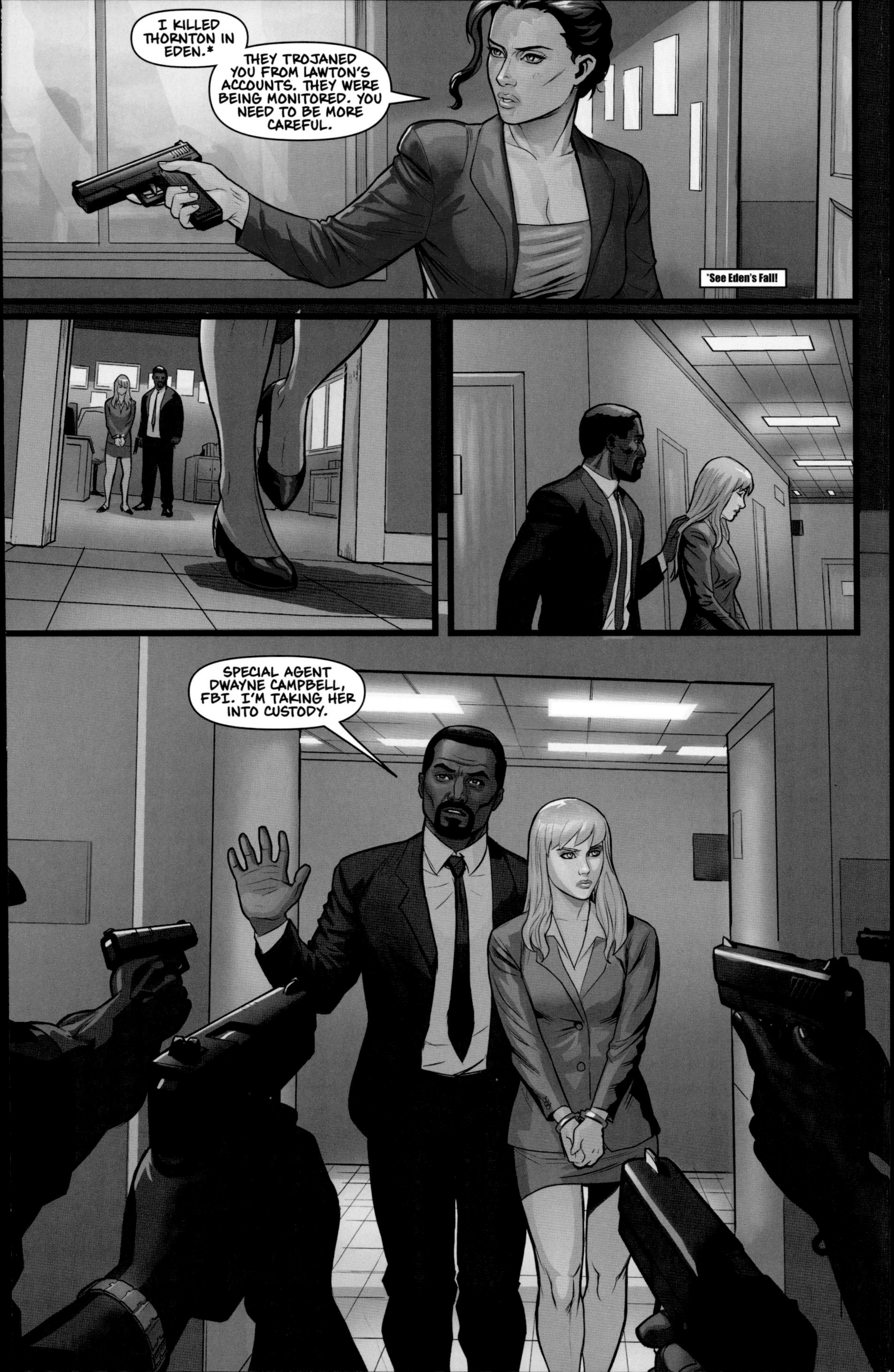
I KILLED THORNTON IN EDEN.*
THEY TROJANED YOU FROM LAWTON'S ACCOUNTS. THEY WERE BEING MONITORED. YOU NEED TO BE MORE CAREFUL.
*See Eden's Fall!
SPECIAL AGENT DWAYNE CAMPBELL, FBI. I'M TAKING HER INTO CUSTODY.

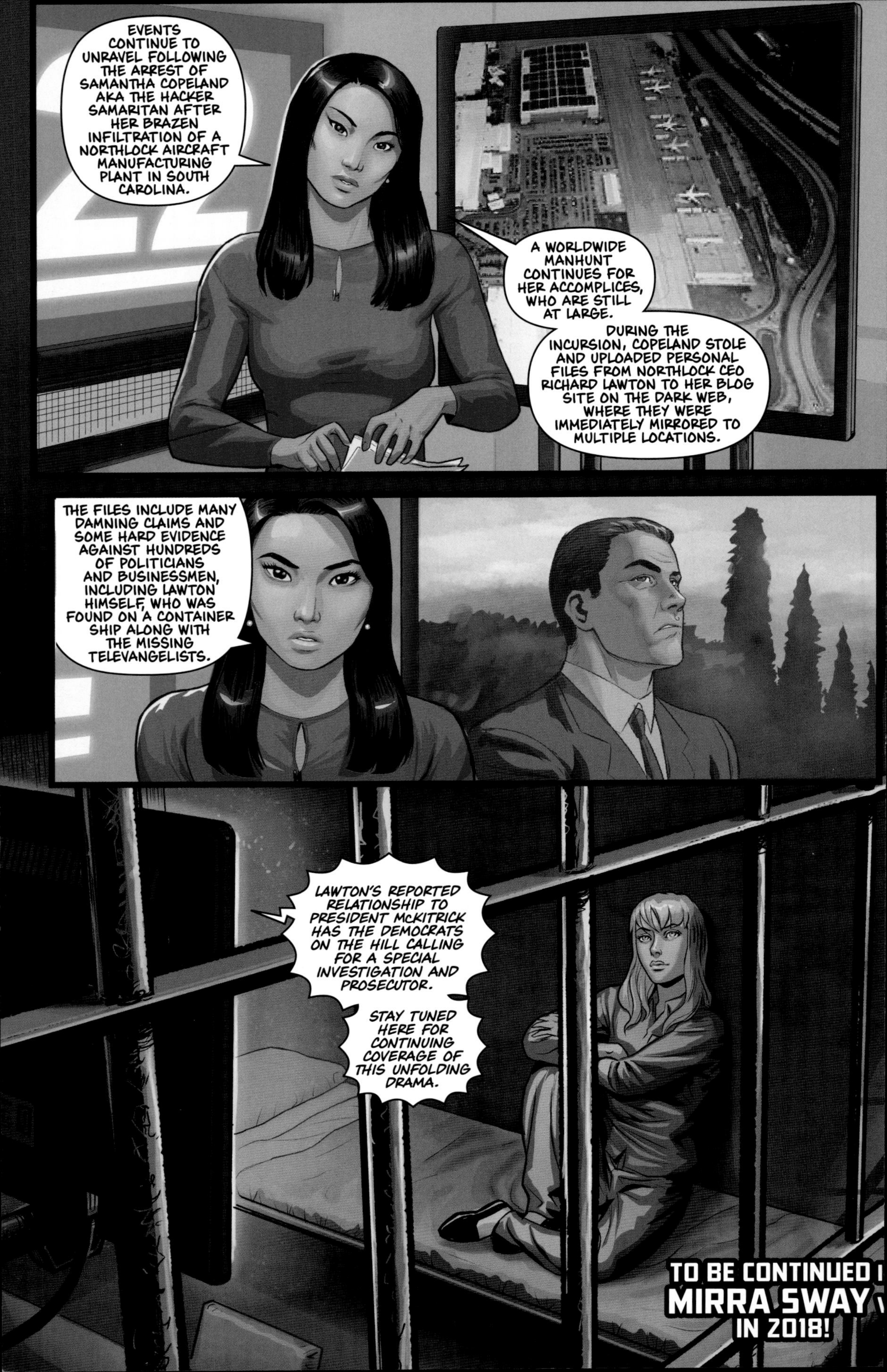
EVENTS CONTINUE TO UNRAVEL FOLLOWING THE ARREST OF SAMANTHA COPELAND AKA THE HACKER SAMARITAN AFTER HER BRAZEN INFILTRATION OF A NORTHLOCK AIRCRAFT MANUFACTURING PLANT IN SOUTH CAROLINA.
A WORLDWIDE MANHUNT CONTINUES FOR HER ACCOMPLICES, WHO ARE STILL AT LARGE.
DURING THE INCURSION, COPELAND STOLE AND UPLOADED PERSONAL FILES FROM NORTHLOCK CEO RICHARD LAWTON TO HER BLOG SITE ON THE DARK WEB, WHERE THEY WERE IMMEDIATELY MIRRORED TO MULTIPLE LOCATIONS.
THE FILES INCLUDE MANY DAMNING CLAIMS AND SOME HARD EVIDENCE AGAINST HUNDREDS OF POLITICIANS AND BUSINESSMEN, INCLUDING LAWTON HIMSELF, WHO WAS FOUND ON A CONTAINER SHIP ALONG WITH THE MISSING TELEVANGELISTS.
LAWTON'S REPORTED RELATIONSHIP TO PRESIDENT McKITRICK HAS THE DEMOCRATS ON THE HILL CALLING FOR A SPECIAL INVESTIGATION AND PROSECUTOR.
STAY TUNED HERE FOR CONTINUING COVERAGE OF THIS UNFOLDING DRAMA.
TO BE CONTINUED I
MIRRA SWAY V
IN 2018!

EDEN'S FALL

**MATT HAWKINS &
BRYAN HILL**
WRITERS

ATILIO ROJO
ARTIST

TROY PETERI
LETTERER

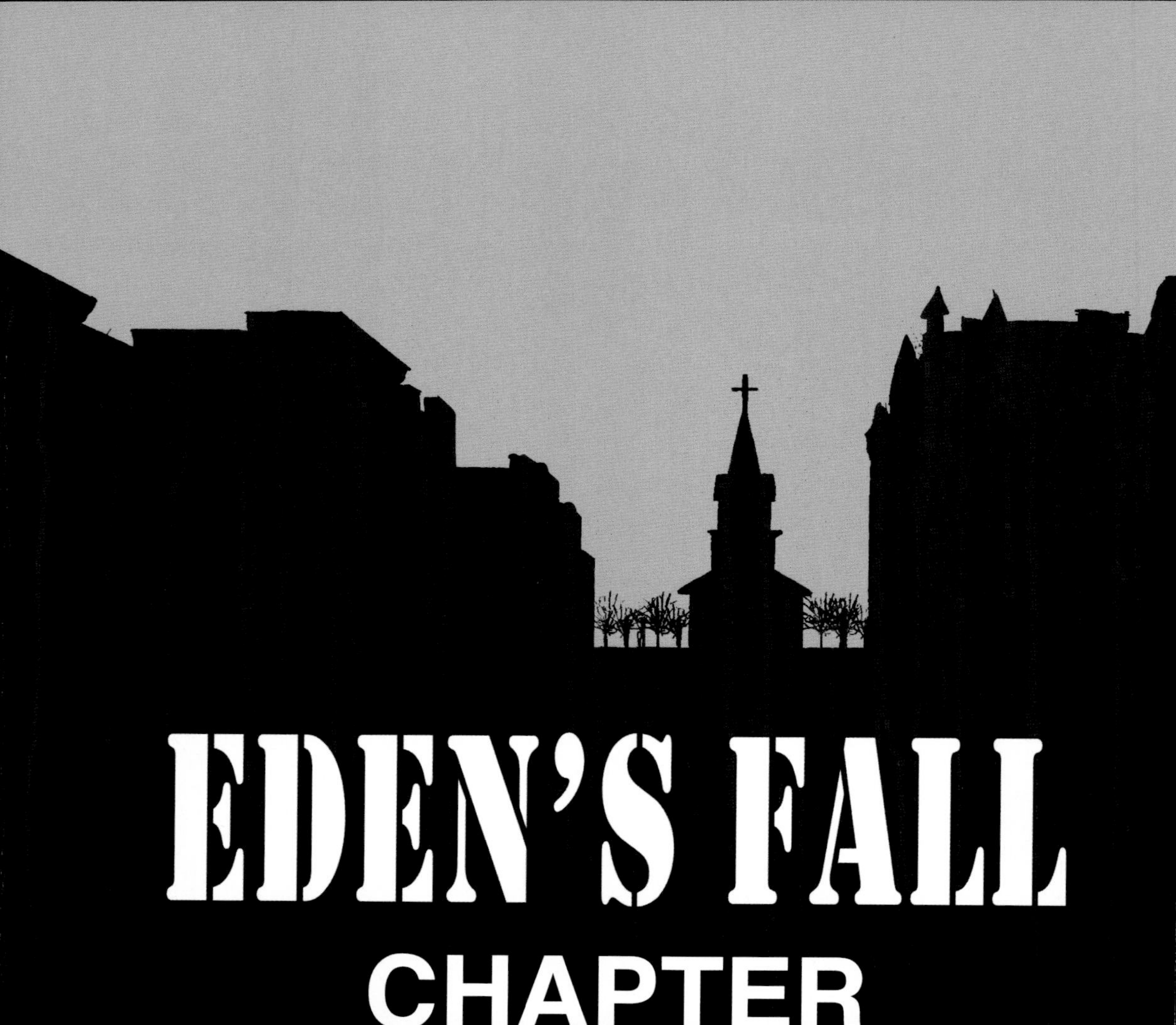

EDEN'S FALL
CHAPTER

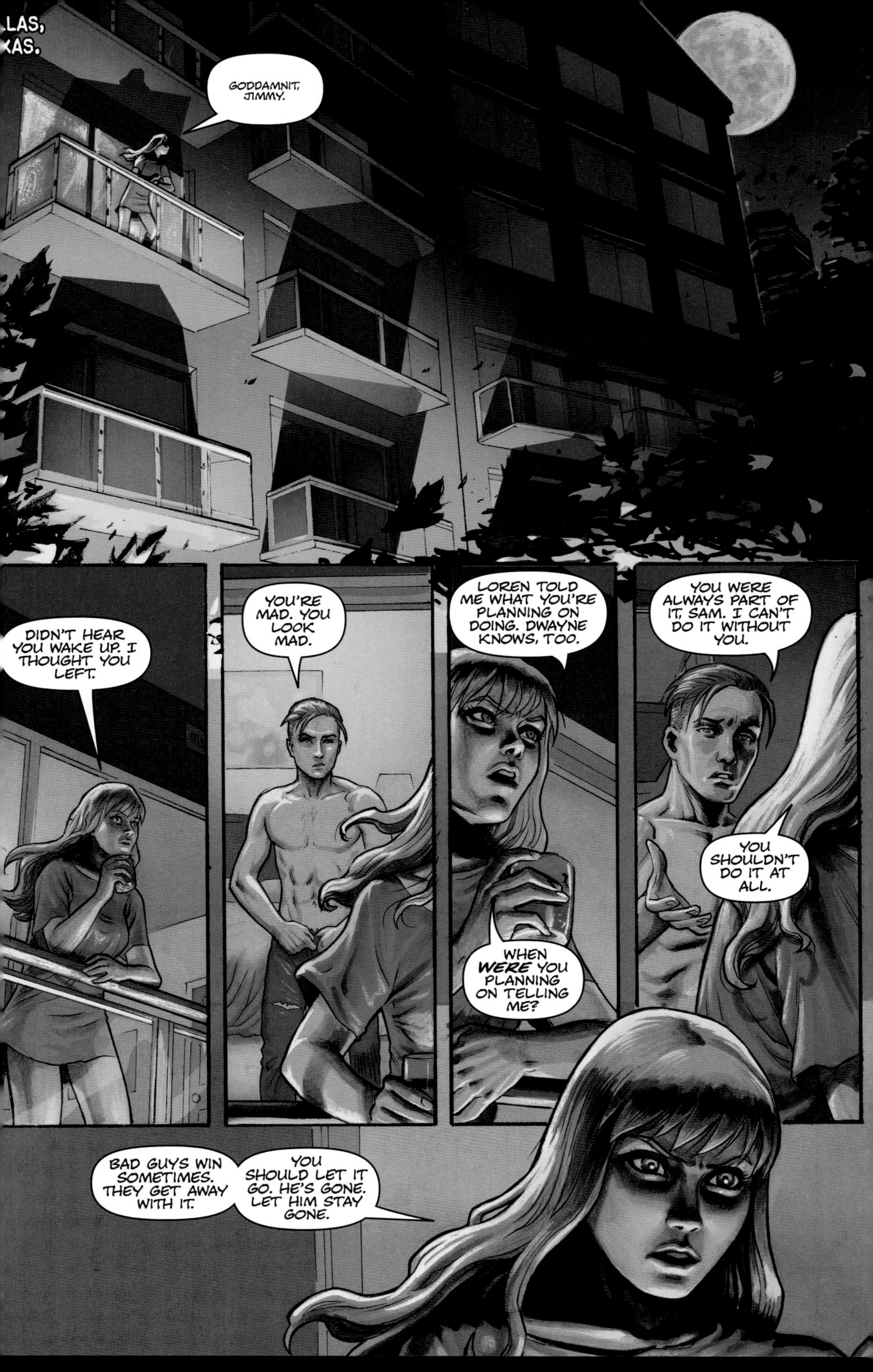

LAS,
XAS.
GODDAMNIT, JIMMY.
DIDN'T HEAR YOU WAKE UP. I THOUGHT YOU LEFT.
YOU'RE MAD. YOU LOOK MAD.
LOREN TOLD ME WHAT YOU'RE PLANNING ON DOING. DWAYNE KNOWS, TOO.
WHEN *WERE* YOU PLANNING ON TELLING ME?
YOU WERE ALWAYS PART OF IT, SAM. I CAN'T DO IT WITHOUT YOU.
YOU SHOULDN'T DO IT AT ALL.
BAD GUYS WIN SOMETIMES. THEY GET AWAY WITH IT.
YOU SHOULD LET IT GO. HE'S GONE. LET HIM STAY GONE.

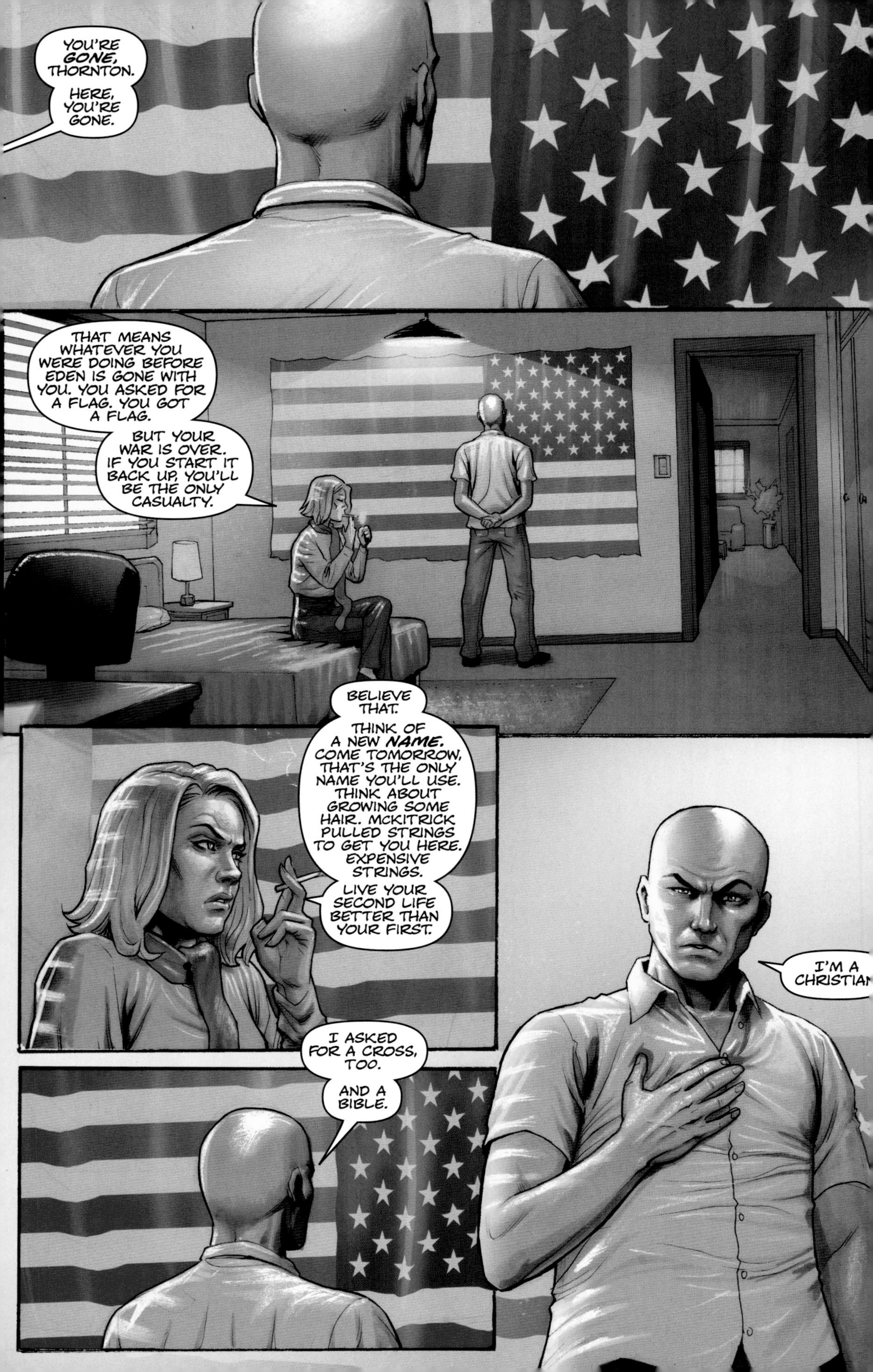
YOU'RE *GONE,* THORNTON.
HERE, YOU'RE GONE.
THAT MEANS WHATEVER YOU WERE DOING BEFORE EDEN IS GONE WITH YOU. YOU ASKED FOR A FLAG. YOU GOT A FLAG.
BUT YOUR WAR IS OVER. IF YOU START IT BACK UP, YOU'LL BE THE ONLY CASUALTY.
BELIEVE THAT.
THINK OF A NEW *NAME.* COME TOMORROW, THAT'S THE ONLY NAME YOU'LL USE. THINK ABOUT GROWING SOME HAIR. MCKITRICK PULLED STRINGS TO GET YOU HERE. EXPENSIVE STRINGS.
LIVE YOUR SECOND LIFE BETTER THAN YOUR FIRST.
I ASKED FOR A CROSS, TOO.
AND A BIBLE.
I'M A CHRISTIAN

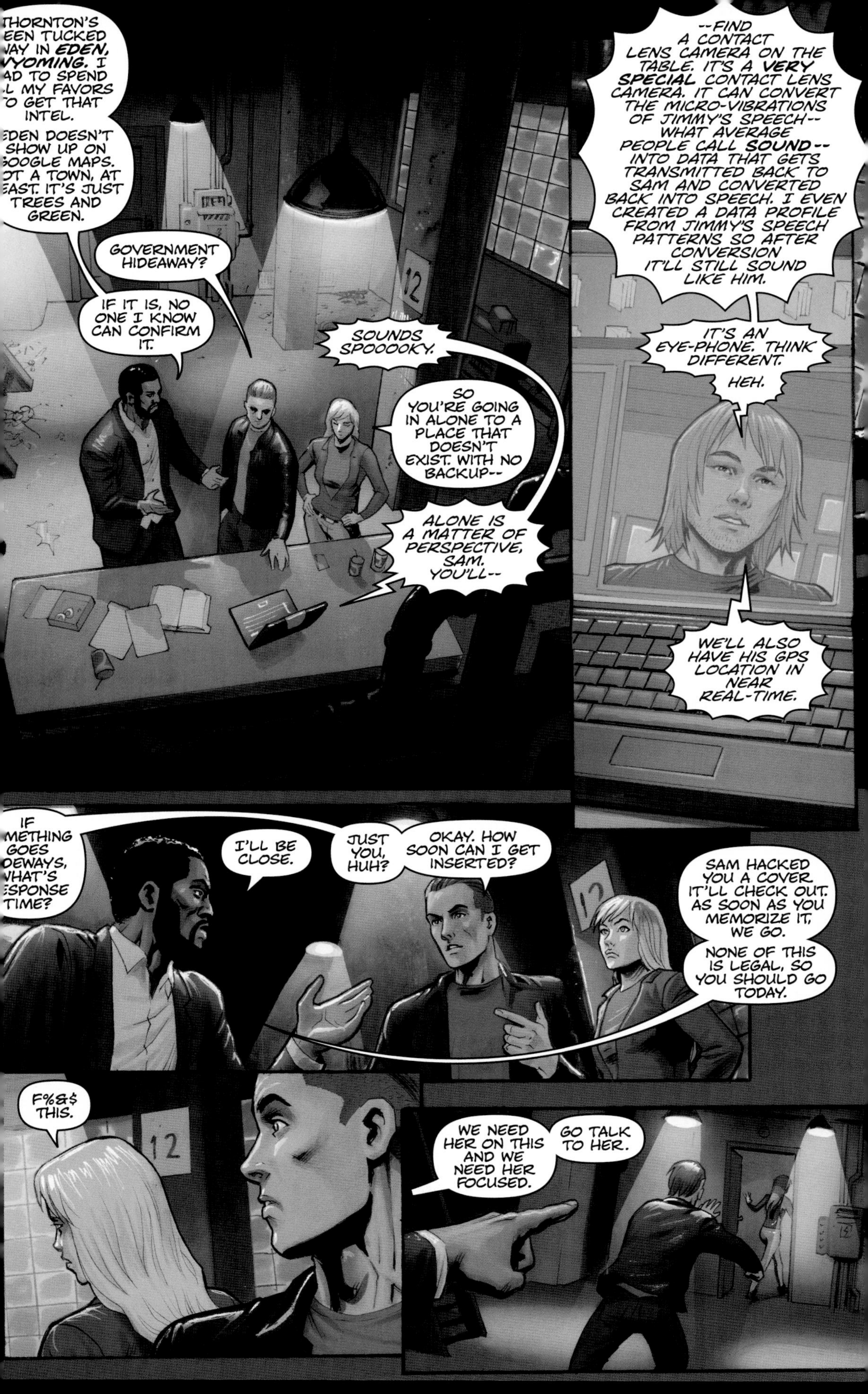
THORNTON'S BEEN TUCKED AWAY IN EDEN, WYOMING. I HAD TO SPEND ALL MY FAVORS TO GET THAT INTEL.
EDEN DOESN'T SHOW UP ON GOOGLE MAPS. NOT A TOWN, AT LEAST. IT'S JUST TREES AND GREEN.
GOVERNMENT HIDEAWAY?
IF IT IS, NO ONE I KNOW CAN CONFIRM IT.
SOUNDS SPOOOOKY.
SO YOU'RE GOING IN ALONE TO A PLACE THAT DOESN'T EXIST. WITH NO BACKUP--
ALONE IS A MATTER OF PERSPECTIVE, SAM. YOU'LL--
--FIND A CONTACT LENS CAMERA ON THE TABLE. IT'S A VERY SPECIAL CONTACT LENS CAMERA. IT CAN CONVERT THE MICRO-VIBRATIONS OF JIMMY'S SPEECH-- WHAT AVERAGE PEOPLE CALL SOUND-- INTO DATA THAT GETS TRANSMITTED BACK TO SAM AND CONVERTED BACK INTO SPEECH. I EVEN CREATED A DATA PROFILE FROM JIMMY'S SPEECH PATTERNS SO AFTER CONVERSION IT'LL STILL SOUND LIKE HIM.
IT'S AN EYE-PHONE. THINK DIFFERENT.
HEH.
WE'LL ALSO HAVE HIS GPS LOCATION IN NEAR REAL-TIME.
IF SOMETHING GOES SIDEWAYS, WHAT'S RESPONSE TIME?
I'LL BE CLOSE.
JUST YOU, HUH?
OKAY. HOW SOON CAN I GET INSERTED?
SAM HACKED YOU A COVER IT'LL CHECK OUT. AS SOON AS YOU MEMORIZE IT, WE GO.
NONE OF THIS IS LEGAL, SO YOU SHOULD GO TODAY.
F%&$ THIS.
WE NEED HER ON THIS AND WE NEED HER FOCUSED.
GO TALK TO HER.

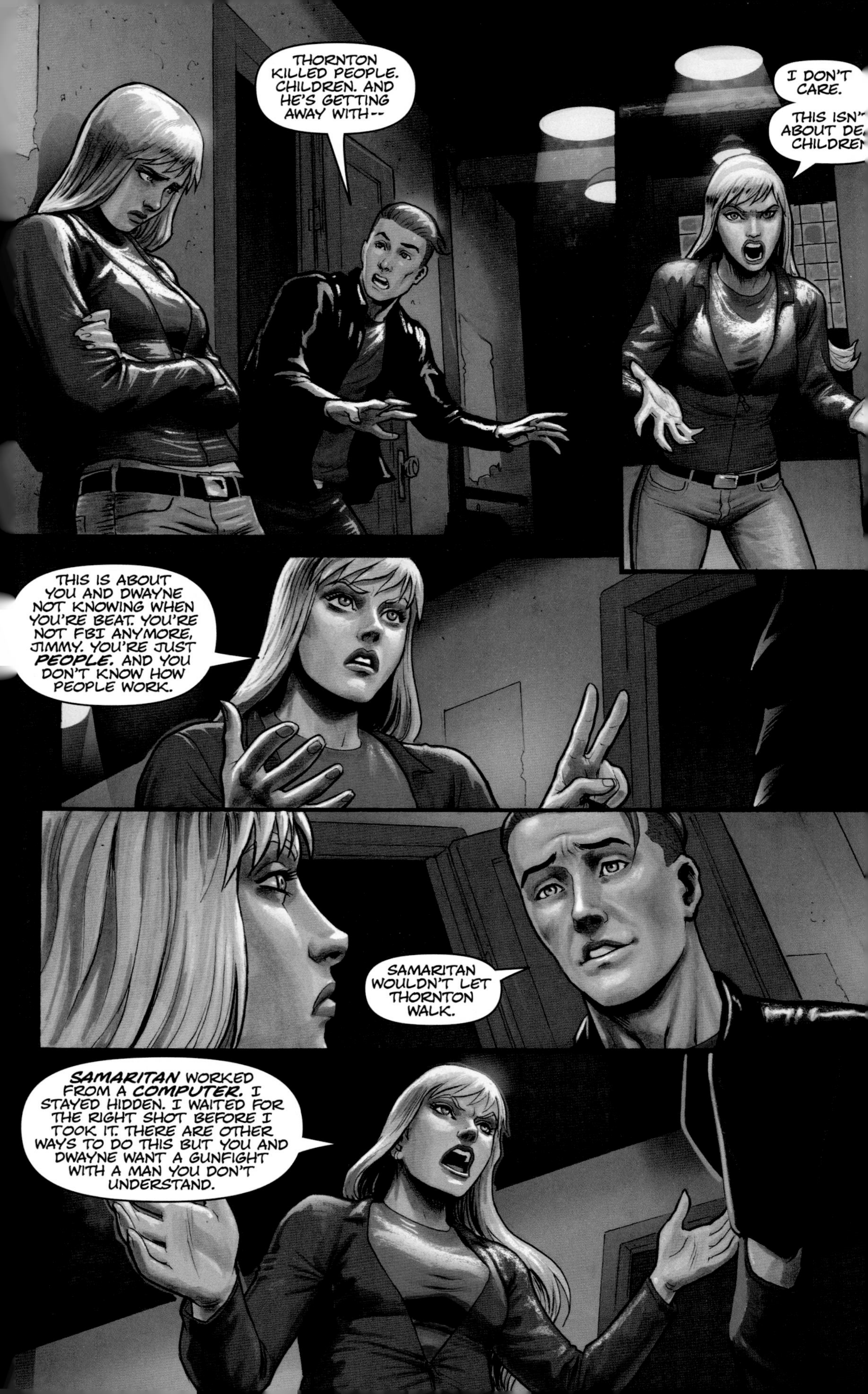
THORNTON KILLED PEOPLE. CHILDREN. AND HE'S GETTING AWAY WITH--
I DON'T CARE.
THIS ISN'T ABOUT DE CHILDREN
THIS IS ABOUT YOU AND DWAYNE NOT KNOWING WHEN YOU'RE BEAT. YOU'RE NOT FBI ANYMORE, JIMMY. YOU'RE JUST PEOPLE. AND YOU DON'T KNOW HOW PEOPLE WORK.
SAMARITAN WOULDN'T LET THORNTON WALK.
SAMARITAN WORKED FROM A COMPUTER. I STAYED HIDDEN. I WAITED FOR THE RIGHT SHOT BEFORE I TOOK IT. THERE ARE OTHER WAYS TO DO THIS BUT YOU AND DWAYNE WANT A GUNFIGHT WITH A MAN YOU DON'T UNDERSTAND.

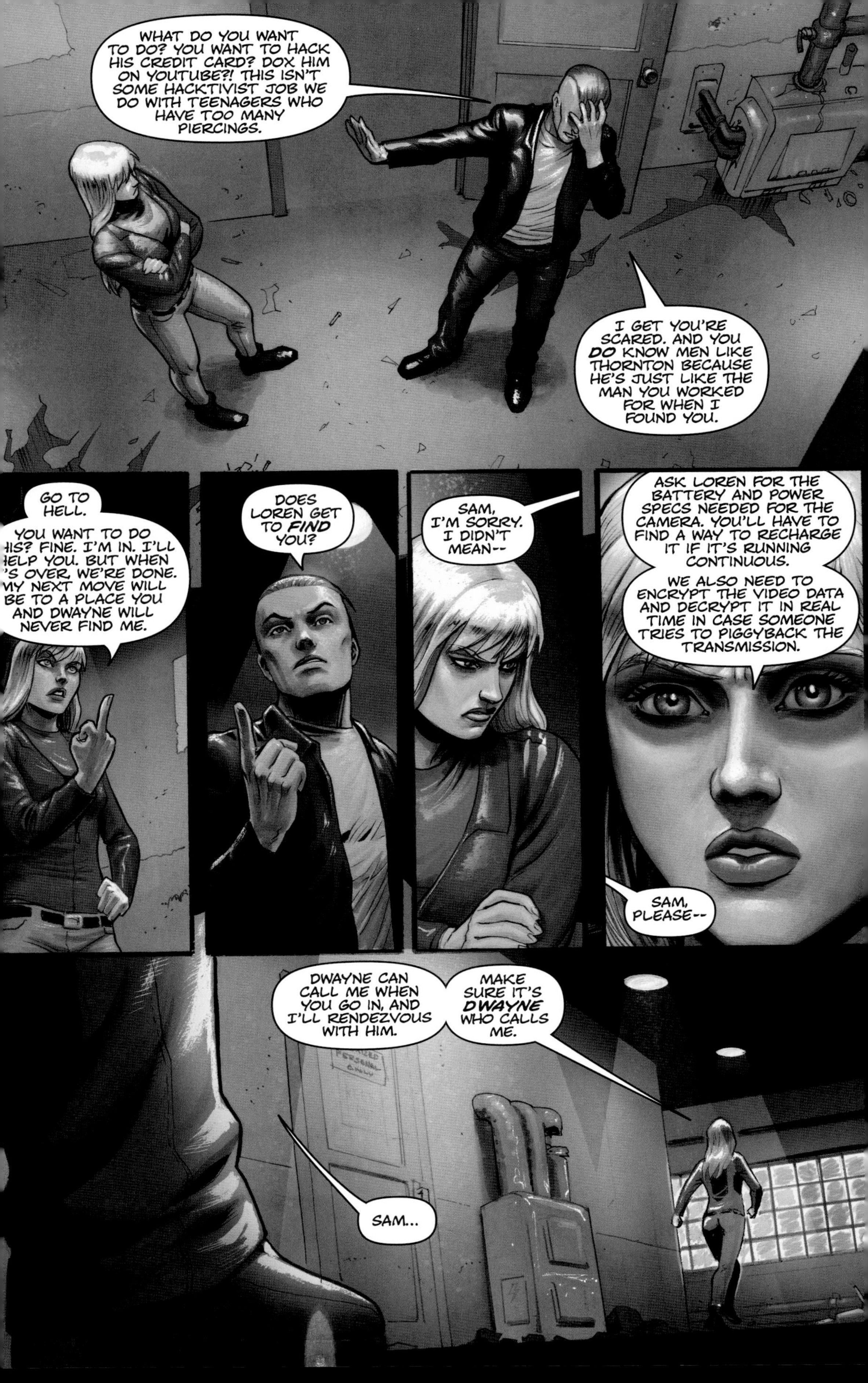
WHAT DO YOU WANT TO DO? YOU WANT TO HACK HIS CREDIT CARD? DOX HIM ON YOUTUBE?! THIS ISN'T SOME HACKTIVIST JOB WE DO WITH TEENAGERS WHO HAVE TOO MANY PIERCINGS.
I GET YOU'RE SCARED. AND YOU DO KNOW MEN LIKE THORNTON BECAUSE HE'S JUST LIKE THE MAN YOU WORKED FOR WHEN I FOUND YOU.
GO TO HELL.
YOU WANT TO DO HIS? FINE. I'M IN. I'LL HELP YOU. BUT WHEN 'S OVER, WE'RE DONE. MY NEXT MOVE WILL BE TO A PLACE YOU AND DWAYNE WILL NEVER FIND ME.
DOES LOREN GET TO FIND YOU?
SAM, I'M SORRY. I DIDN'T MEAN--
ASK LOREN FOR THE BATTERY AND POWER SPECS NEEDED FOR THE CAMERA. YOU'LL HAVE TO FIND A WAY TO RECHARGE IT IF IT'S RUNNING CONTINUOUS.
WE ALSO NEED TO ENCRYPT THE VIDEO DATA AND DECRYPT IT IN REAL TIME IN CASE SOMEONE TRIES TO PIGGYBACK THE TRANSMISSION.
SAM, PLEASE--
DWAYNE CAN CALL ME WHEN YOU GO IN, AND I'LL RENDEZVOUS WITH HIM.
MAKE SURE IT'S DWAYNE WHO CALLS ME.
SAM...

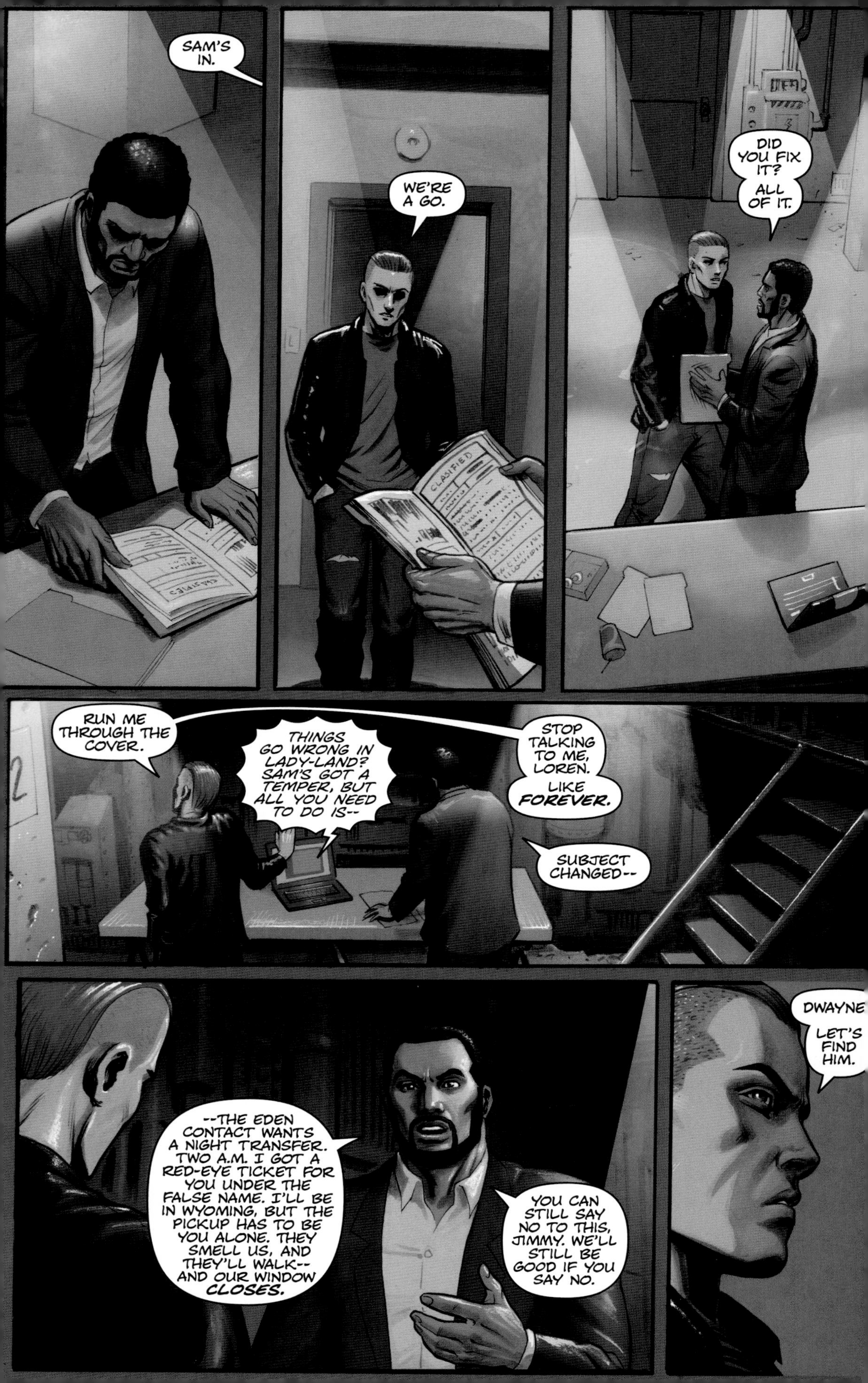
SAM'S IN.
WE'RE A GO.
DID YOU FIX IT?
ALL OF IT.
RUN ME THROUGH THE COVER.
THINGS GO WRONG IN LADY-LAND? SAM'S GOT A TEMPER, BUT ALL YOU NEED TO DO IS--
STOP TALKING TO ME, LOREN.
LIKE *FOREVER.*
SUBJECT CHANGED--
--THE EDEN CONTACT WANTS A NIGHT TRANSFER. TWO A.M. I GOT A RED-EYE TICKET FOR YOU UNDER THE FALSE NAME. I'LL BE IN WYOMING, BUT THE PICKUP HAS TO BE YOU ALONE. THEY SMELL US, AND THEY'LL WALK-- AND OUR WINDOW *CLOSES.*
YOU CAN STILL SAY NO TO THIS, JIMMY. WE'LL STILL BE GOOD IF YOU SAY NO.
DWAYNE
LET'S FIND HIM.

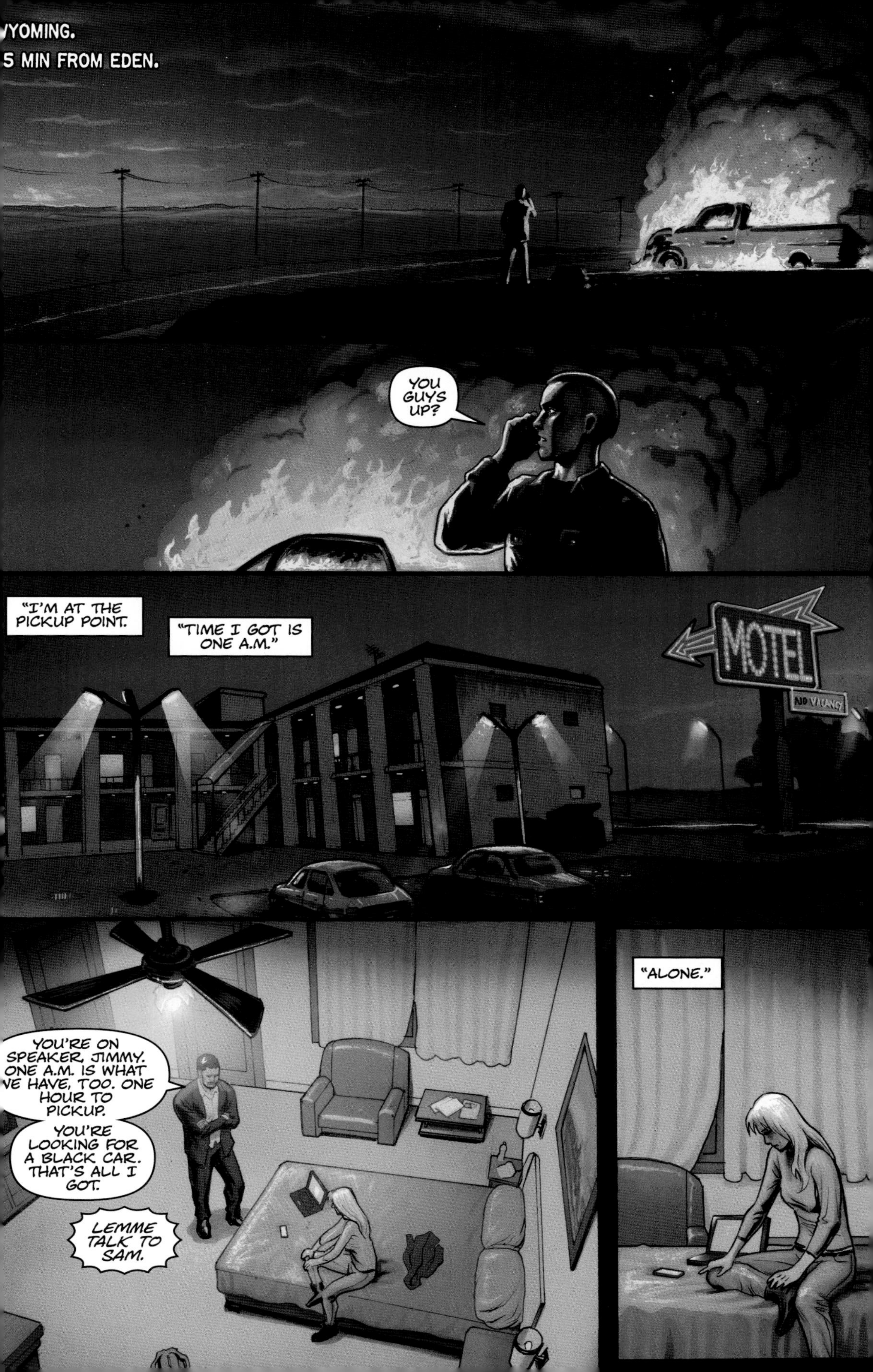

YOMING.
5 MIN FROM EDEN.
YOU GUYS UP?
"I'M AT THE PICKUP POINT.
"TIME I GOT IS ONE A.M."
MOTEL
NO VACANCY
YOU'RE ON SPEAKER, JIMMY. ONE A.M. IS WHAT E HAVE, TOO. ONE HOUR TO PICKUP.
YOU'RE LOOKING FOR A BLACK CAR. THAT'S ALL I GOT.
LEMME TALK TO SAM.
"ALONE."

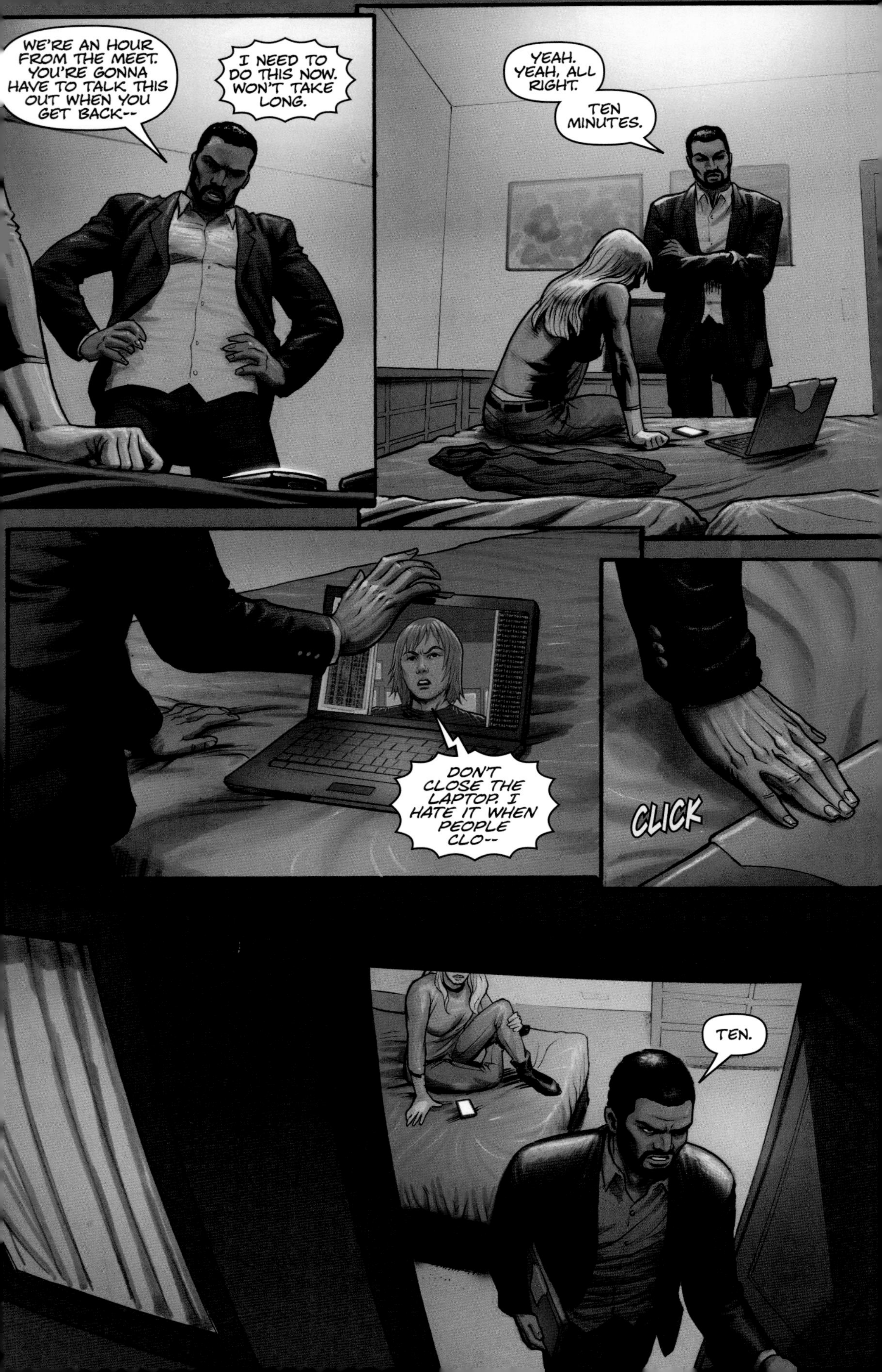
WE'RE AN HOUR FROM THE MEET. YOU'RE GONNA HAVE TO TALK THIS OUT WHEN YOU GET BACK--
I NEED TO DO THIS NOW. WON'T TAKE LONG.
YEAH. YEAH, ALL RIGHT.
TEN MINUTES.
DON'T CLOSE THE LAPTOP. I HATE IT WHEN PEOPLE CLO--
CLICK
TEN.

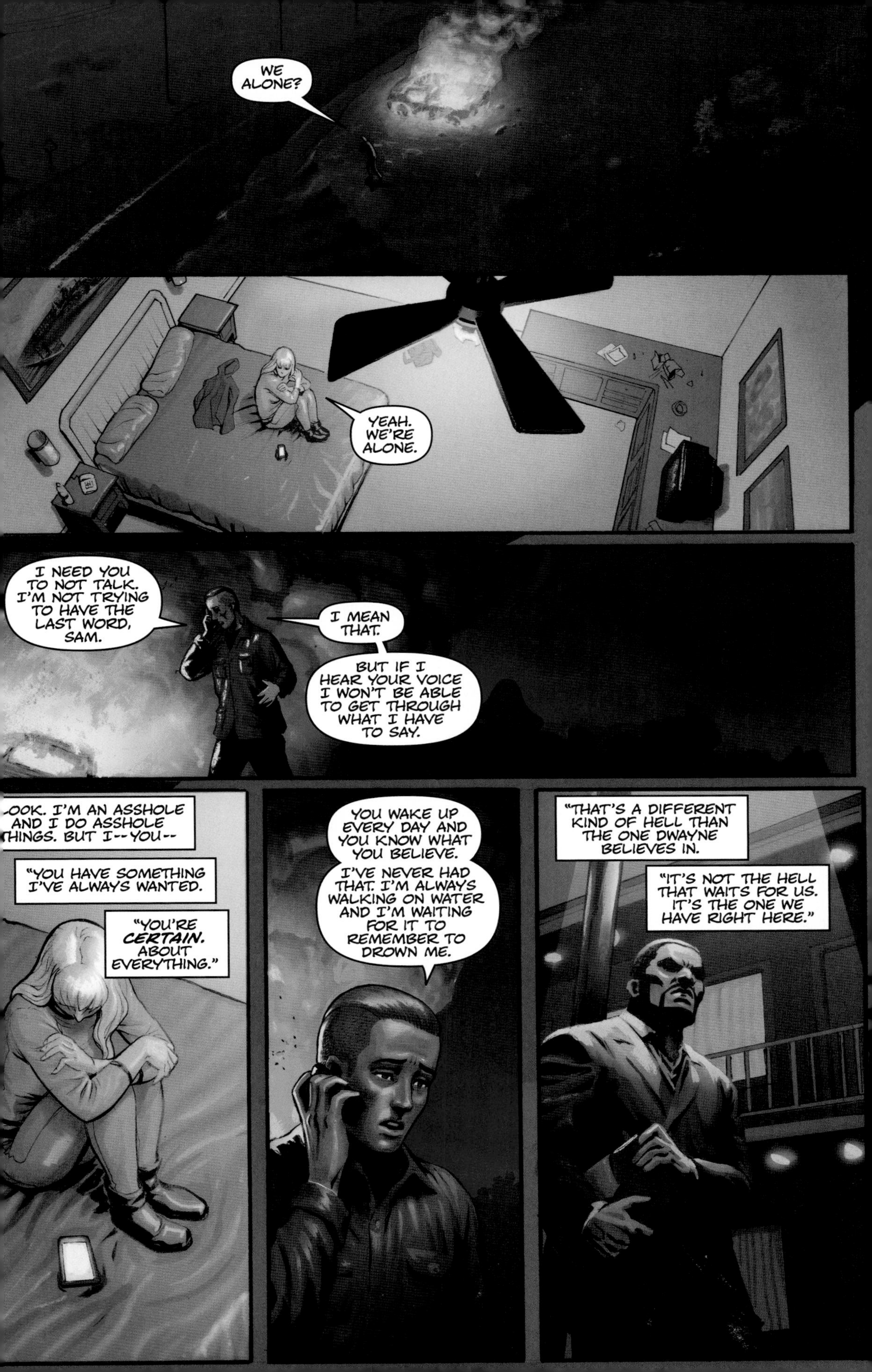
WE ALONE?
YEAH. WE'RE ALONE.
I NEED YOU TO NOT TALK. I'M NOT TRYING TO HAVE THE LAST WORD, SAM.
I MEAN THAT.
BUT IF I HEAR YOUR VOICE I WON'T BE ABLE TO GET THROUGH WHAT I HAVE TO SAY.
OOK. I'M AN ASSHOLE AND I DO ASSHOLE THINGS. BUT I--YOU--
"YOU HAVE SOMETHING I'VE ALWAYS WANTED.
"YOU'RE CERTAIN. ABOUT EVERYTHING."
YOU WAKE UP EVERY DAY AND YOU KNOW WHAT YOU BELIEVE.
I'VE NEVER HAD THAT. I'M ALWAYS WALKING ON WATER AND I'M WAITING FOR IT TO REMEMBER TO DROWN ME.
"THAT'S A DIFFERENT KIND OF HELL THAN THE ONE DWAYNE BELIEVES IN.
"IT'S NOT THE HELL THAT WAITS FOR US. IT'S THE ONE WE HAVE RIGHT HERE."

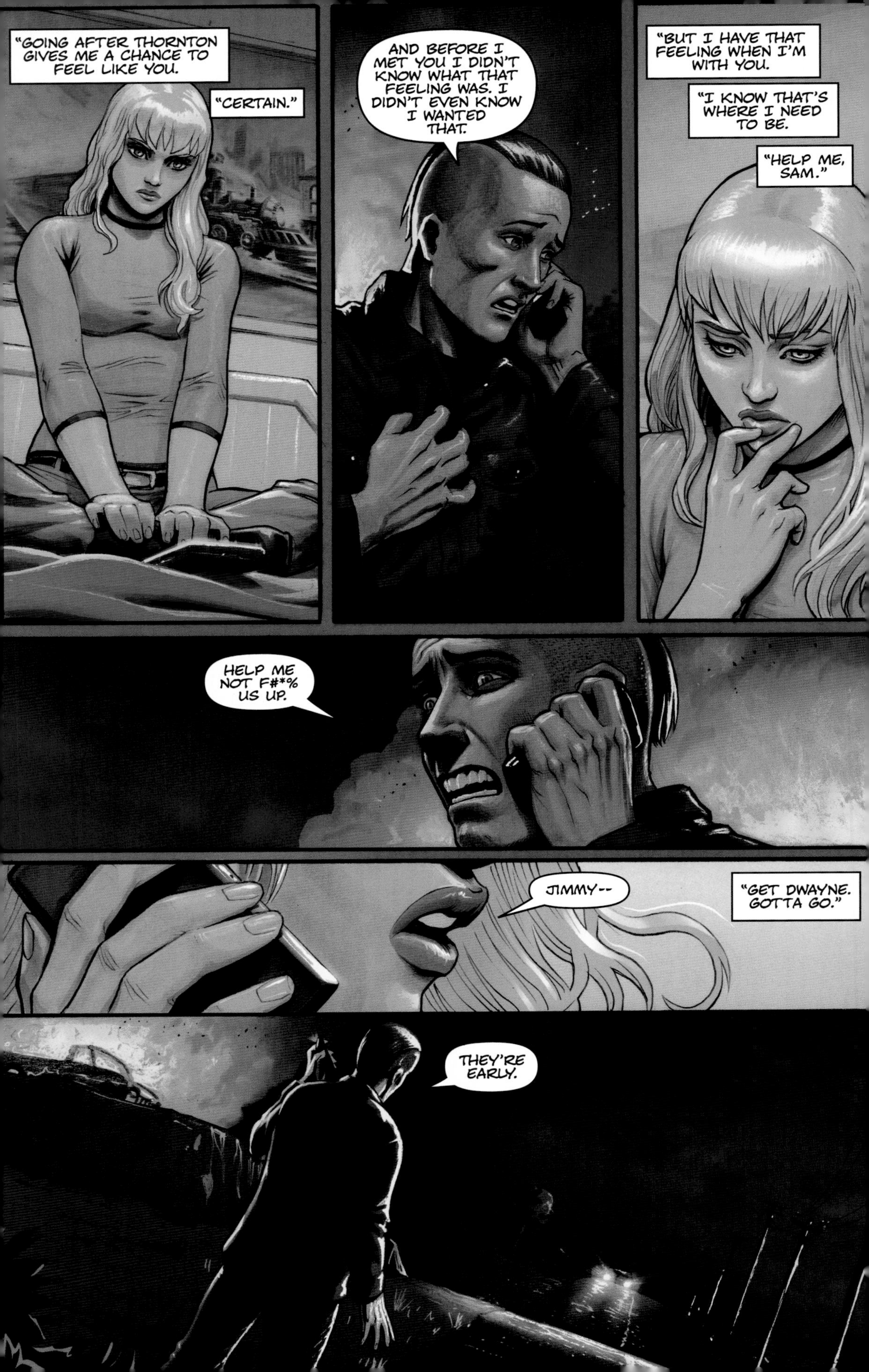
"GOING AFTER THORNTON GIVES ME A CHANCE TO FEEL LIKE YOU.
"CERTAIN."
AND BEFORE I MET YOU I DIDN'T KNOW WHAT THAT FEELING WAS. I DIDN'T EVEN KNOW I WANTED THAT.
"BUT I HAVE THAT FEELING WHEN I'M WITH YOU.
"I KNOW THAT'S WHERE I NEED TO BE.
"HELP ME, SAM."
HELP ME NOT F#*% US UP.
JIMMY--
"GET DWAYNE. GOTTA GO."
THEY'RE EARLY.

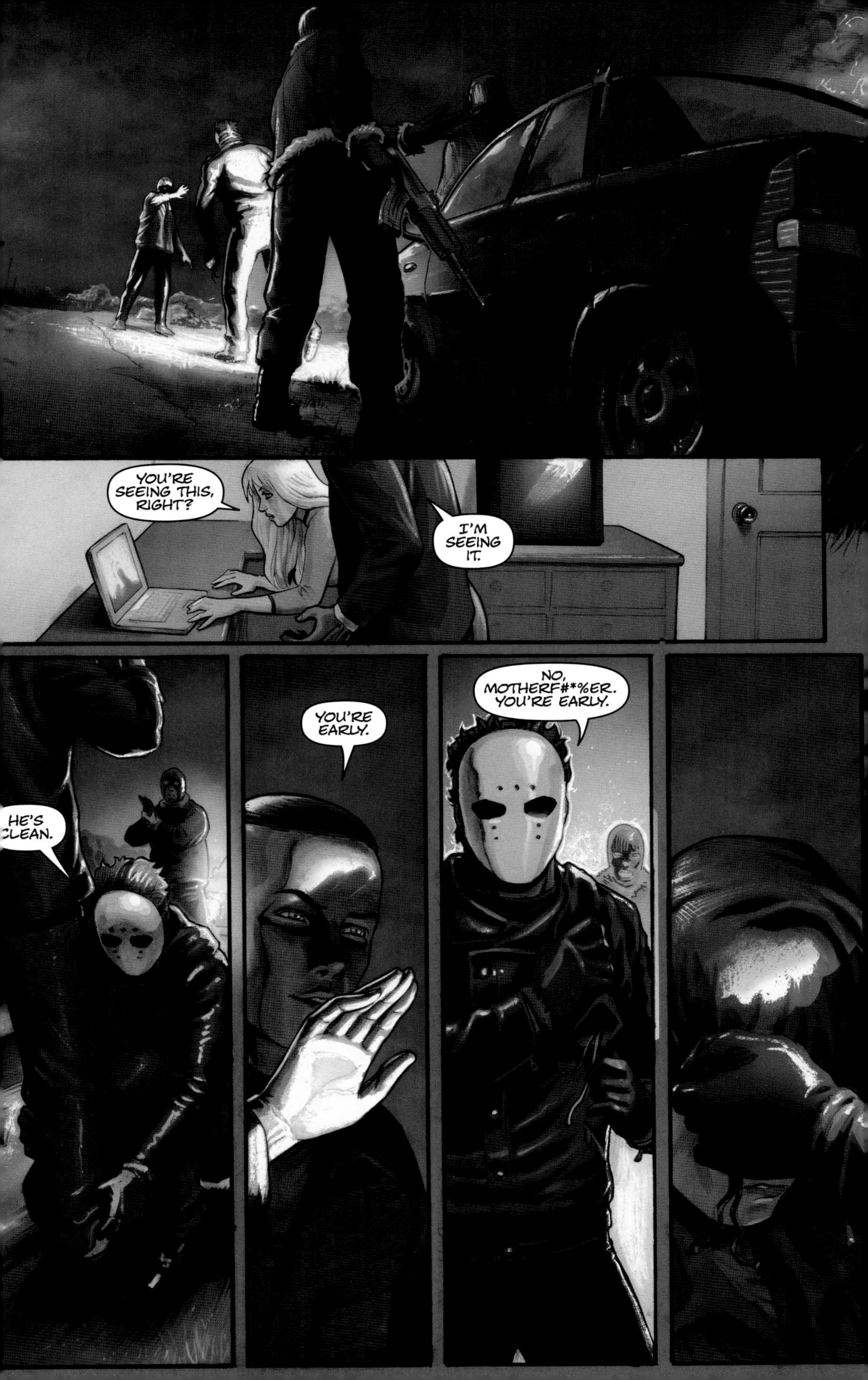
YOU'RE SEEING THIS, RIGHT?
I'M SEEING IT.
HE'S CLEAN.
YOU'RE EARLY.
NO, MOTHERF#*%ER. YOU'RE EARLY.

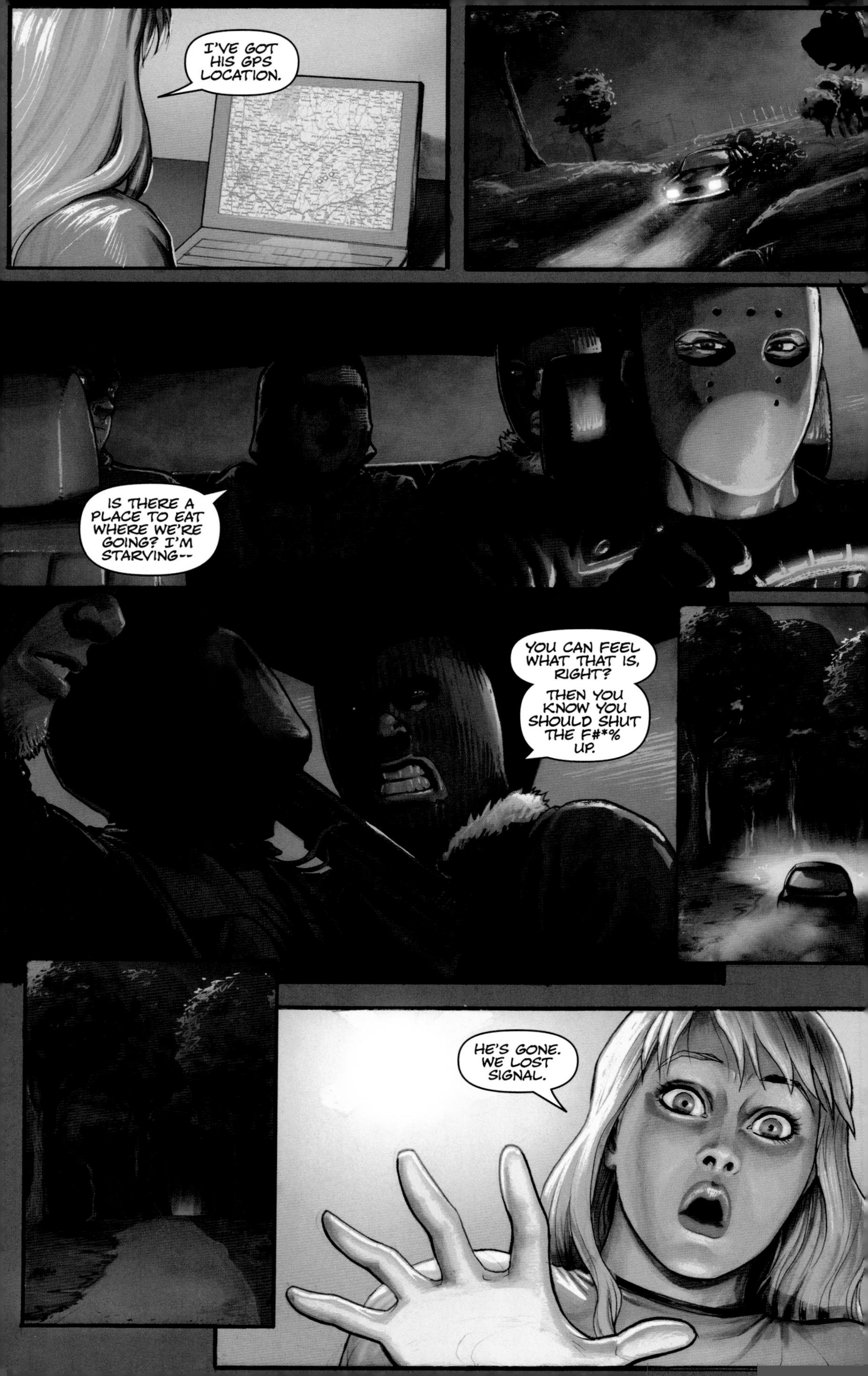
I'VE GOT HIS GPS LOCATION.
IS THERE A PLACE TO EAT WHERE WE'RE GOING? I'M STARVING--
YOU CAN FEEL WHAT THAT IS, RIGHT?
THEN YOU KNOW YOU SHOULD SHUT THE F#*% UP.
HE'S GONE. WE LOST SIGNAL.

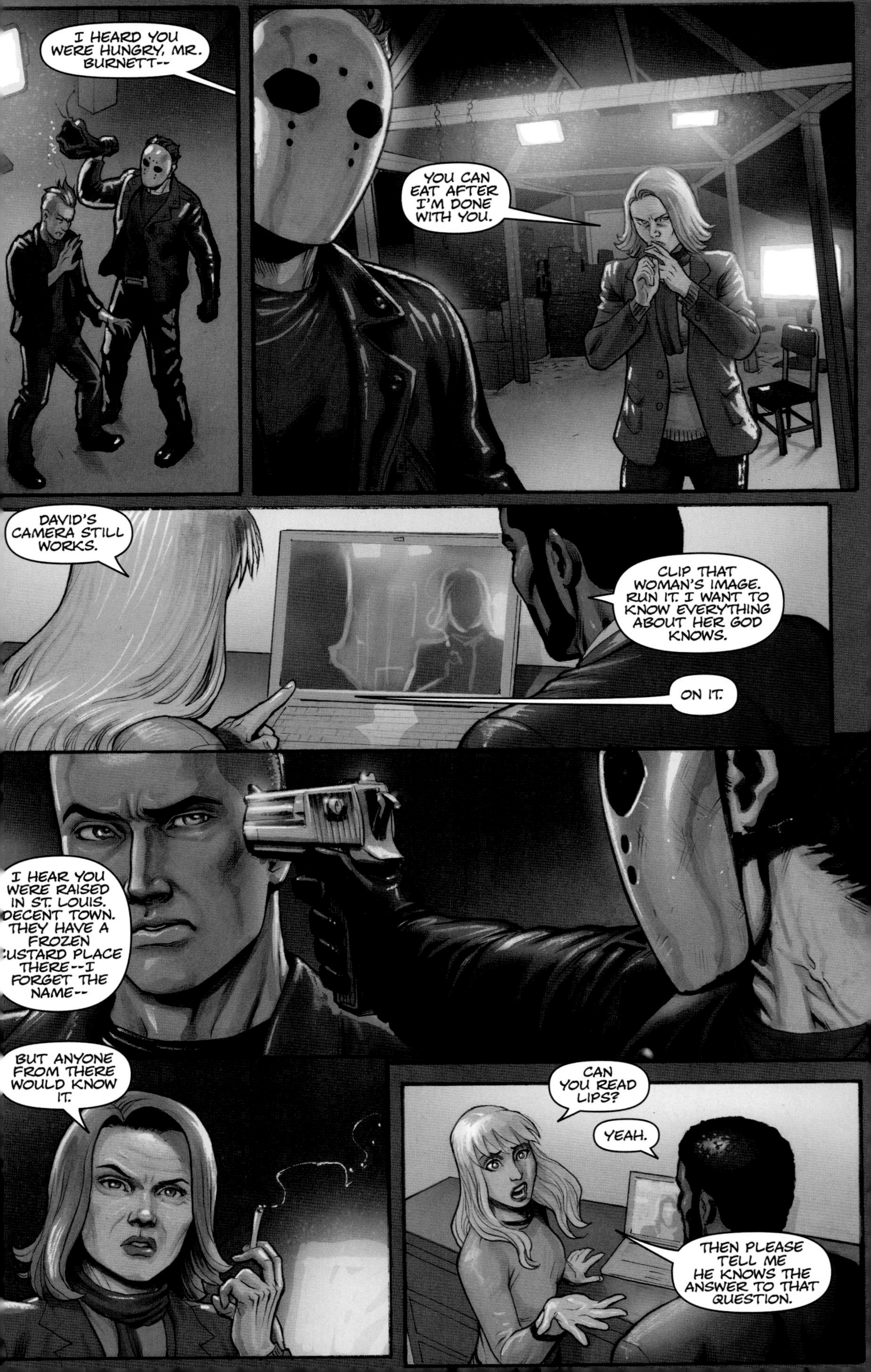
I HEARD YOU WERE HUNGRY, MR. BURNETT--
YOU CAN EAT AFTER I'M DONE WITH YOU.
DAVID'S CAMERA STILL WORKS.
CLIP THAT WOMAN'S IMAGE. RUN IT. I WANT TO KNOW EVERYTHING ABOUT HER GOD KNOWS.
ON IT.
I HEAR YOU WERE RAISED IN ST. LOUIS. DECENT TOWN. THEY HAVE A FROZEN CUSTARD PLACE THERE--I FORGET THE NAME--
BUT ANYONE FROM THERE WOULD KNOW IT.
CAN YOU READ LIPS?
YEAH.
THEN PLEASE TELL ME HE KNOWS THE ANSWER TO THAT QUESTION.

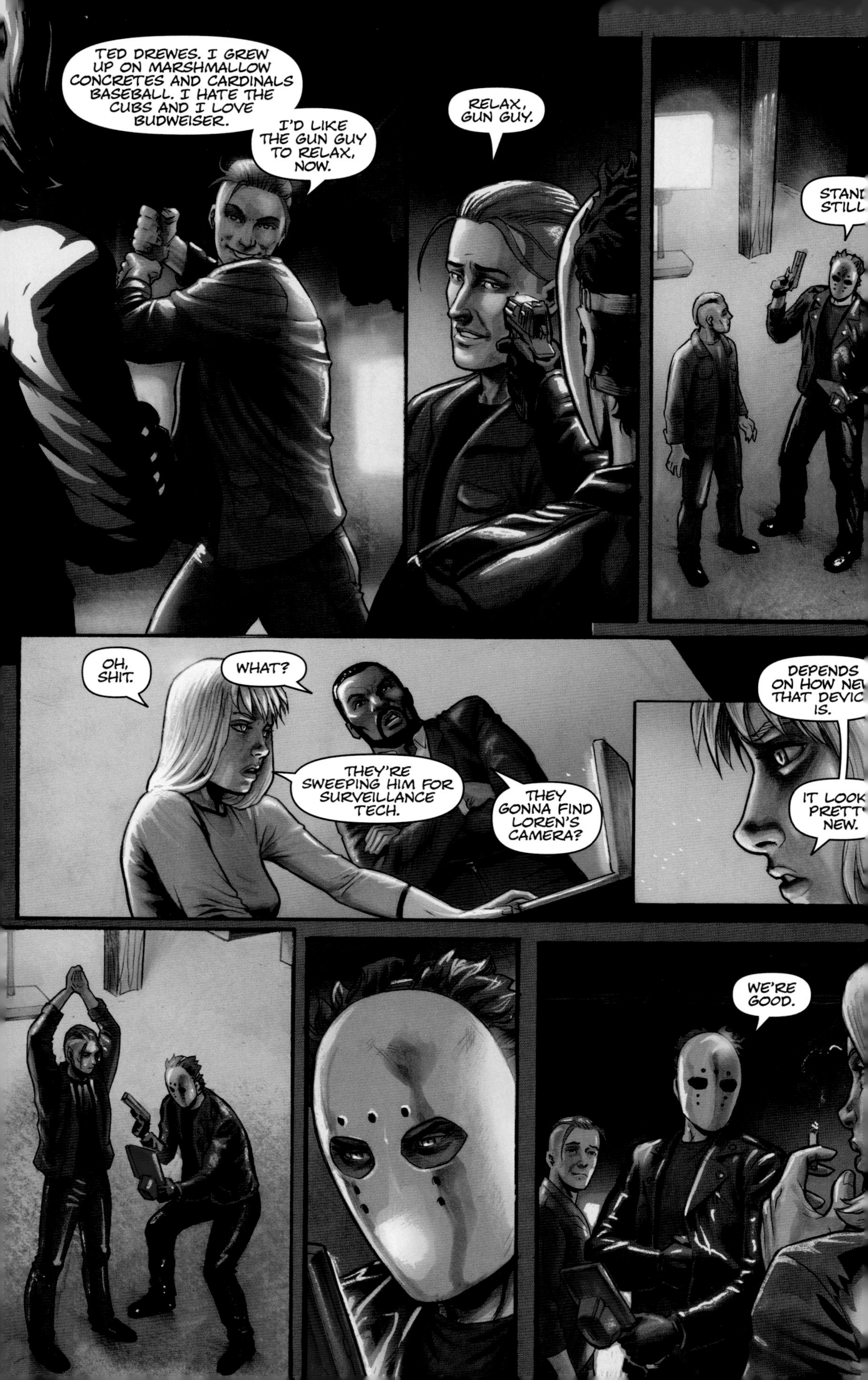
TED DREWES. I GREW UP ON MARSHMALLOW CONCRETES AND CARDINALS BASEBALL. I HATE THE CUBS AND I LOVE BUDWEISER.
I'D LIKE THE GUN GUY TO RELAX, NOW.
RELAX, GUN GUY.
STAND STILL
OH, SHIT.
WHAT?
THEY'RE SWEEPING HIM FOR SURVEILLANCE TECH.
THEY GONNA FIND LOREN'S CAMERA?
DEPENDS ON HOW NEW THAT DEVICE IS.
IT LOOKS PRETTY NEW.
WE'RE GOOD.

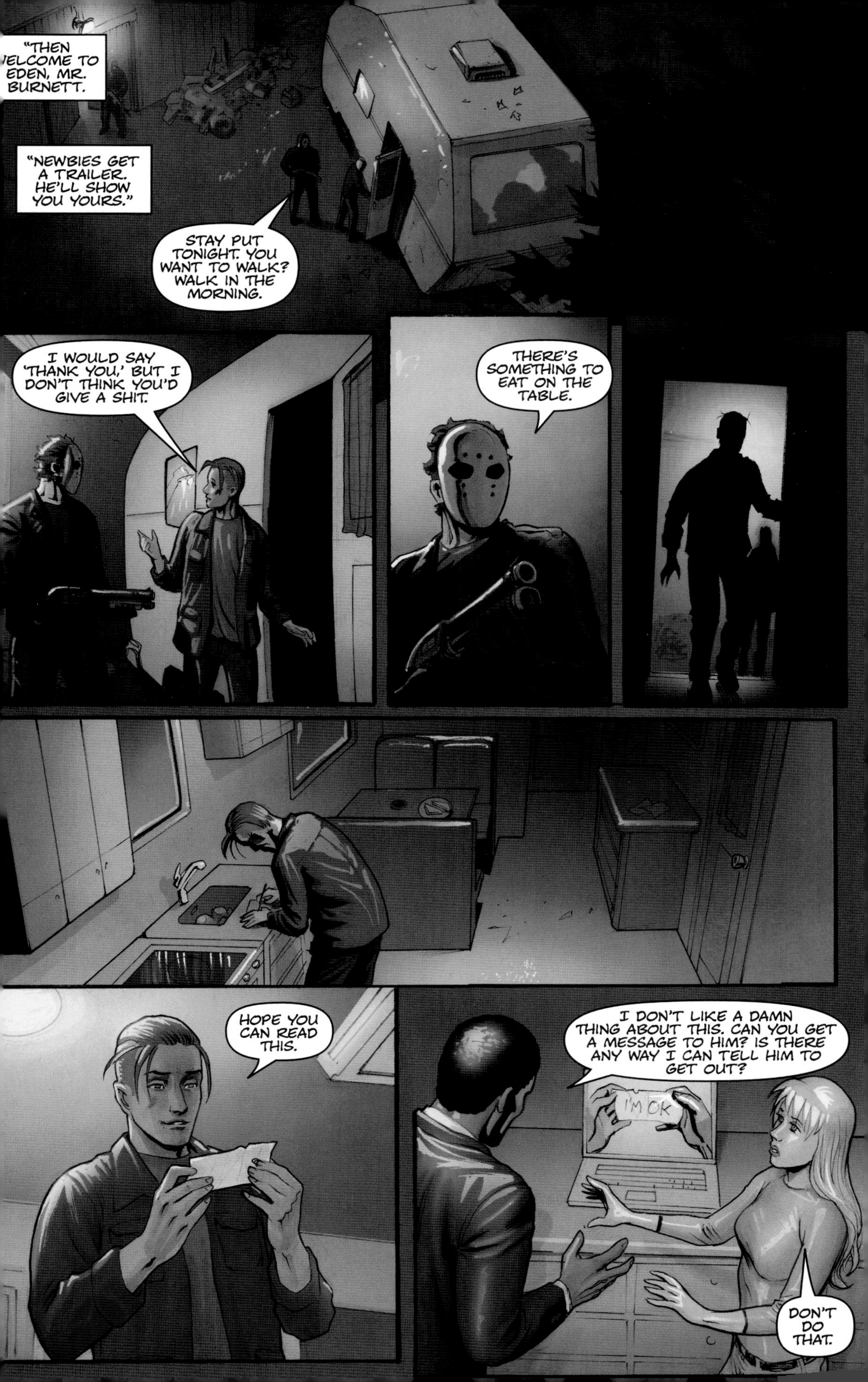
"THEN WELCOME TO EDEN, MR. BURNETT.
"NEWBIES GET A TRAILER. HE'LL SHOW YOU YOURS."
STAY PUT TONIGHT. YOU WANT TO WALK? WALK IN THE MORNING.
I WOULD SAY 'THANK YOU,' BUT I DON'T THINK YOU'D GIVE A SHIT.
THERE'S SOMETHING TO EAT ON THE TABLE.
HOPE YOU CAN READ THIS.
I DON'T LIKE A DAMN THING ABOUT THIS. CAN YOU GET A MESSAGE TO HIM? IS THERE ANY WAY I CAN TELL HIM TO GET OUT?
I'M OK
DON'T DO THAT.

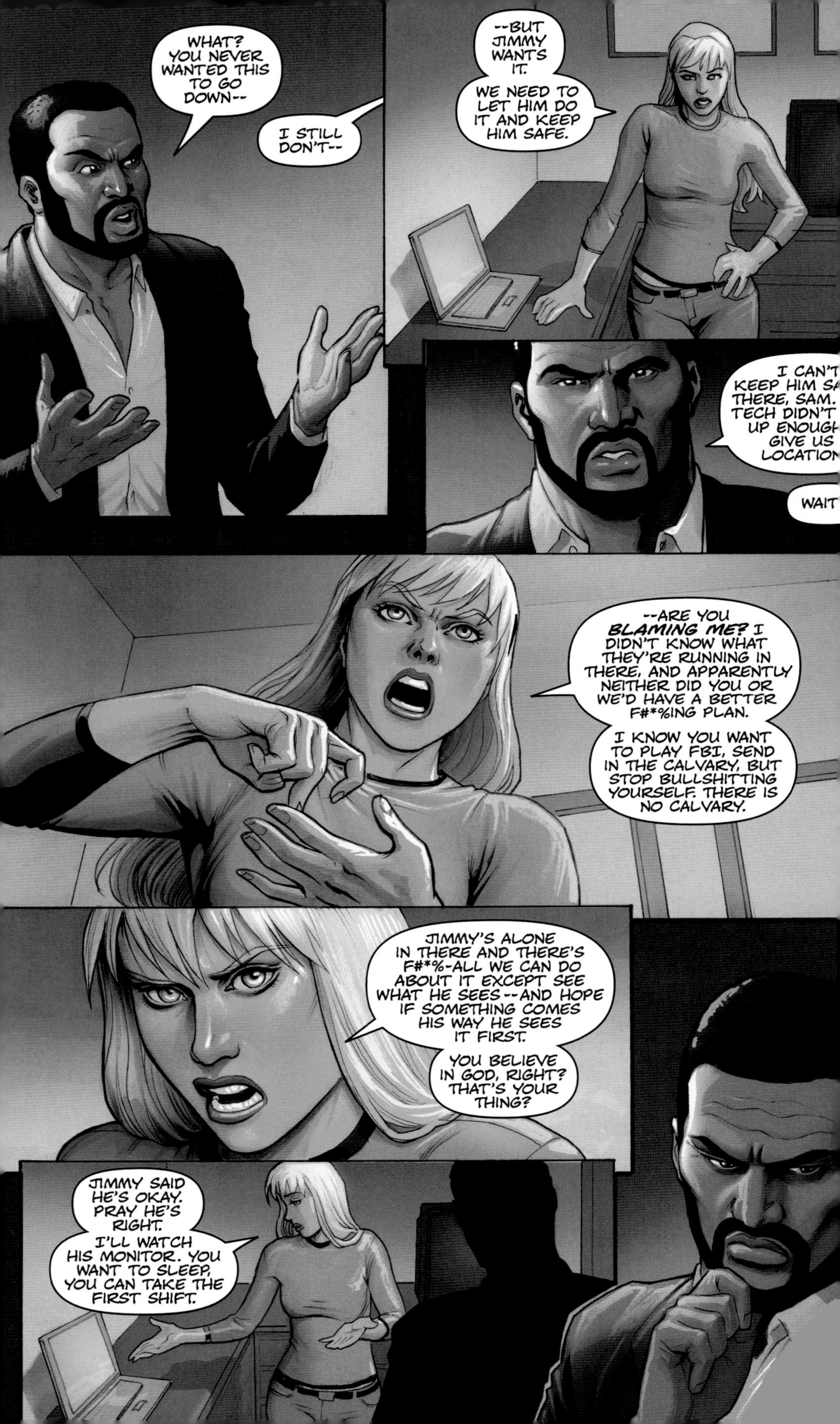
WHAT? YOU NEVER WANTED THIS TO GO DOWN--
I STILL DON'T--
--BUT JIMMY WANTS IT.
WE NEED TO LET HIM DO IT AND KEEP HIM SAFE.
I CAN'T KEEP HIM SA THERE, SAM. TECH DIDN'T UP ENOUGH GIVE US LOCATION
WAIT
--ARE YOU **BLAMING ME?** I DIDN'T KNOW WHAT THEY'RE RUNNING IN THERE, AND APPARENTLY NEITHER DID YOU OR WE'D HAVE A BETTER F#*%ING PLAN.
I KNOW YOU WANT TO PLAY FBI, SEND IN THE CALVARY, BUT STOP BULLSHITTING YOURSELF. THERE IS NO CALVARY.
JIMMY'S ALONE IN THERE AND THERE'S F#*%-ALL WE CAN DO ABOUT IT EXCEPT SEE WHAT HE SEES--AND HOPE IF SOMETHING COMES HIS WAY HE SEES IT FIRST.
YOU BELIEVE IN GOD, RIGHT? THAT'S YOUR THING?
JIMMY SAID HE'S OKAY. PRAY HE'S RIGHT.
I'LL WATCH HIS MONITOR. YOU WANT TO SLEEP, YOU CAN TAKE THE FIRST SHIFT.

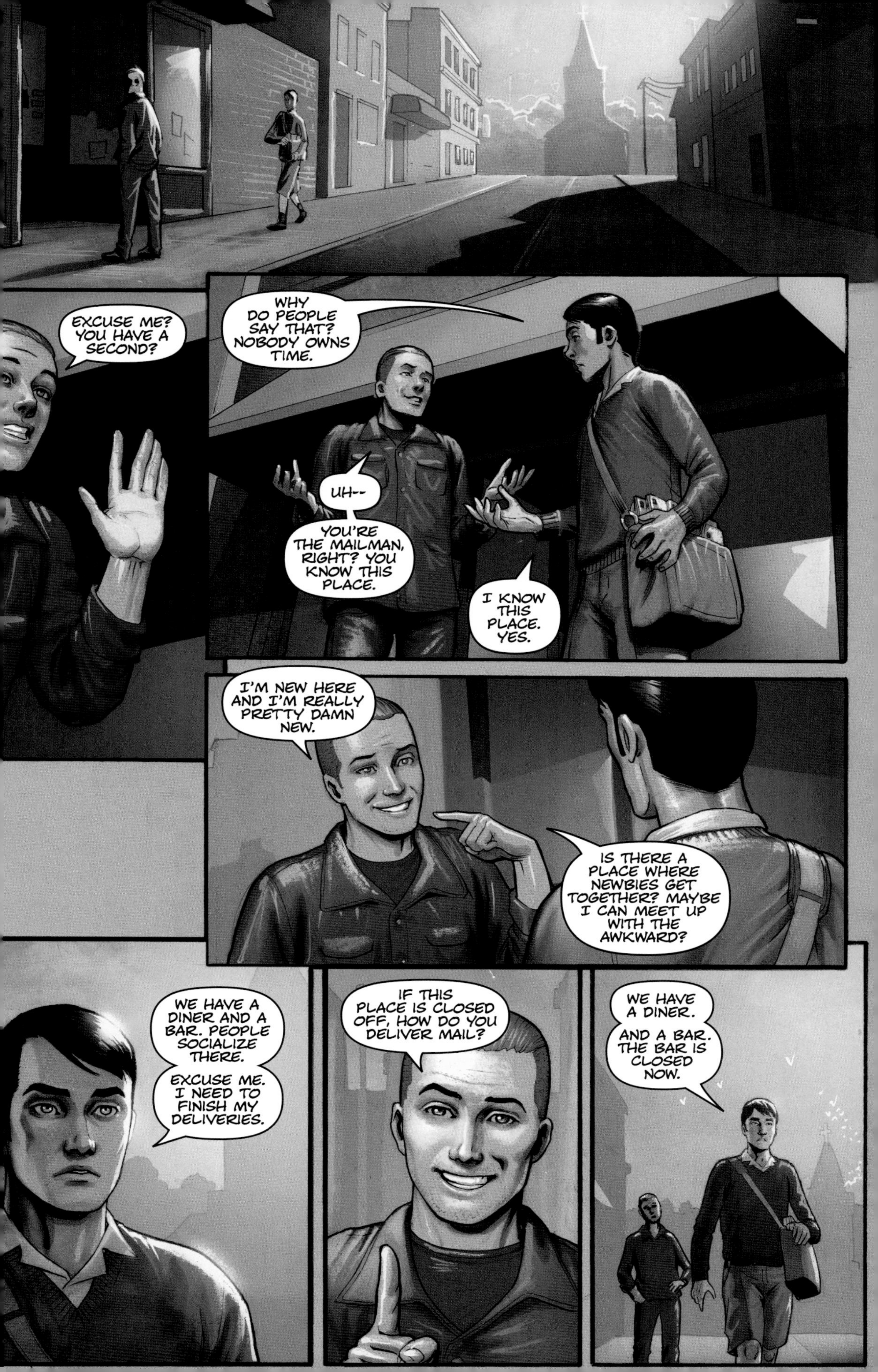
EXCUSE ME? YOU HAVE A SECOND?
WHY DO PEOPLE SAY THAT? NOBODY OWNS TIME.
UH--
YOU'RE THE MAILMAN, RIGHT? YOU KNOW THIS PLACE.
I KNOW THIS PLACE. YES.
I'M NEW HERE AND I'M REALLY PRETTY DAMN NEW.
IS THERE A PLACE WHERE NEWBIES GET TOGETHER? MAYBE I CAN MEET UP WITH THE AWKWARD?
WE HAVE A DINER AND A BAR. PEOPLE SOCIALIZE THERE.
EXCUSE ME. I NEED TO FINISH MY DELIVERIES.
IF THIS PLACE IS CLOSED OFF, HOW DO YOU DELIVER MAIL?
WE HAVE A DINER.
AND A BAR. THE BAR IS CLOSED NOW.

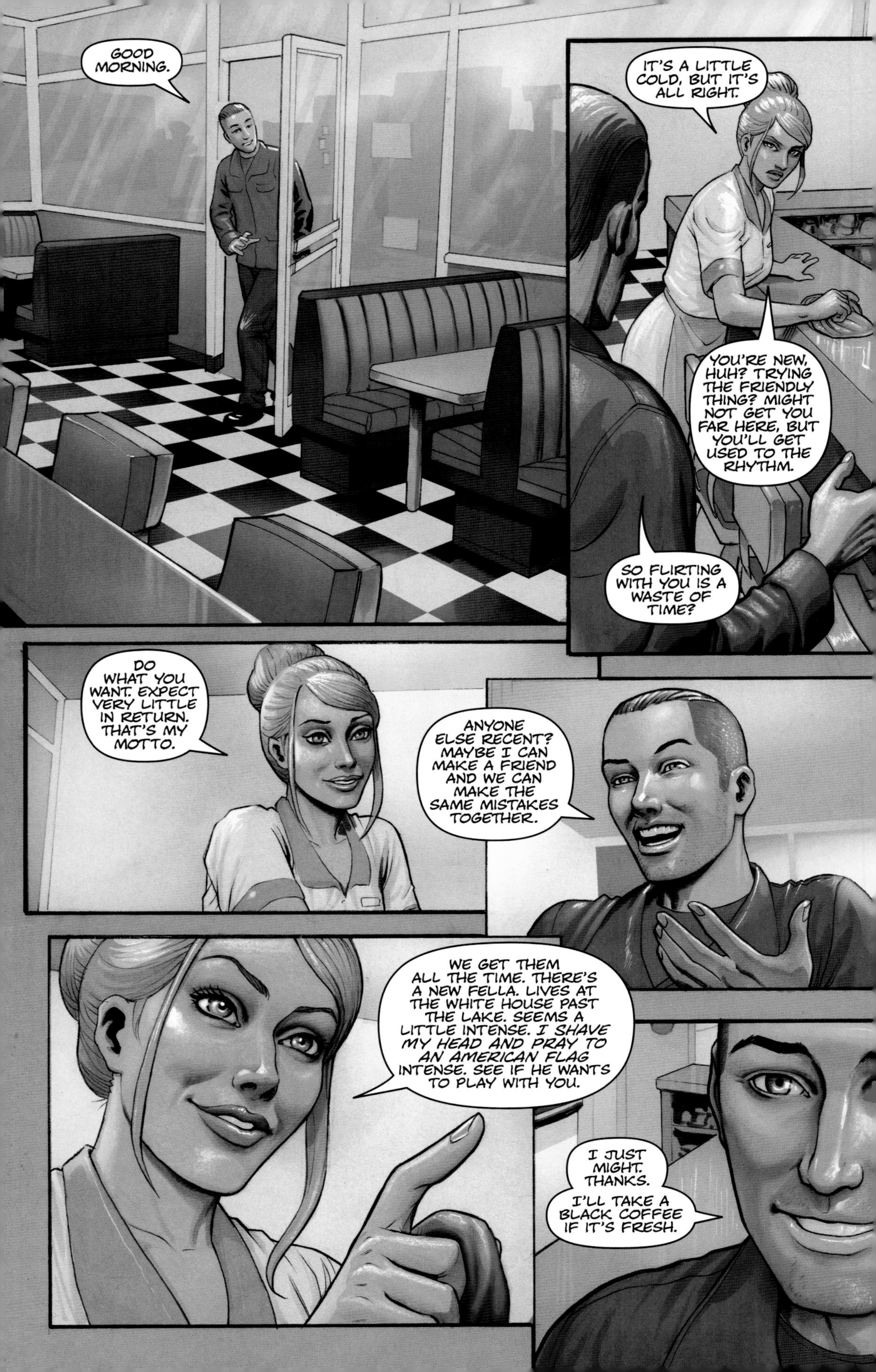
GOOD MORNING.
IT'S A LITTLE COLD, BUT IT'S ALL RIGHT.
YOU'RE NEW, HUH? TRYING THE FRIENDLY THING? MIGHT NOT GET YOU FAR HERE, BUT YOU'LL GET USED TO THE RHYTHM.
SO FLIRTING WITH YOU IS A WASTE OF TIME?
DO WHAT YOU WANT. EXPECT VERY LITTLE IN RETURN. THAT'S MY MOTTO.
ANYONE ELSE RECENT? MAYBE I CAN MAKE A FRIEND AND WE CAN MAKE THE SAME MISTAKES TOGETHER.
WE GET THEM ALL THE TIME. THERE'S A NEW FELLA. LIVES AT THE WHITE HOUSE PAST THE LAKE. SEEMS A LITTLE INTENSE. *I SHAVE MY HEAD AND PRAY TO AN AMERICAN FLAG* INTENSE. SEE IF HE WANTS TO PLAY WITH YOU.
I JUST MIGHT. THANKS.
I'LL TAKE A BLACK COFFEE IF IT'S FRESH.

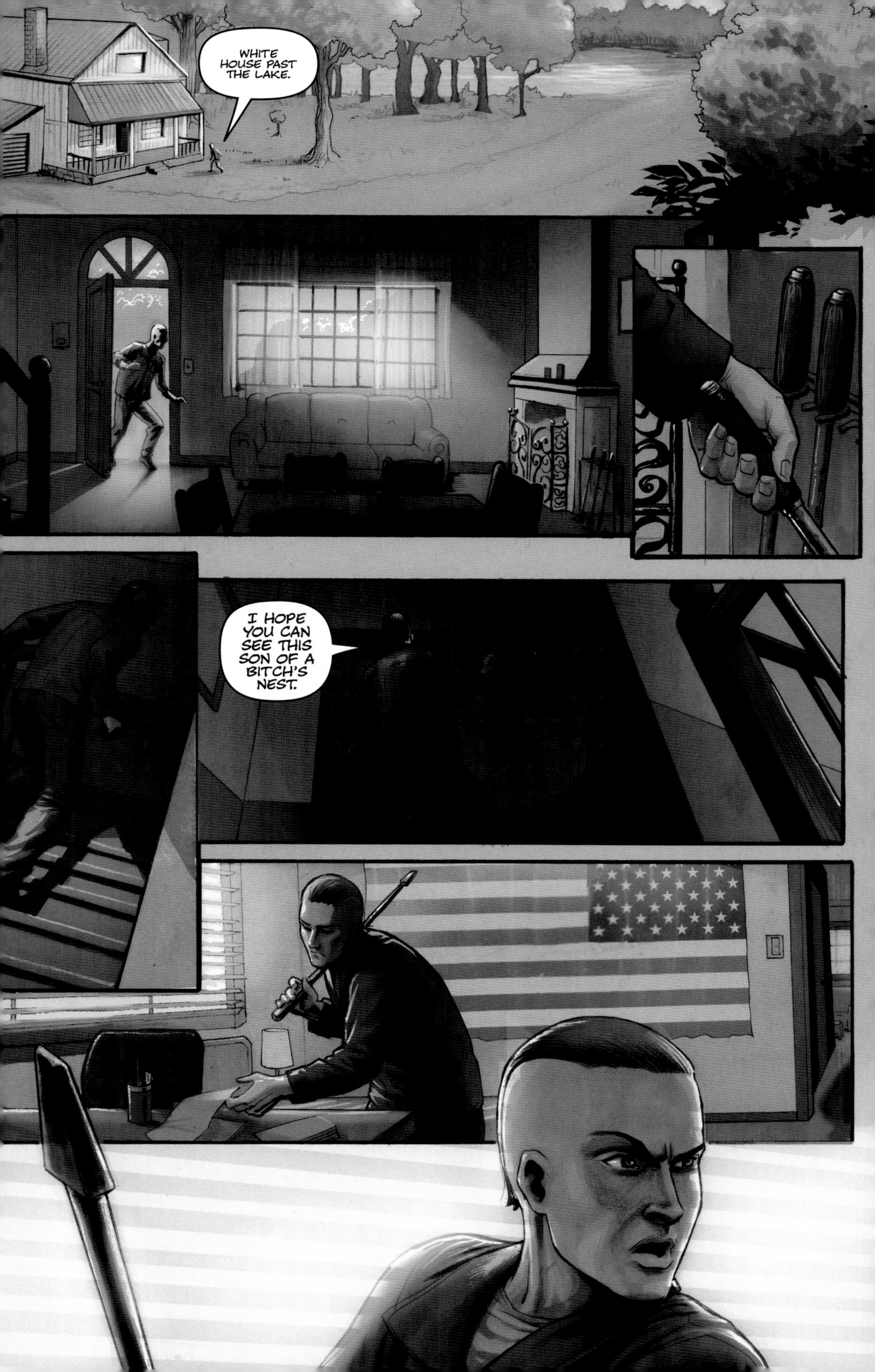
WHITE HOUSE PAST THE LAKE.
I HOPE YOU CAN SEE THIS SON OF A BITCH'S NEST.

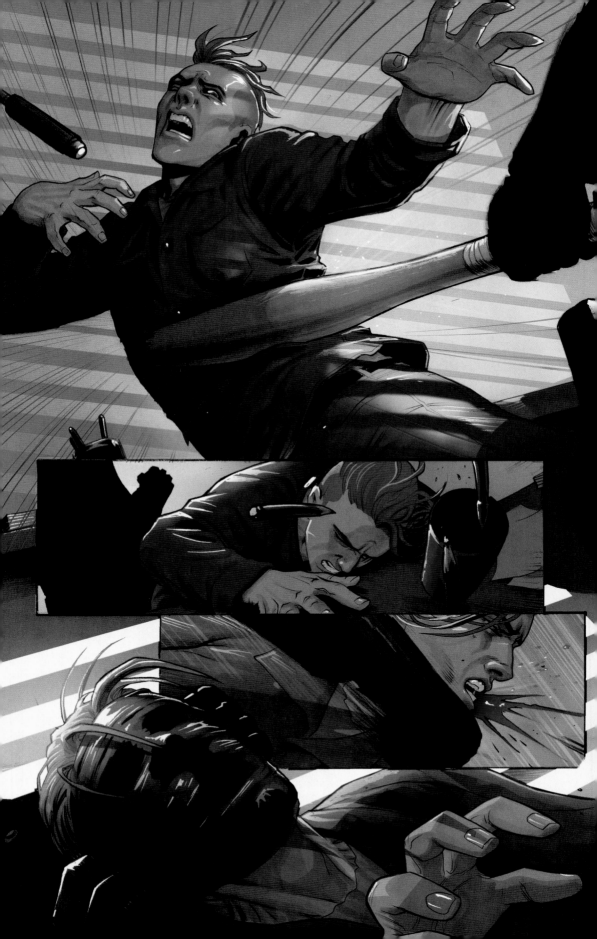

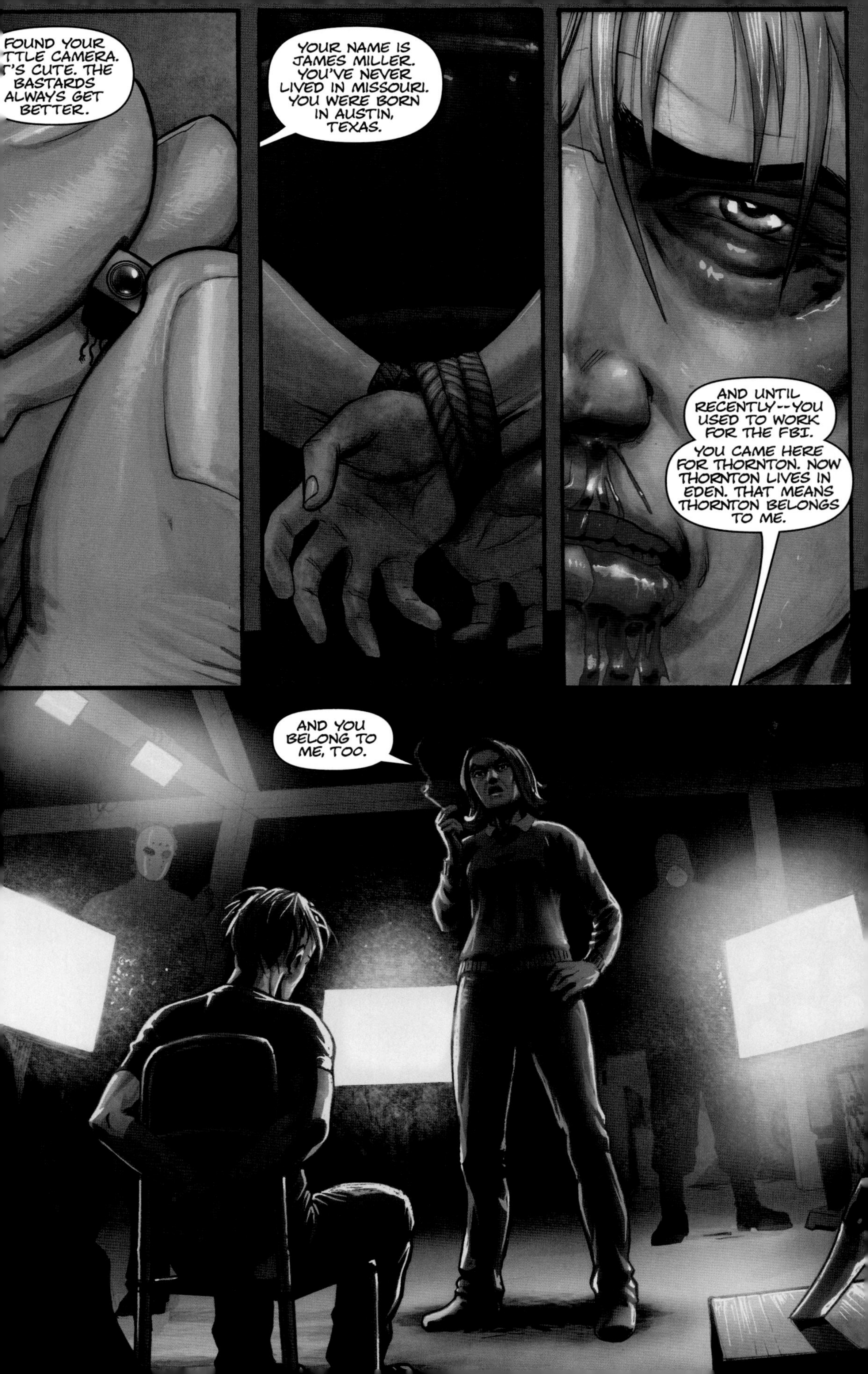
FOUND YOUR TTLE CAMERA. 'S CUTE. THE BASTARDS ALWAYS GET BETTER.
YOUR NAME IS JAMES MILLER. YOU'VE NEVER LIVED IN MISSOURI. YOU WERE BORN IN AUSTIN, TEXAS.
AND UNTIL RECENTLY--YOU USED TO WORK FOR THE FBI.
YOU CAME HERE FOR THORNTON. NOW THORNTON LIVES IN EDEN. THAT MEANS THORNTON BELONGS TO ME.
AND YOU BELONG TO ME, TOO.

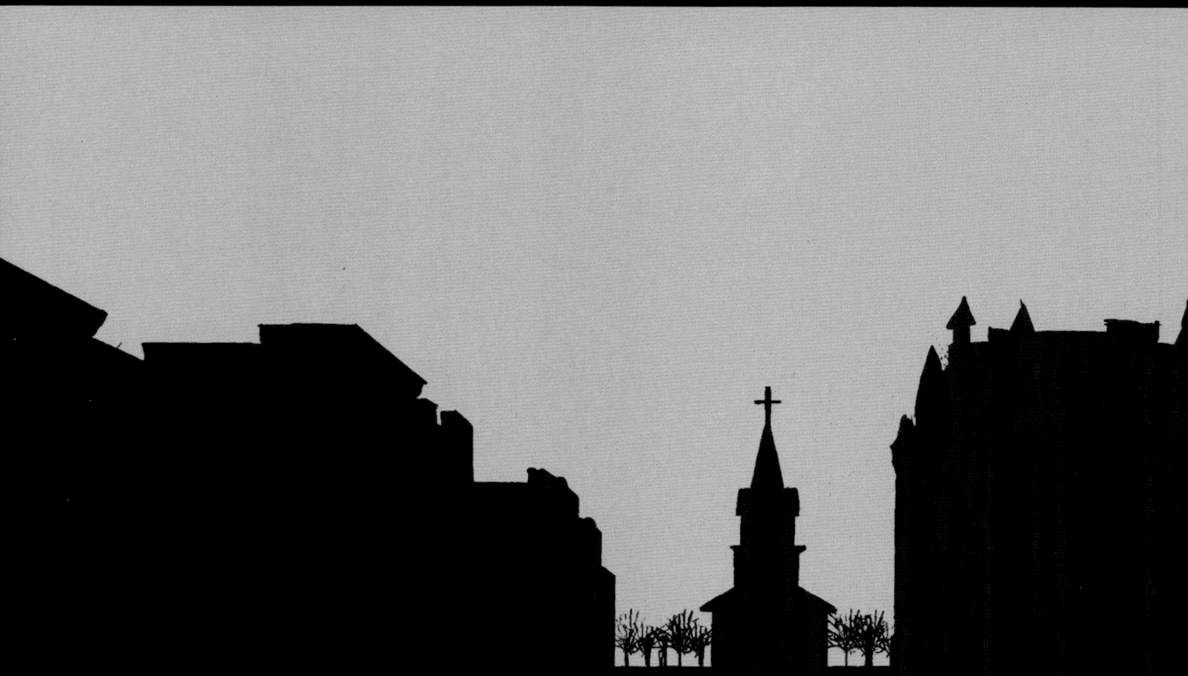

EDEN'S FALL

CHAPTER 2

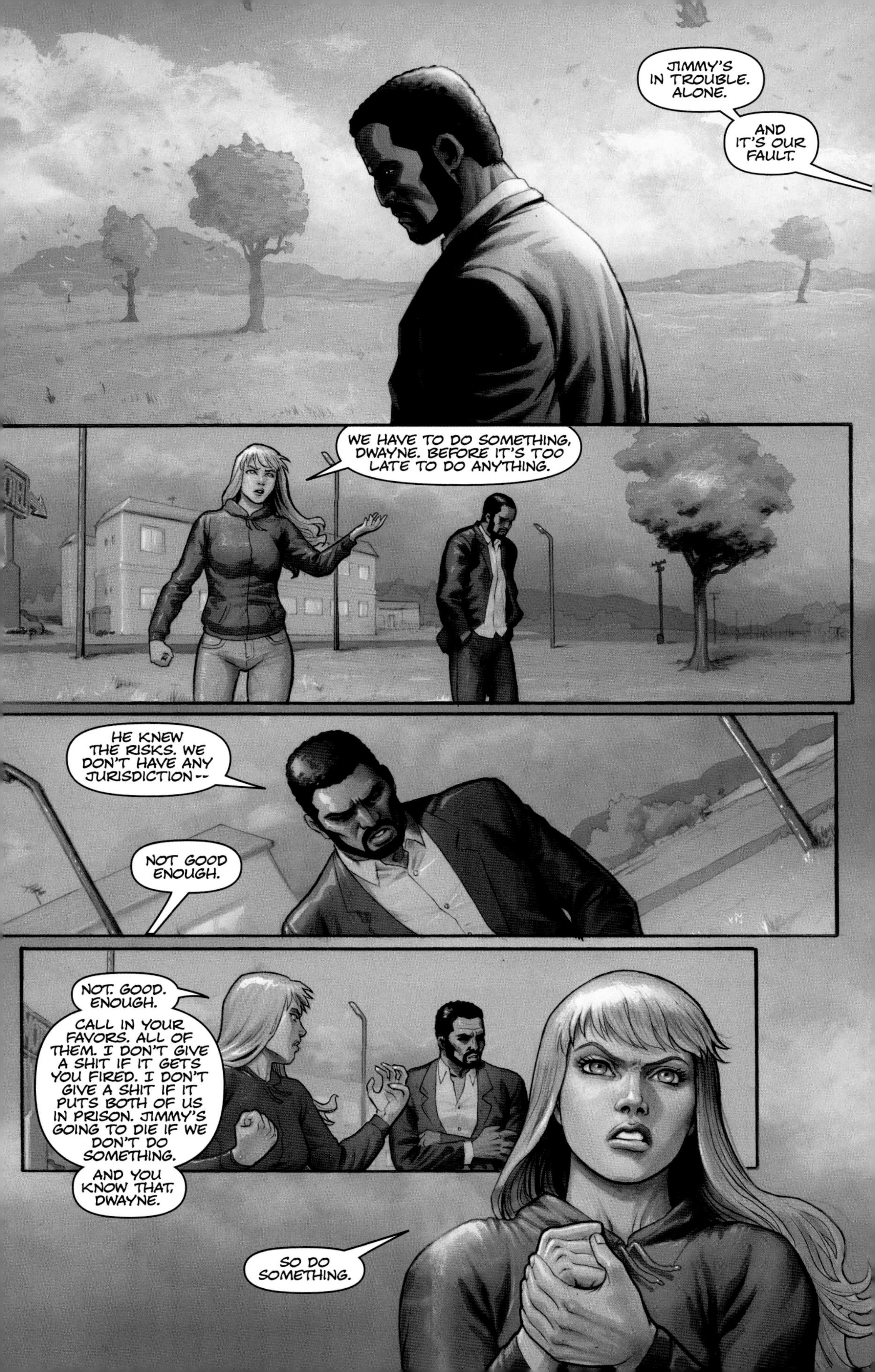
JIMMY'S IN TROUBLE. ALONE.
AND IT'S OUR FAULT.
WE HAVE TO DO SOMETHING, DWAYNE. BEFORE IT'S TOO LATE TO DO ANYTHING.
HE KNEW THE RISKS. WE DON'T HAVE ANY JURISDICTION--
NOT GOOD ENOUGH.
NOT. GOOD. ENOUGH.
CALL IN YOUR FAVORS. ALL OF THEM. I DON'T GIVE A SHIT IF IT GETS YOU FIRED. I DON'T GIVE A SHIT IF IT PUTS BOTH OF US IN PRISON. JIMMY'S GOING TO DIE IF WE DON'T DO SOMETHING.
AND YOU KNOW THAT, DWAYNE.
SO DO SOMETHING.

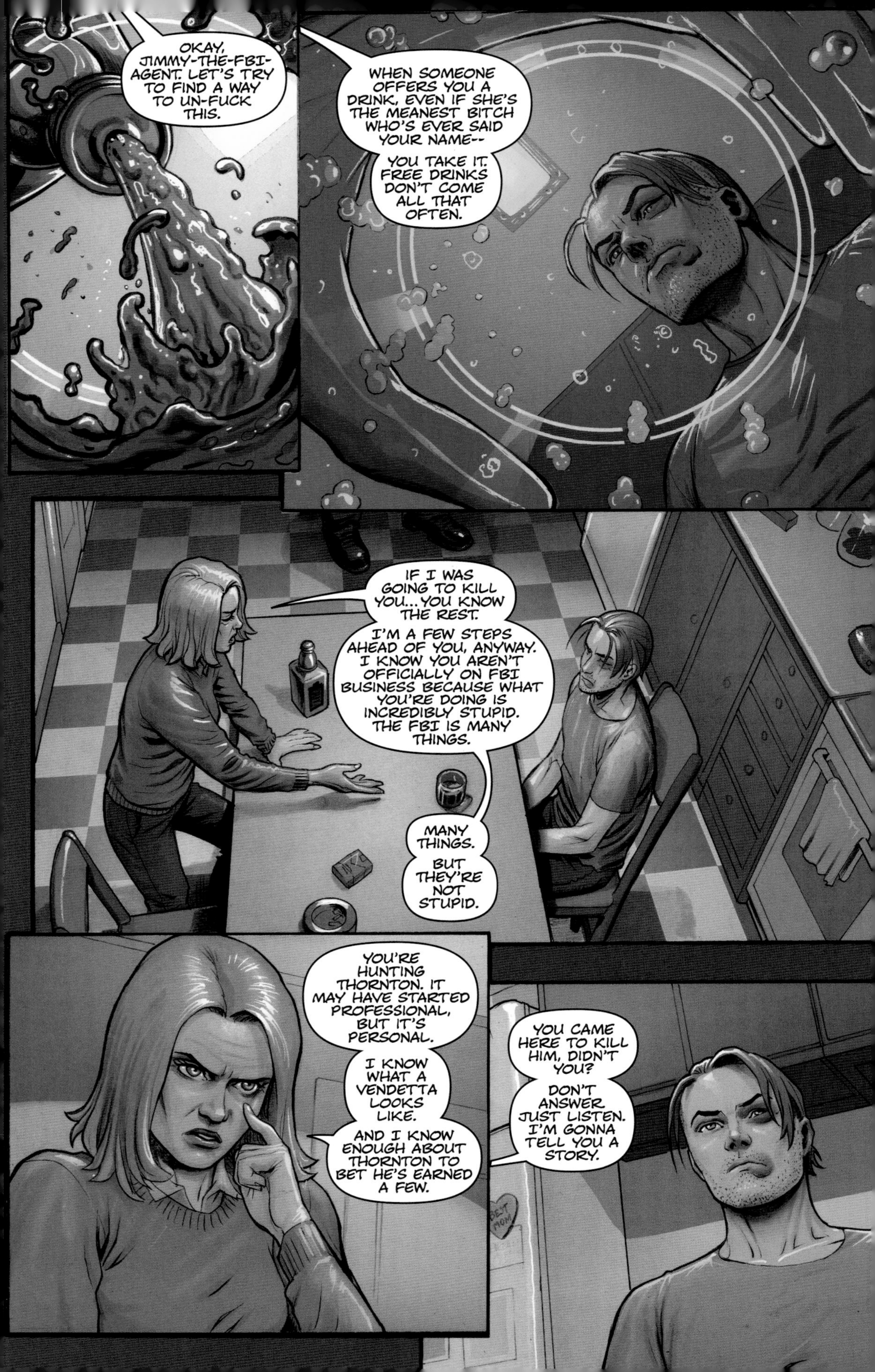

OKAY, JIMMY-THE-FBI-AGENT. LET'S TRY TO FIND A WAY TO UN-FUCK THIS.
WHEN SOMEONE OFFERS YOU A DRINK, EVEN IF SHE'S THE MEANEST BITCH WHO'S EVER SAID YOUR NAME--
YOU TAKE IT. FREE DRINKS DON'T COME ALL THAT OFTEN.
IF I WAS GOING TO KILL YOU...YOU KNOW THE REST.
I'M A FEW STEPS AHEAD OF YOU, ANYWAY. I KNOW YOU AREN'T OFFICIALLY ON FBI BUSINESS BECAUSE WHAT YOU'RE DOING IS INCREDIBLY STUPID. THE FBI IS MANY THINGS.
MANY THINGS.
BUT THEY'RE NOT STUPID.
YOU'RE HUNTING THORNTON. IT MAY HAVE STARTED PROFESSIONAL, BUT IT'S PERSONAL.
I KNOW WHAT A VENDETTA LOOKS LIKE.
AND I KNOW ENOUGH ABOUT THORNTON TO BET HE'S EARNED A FEW.
YOU CAME HERE TO KILL HIM, DIDN'T YOU?
DON'T ANSWER JUST LISTEN. I'M GONNA TELL YOU A STORY.
BEST MOM

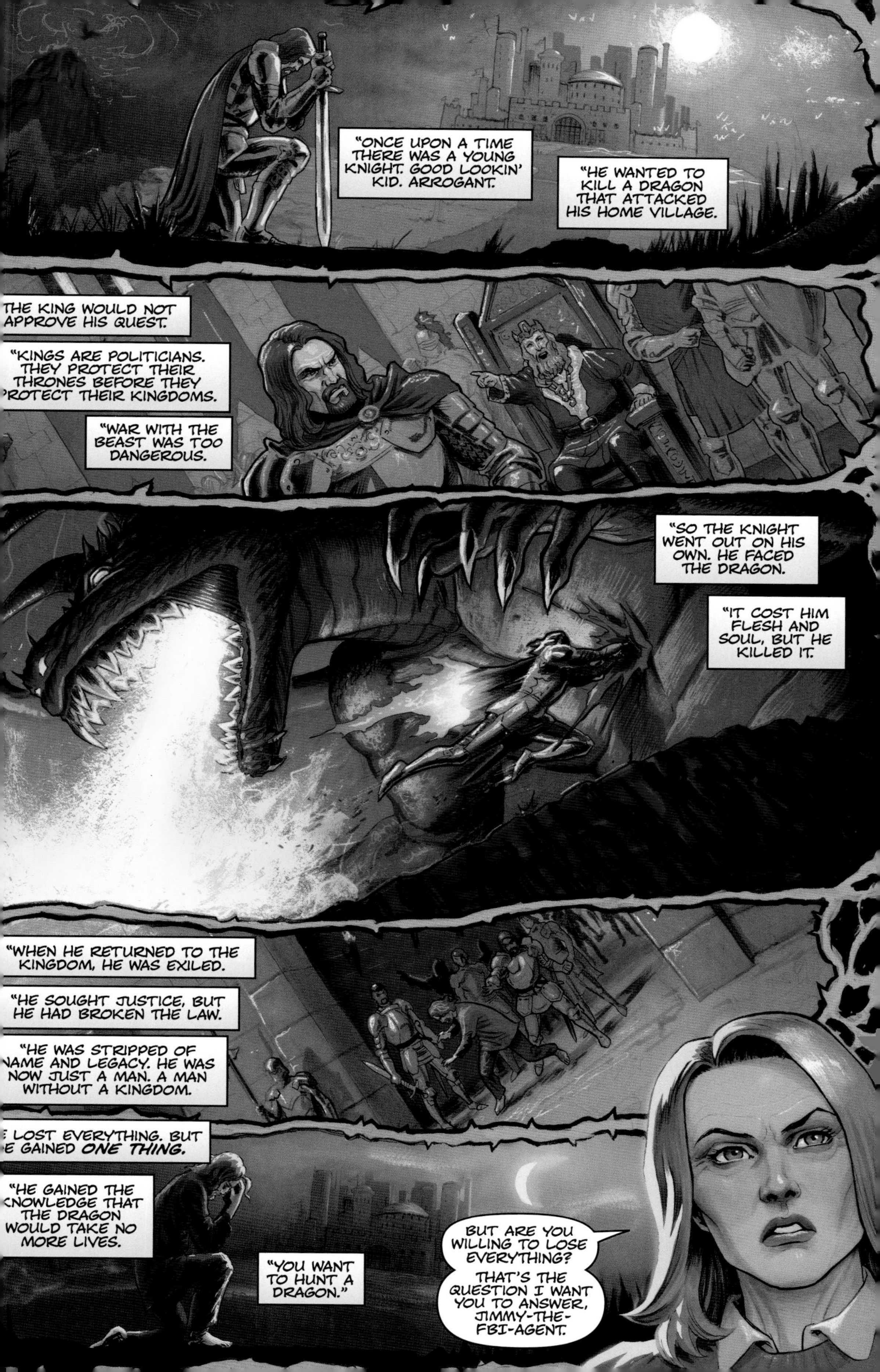

"ONCE UPON A TIME THERE WAS A YOUNG KNIGHT. GOOD LOOKIN' KID. ARROGANT.
"HE WANTED TO KILL A DRAGON THAT ATTACKED HIS HOME VILLAGE.
THE KING WOULD NOT APPROVE HIS QUEST.
"KINGS ARE POLITICIANS. THEY PROTECT THEIR THRONES BEFORE THEY PROTECT THEIR KINGDOMS.
"WAR WITH THE BEAST WAS TOO DANGEROUS.
"SO THE KNIGHT WENT OUT ON HIS OWN. HE FACED THE DRAGON.
"IT COST HIM FLESH AND SOUL, BUT HE KILLED IT.
"WHEN HE RETURNED TO THE KINGDOM, HE WAS EXILED.
"HE SOUGHT JUSTICE, BUT HE HAD BROKEN THE LAW.
"HE WAS STRIPPED OF NAME AND LEGACY. HE WAS NOW JUST A MAN. A MAN WITHOUT A KINGDOM.
LOST EVERYTHING. BUT GAINED *ONE THING.*
"HE GAINED THE KNOWLEDGE THAT THE DRAGON WOULD TAKE NO MORE LIVES.
"YOU WANT TO HUNT A DRAGON."
BUT ARE YOU WILLING TO LOSE EVERYTHING?
THAT'S THE QUESTION I WANT YOU TO ANSWER, JIMMY-THE-FBI-AGENT.

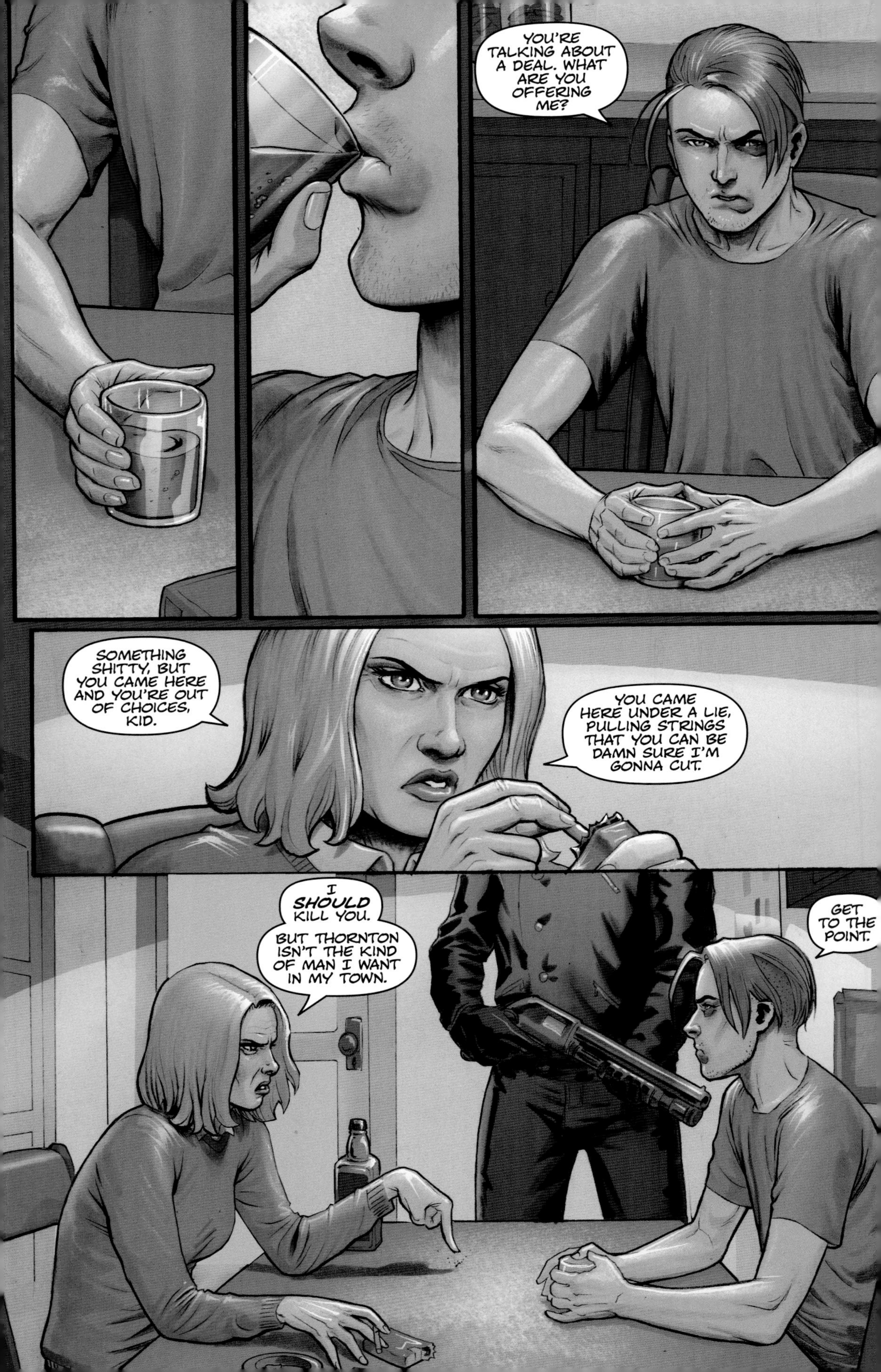
YOU'RE TALKING ABOUT A DEAL. WHAT ARE YOU OFFERING ME?
SOMETHING SHITTY, BUT YOU CAME HERE AND YOU'RE OUT OF CHOICES, KID.
YOU CAME HERE UNDER A LIE, PULLING STRINGS THAT YOU CAN BE DAMN SURE I'M GONNA CUT.
I *SHOULD* KILL YOU.
BUT THORNTON ISN'T THE KIND OF MAN I WANT IN MY TOWN.
GET TO THE POINT.

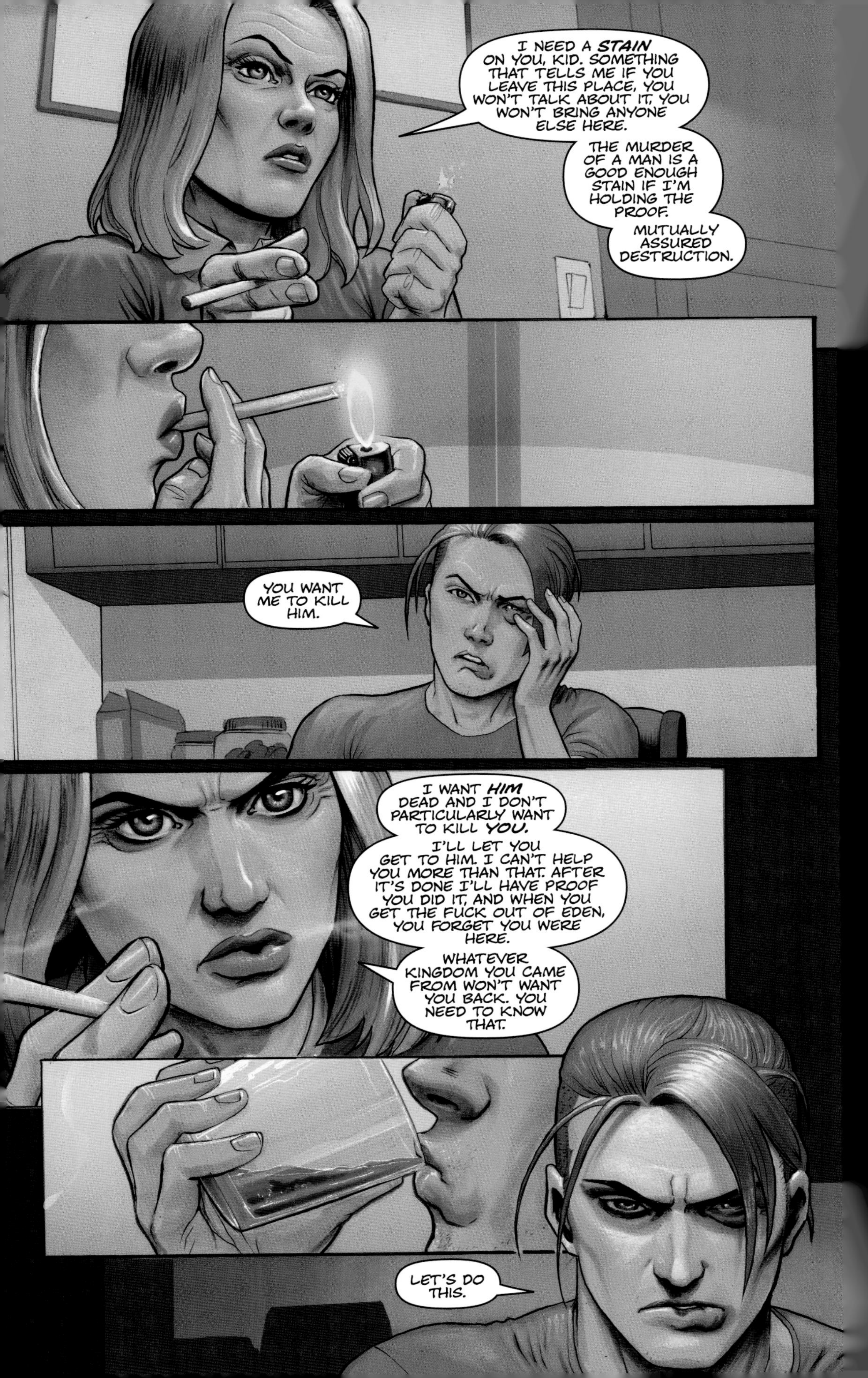
I NEED A STAIN ON YOU, KID. SOMETHING THAT TELLS ME IF YOU LEAVE THIS PLACE, YOU WON'T TALK ABOUT IT, YOU WON'T BRING ANYONE ELSE HERE.
THE MURDER OF A MAN IS A GOOD ENOUGH STAIN IF I'M HOLDING THE PROOF.
MUTUALLY ASSURED DESTRUCTION.
YOU WANT ME TO KILL HIM.
I WANT HIM DEAD AND I DON'T PARTICULARLY WANT TO KILL YOU.
I'LL LET YOU GET TO HIM. I CAN'T HELP YOU MORE THAN THAT. AFTER IT'S DONE I'LL HAVE PROOF YOU DID IT, AND WHEN YOU GET THE FUCK OUT OF EDEN, YOU FORGET YOU WERE HERE.
WHATEVER KINGDOM YOU CAME FROM WON'T WANT YOU BACK. YOU NEED TO KNOW THAT.
LET'S DO THIS.

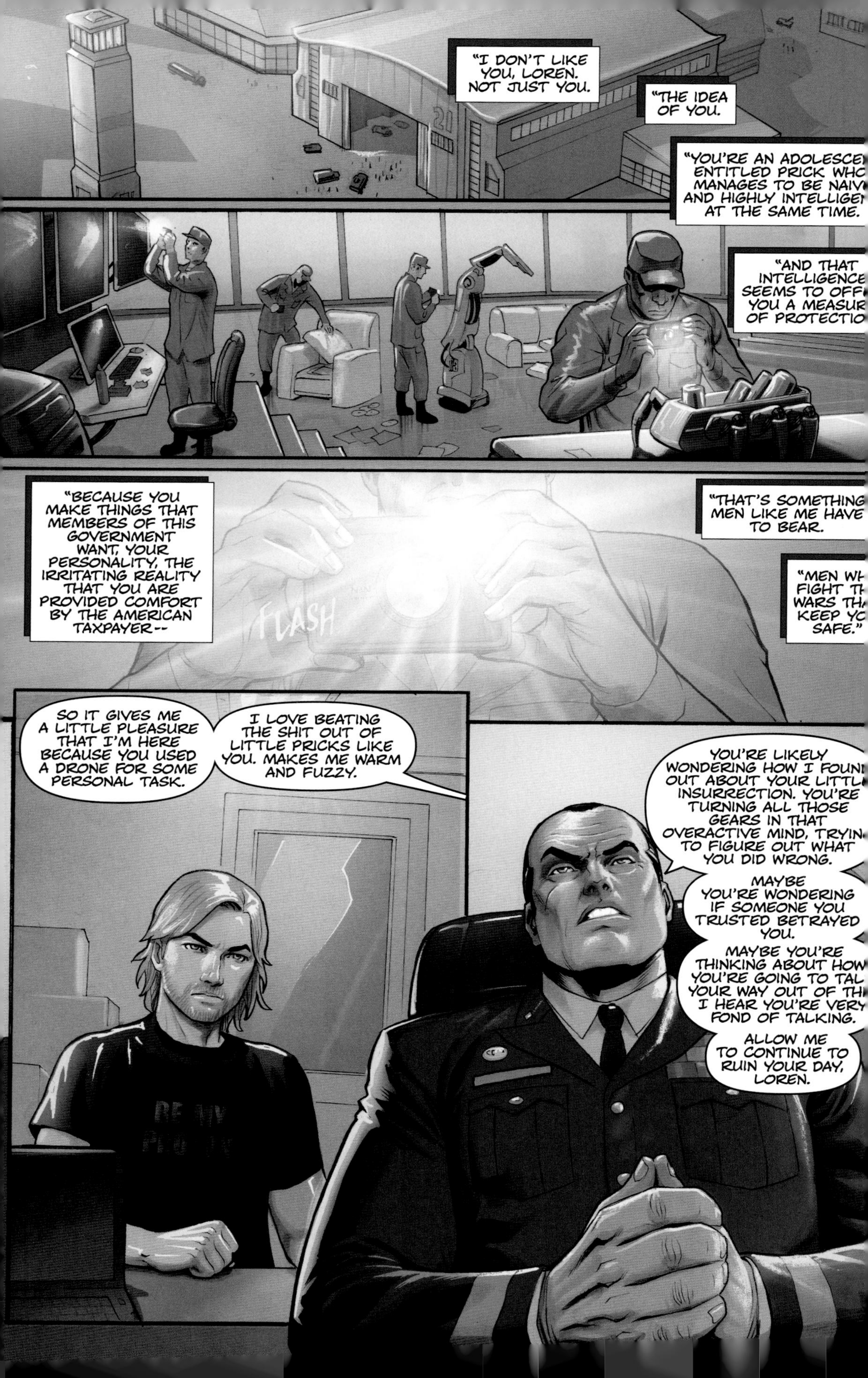
"I DON'T LIKE YOU, LOREN. NOT JUST YOU.
"THE IDEA OF YOU.
"YOU'RE AN ADOLESCE ENTITLED PRICK WHO MANAGES TO BE NAIV AND HIGHLY INTELLIGE AT THE SAME TIME.
"AND THAT INTELLIGENCE SEEMS TO OFF YOU A MEASUR OF PROTECTIO
"BECAUSE YOU MAKE THINGS THAT MEMBERS OF THIS GOVERNMENT WANT, YOUR PERSONALITY, THE IRRITATING REALITY THAT YOU ARE PROVIDED COMFORT BY THE AMERICAN TAXPAYER--
FLASH
"THAT'S SOMETHING MEN LIKE ME HAVE TO BEAR.
"MEN WH FIGHT TH WARS TH KEEP YO SAFE."
SO IT GIVES ME A LITTLE PLEASURE THAT I'M HERE BECAUSE YOU USED A DRONE FOR SOME PERSONAL TASK.
I LOVE BEATING THE SHIT OUT OF LITTLE PRICKS LIKE YOU. MAKES ME WARM AND FUZZY.
YOU'RE LIKELY WONDERING HOW I FOUN OUT ABOUT YOUR LITTL INSURRECTION. YOU'RE TURNING ALL THOSE GEARS IN THAT OVERACTIVE MIND, TRYIN TO FIGURE OUT WHAT YOU DID WRONG.
MAYBE YOU'RE WONDERING IF SOMEONE YOU TRUSTED BETRAYED YOU.
MAYBE YOU'RE THINKING ABOUT HOW YOU'RE GOING TO TAL YOUR WAY OUT OF TH I HEAR YOU'RE VERY FOND OF TALKING.
ALLOW ME TO CONTINUE TO RUIN YOUR DAY, LOREN.

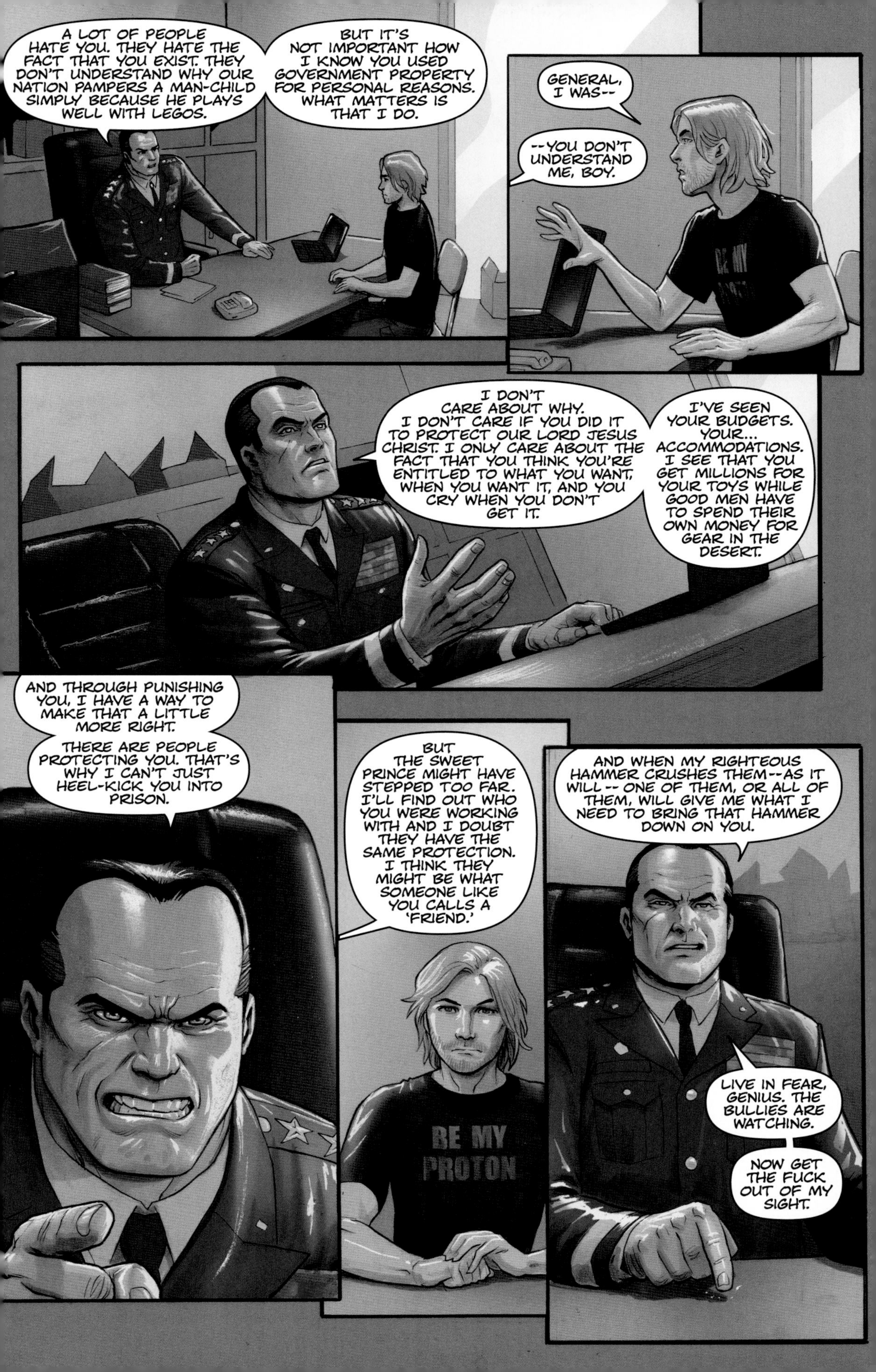
A LOT OF PEOPLE HATE YOU. THEY HATE THE FACT THAT YOU EXIST. THEY DON'T UNDERSTAND WHY OUR NATION PAMPERS A MAN-CHILD SIMPLY BECAUSE HE PLAYS WELL WITH LEGOS.
BUT IT'S NOT IMPORTANT HOW I KNOW YOU USED GOVERNMENT PROPERTY FOR PERSONAL REASONS. WHAT MATTERS IS THAT I DO.
GENERAL, I WAS--
--YOU DON'T UNDERSTAND ME, BOY.
I DON'T CARE ABOUT WHY. I DON'T CARE IF YOU DID IT TO PROTECT OUR LORD JESUS CHRIST. I ONLY CARE ABOUT THE FACT THAT YOU THINK YOU'RE ENTITLED TO WHAT YOU WANT, WHEN YOU WANT IT, AND YOU CRY WHEN YOU DON'T GET IT.
I'VE SEEN YOUR BUDGETS. YOUR... ACCOMMODATIONS. I SEE THAT YOU GET MILLIONS FOR YOUR TOYS WHILE GOOD MEN HAVE TO SPEND THEIR OWN MONEY FOR GEAR IN THE DESERT.
AND THROUGH PUNISHING YOU, I HAVE A WAY TO MAKE THAT A LITTLE MORE RIGHT.
THERE ARE PEOPLE PROTECTING YOU. THAT'S WHY I CAN'T JUST HEEL-KICK YOU INTO PRISON.
BUT THE SWEET PRINCE MIGHT HAVE STEPPED TOO FAR. I'LL FIND OUT WHO YOU WERE WORKING WITH AND I DOUBT THEY HAVE THE SAME PROTECTION. I THINK THEY MIGHT BE WHAT SOMEONE LIKE YOU CALLS A 'FRIEND.'
BE MY PROTON
AND WHEN MY RIGHTEOUS HAMMER CRUSHES THEM--AS IT WILL--ONE OF THEM, OR ALL OF THEM, WILL GIVE ME WHAT I NEED TO BRING THAT HAMMER DOWN ON YOU.
LIVE IN FEAR, GENIUS. THE BULLIES ARE WATCHING.
NOW GET THE FUCK OUT OF MY SIGHT.

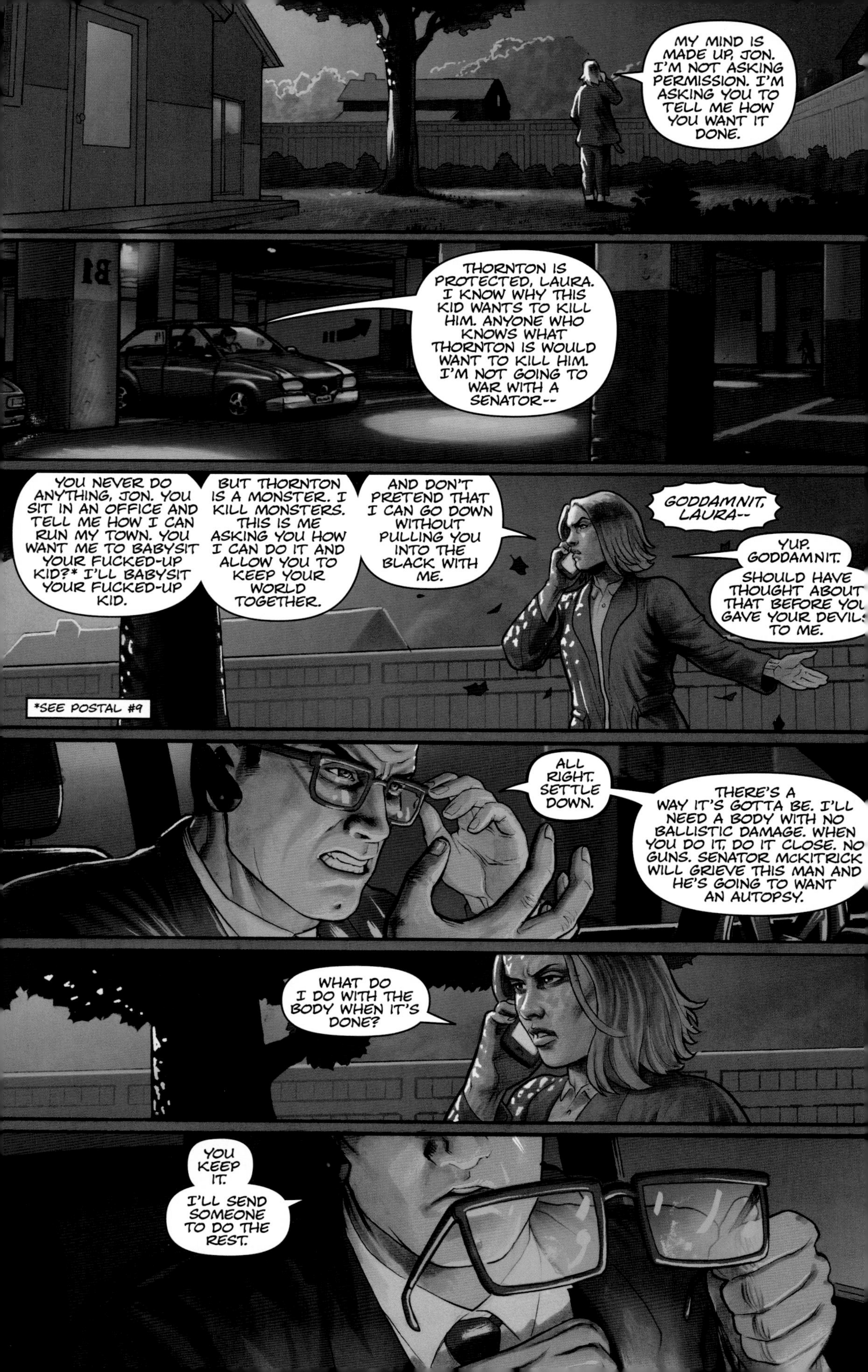
MY MIND IS MADE UP, JON. I'M NOT ASKING PERMISSION. I'M ASKING YOU TO TELL ME HOW YOU WANT IT DONE.
B1
THORNTON IS PROTECTED, LAURA. I KNOW WHY THIS KID WANTS TO KILL HIM. ANYONE WHO KNOWS WHAT THORNTON IS WOULD WANT TO KILL HIM. I'M NOT GOING TO WAR WITH A SENATOR--
YOU NEVER DO ANYTHING, JON. YOU SIT IN AN OFFICE AND TELL ME HOW I CAN RUN MY TOWN. YOU WANT ME TO BABYSIT YOUR FUCKED-UP KID?* I'LL BABYSIT YOUR FUCKED-UP KID.
BUT THORNTON IS A MONSTER. I KILL MONSTERS. THIS IS ME ASKING YOU HOW I CAN DO IT AND ALLOW YOU TO KEEP YOUR WORLD TOGETHER.
AND DON'T PRETEND THAT I CAN GO DOWN WITHOUT PULLING YOU INTO THE BLACK WITH ME.
GODDAMNIT, LAURA--
YUP. GODDAMNIT.
SHOULD HAVE THOUGHT ABOUT THAT BEFORE YOU GAVE YOUR DEVILS TO ME.
*SEE POSTAL #9
ALL RIGHT. SETTLE DOWN.
THERE'S A WAY IT'S GOTTA BE. I'LL NEED A BODY WITH NO BALLISTIC DAMAGE. WHEN YOU DO IT, DO IT CLOSE. NO GUNS. SENATOR MCKITRICK WILL GRIEVE THIS MAN AND HE'S GOING TO WANT AN AUTOPSY.
WHAT DO I DO WITH THE BODY WHEN IT'S DONE?
YOU KEEP IT.
I'LL SEND SOMEONE TO DO THE REST.

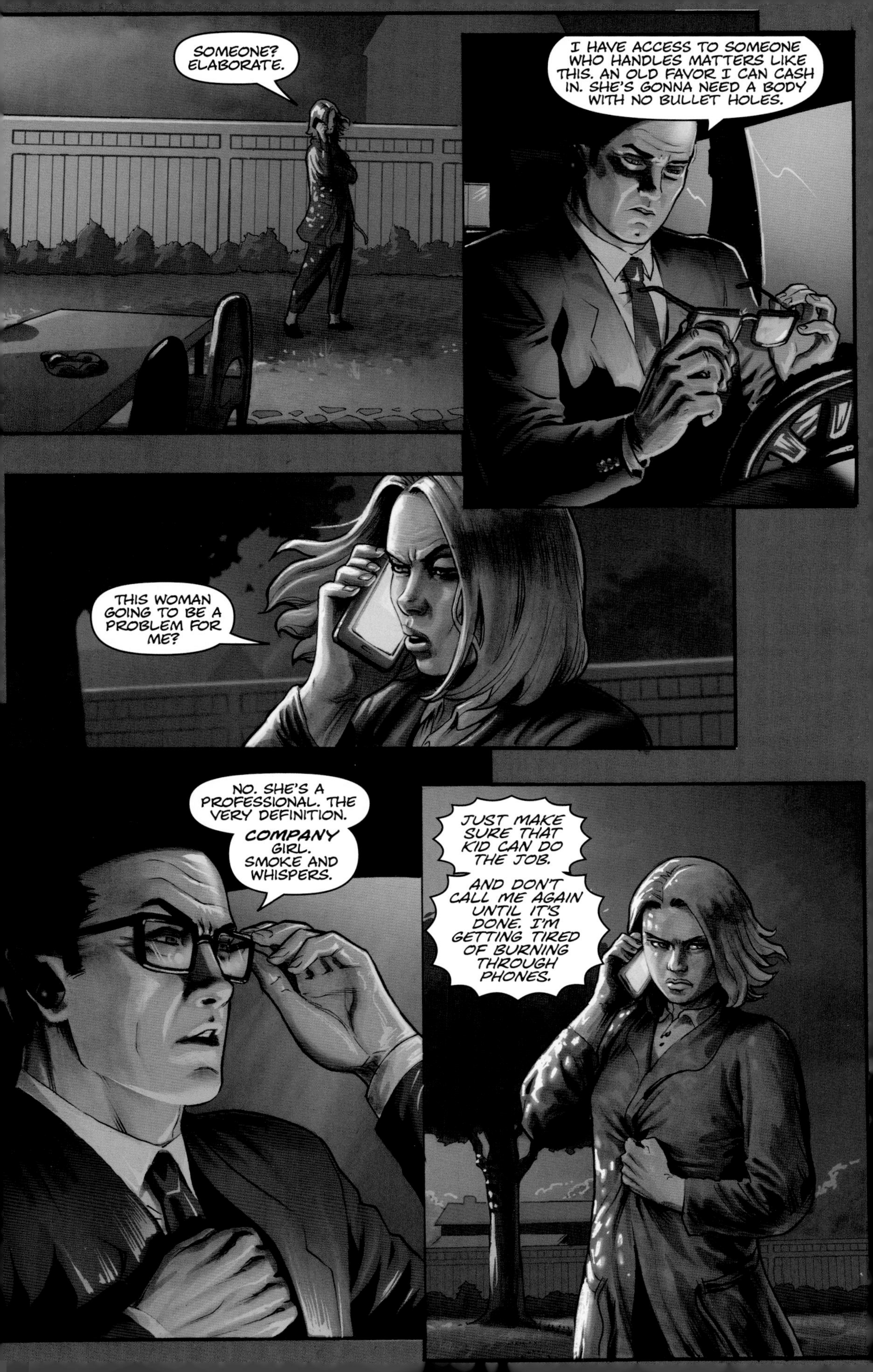
SOMEONE? ELABORATE.
I HAVE ACCESS TO SOMEONE WHO HANDLES MATTERS LIKE THIS. AN OLD FAVOR I CAN CASH IN. SHE'S GONNA NEED A BODY WITH NO BULLET HOLES.
THIS WOMAN GOING TO BE A PROBLEM FOR ME?
NO. SHE'S A PROFESSIONAL. THE VERY DEFINITION.
COMPANY GIRL. SMOKE AND WHISPERS.
JUST MAKE SURE THAT KID CAN DO THE JOB.
AND DON'T CALL ME AGAIN UNTIL IT'S DONE. I'M GETTING TIRED OF BURNING THROUGH PHONES.

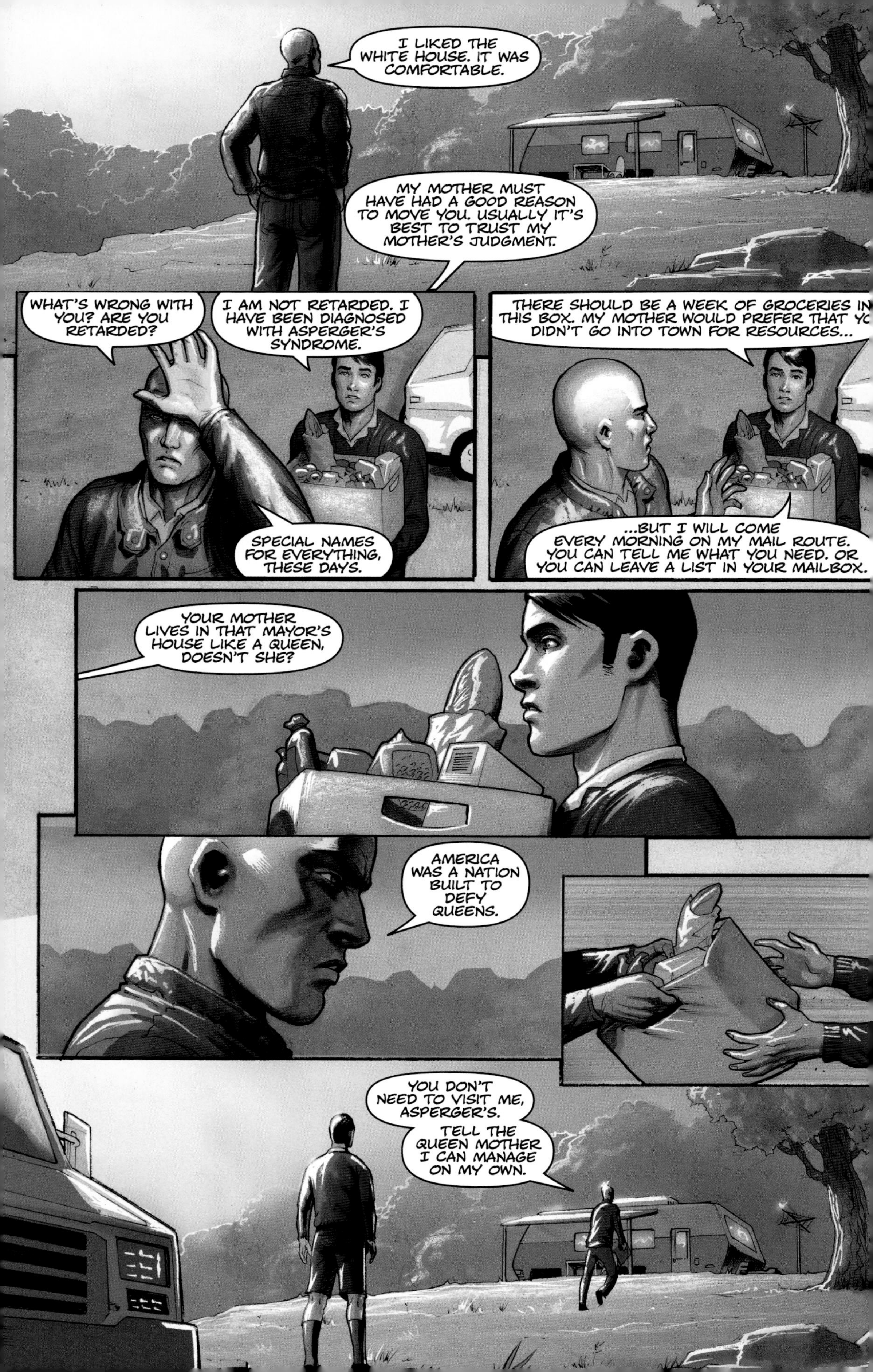
I LIKED THE WHITE HOUSE. IT WAS COMFORTABLE.
MY MOTHER MUST HAVE HAD A GOOD REASON TO MOVE YOU. USUALLY IT'S BEST TO TRUST MY MOTHER'S JUDGMENT.
WHAT'S WRONG WITH YOU? ARE YOU RETARDED?
I AM NOT RETARDED. I HAVE BEEN DIAGNOSED WITH ASPERGER'S SYNDROME.
SPECIAL NAMES FOR EVERYTHING, THESE DAYS.
THERE SHOULD BE A WEEK OF GROCERIES IN THIS BOX. MY MOTHER WOULD PREFER THAT YO DIDN'T GO INTO TOWN FOR RESOURCES...
...BUT I WILL COME EVERY MORNING ON MY MAIL ROUTE. YOU CAN TELL ME WHAT YOU NEED. OR YOU CAN LEAVE A LIST IN YOUR MAILBOX.
YOUR MOTHER LIVES IN THAT MAYOR'S HOUSE LIKE A QUEEN, DOESN'T SHE?
AMERICA WAS A NATION BUILT TO DEFY QUEENS.
YOU DON'T NEED TO VISIT ME, ASPERGER'S.
TELL THE QUEEN MOTHER I CAN MANAGE ON MY OWN.

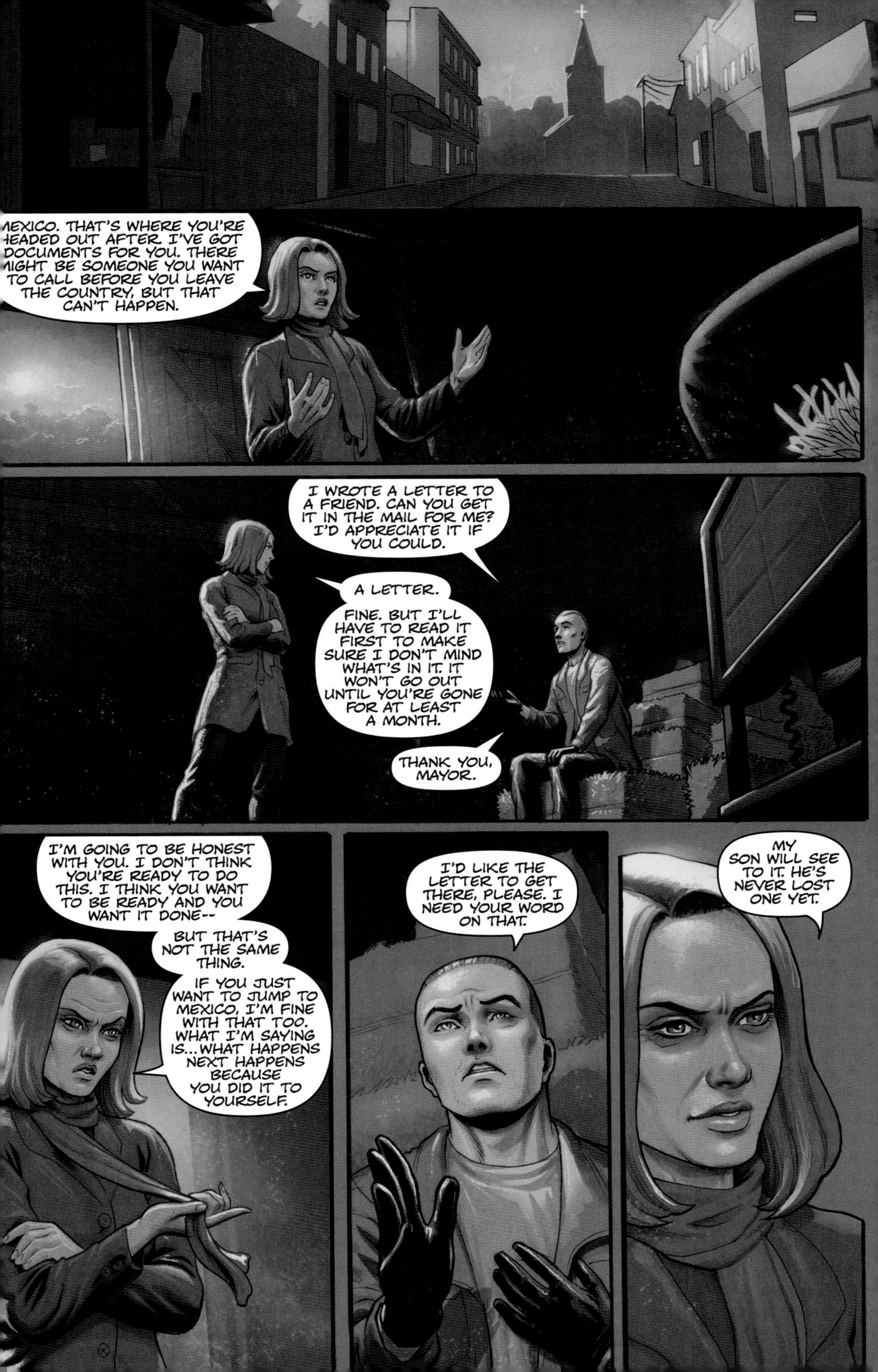

MEXICO. THAT'S WHERE YOU'RE HEADED OUT AFTER I'VE GOT DOCUMENTS FOR YOU. THERE MIGHT BE SOMEONE YOU WANT TO CALL BEFORE YOU LEAVE THE COUNTRY, BUT THAT CAN'T HAPPEN.
I WROTE A LETTER TO A FRIEND. CAN YOU GET IT IN THE MAIL FOR ME? I'D APPRECIATE IT IF YOU COULD.
A LETTER.
FINE. BUT I'LL HAVE TO READ IT FIRST TO MAKE SURE I DON'T MIND WHAT'S IN IT. IT WON'T GO OUT UNTIL YOU'RE GONE FOR AT LEAST A MONTH.
THANK YOU, MAYOR.
I'M GOING TO BE HONEST WITH YOU. I DON'T THINK YOU'RE READY TO DO THIS. I THINK YOU WANT TO BE READY AND YOU WANT IT DONE--
BUT THAT'S NOT THE SAME THING.
IF YOU JUST WANT TO JUMP TO MEXICO, I'M FINE WITH THAT TOO. WHAT I'M SAYING IS...WHAT HAPPENS NEXT HAPPENS BECAUSE YOU DID IT TO YOURSELF.
I'D LIKE THE LETTER TO GET THERE, PLEASE. I NEED YOUR WORD ON THAT.
MY SON WILL SEE TO IT. HE'S NEVER LOST ONE YET.

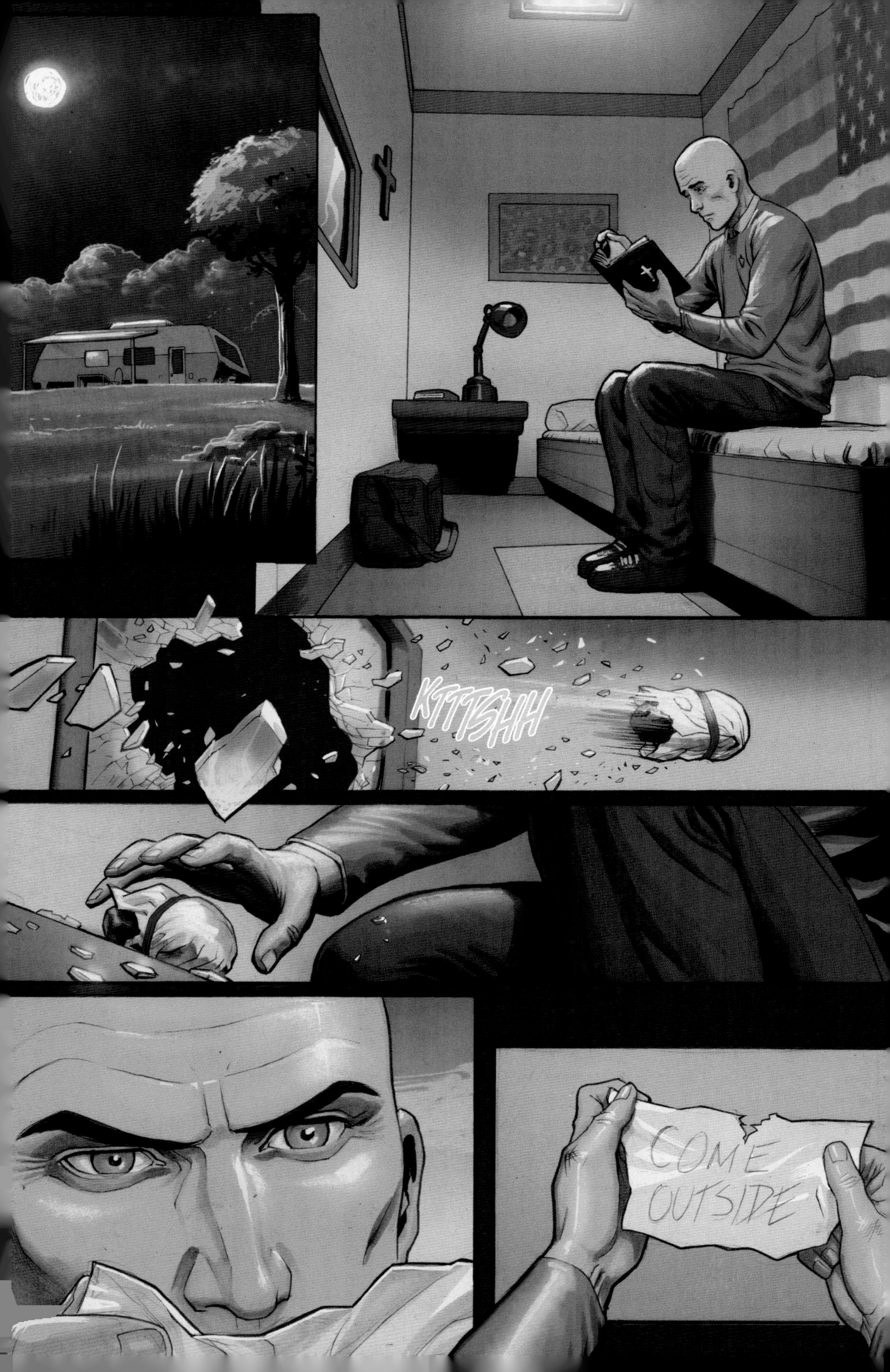
KTTTSHH
COME
OUTSIDE

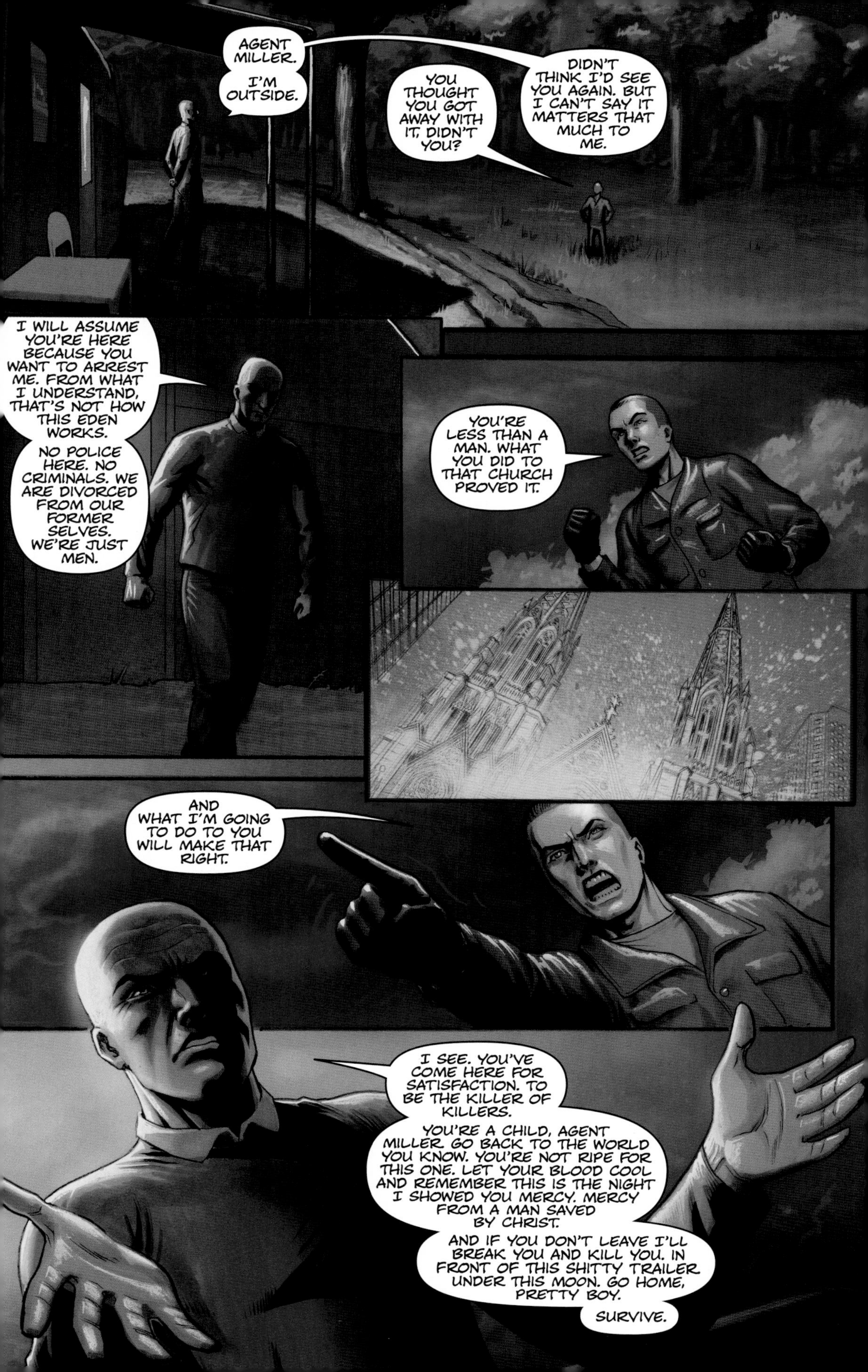
AGENT MILLER.
I'M OUTSIDE.
DIDN'T THINK I'D SEE YOU AGAIN. BUT I CAN'T SAY IT MATTERS THAT MUCH TO ME.
YOU THOUGHT YOU GOT AWAY WITH IT, DIDN'T YOU?
I WILL ASSUME YOU'RE HERE BECAUSE YOU WANT TO ARREST ME. FROM WHAT I UNDERSTAND, THAT'S NOT HOW THIS EDEN WORKS.
NO POLICE HERE. NO CRIMINALS. WE ARE DIVORCED FROM OUR FORMER SELVES. WE'RE JUST MEN.
YOU'RE LESS THAN A MAN. WHAT YOU DID TO THAT CHURCH PROVED IT.
AND WHAT I'M GOING TO DO TO YOU WILL MAKE THAT RIGHT.
I SEE. YOU'VE COME HERE FOR SATISFACTION. TO BE THE KILLER OF KILLERS.
YOU'RE A CHILD, AGENT MILLER. GO BACK TO THE WORLD YOU KNOW. YOU'RE NOT RIPE FOR THIS ONE. LET YOUR BLOOD COOL AND REMEMBER THIS IS THE NIGHT I SHOWED YOU MERCY. MERCY FROM A MAN SAVED BY CHRIST.
AND IF YOU DON'T LEAVE I'LL BREAK YOU AND KILL YOU. IN FRONT OF THIS SHITTY TRAILER UNDER THIS MOON. GO HOME, PRETTY BOY.
SURVIVE.

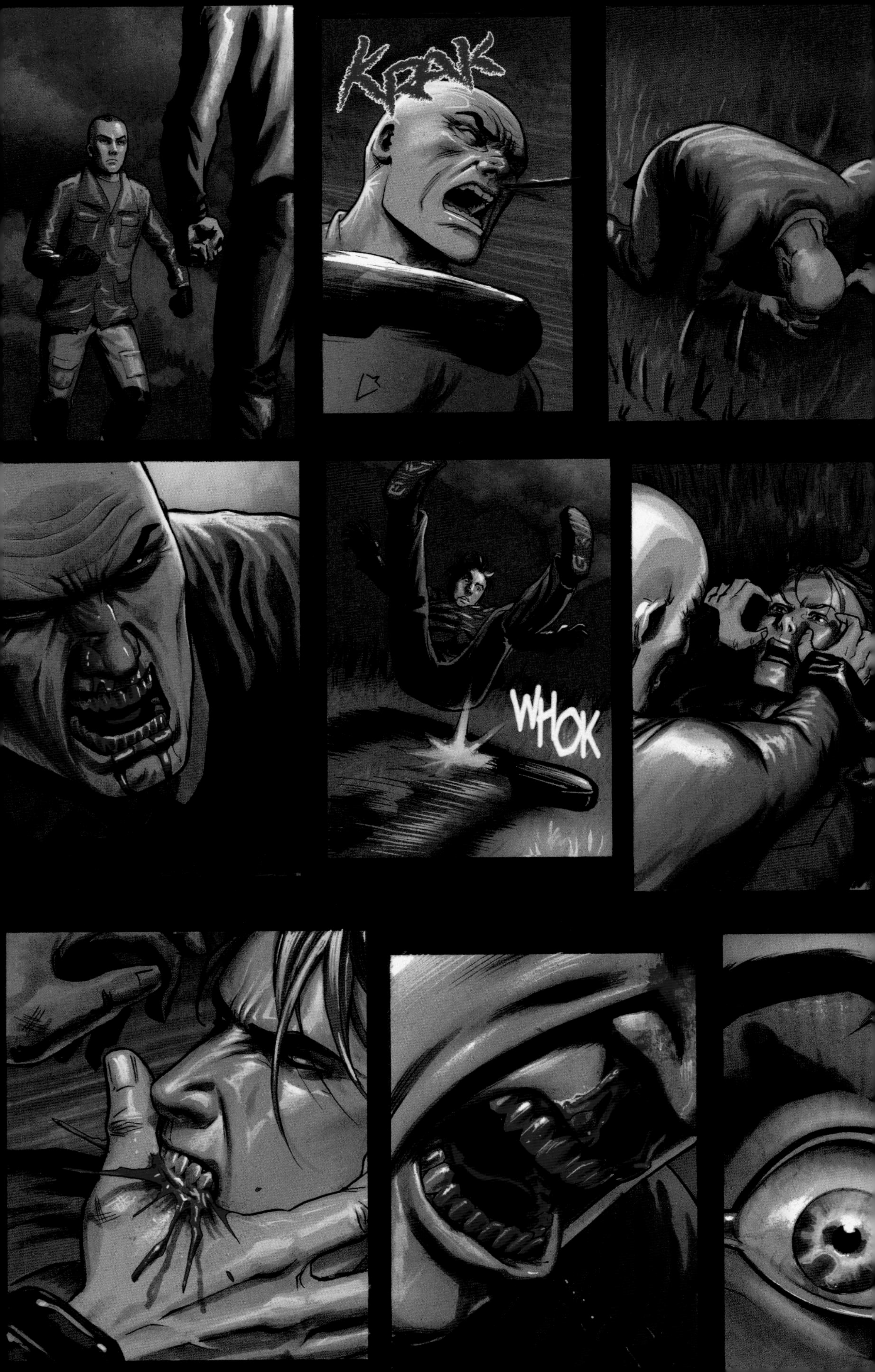
KRAK
WHOK

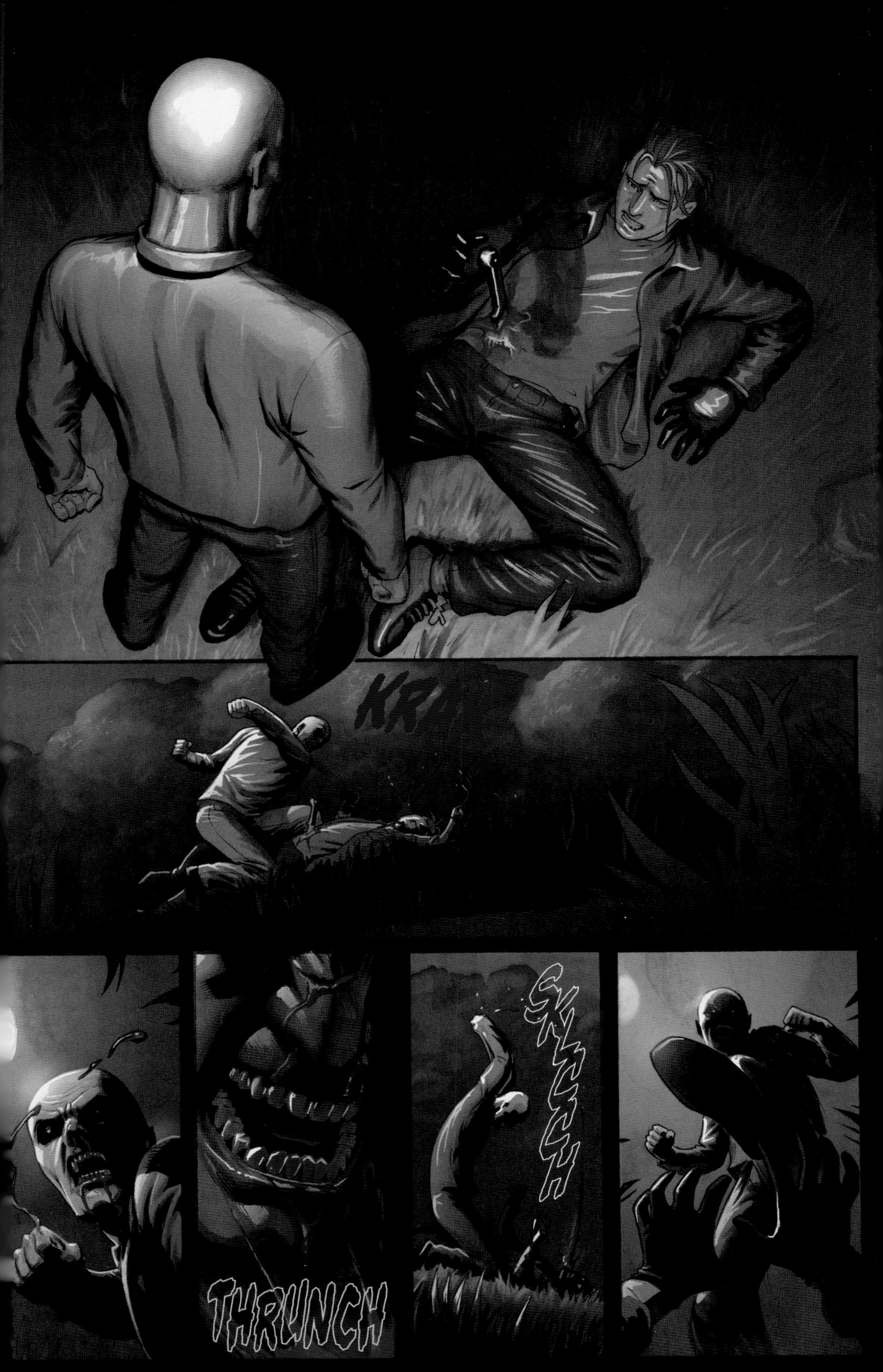
KRA
THRUNCH
SKWUNCH

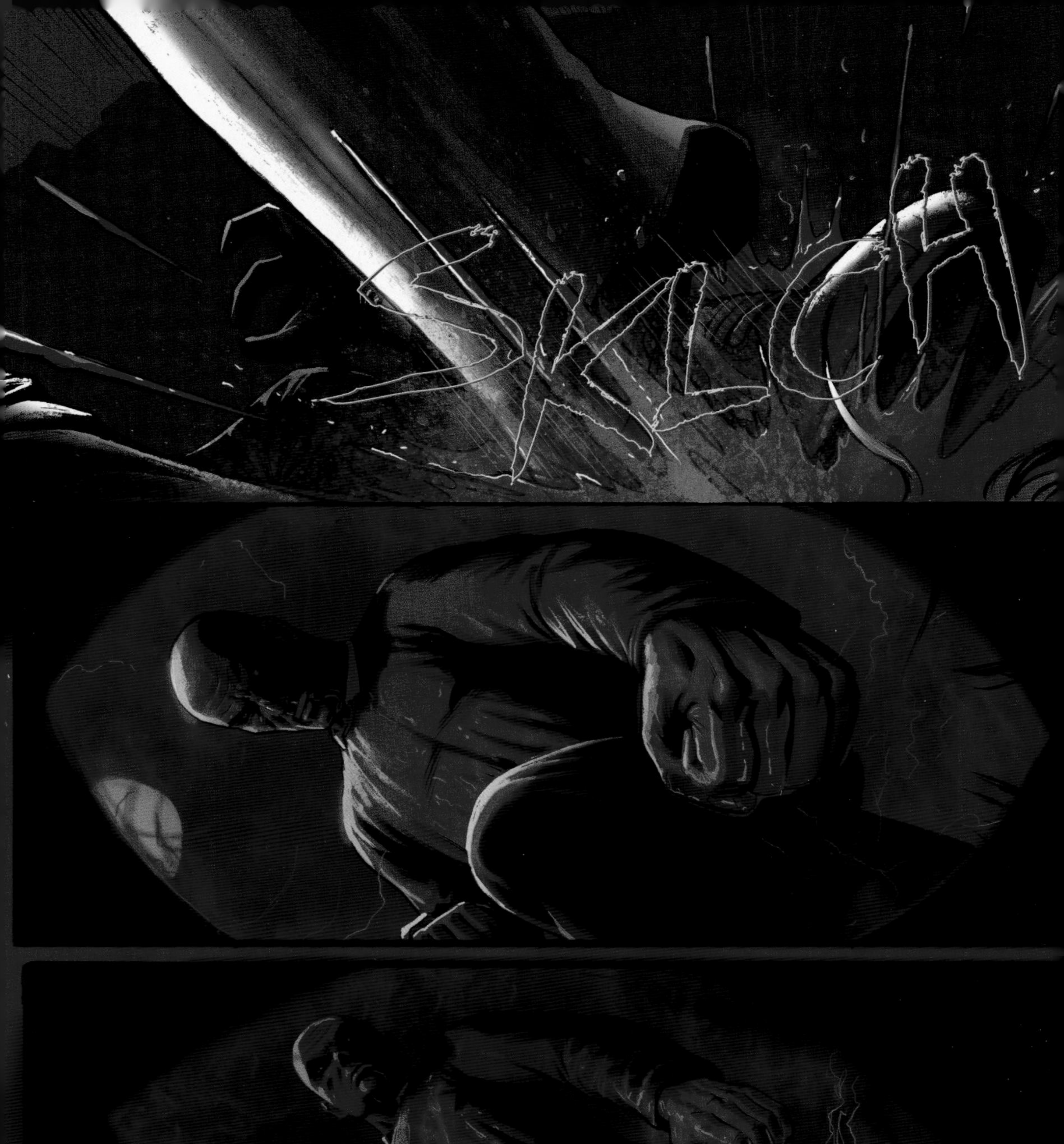
SKLCH

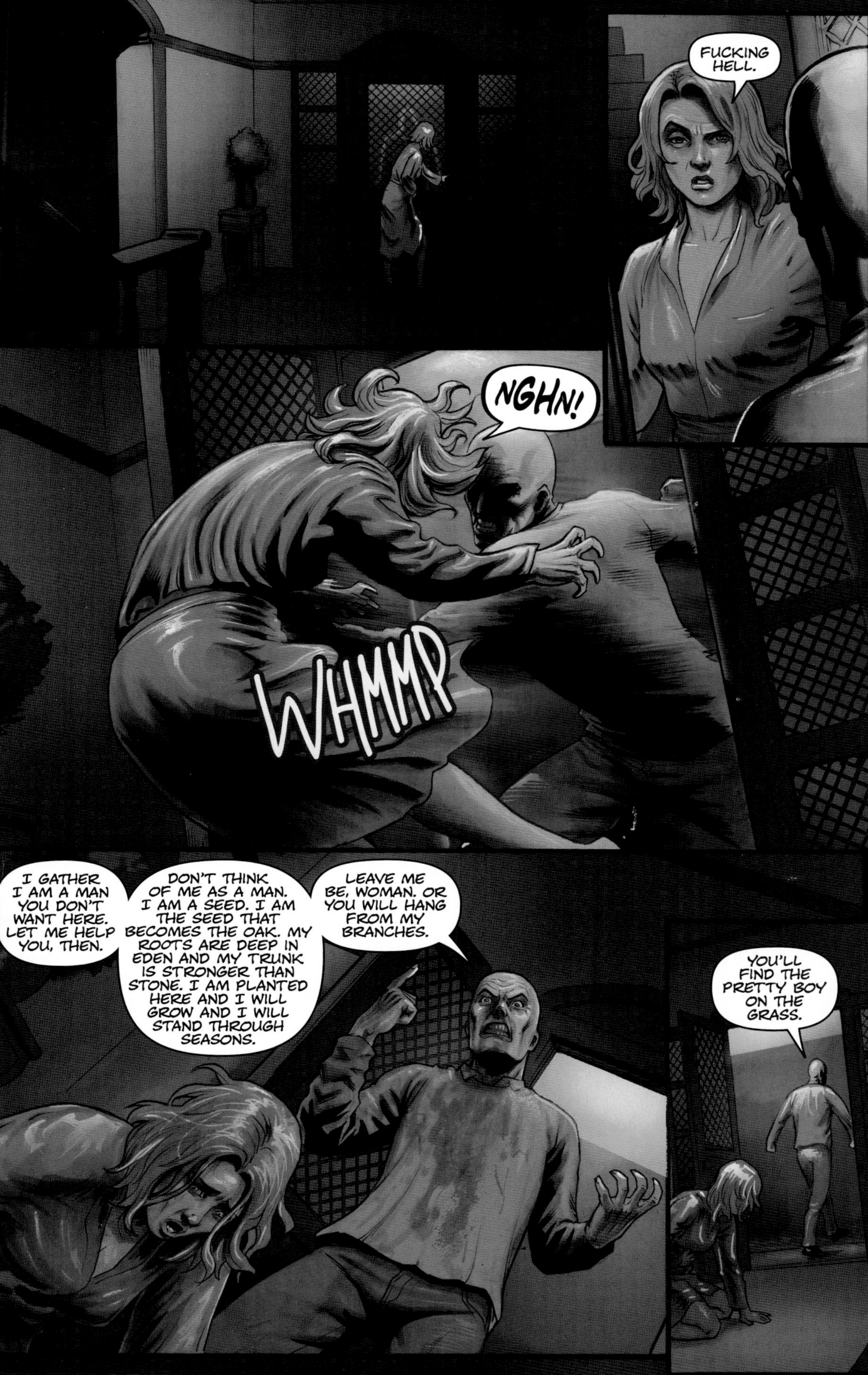
FUCKING HELL.
NGHN!
WHMMP
I GATHER I AM A MAN YOU DON'T WANT HERE. LET ME HELP YOU, THEN.
DON'T THINK OF ME AS A MAN. I AM A SEED. I AM THE SEED THAT BECOMES THE OAK. MY ROOTS ARE DEEP IN EDEN AND MY TRUNK IS STRONGER THAN STONE. I AM PLANTED HERE AND I WILL GROW AND I WILL STAND THROUGH SEASONS.
LEAVE ME BE, WOMAN. OR YOU WILL HANG FROM MY BRANCHES.
YOU'LL FIND THE PRETTY BOY ON THE GRASS.

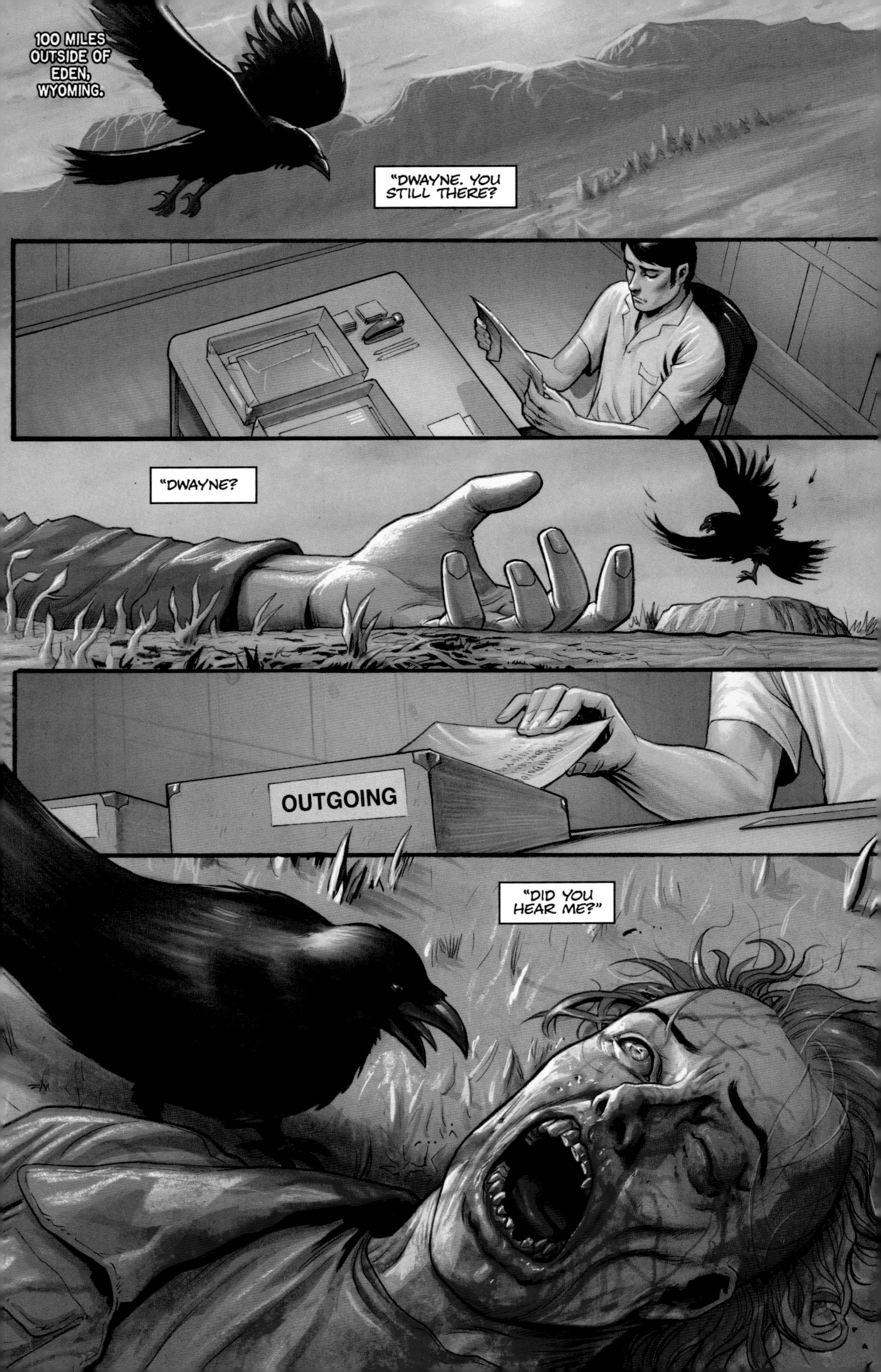
100 MILES OUTSIDE OF EDEN, WYOMING.
"DWAYNE. YOU STILL THERE?
"DWAYNE?
OUTGOING
"DID YOU HEAR ME?"

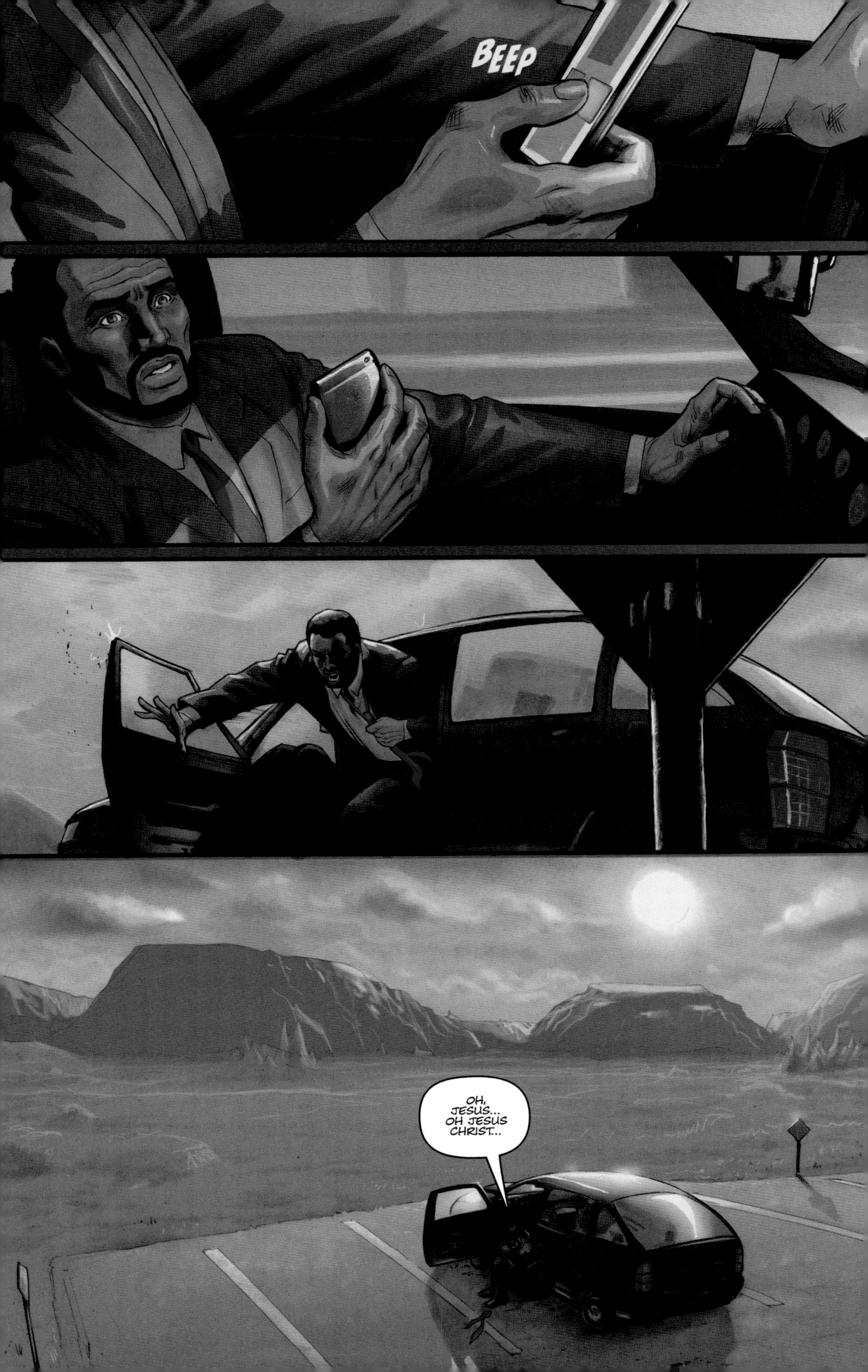
BEEP
OH, JESUS... OH JESUS CHRIST...

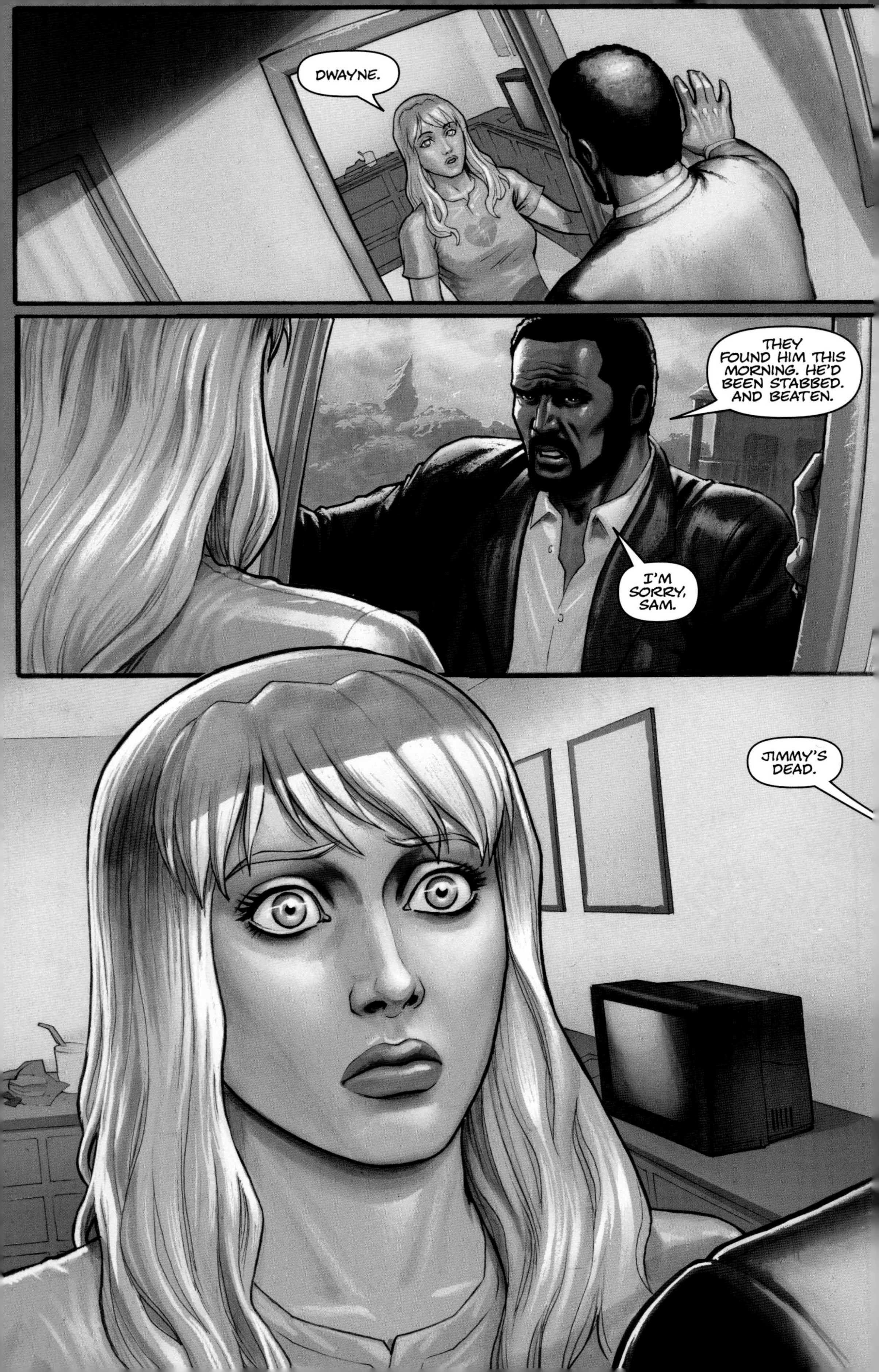
DWAYNE.
THEY FOUND HIM THIS MORNING. HE'D BEEN STABBED. AND BEATEN.
I'M SORRY, SAM.
JIMMY'S DEAD.

EDEN'S FALL
CHAPTER
3

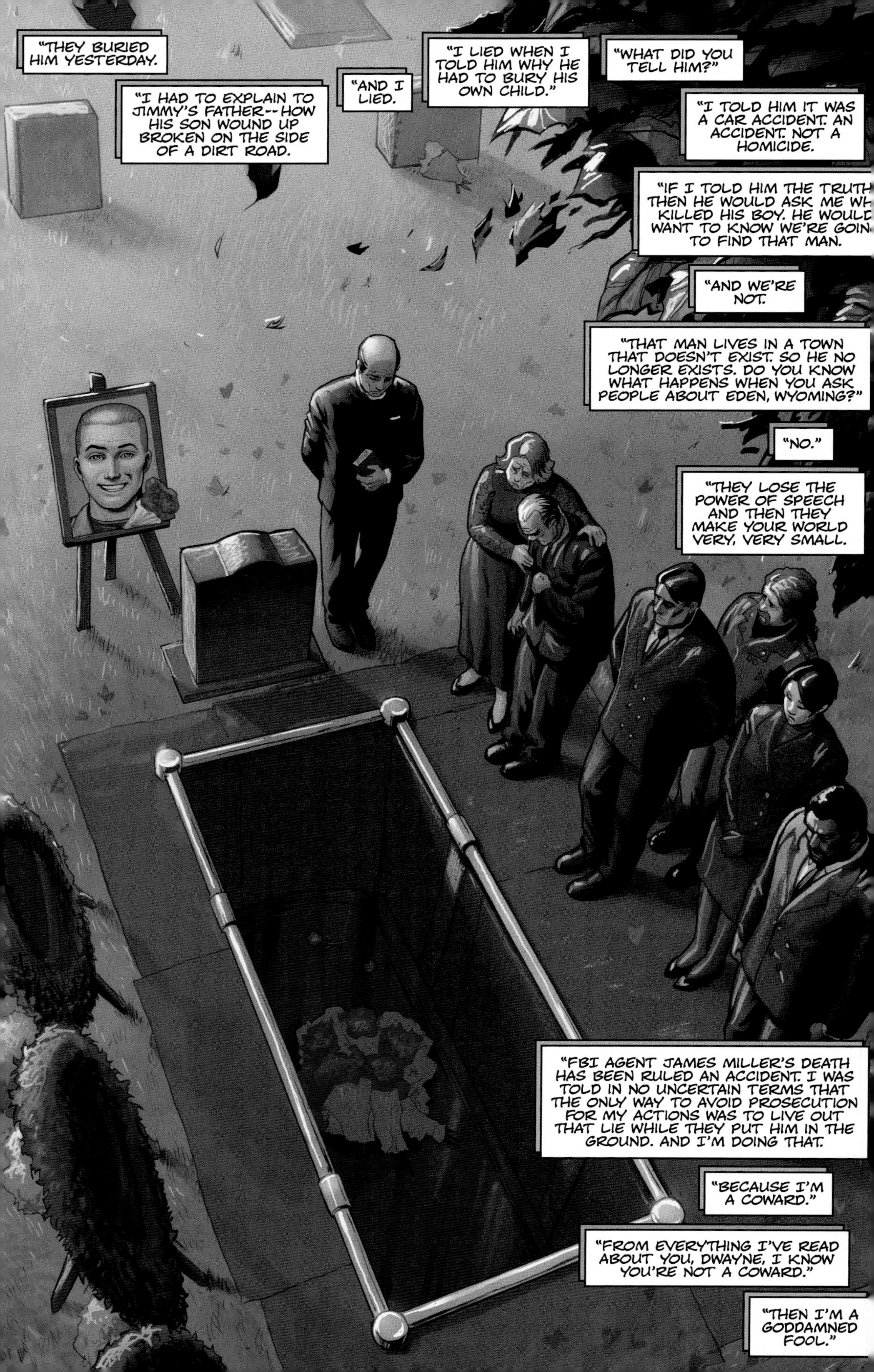

"THEY BURIED HIM YESTERDAY.
"I HAD TO EXPLAIN TO JIMMY'S FATHER--HOW HIS SON WOUND UP BROKEN ON THE SIDE OF A DIRT ROAD.
"AND I LIED.
"I LIED WHEN I TOLD HIM WHY HE HAD TO BURY HIS OWN CHILD."
"WHAT DID YOU TELL HIM?"
"I TOLD HIM IT WAS A CAR ACCIDENT. AN ACCIDENT. NOT A HOMICIDE.
"IF I TOLD HIM THE TRUTH THEN HE WOULD ASK ME WH KILLED HIS BOY. HE WOULD WANT TO KNOW WE'RE GOIN TO FIND THAT MAN.
"AND WE'RE NOT.
"THAT MAN LIVES IN A TOWN THAT DOESN'T EXISTS EXIST. SO HE NO LONGER EXISTS. DO YOU KNOW WHAT HAPPENS WHEN YOU ASK PEOPLE ABOUT EDEN, WYOMING?"
"NO."
"THEY LOSE THE POWER OF SPEECH AND THEN THEY MAKE YOUR WORLD VERY, VERY SMALL.
"FBI AGENT JAMES MILLER'S DEATH HAS BEEN RULED AN ACCIDENT. I WAS TOLD IN NO UNCERTAIN TERMS THAT THE ONLY WAY TO AVOID PROSECUTION FOR MY ACTIONS WAS TO LIVE OUT THAT LIE WHILE THEY PUT HIM IN THE GROUND. AND I'M DOING THAT.
"BECAUSE I'M A COWARD."
"FROM EVERYTHING I'VE READ ABOUT YOU, DWAYNE, I KNOW YOU'RE NOT A COWARD."
"THEN I'M A GODDAMNED FOOL."

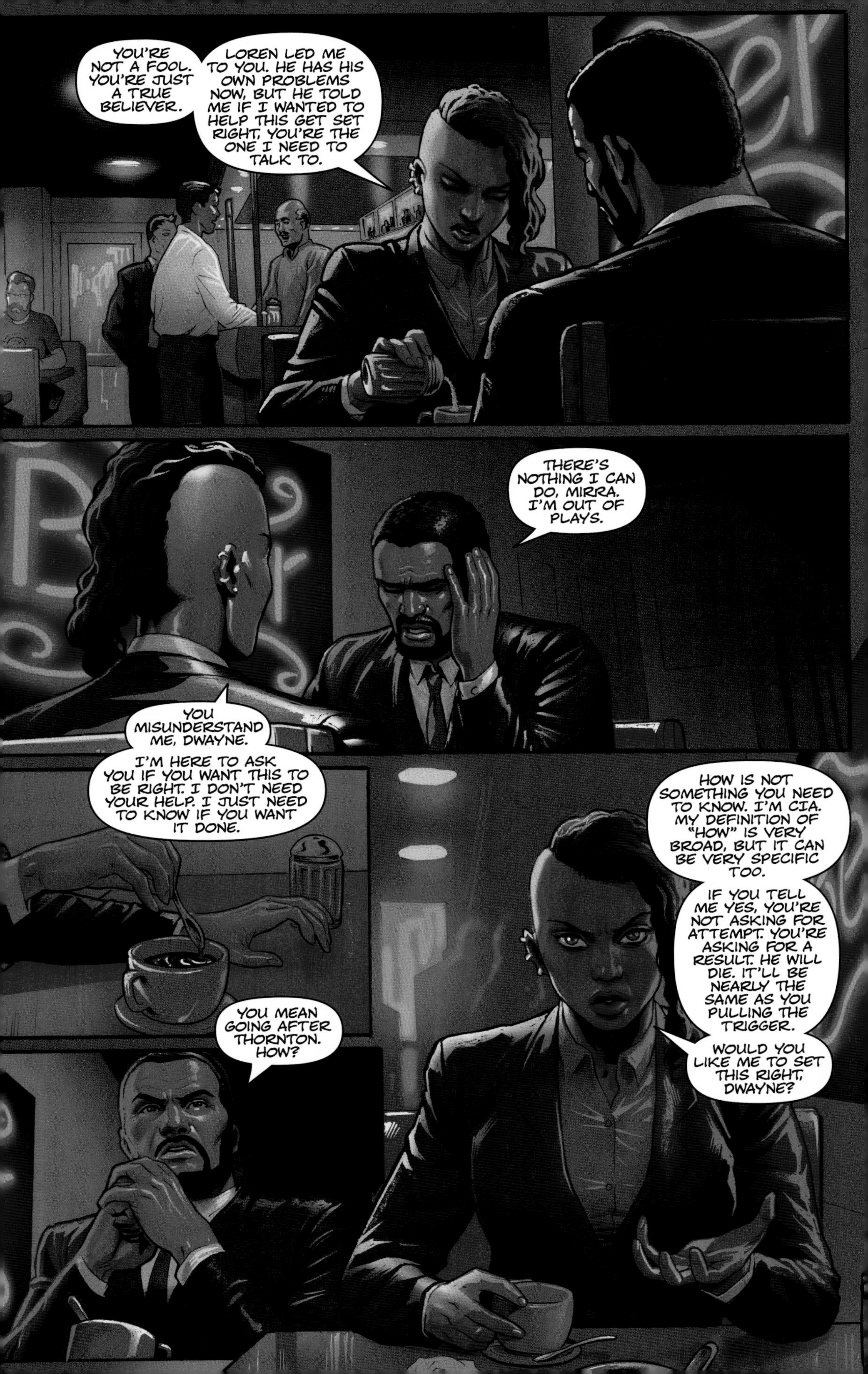
YOU'RE NOT A FOOL. YOU'RE JUST A TRUE BELIEVER.
LOREN LED ME TO YOU. HE HAS HIS OWN PROBLEMS NOW, BUT HE TOLD ME IF I WANTED TO HELP THIS GET SET RIGHT, YOU'RE THE ONE I NEED TO TALK TO.
THERE'S NOTHING I CAN DO, MIRRA. I'M OUT OF PLAYS.
YOU MISUNDERSTAND ME, DWAYNE.
I'M HERE TO ASK YOU IF YOU WANT THIS TO BE RIGHT. I DON'T NEED YOUR HELP. I JUST NEED TO KNOW IF YOU WANT IT DONE.
YOU MEAN GOING AFTER THORNTON. HOW?
HOW IS NOT SOMETHING YOU NEED TO KNOW. I'M CIA. MY DEFINITION OF "HOW" IS VERY BROAD, BUT IT CAN BE VERY SPECIFIC TOO.
IF YOU TELL ME YES, YOU'RE NOT ASKING FOR ATTEMPT. YOU'RE ASKING FOR A RESULT. HE WILL DIE. IT'LL BE NEARLY THE SAME AS YOU PULLING THE TRIGGER.
WOULD YOU LIKE ME TO SET THIS RIGHT, DWAYNE?

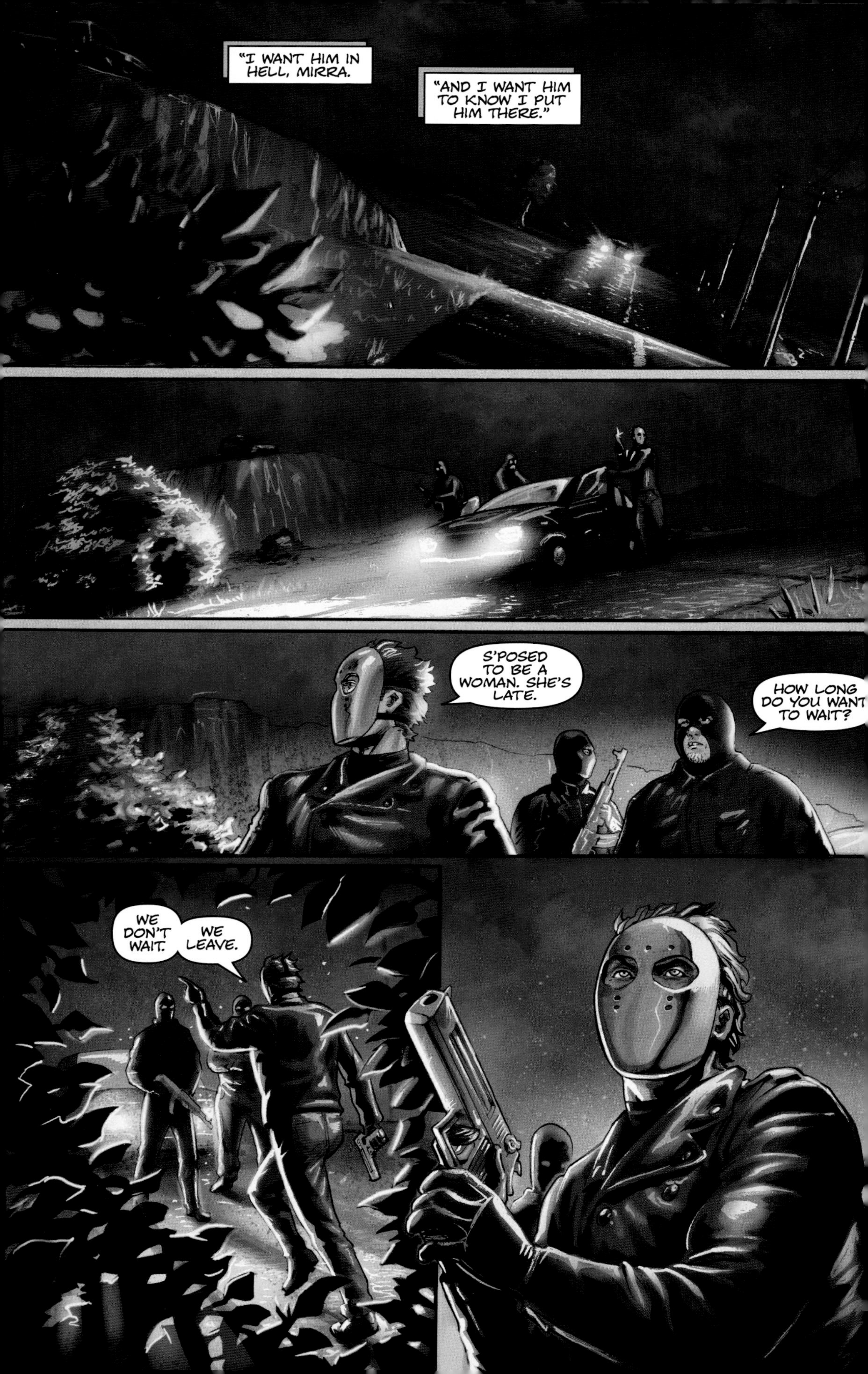
"I WANT HIM IN HELL, MIRRA.
"AND I WANT HIM TO KNOW I PUT HIM THERE."
S'POSED TO BE A WOMAN. SHE'S LATE.
HOW LONG DO YOU WANT TO WAIT?
WE DON'T WAIT.
WE LEAVE.

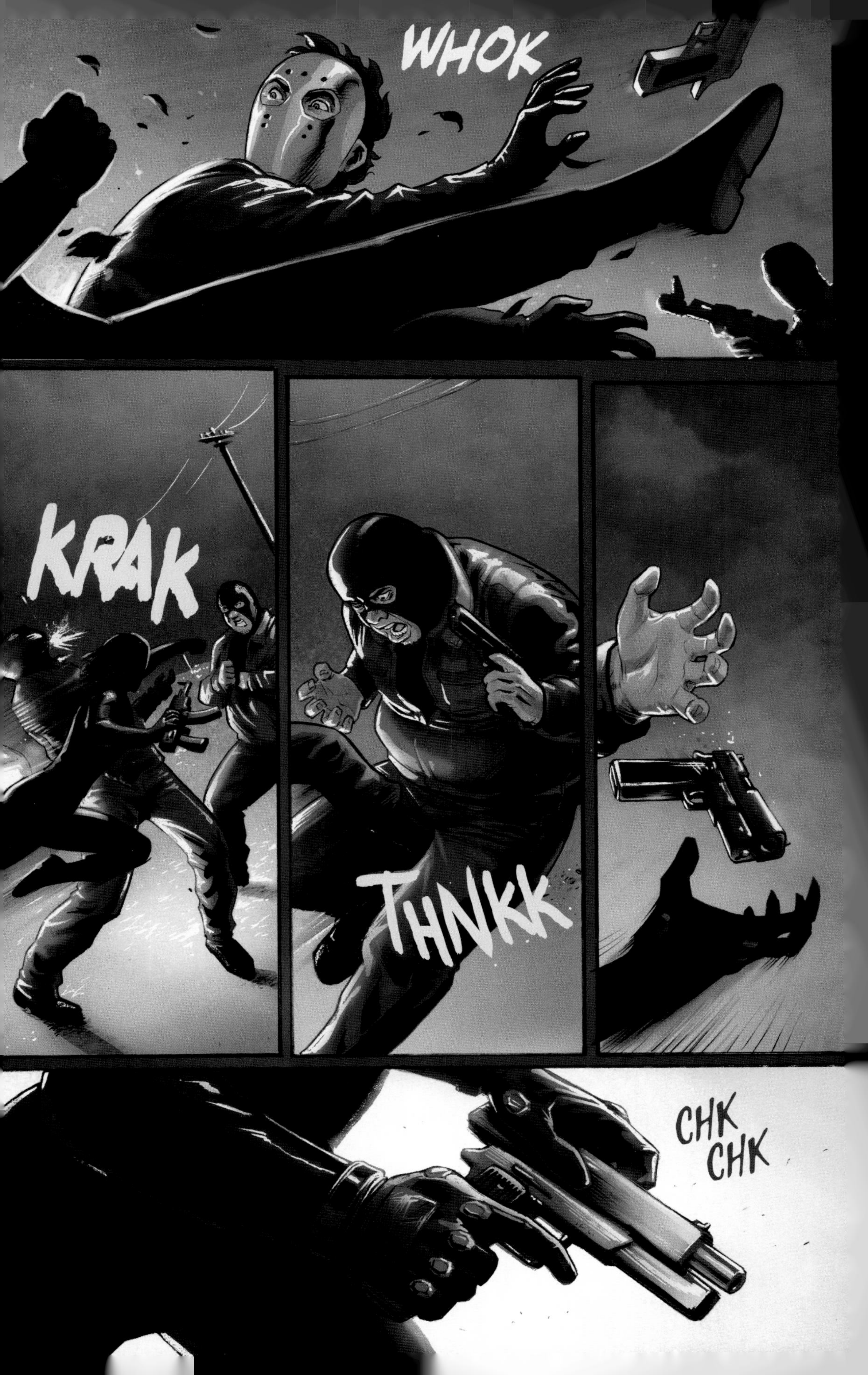
WHOK
KRAK
THNKK
CHK
CHK

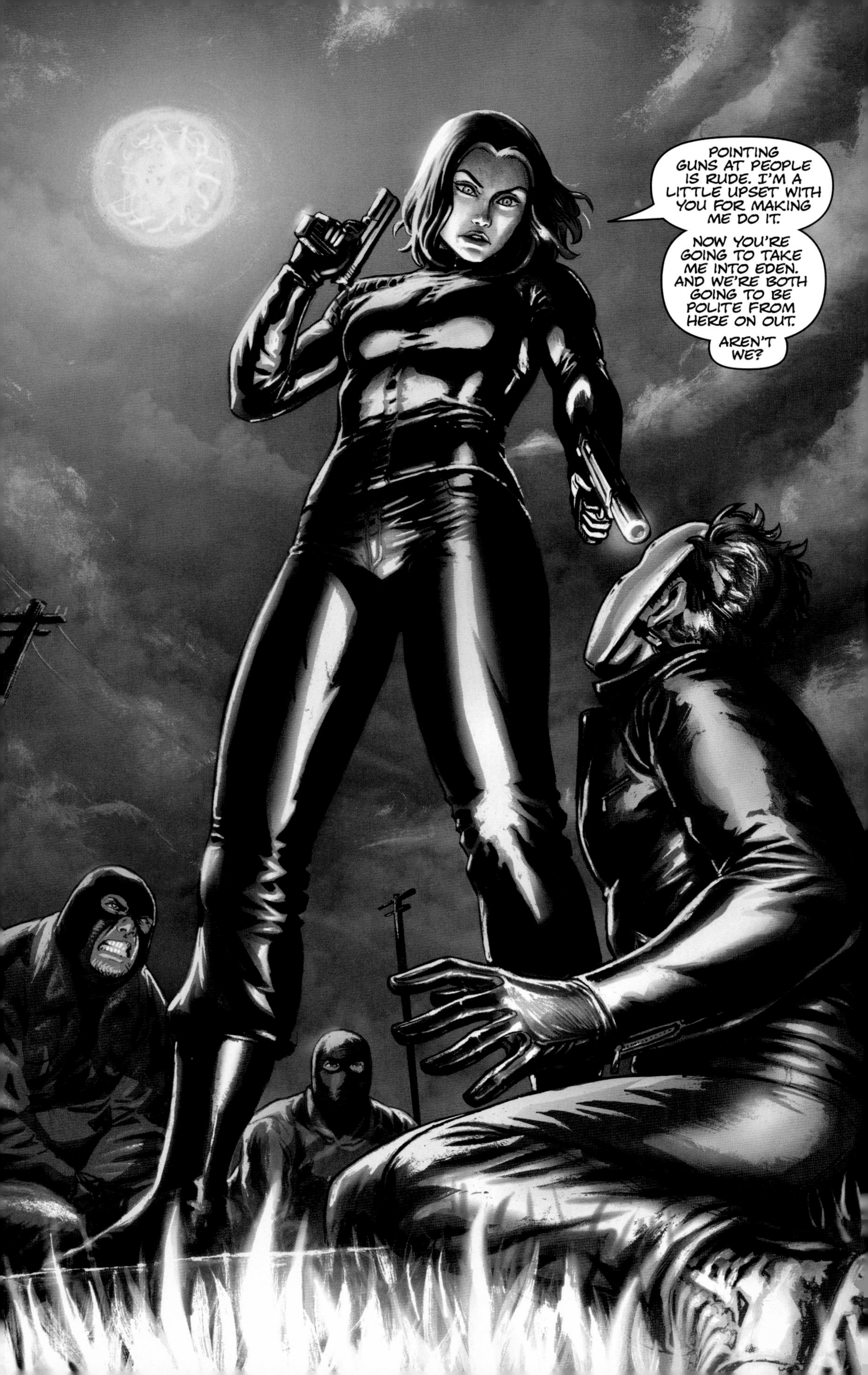
POINTING GUNS AT PEOPLE IS RUDE. I'M A LITTLE UPSET WITH YOU FOR MAKING ME DO IT.
NOW YOU'RE GOING TO TAKE ME INTO EDEN. AND WE'RE BOTH GOING TO BE POLITE FROM HERE ON OUT.
AREN'T WE?

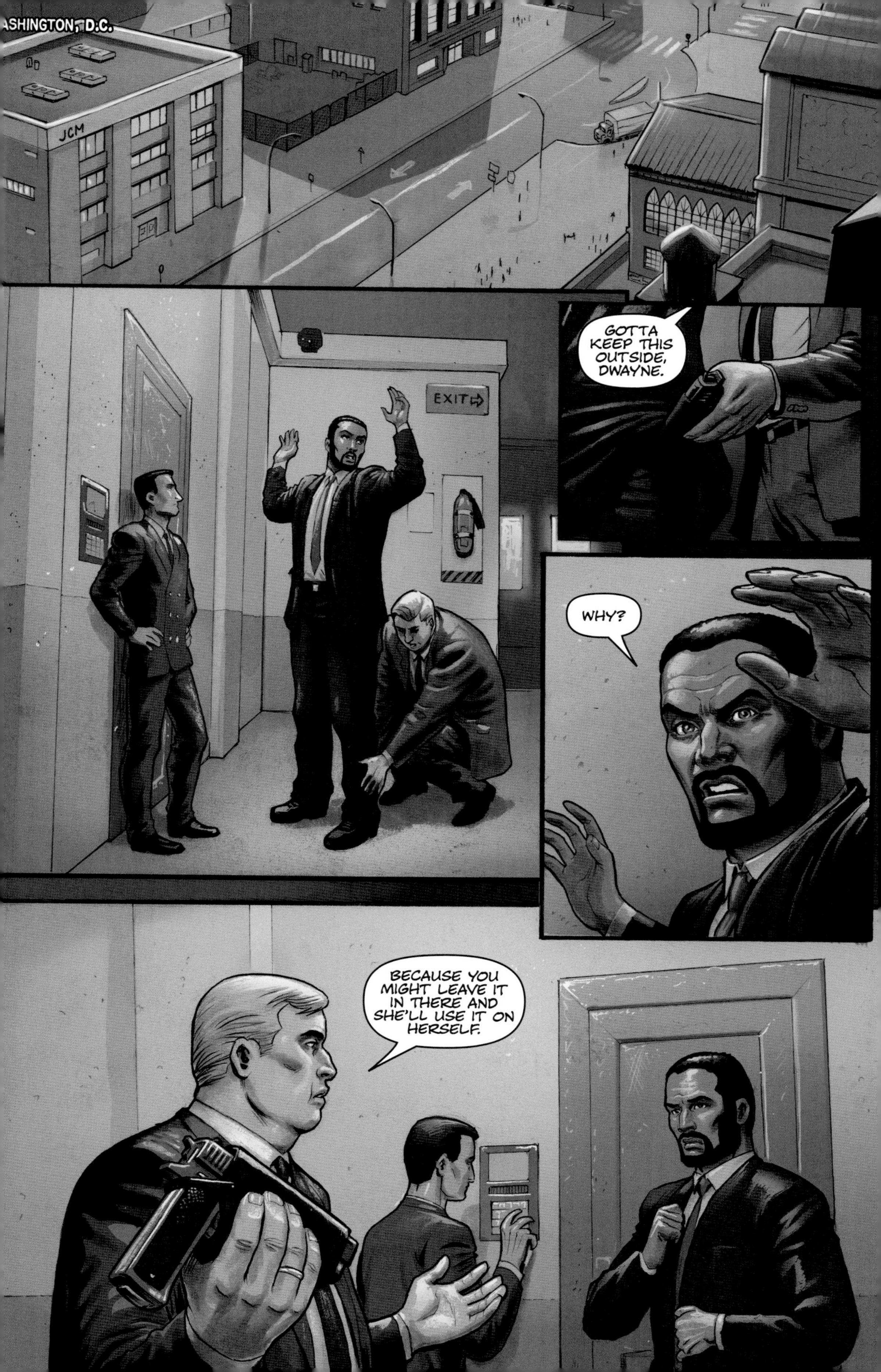
ASHINGTON, D.C.
JCM
EXIT
GOTTA KEEP THIS OUTSIDE, DWAYNE.
WHY?
BECAUSE YOU MIGHT LEAVE IT IN THERE AND SHE'LL USE IT ON HERSELF.

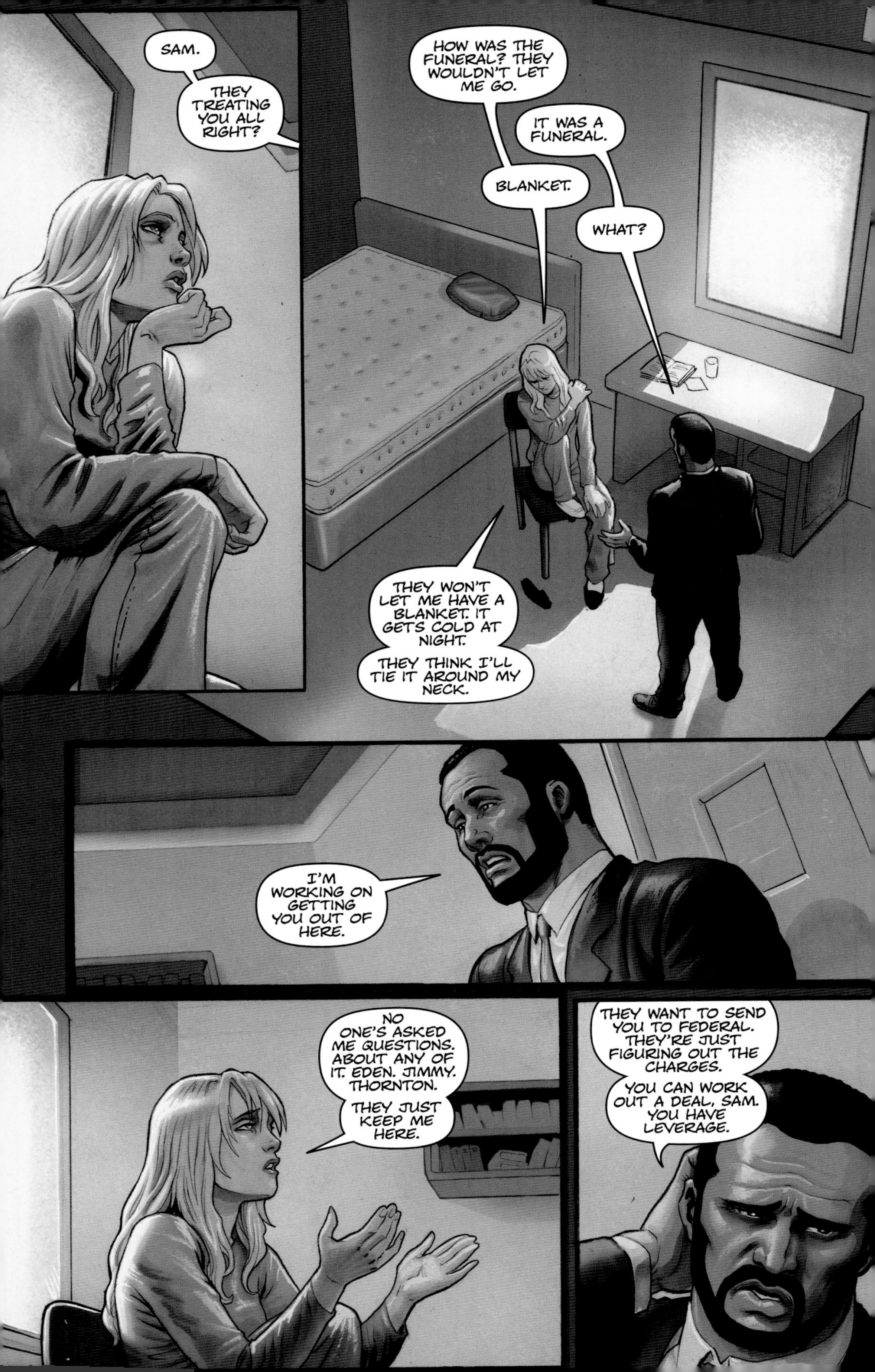
SAM.
THEY TREATING YOU ALL RIGHT?
HOW WAS THE FUNERAL? THEY WOULDN'T LET ME GO.
IT WAS A FUNERAL.
BLANKET.
WHAT?
THEY WON'T LET ME HAVE A BLANKET. IT GETS COLD AT NIGHT.
THEY THINK I'LL TIE IT AROUND MY NECK.
I'M WORKING ON GETTING YOU OUT OF HERE.
NO ONE'S ASKED ME QUESTIONS. ABOUT ANY OF IT. EDEN. JIMMY. THORNTON.
THEY JUST KEEP ME HERE.
THEY WANT TO SEND YOU TO FEDERAL. THEY'RE JUST FIGURING OUT THE CHARGES.
YOU CAN WORK OUT A DEAL, SAM. YOU HAVE LEVERAGE.

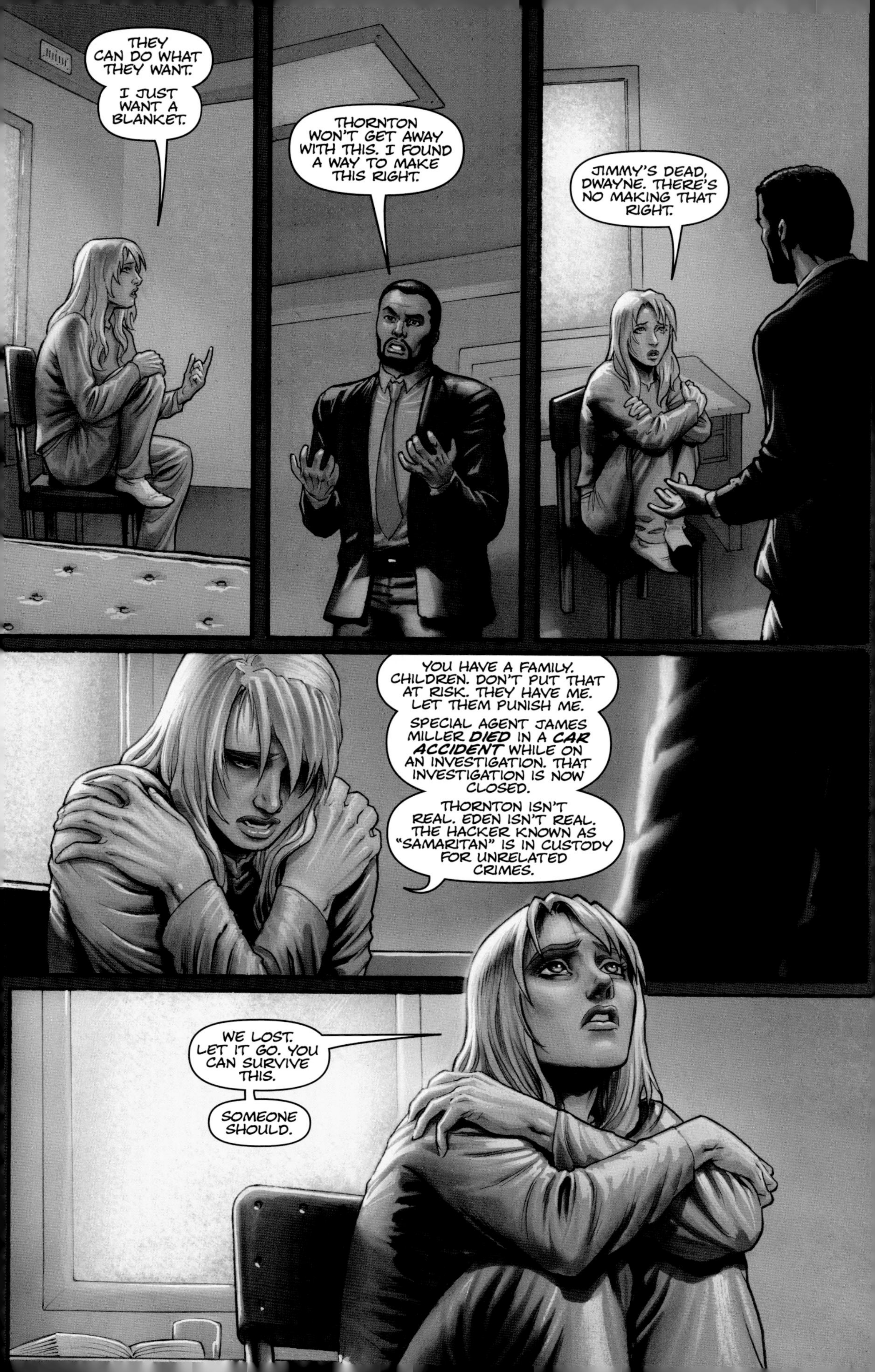
THEY CAN DO WHAT THEY WANT.
I JUST WANT A BLANKET.
THORNTON WON'T GET AWAY WITH THIS. I FOUND A WAY TO MAKE THIS RIGHT.
JIMMY'S DEAD, DWAYNE. THERE'S NO MAKING THAT RIGHT.
YOU HAVE A FAMILY. CHILDREN. DON'T PUT THAT AT RISK. THEY HAVE ME. LET THEM PUNISH ME.
SPECIAL AGENT JAMES MILLER DIED IN A CAR ACCIDENT WHILE ON AN INVESTIGATION. THAT INVESTIGATION IS NOW CLOSED.
THORNTON ISN'T REAL. EDEN ISN'T REAL. THE HACKER KNOWN AS "SAMARITAN" IS IN CUSTODY FOR UNRELATED CRIMES.
WE LOST. LET IT GO. YOU CAN SURVIVE THIS.
SOMEONE SHOULD.

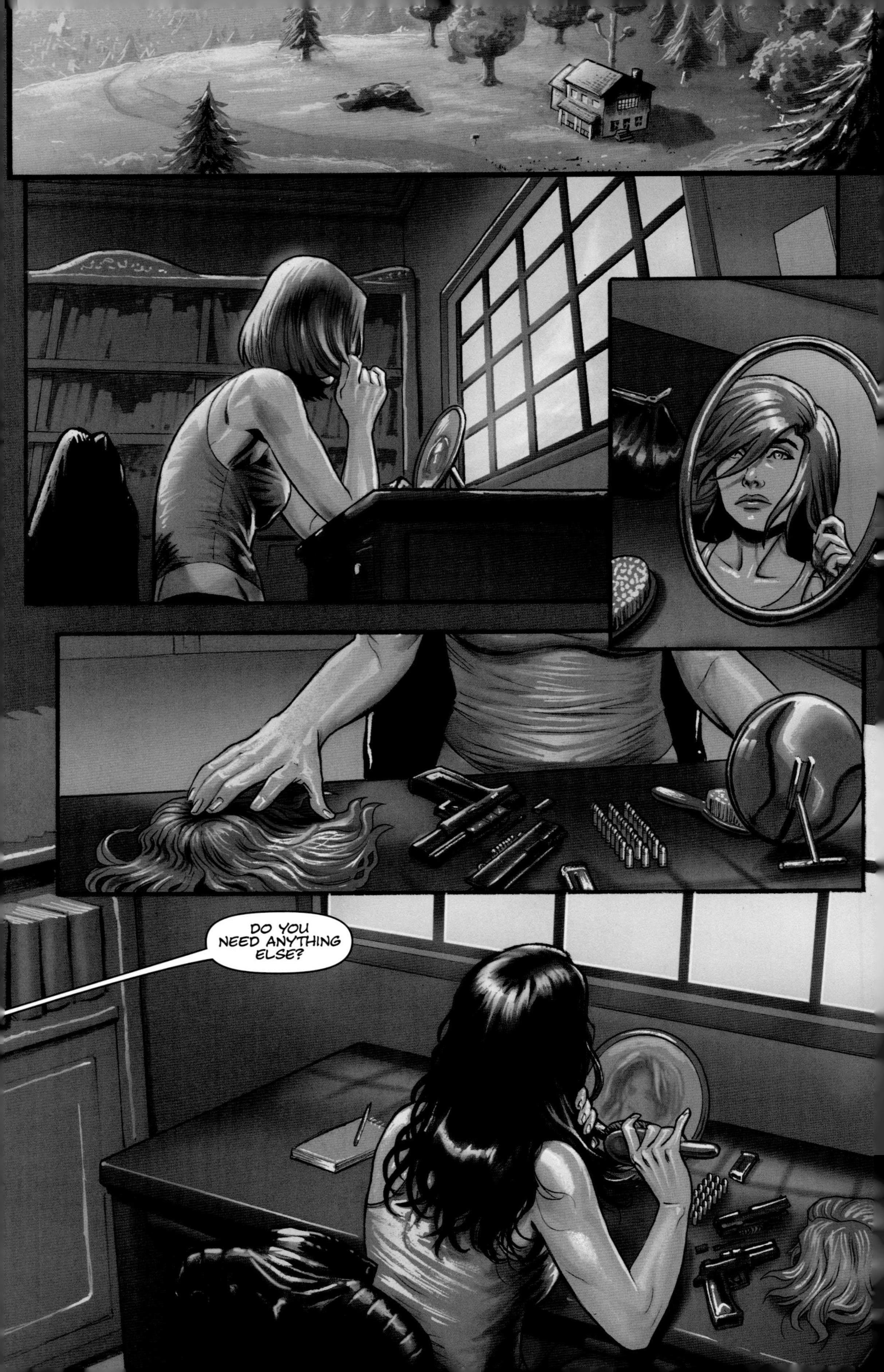
DO YOU NEED ANYTHING ELSE?

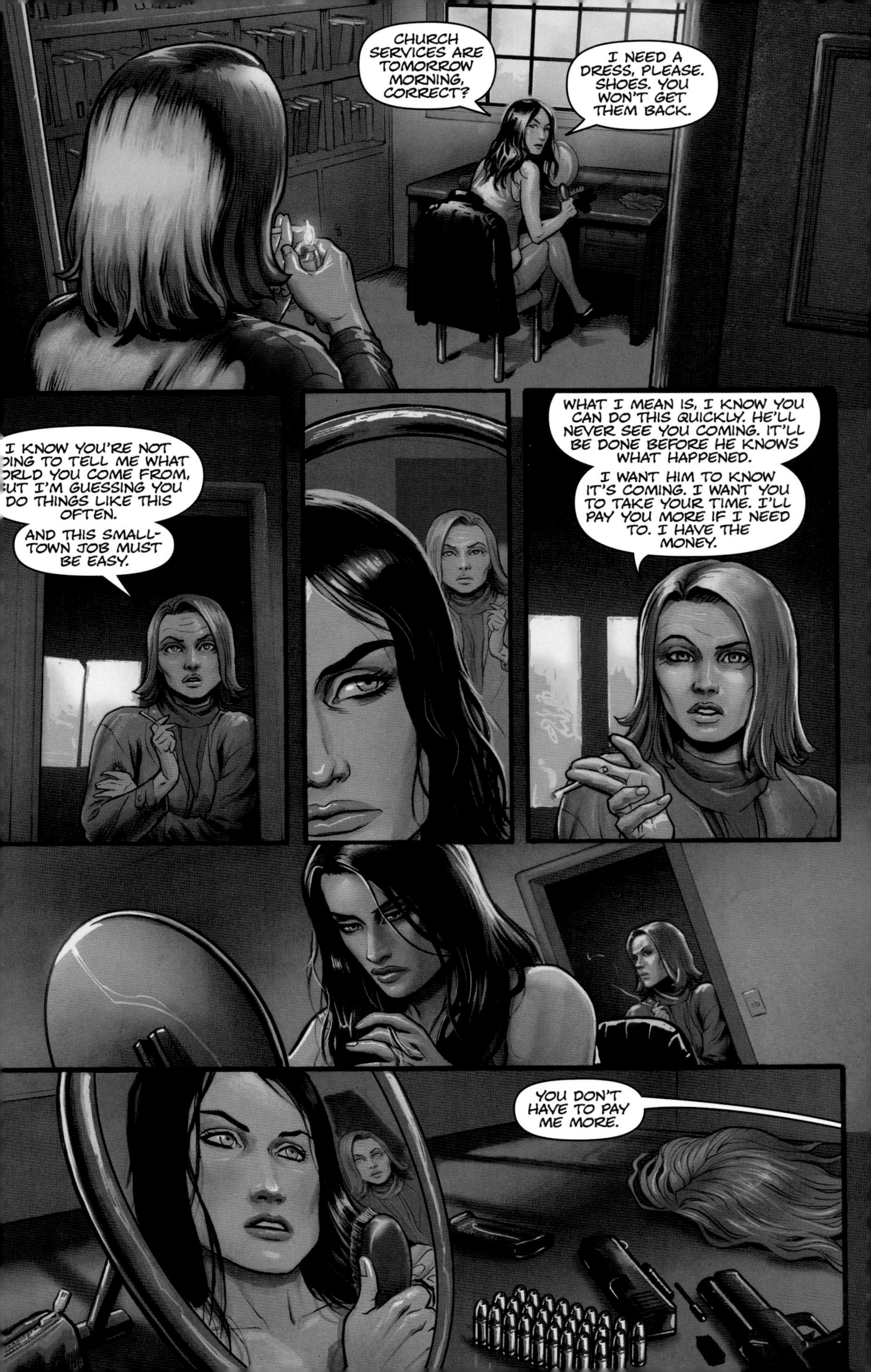
CHURCH SERVICES ARE TOMORROW MORNING, CORRECT?
I NEED A DRESS, PLEASE. SHOES. YOU WON'T GET THEM BACK.
I KNOW YOU'RE NOT OING TO TELL ME WHAT ORLD YOU COME FROM, UT I'M GUESSING YOU DO THINGS LIKE THIS OFTEN.
AND THIS SMALL-TOWN JOB MUST BE EASY.
WHAT I MEAN IS, I KNOW YOU CAN DO THIS QUICKLY. HE'LL NEVER SEE YOU COMING. IT'LL BE DONE BEFORE HE KNOWS WHAT HAPPENED.
I WANT HIM TO KNOW IT'S COMING. I WANT YOU TO TAKE YOUR TIME. I'LL PAY YOU MORE IF I NEED TO. I HAVE THE MONEY.
YOU DON'T HAVE TO PAY ME MORE.

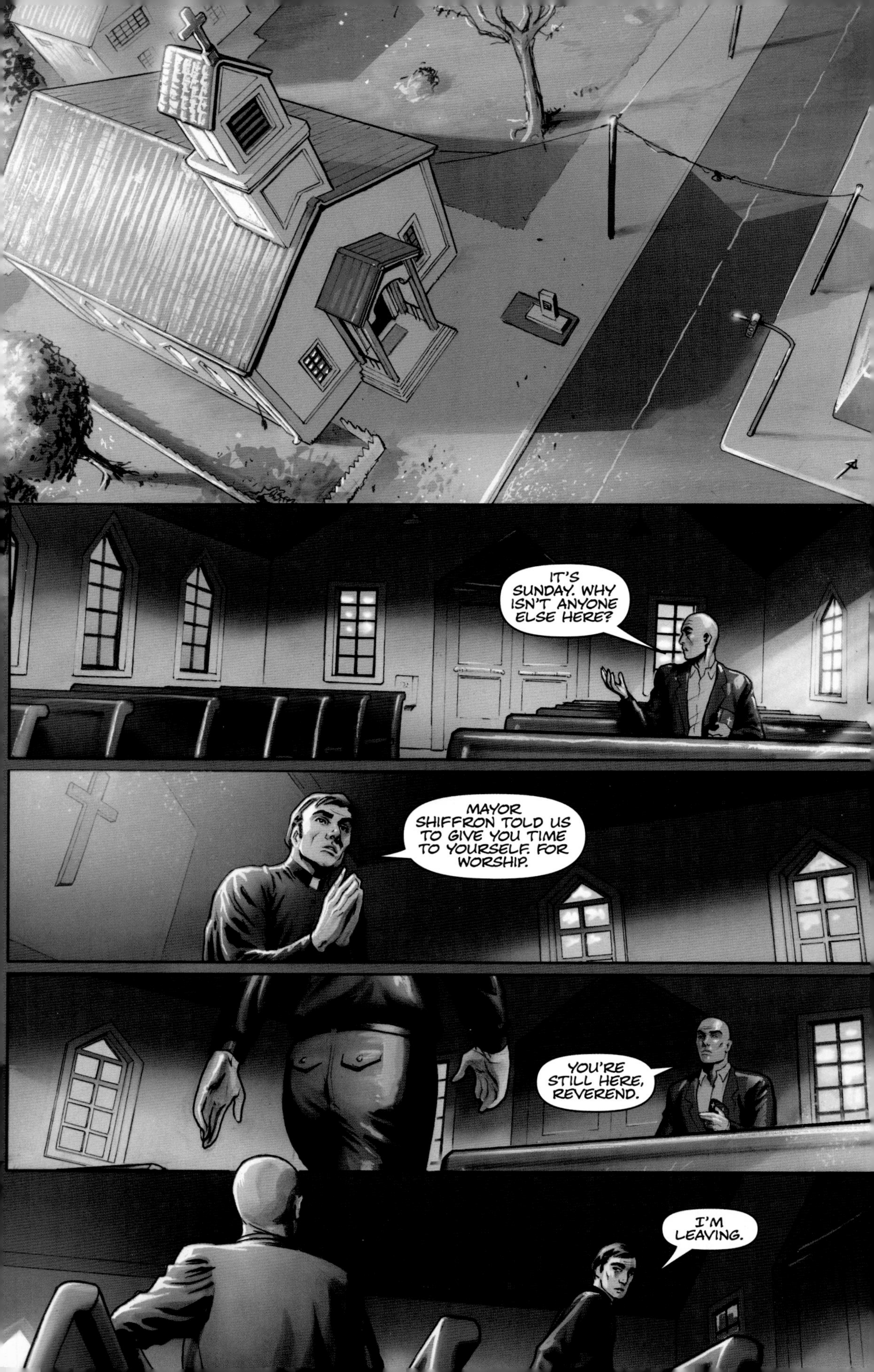
IT'S SUNDAY. WHY ISN'T ANYONE ELSE HERE?
MAYOR SHIFFRON TOLD US TO GIVE YOU TIME TO YOURSELF. FOR WORSHIP.
YOU'RE STILL HERE, REVEREND.
I'M LEAVING.

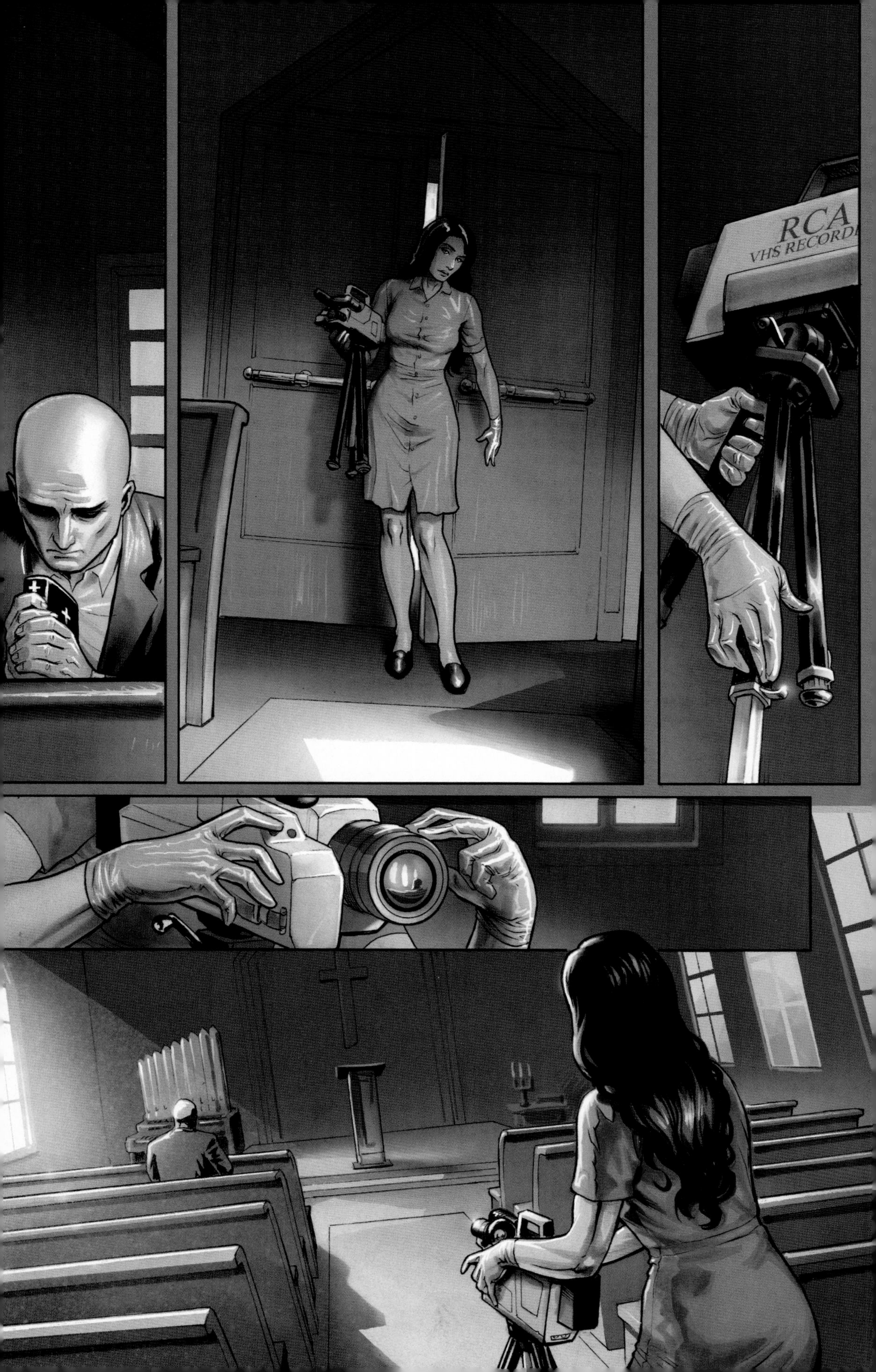
RCA

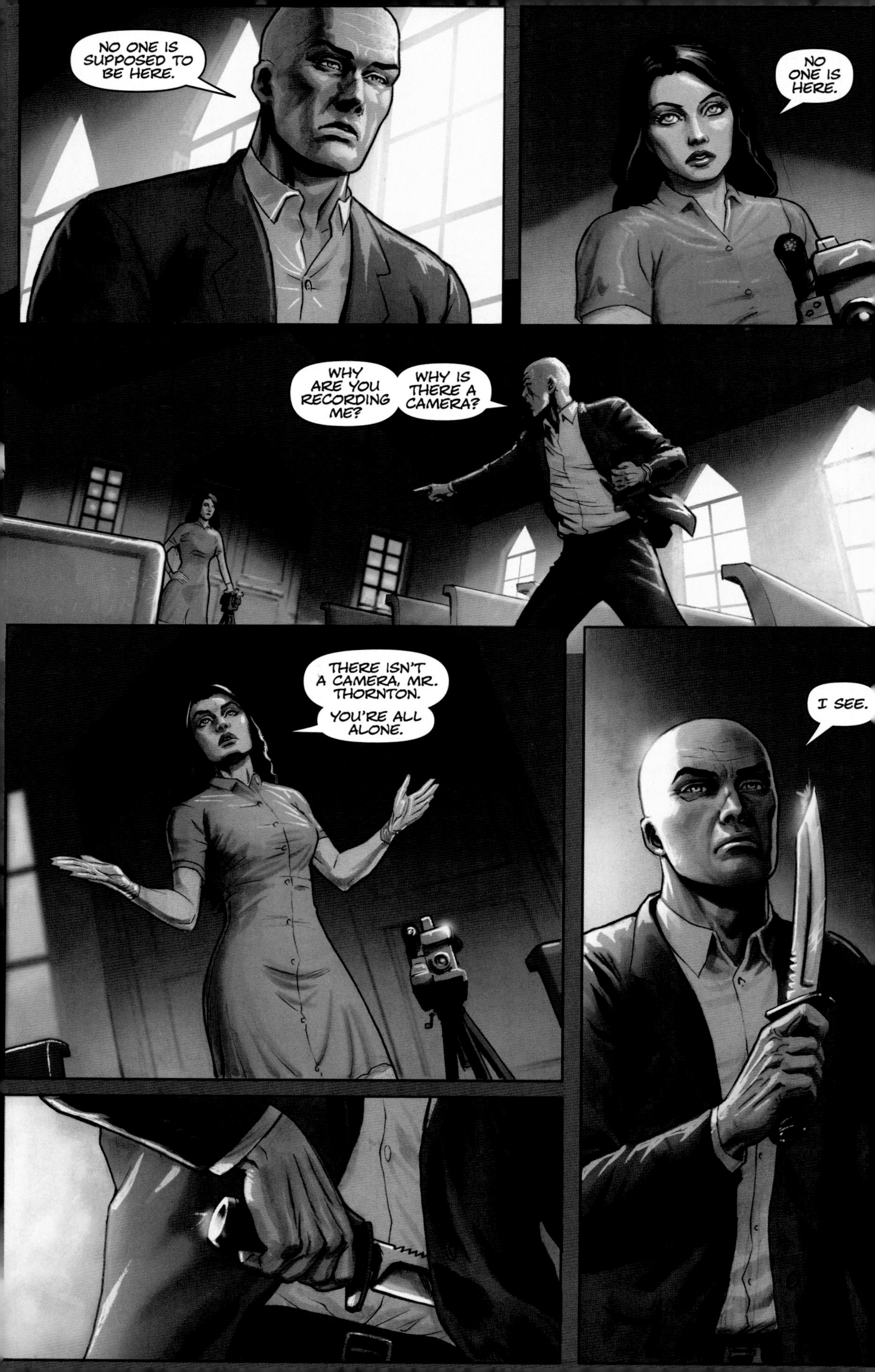
NO ONE IS SUPPOSED TO BE HERE.
NO ONE IS HERE.
WHY IS THERE A CAMERA?
WHY ARE YOU RECORDING ME?
THERE ISN'T A CAMERA, MR. THORNTON.
YOU'RE ALL ALONE.
I SEE.

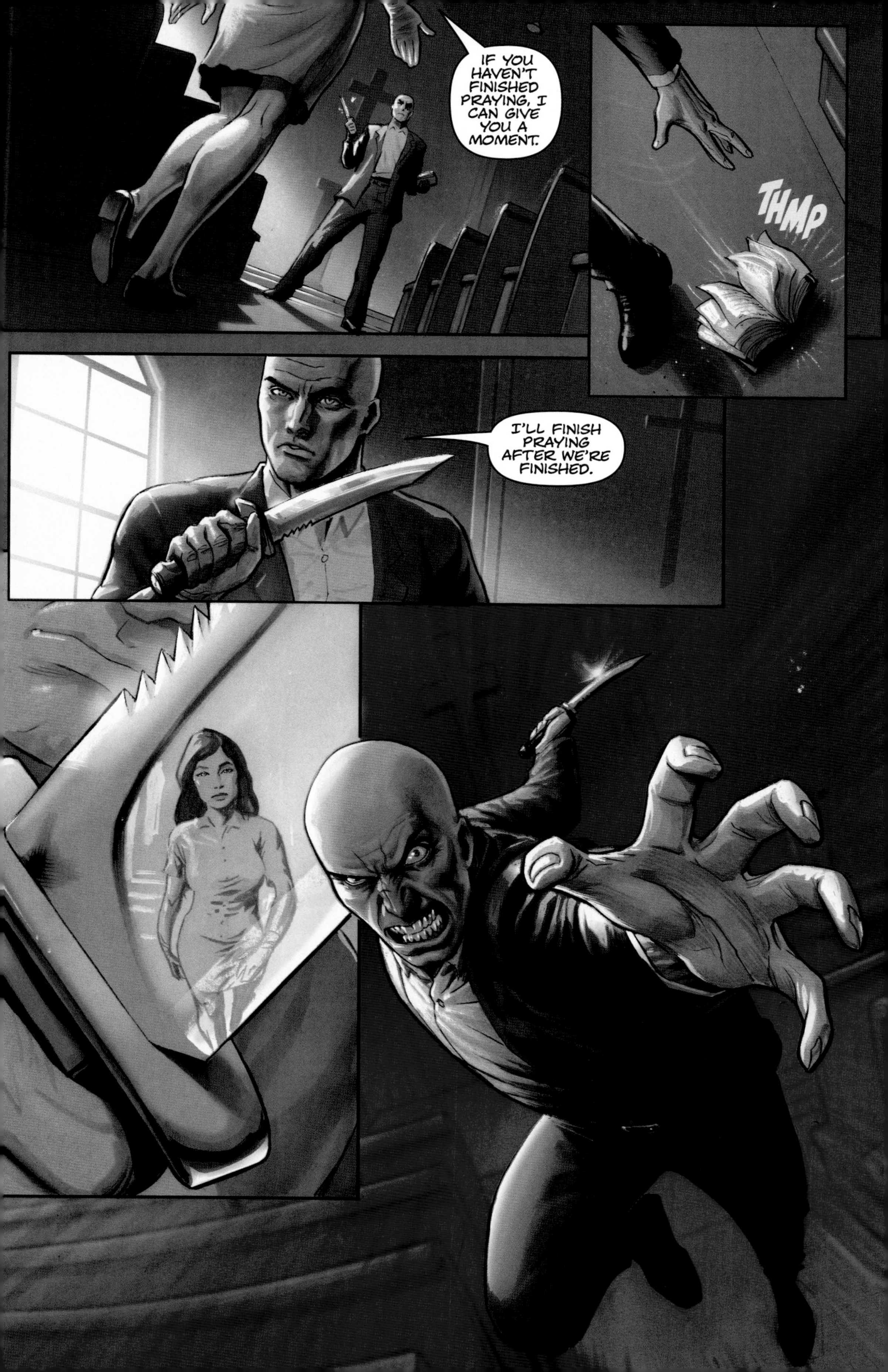
IF YOU HAVEN'T FINISHED PRAYING, I CAN GIVE YOU A MOMENT.
THMP
I'LL FINISH PRAYING AFTER WE'RE FINISHED.

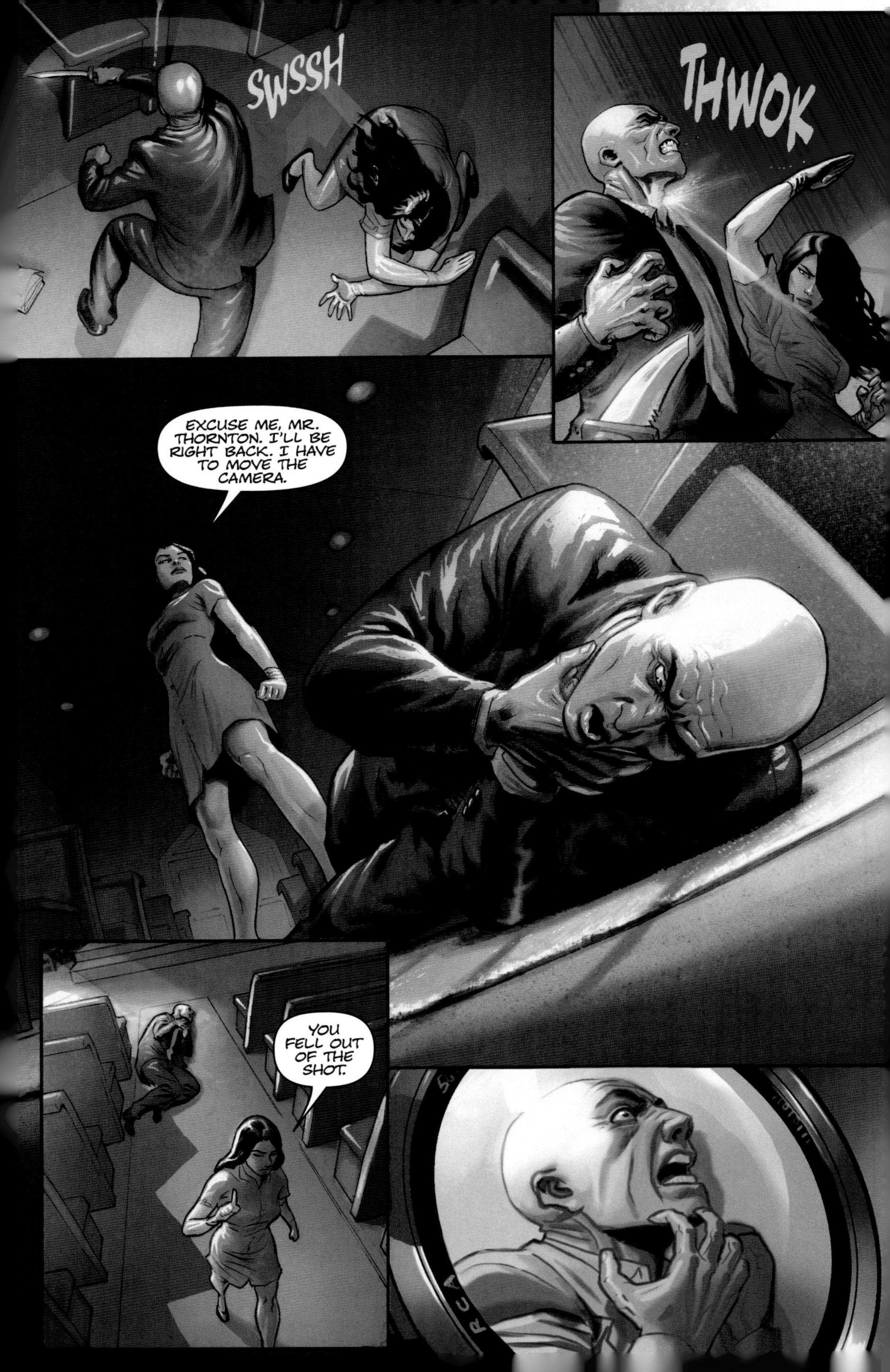
SWSSH
THWOK
EXCUSE ME, MR. THORNTON. I'LL BE RIGHT BACK. I HAVE TO MOVE THE CAMERA.
YOU FELL OUT OF THE SHOT.
RCA

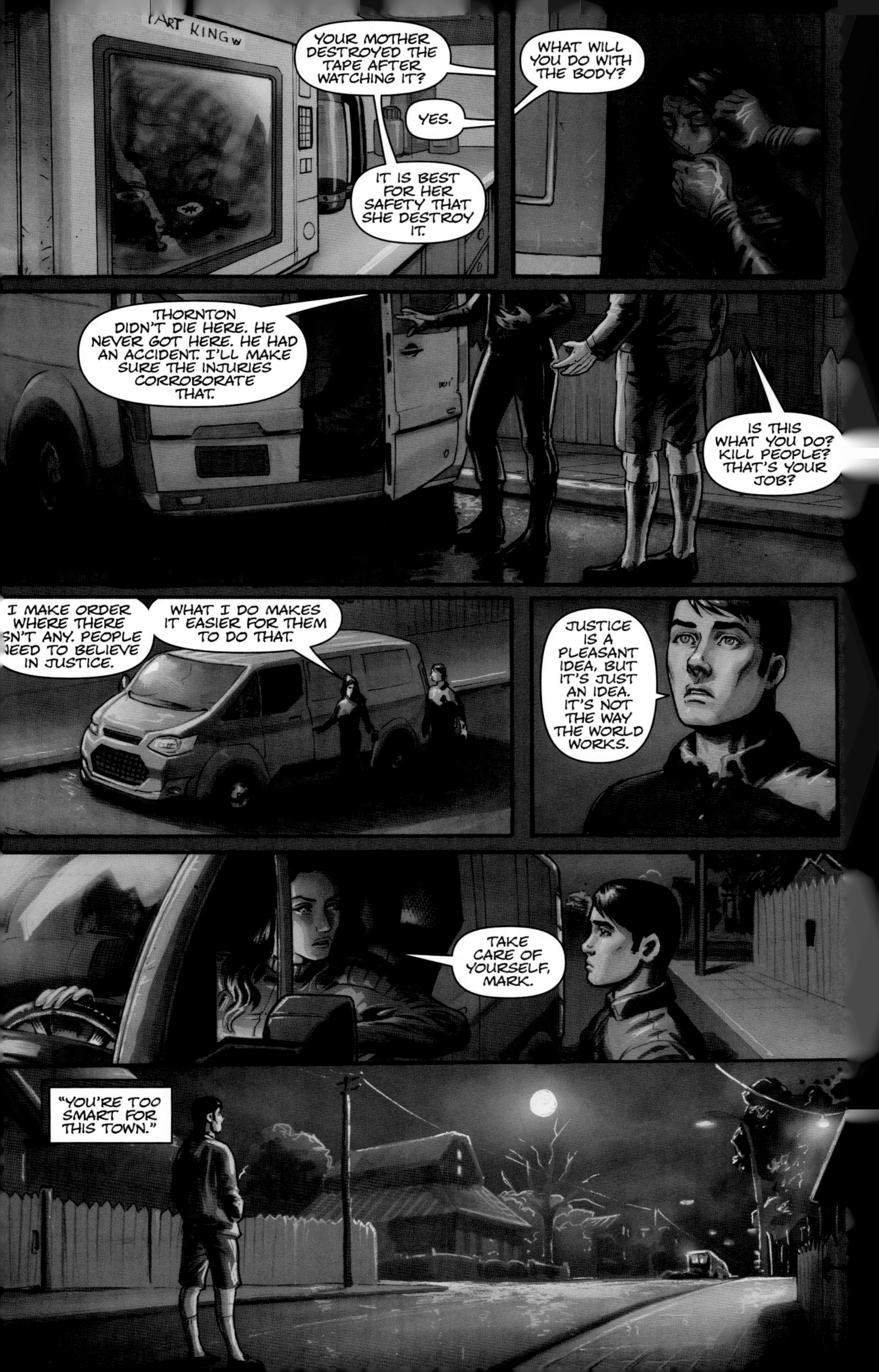
ART KING
YOUR MOTHER DESTROYED THE TAPE AFTER WATCHING IT?
YES.
IT IS BEST FOR HER SAFETY THAT SHE DESTROY IT.
WHAT WILL YOU DO WITH THE BODY?
THORNTON DIDN'T DIE HERE. HE NEVER GOT HERE. HE HAD AN ACCIDENT. I'LL MAKE SURE THE INJURIES CORROBORATE THAT.
IS THIS WHAT YOU DO? KILL PEOPLE? THAT'S YOUR JOB?
I MAKE ORDER WHERE THERE ISN'T ANY. PEOPLE NEED TO BELIEVE IN JUSTICE.
WHAT I DO MAKES IT EASIER FOR THEM TO DO THAT.
JUSTICE IS A PLEASANT IDEA, BUT IT'S JUST AN IDEA. IT'S NOT THE WAY THE WORLD WORKS.
TAKE CARE OF YOURSELF, MARK.
"YOU'RE TOO SMART FOR THIS TOWN."

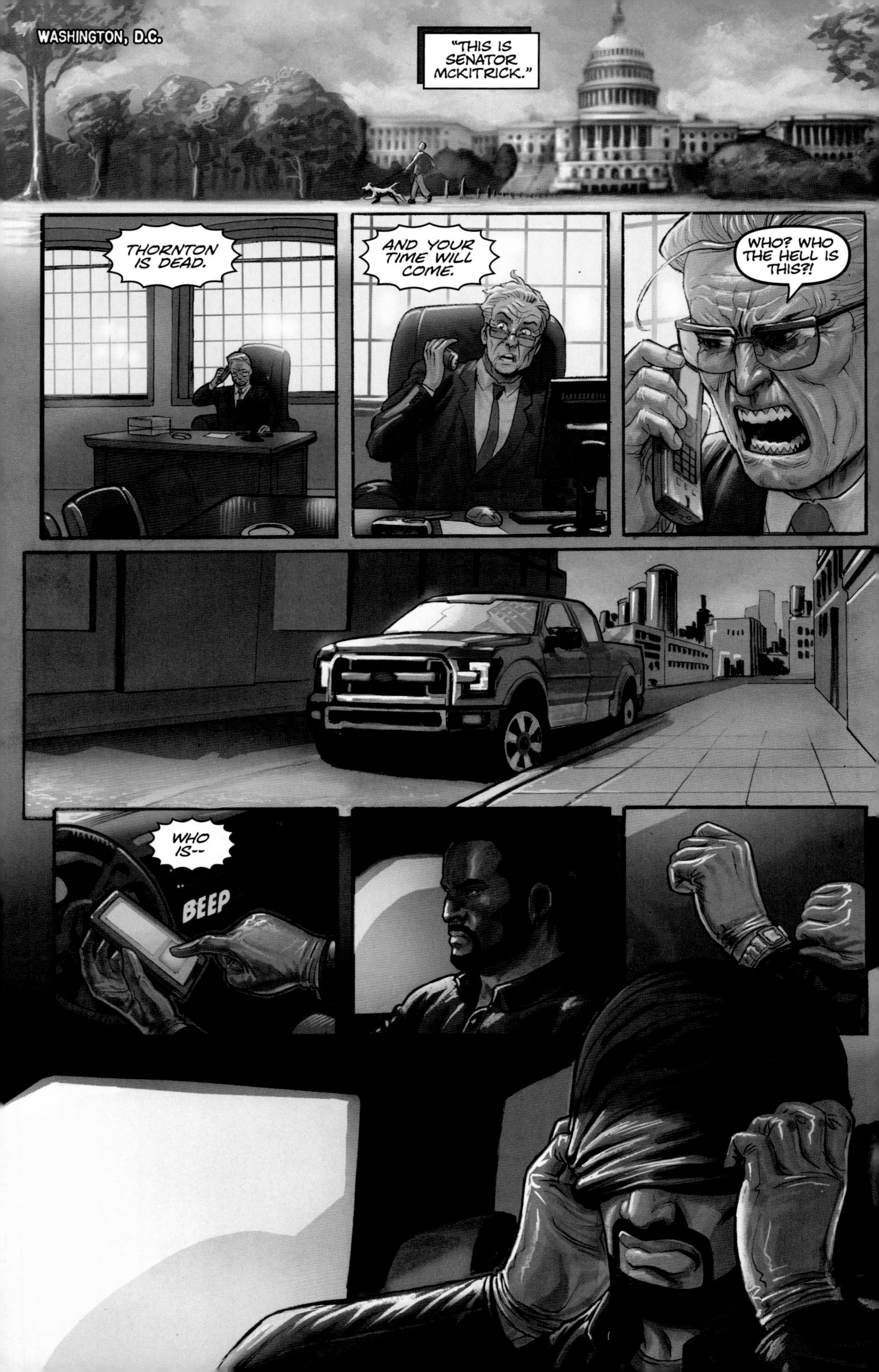
WASHINGTON, D.C.
"THIS IS SENATOR MCKITRICK."
THORNTON IS DEAD.
AND YOUR TIME WILL COME.
WHO? WHO THE HELL IS THIS?!
WHO IS--
BEEP

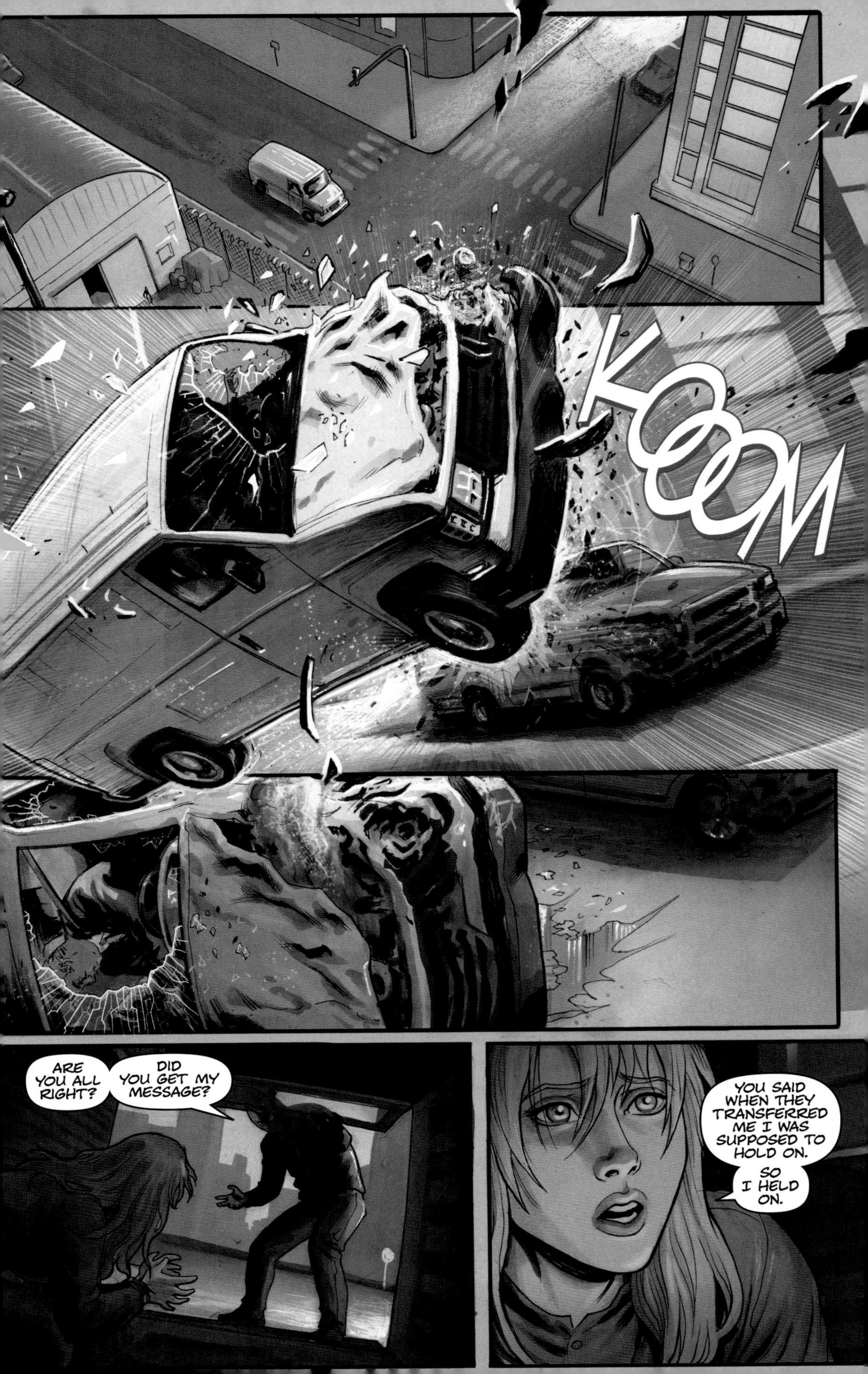
KOOOM
ARE YOU ALL RIGHT?
DID YOU GET MY MESSAGE?
YOU SAID WHEN THEY TRANSFERRED ME I WAS SUPPOSED TO HOLD ON.
SO I HELD ON.

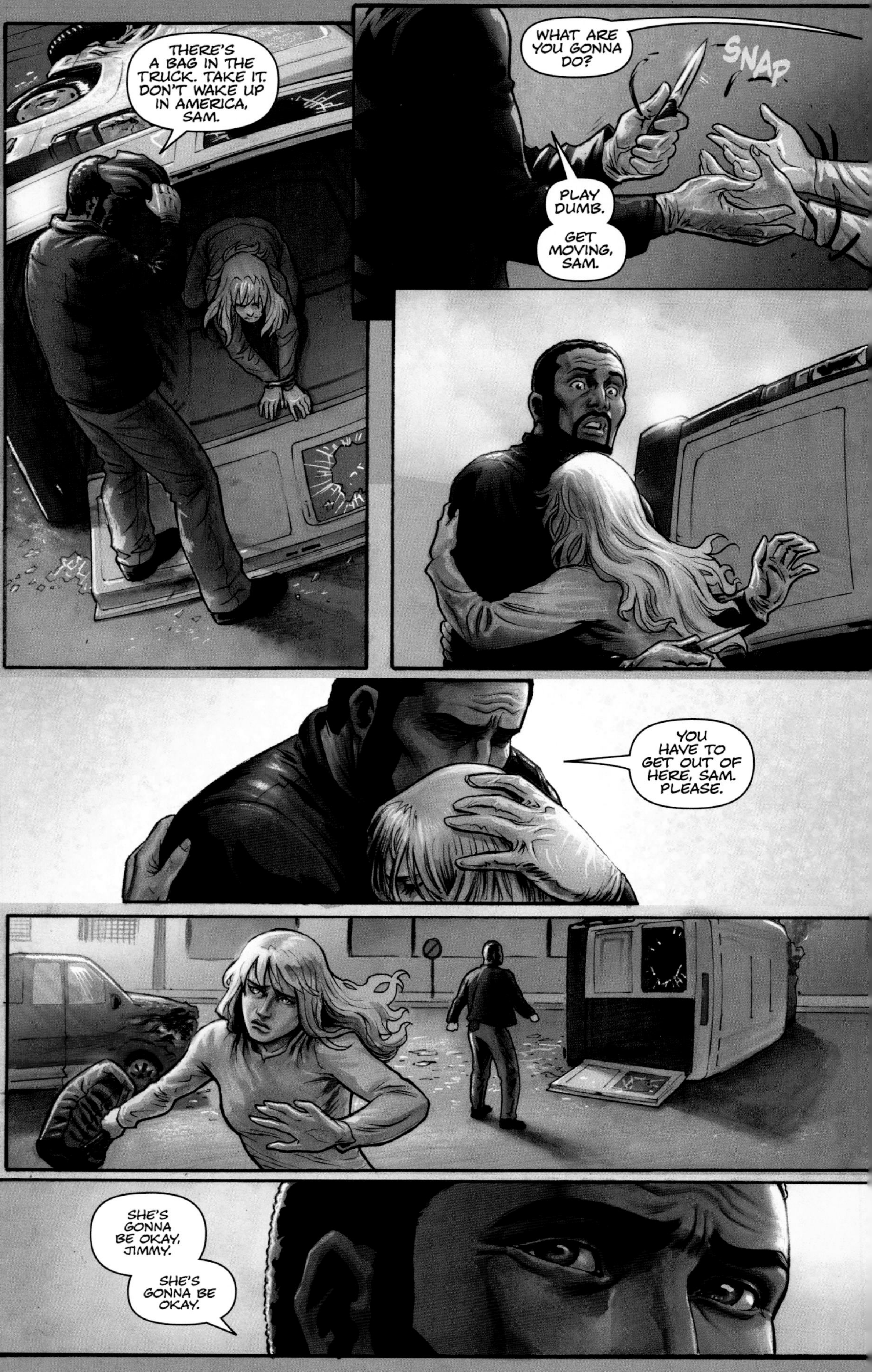
THERE'S A BAG IN THE TRUCK. TAKE IT. DON'T WAKE UP IN AMERICA, SAM.
WHAT ARE YOU GONNA DO?
SNAP
PLAY DUMB.
GET MOVING, SAM.
YOU HAVE TO GET OUT OF HERE, SAM. PLEASE.
SHE'S GONNA BE OKAY, JIMMY.
SHE'S GONNA BE OKAY.

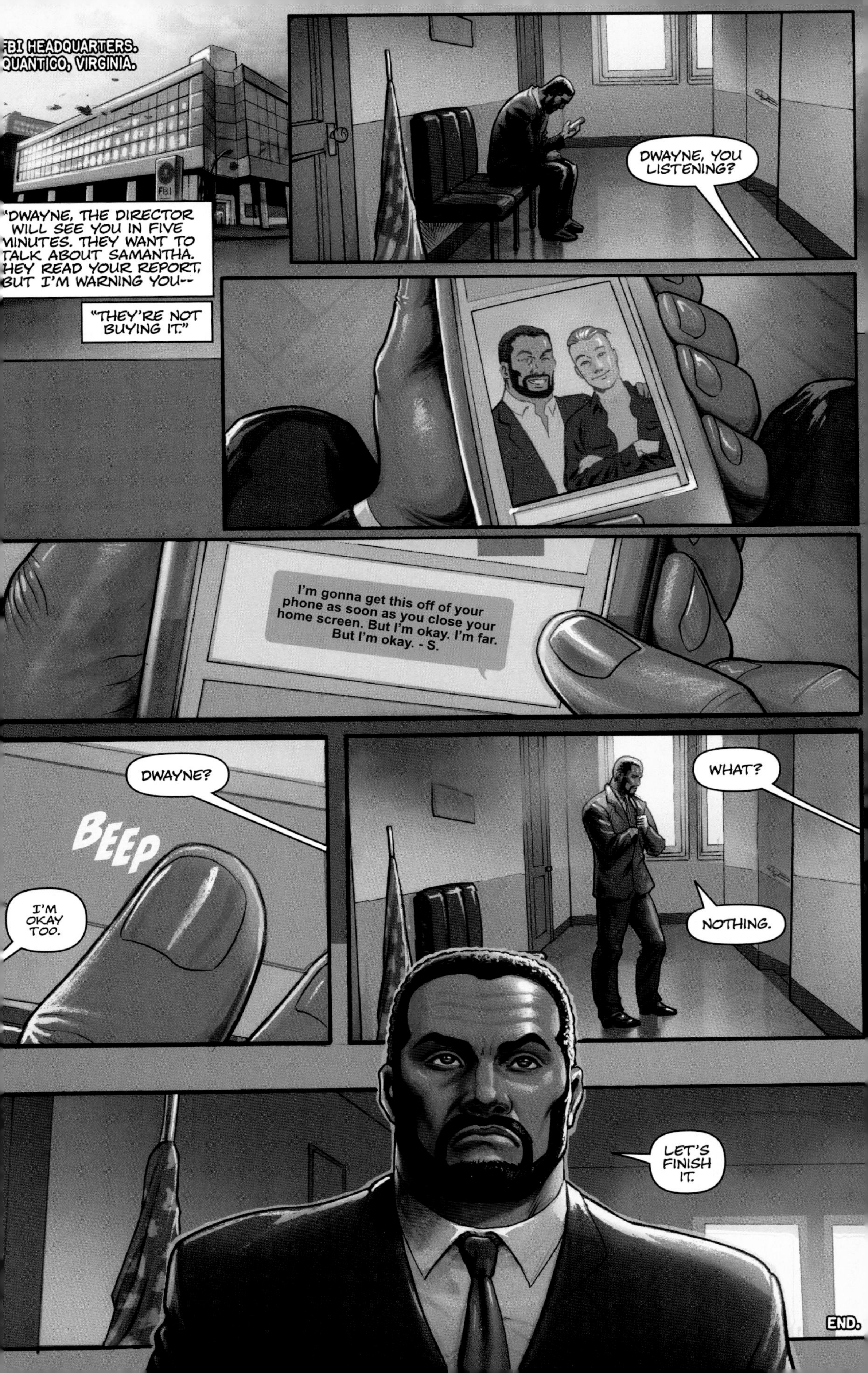
FBI HEADQUARTERS.
QUANTICO, VIRGINIA.
FBI
"DWAYNE, THE DIRECTOR WILL SEE YOU IN FIVE MINUTES. THEY WANT TO TALK ABOUT SAMANTHA. THEY READ YOUR REPORT, BUT I'M WARNING YOU--
"THEY'RE NOT BUYING IT."
DWAYNE, YOU LISTENING?
I'm gonna get this off of your phone as soon as you close your home screen. But I'm okay. I'm far. But I'm okay. - S.
DWAYNE?
BEEP
I'M OKAY TOO.
WHAT?
NOTHING.
LET'S FINISH IT.
END.

SAMARITAN

COVER
GALLERY

Samaritan: Veritas Issue 1 Cover
Art by Atilio Rojo

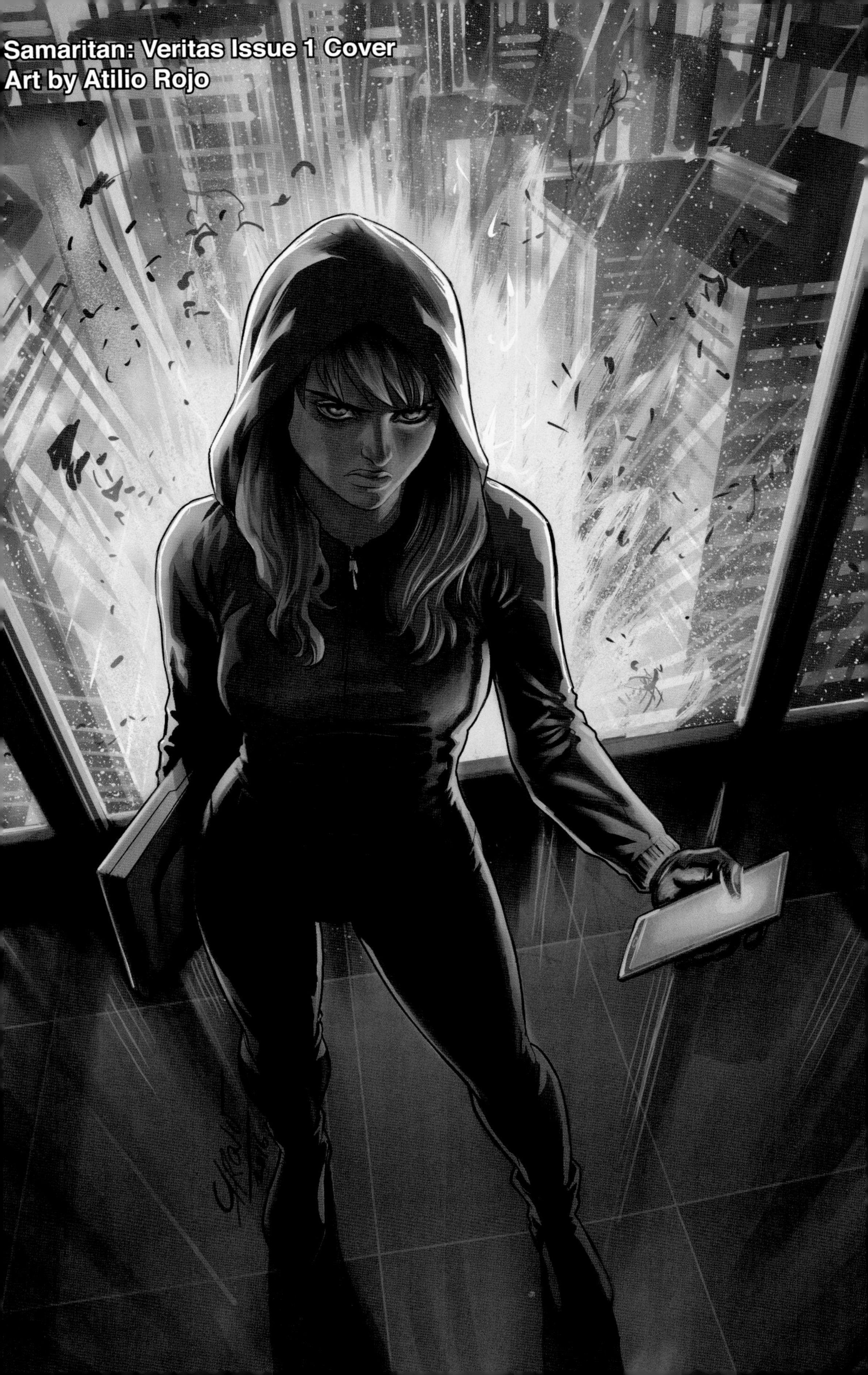

Samaritan: Veritas Issue 2 Cover
Art by Atilio Rojo

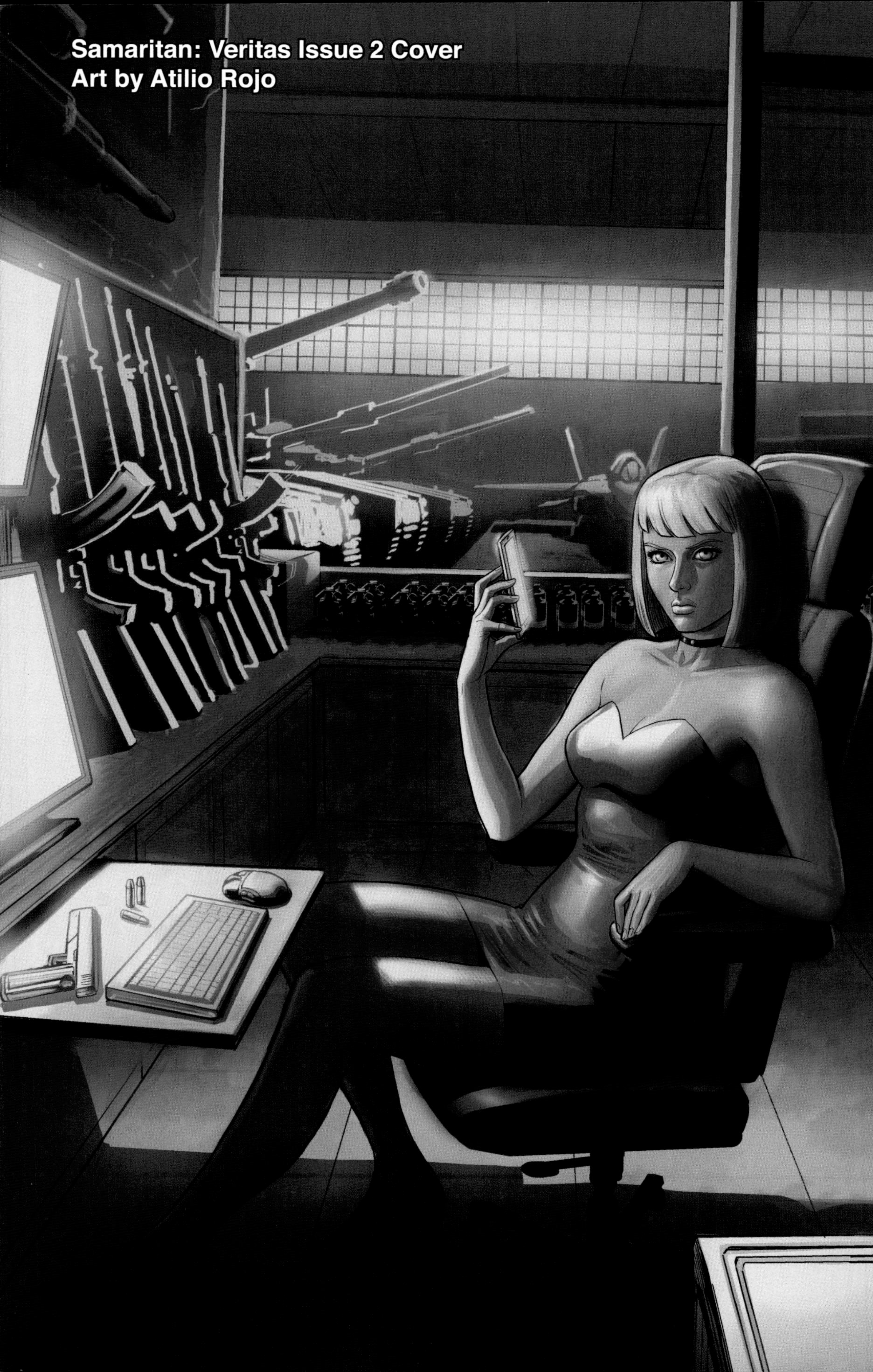

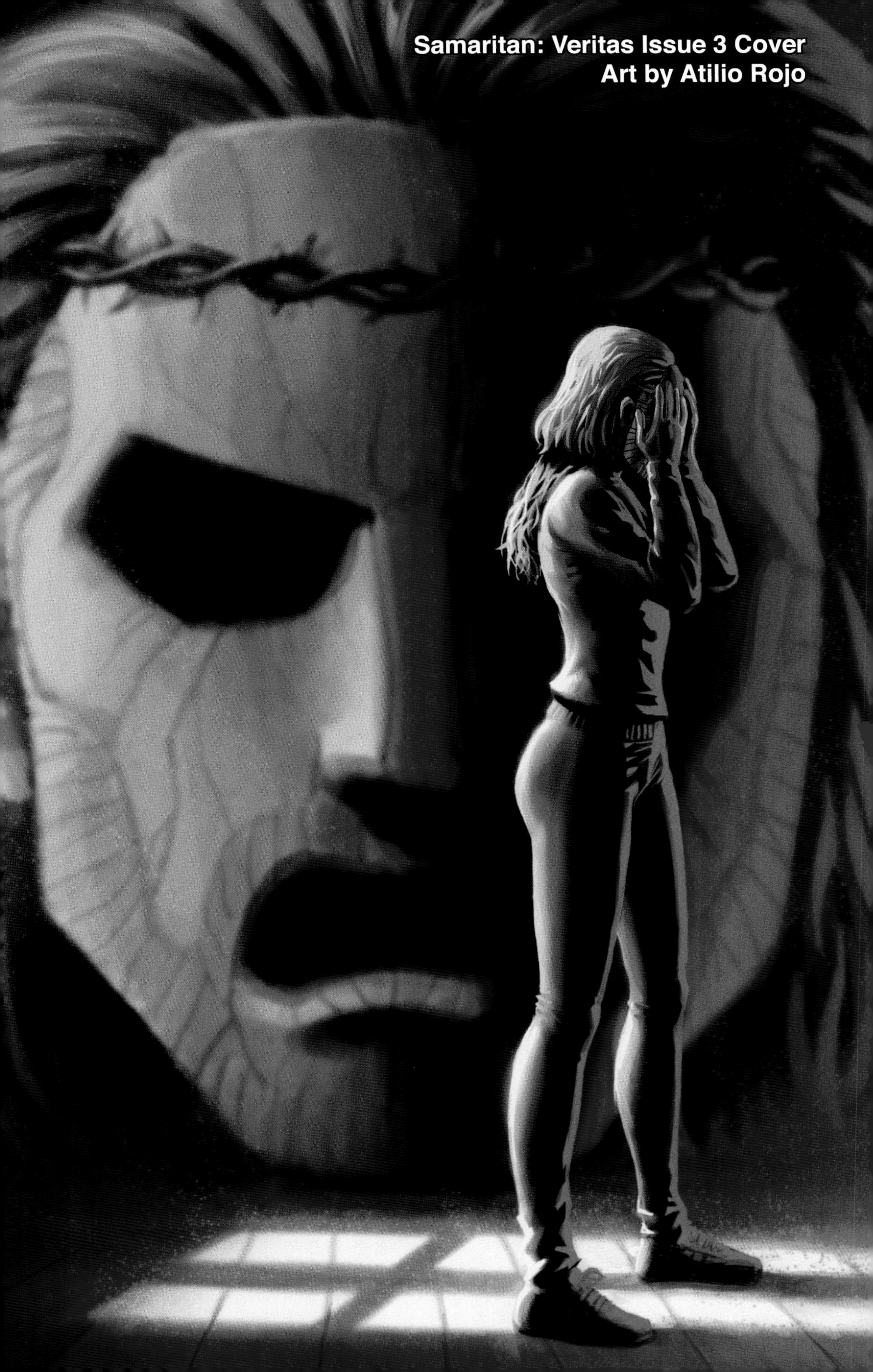

Samaritan: Veritas Issue 3 Cover
Art by Atilio Rojo

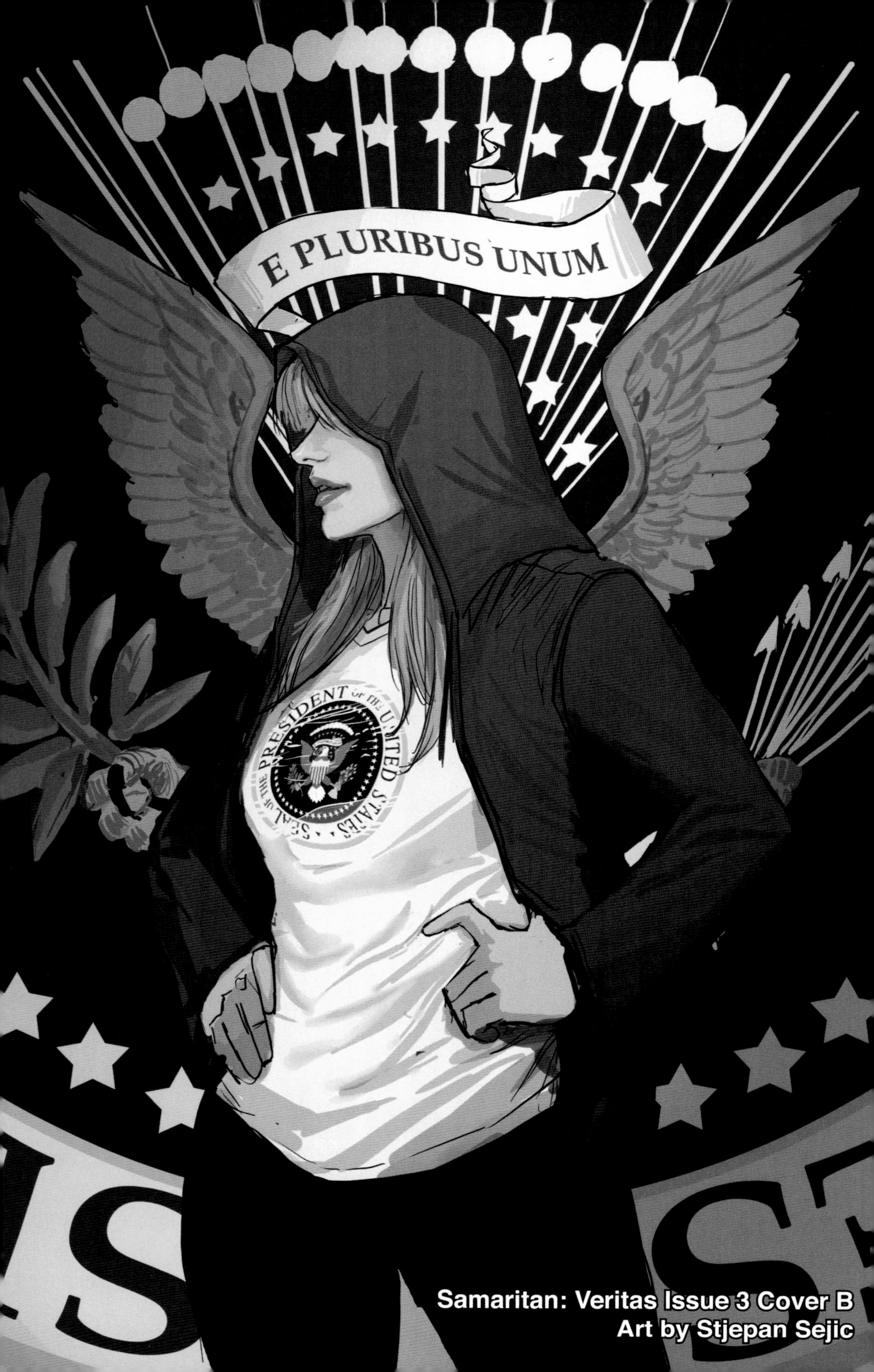
E PLURIBUS UNUM
SEAL OF THE PRESIDENT OF THE UNITED STATES

Samaritan: Veritas Issue 3 Cover B
Art by Stjepan Sejic

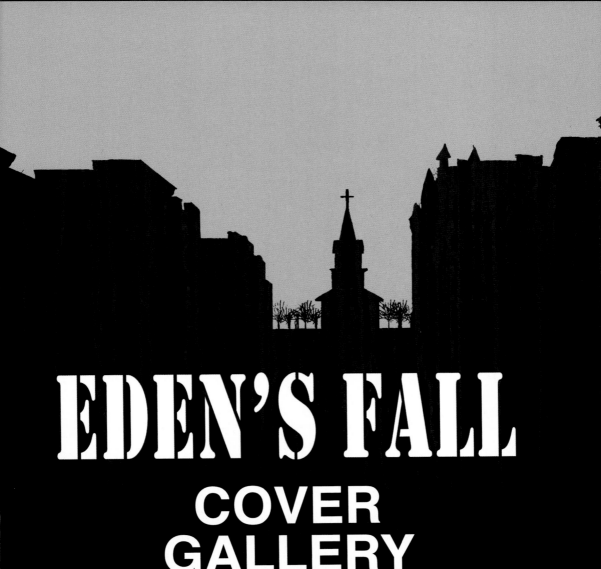

EDEN'S FALL
COVER
GALLERY

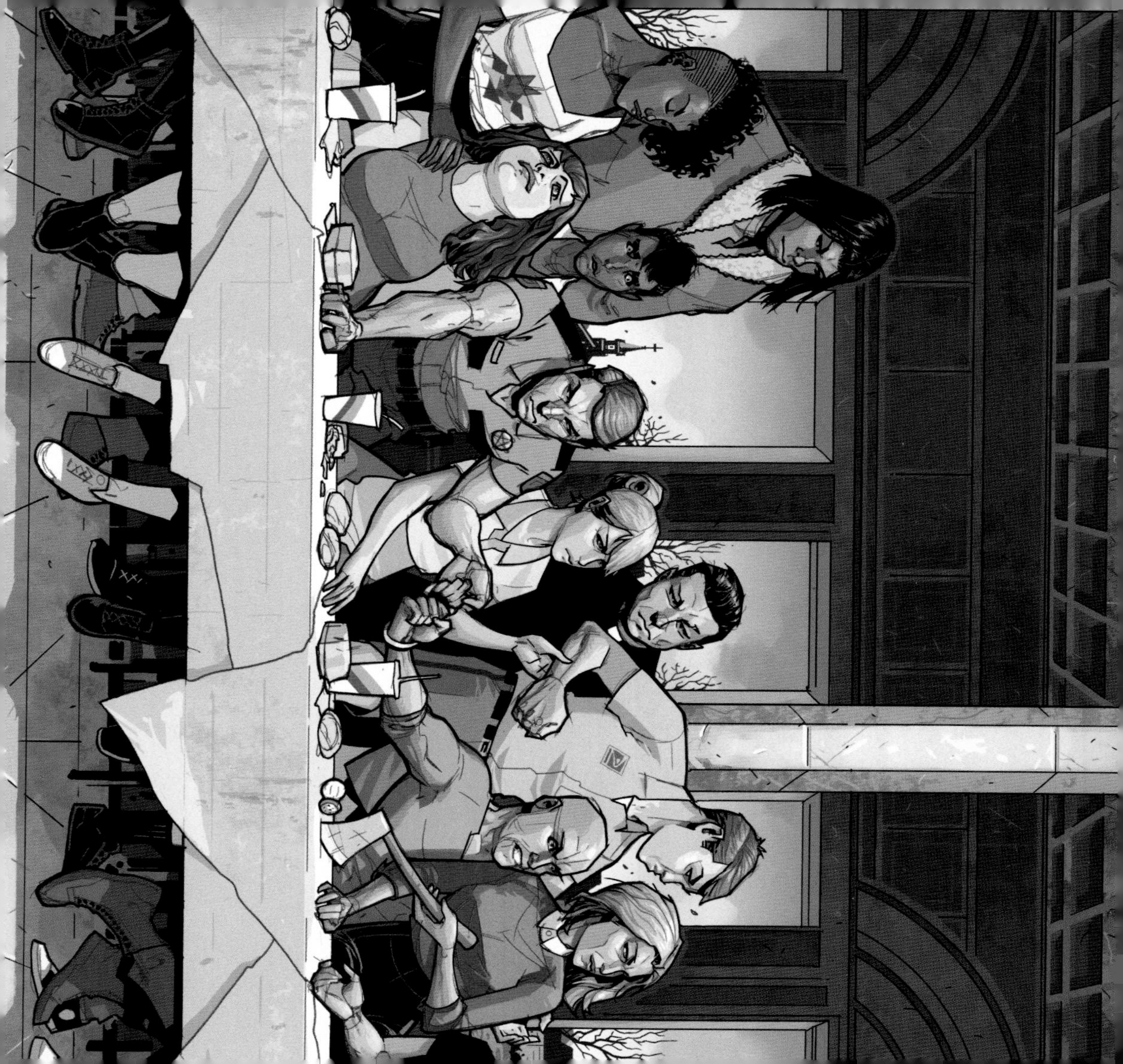

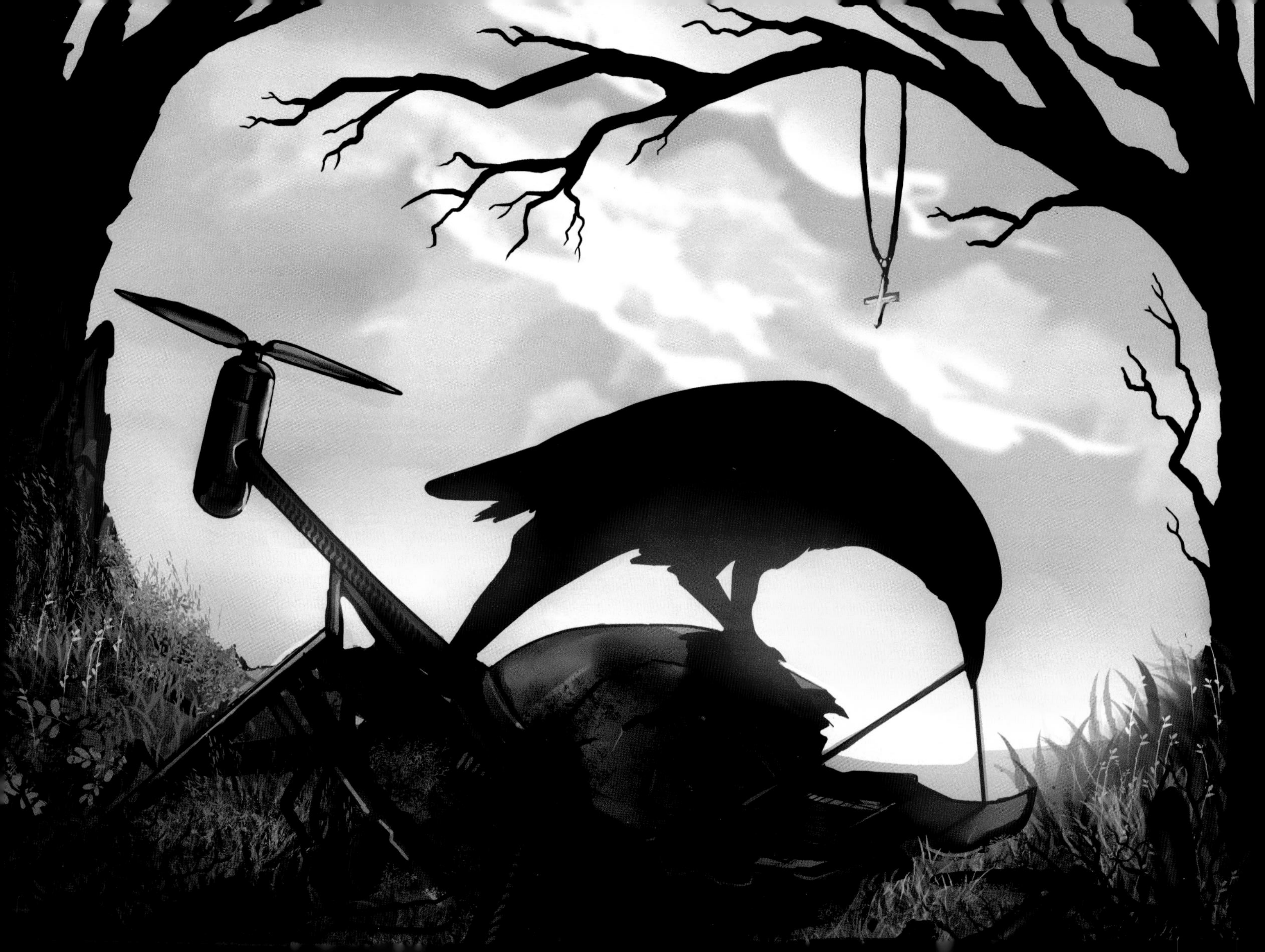

Eden's Fall
Issue 1
Wraparound
Cover B
Art by

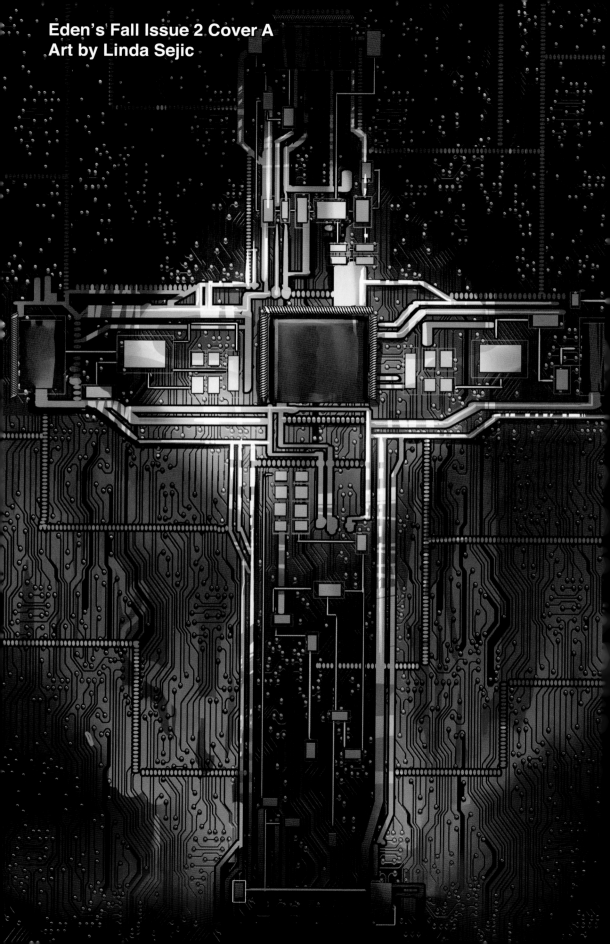

Eden's Fall Issue 2 Cover A
Art by Linda Sejic

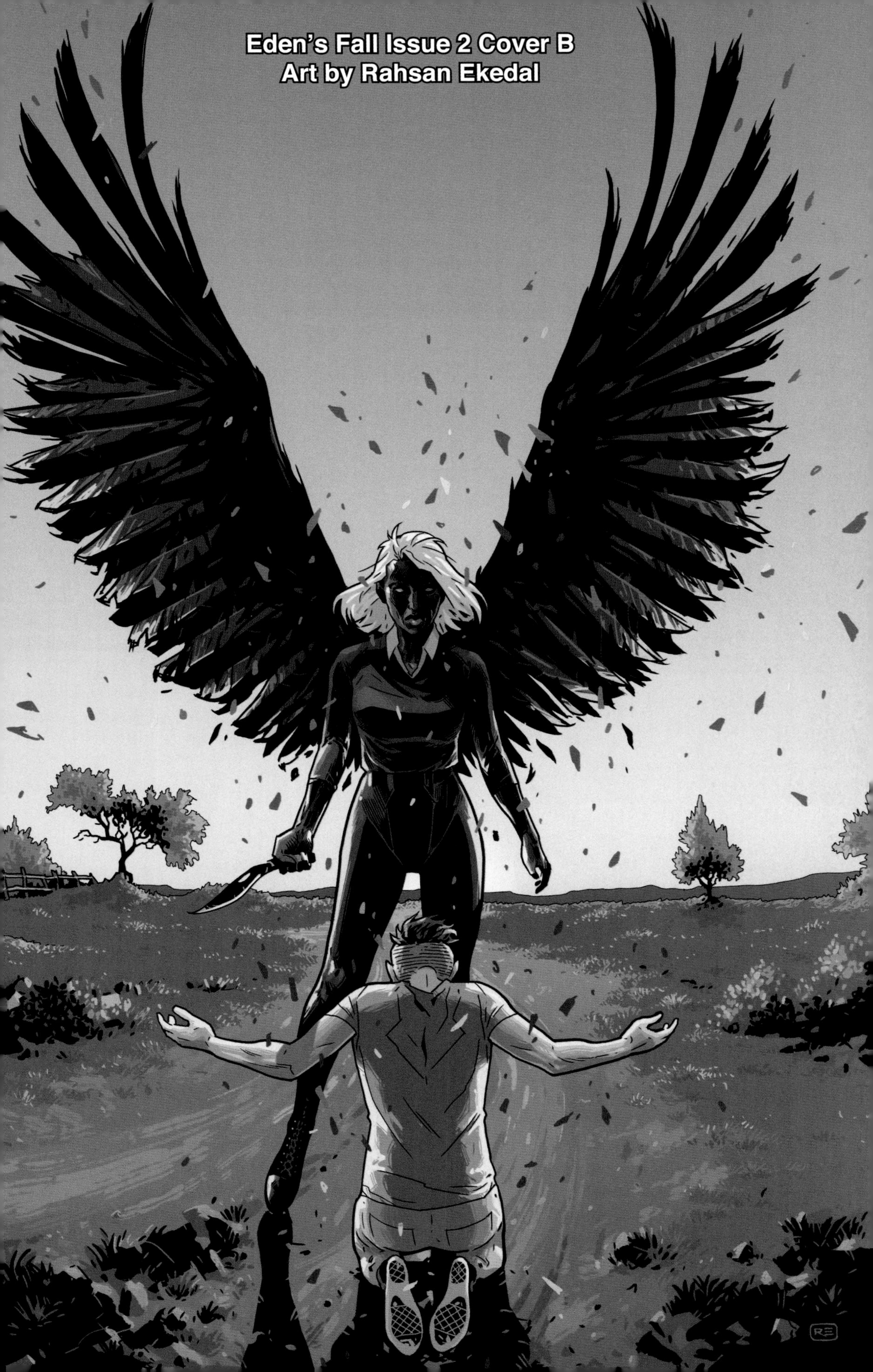

Eden’s Fall Issue 2 Cover B
Art by Rahsan Ekedal

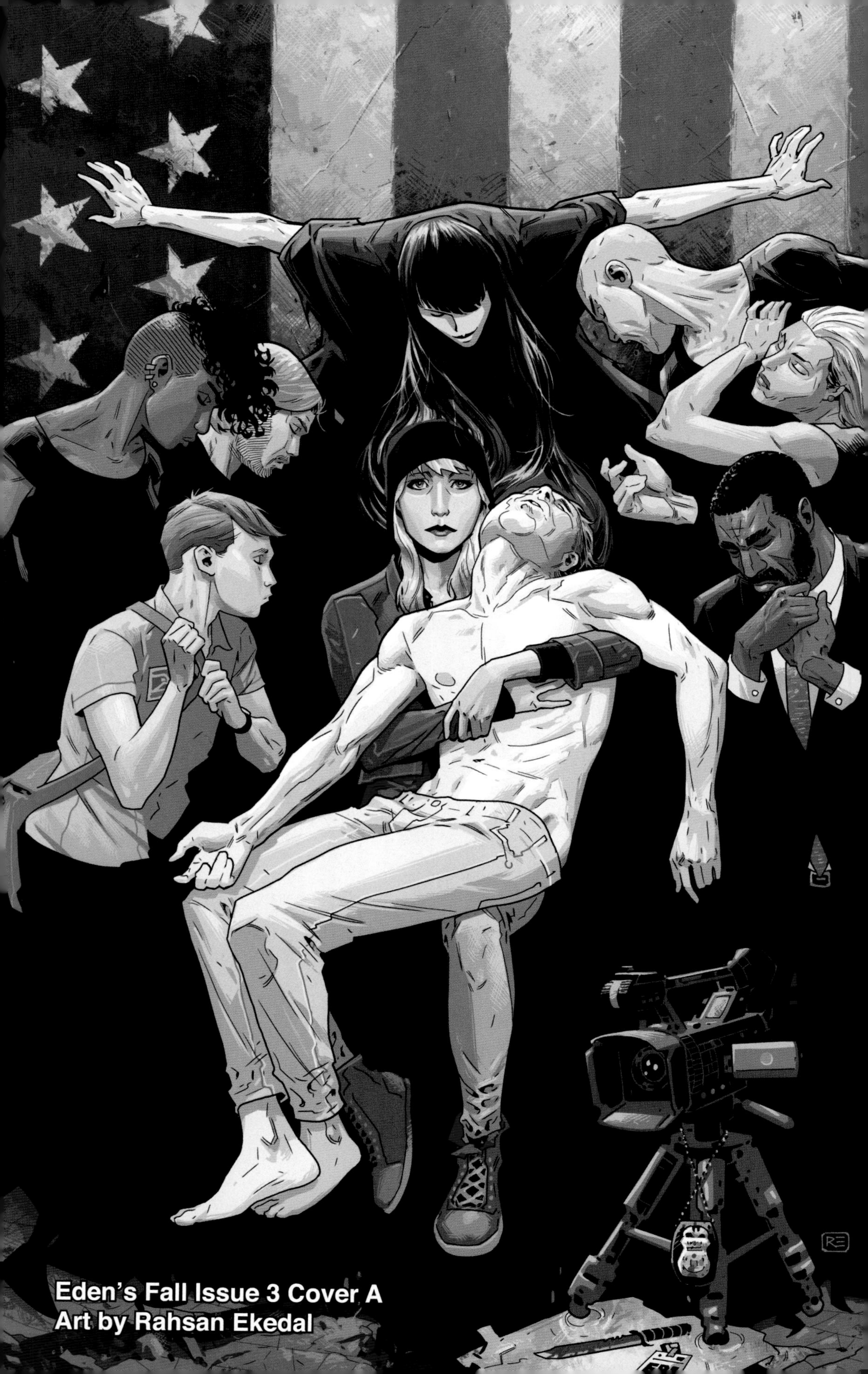

Eden's Fall Issue 3 Cover A
Art by Rahsan Ekedal

Eden's Fall Issue 3 Cover B
Art by Linda Sejic

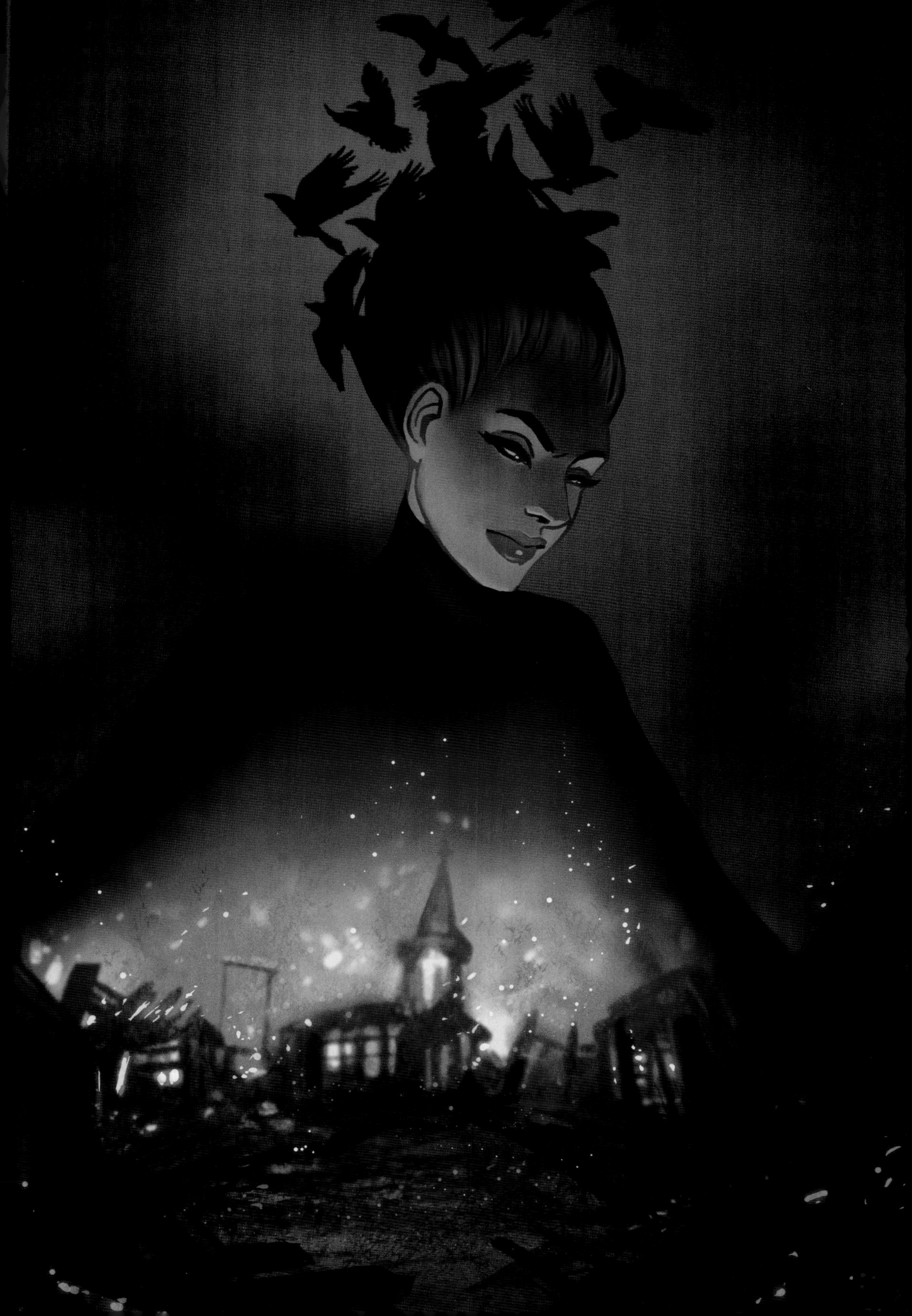

SUNDAY SCHOOL

Howdy! Thanks for picking up and reading this book. If you enjoyed it, please recommend it to your friends and talk it up on your social media. Publishing origina ideas is tough, especially in this crowded publishing world. There are roughly 2,00 comic books and 200 trade paperbacks coming out every month. Nothing sells better than word of mouth so anything you can do is appreciated.

I've include a lot of links below, if you want to click on them to check it out without having to type them in you can go to http://matttalks.com/ I post this backup article there the same day the book releases into stores. I'm an atheist but I try to be respectful of people's beliefs, so if I say something that offends you, apologies!

If this is the first time you've read an Edenverse title, there are other books you can read. They're listed below and in order. You don't have to read them to get this series, but they'd certainly flesh out the world and tell other stories you might like.

SEASON 1

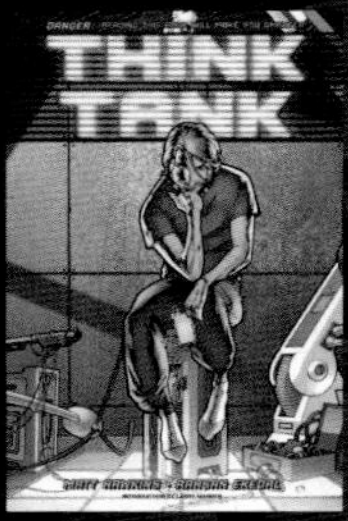
THINK TANK
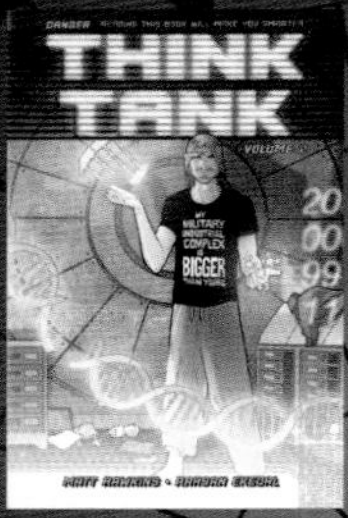
THINK TANK
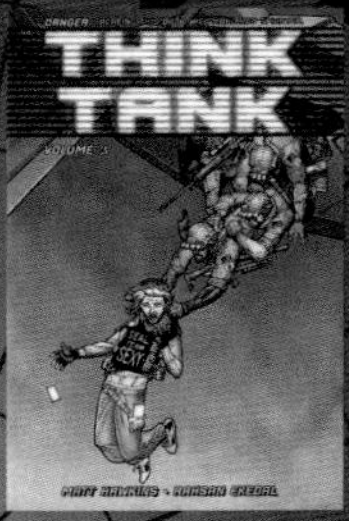
THINK TANK
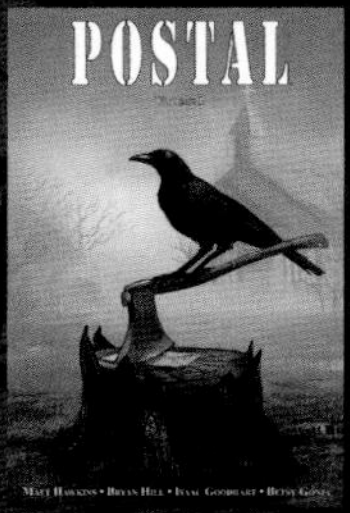
POSTAL
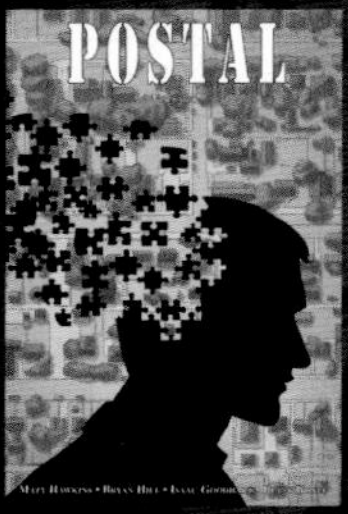
POSTAL
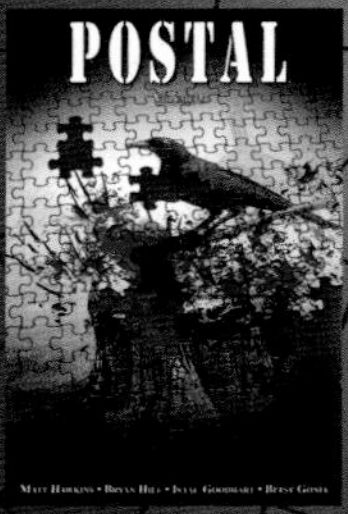
POSTAL
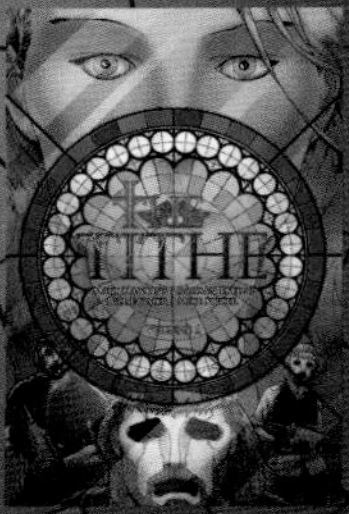
TITHE
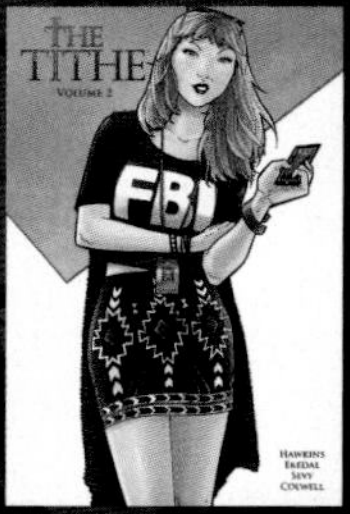
THE TITHE

SEASON 2

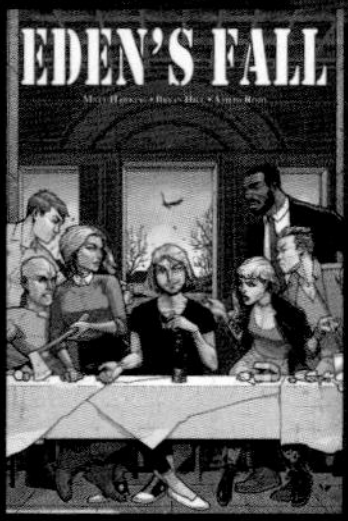
EDEN'S FALL
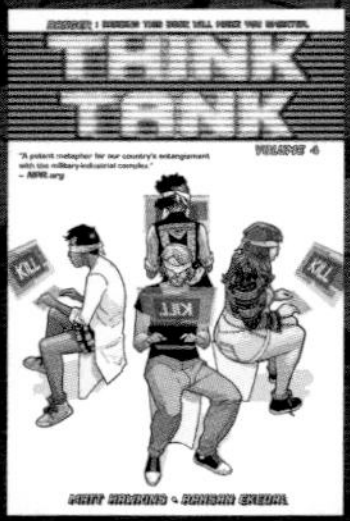
THINK TANK
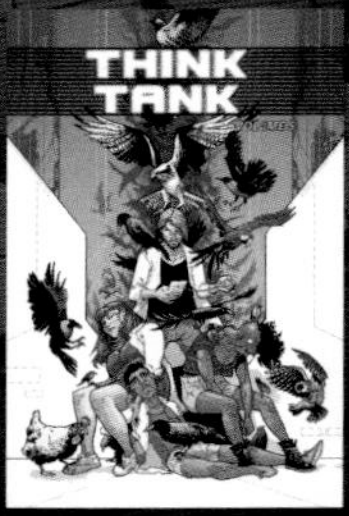
THINK TANK
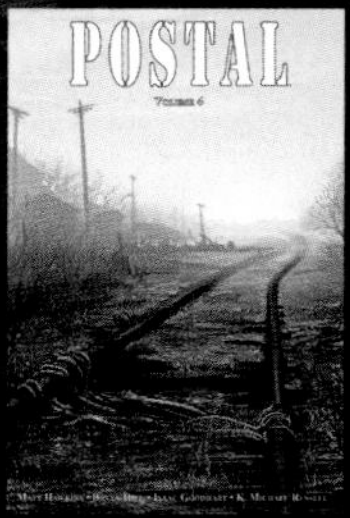
POSTAL

SEASON 3

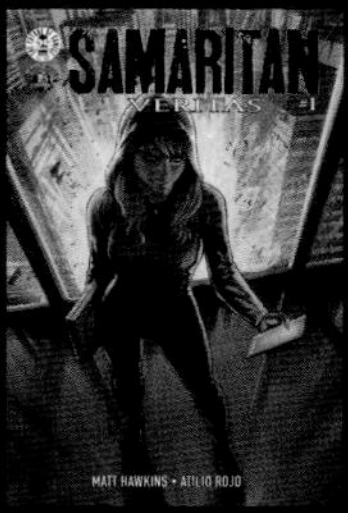
SAMARITAN
VERITAS
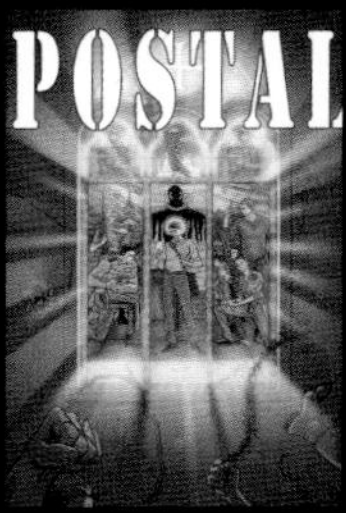
POSTAL

in the Bible verses attributed to Jesus
dence Jesus really said this. The basic
but loving ones neighbor, it's meant to b
be considered a neighbor. The Jews a
Good Samaritan" showed how people
passionate.

6/the-origin-of-the-good-samaritan-parable-

blogs/christiancrier/2014/04/21/parable-of-th
ommentary/

amantha as a modern day Robin Hood,
myth as well. The first clear reference to
bem *Piers Plowman*. The idea of someo
e poor is as timeless as income inequal

opics/british-history/robin-hood
viki/Robin_Hood

CUBE
e one. They're fun. You can buy one for

e Darknet, which you can access from a
an't access it from regular browsers. Be c
ople off there you're likely to regret it. Yo
u can imagine there, but they have a pret
 jump through to earn trust. If you want to
ping there, these Reddit forums give you

ACKING

Vhat is hacking? Merriam-Webster's most recent definitic legally gains access to and sometimes tampers with info ystem." This is such a broad category now encompassin nings that it's hard to discuss quickly. If you want to learn heck the first link. The third link there breaks down the di

http://www.catb.org/esr/faqs/hacker-howto.html

https://www.technologyreview.com/s/603045/mr-robot-killed-t

https://www.cybrary.it/0p3n/types-of-hackers/

ENRE REFERENCES

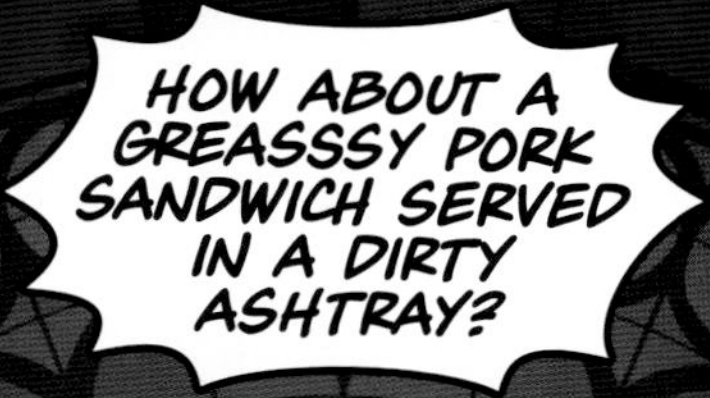
HOW ABOUT A GREASSSY PORK SANDWICH SERVED IN A DIRTY ASHTRAY?

his is from *Weird Science* by the character *Chet* played b *axton (RIP).*

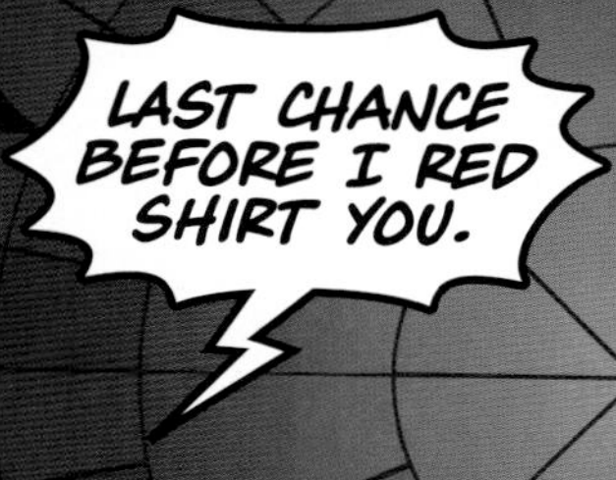
LAST CHANCE BEFORE I RED SHIRT YOU.

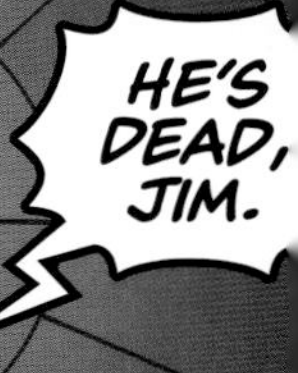
HE'S DEAD, JIM.

om the original *Star Trek* TV series of course.

)*bert.exe"

homage to the Atari video game.

on't call the leader Hannibal though; he's had enoug kes."

is one seems obvious =)

ESTLEY = *Princess Bride*
CARD = *Star Trek TNG*
PLEY = *Alien*
NDO = *Empire Strikes Back*
CKARD = *Blade Runner*
TSUO = *Akira*

ISSOURI SENATOR AS BAD GUY

o my parents are from Wichita, Kansas and I lived in Warrensburg, Missouri for our years while my dad was at Whiteman AFB, so I don't really have anything gainst Missouri. Although I was amused at how some of my friends there would ronounce it "Mizz--urrr--rah", others like "misery"…I guess depending on how they elt! I needed a place for a religious ideologue to come from and since I'd lived ere I chose it. =p

---

fter The Tithe V2 was released I got my first real death threat. It was a sobering noment and did actually scare me a bit. I reported it to the police and increased ny vigilance. As a public person who uses social media and does many public ppearances that are posted in advance, it's going to be fairly easy to take me out someone really wanted to. Ultimately I upped my life insurance to make sure my vife and kids would be taken care of and moved on with my life. I'll be damned if ome religious ideologue is going to censor me with fear.

respect your religion as long as you don't try to force it down my throat or it nakes you want to kill me for not believing it. As an atheist, all religions tend to get umped together in your mind as wishful thinking. Dwayne Campbell is a Christian nd a good advocate for Christianity both in word and deed. I've had to sideline nat for the most part during this story arc because it's not really about that, but nat'll be front and center next arc.

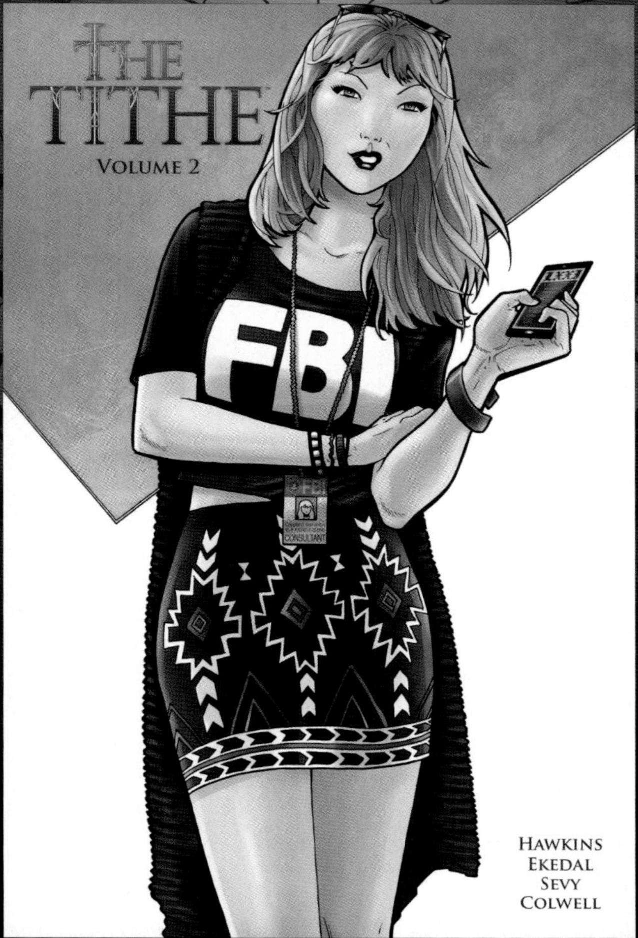
THE TITHE
VOLUME 2
FBI
FBI
CONSULTANT
HAWKINS
EKEDAL
SEVY
COLWELL

TELEVANGELISTS

The Christian televangelists that were kidnapped are secondary to this story and I included it primarily as a nod to the first arc of *The Tithe* where Samaritan first appeared. I am well aware that the vast majority of Christians and their pastors are good people. It makes the bad ones in their midst stand out as even more egregious than they probably even are. There are plenty of snake oil salesmen and businessmen trying to rip people off, but when you cloak it under the guise of religion I find it particularly deplorable. It becomes even more despicable when they convince fixed-income, semi-dementia-addled elderly to give money they can't afford to. The first link has the worst schemes of all time. The Youtube link is John Oliver skewering televangelists and worth a watch.

» http://dustoffthebible.com/Blog-archive/2012/07/25/the-worst-tbn-product-scams-of-all-time/

» http://gawker.com/making-money-off-miracles-the-gospel-of-televangelists-1725330875

» https://www.youtube.com/watch?v=7y1xJAVZxXg

» https://www.youtube.com/watch?v=8dfor8BqFFk

FALLS CHURCH, VIRGINIA

I picked here because it's in the greater Washington D.C. area and where most of the headquarters for the military industrial complex companies are located. They keep them here for tax reasons and to keep their heavy hitters near D.C. for lobbying purposes.

NORTHLOCK INDUSTRIES

This company first appeared in *Think Tank* Volume 4 and I intended it as a mash up of several different real companies with a slightly more evil twist for dramatic effect.

RARE EARTH METALS

This is based on reality. China does dominate this industry. These metals are used in the ubiquity that has become modern electronics. China has dominated this industry for a long time, partially because of the abundance of these elements appearing naturally inside their borders, but also because they're dangerous to extract and China has fewer government regulations.

Definition (from link):

"Rare earth elements are a group of seventeen chemical elements that occur together in the periodic table. The group consists of yttrium and the 15 lanthanide elements (lanthanum, cerium, praseodymium, neodymium, promethium, samariun europium, gadolinium, terbium, dysprosium, holmium, erbium, thulium, ytterbium, and lutetium). Scandium is found in most rare earth element deposits and is sometimes classified as a rare earth element. The International Union of Pure and Applied Chemistry includes scandium in their rare earth element definition.

The rare earth elements are all metals, and the group is often referred to as the 'rare earth metals.' These metals have many similar properties, and that often causes them to be found together in geologic deposits. They are also referred to a 'rare earth oxides' because many of them are typically sold as oxide compounds."

» http://geology.com/articles/rare-earth-elements/

» http://www.prnewswire.com/news-releases/china-rare-earth-industry-report-2017-2021---research-and-markets-300467141.html

» http://www.mining-technology.com/features/featurethe-false-monopoly-china-and-the-rare-earths-trade-4646712/

» http://www.bbc.com/news/world-17357863

PRIVATE CONTRACTING AND SECURITY

It's very common for retired military to go into private security and mercenary contracting. Governments and private corporations hire them all the time. They aren't bound by the same restrictions as many formal military forces so using them skirts the law a bit. Erik Prince's Blackwater is the most notorious for a variety of reasons, but mainly because of the profile. It's now called Academi and a separate group snagged the Blackwater Protection name (both linked below).

http://www.globalresearch.ca/the-privatization-of-war-mercenaries-private-military-and-security-companies-pmsc/21826

https://www.academi.com/

https://blackwaterprotection.com/

ELECTRONIC SWEEPING

In the first issue I used SIGINT 972-A as a means to track Samantha even though she'd taken precautions to have her phone traced to Seattle. SIGINT is an actual term used, it stands for signals intelligence. It's defined as the interception of signals, whether communications between people or from electronic signals not directly used in communication. There are many SIGINTs listed online, most of these are either declassified or were revealed by Wikileaks of Edward Snowden. SIGNINT 972-A I made up, but only after researching whether it was plausible. It might be real, it might be near-term tech, who knows? The concept of this is that if you're using a device, you broadcast a separate signal from that device which connects with every other device in the immediate area. Those devices then give their location, which would allow a triangulation of where the actual device was... regardless of where it's telling you it's at.

https://www.nsa.gov/what-we-do/signals-intelligence/

https://www.cia.gov/news-information/featured-story-archive/2010-featured-story-archive/intelligence-signals-intelligence-1.html

https://journals.law.stanford.edu/stanford-law-policy-review/print/volume-22/issue-1-defense-policy/electronic-surveillance-era-modern-technology-and-evolving

EDWARD SNOWDEN FILES

Everyone should know who he is now, he's the computer programmer who worked for the NSA who leaked documents about PRISM and other government surveillance programs and tactics that were all outside the bounds of what was allowed by U.S. and international law. I have mixed feelings about what he did. Is he a traitor or a heroic whistleblower...or both? The documents he released are here:

http://www.cjfe.org/snowden

SMITHSONIAN MUSEUM

This is a real place and I love it so! Have not been there since I was a kid, but looking forward to going back and spending some real time there. It was founded by British Scientist James Smithson (1765-1829) and was passed down to U.S. government control in 1836.

» https://www.si.edu/museums

BIOMETRIC QUANTUM CRYPTOGRAPHY

"Quantum cryptography uses our current knowledge of physics to develop a cryptosystem that is not able to be defeated — that is, one that is completely secure against being compromised without knowledge of the sender or the receiver of the messages. The word quantum itself refers to the most fundamental behavior of the smallest particles of matter and energy: quantum theory explains everything that exists and nothing can be in violation of it." That's how one security firm described it which turned out not to be true. Security firms have been adding biometrics (retina scans, etc.) combined with quantum crypto to make it harder to combat. The reality is this is an ongoing battle and they're going to always need to improve security to stay one step ahead of the hackers...many of whom are sponsored by governments.

> https://www.researchgate.net/publication/286680772_Quantum_Cryptography_Based_Biometric_Encryption_for_Network_Security
> https://www.technologyreview.com/s/604266/quantum-biometrics-exploits-the-human-eyes-ability-to-detect-single-photons/
> http://www.wiley.com/WileyCDA/WileyTitle/productCd-0470193395,subjectCd-CSH0.html
> http://www.popsci.com/g00/what-is-quantum-cryptography?i10c.referrer=https%3A%2F%2Fwww.google.com%2F

C.I.A. AND F.B.I. SEPARATION

So there's a myth that the C.I.A. can't operate on U.S. soil and F.B.I. can't operate outside of it. I've discovered that neither of those is true. The C.I.A. can pursue foreign intelligence matters inside U.S. boundaries and the F.B.I. can investigate leads in its cases in other countries as well. They have certain jurisdictional limitations, but they both operate worldwide. There are multiple C.I.A. offices inside the U.S.A.

> https://www.quora.com/What-are-the-rules-on-the-CIA-operating-within-the-borders-of-the-United-States
> https://www.fbi.gov/about/faqs
> https://www.cia.gov/about-cia/faqs

LIVES OF RICH SO DIFFERENT

Working in entertainment, I get to meet a lot of rich people. There are super rich people that like my work and will chat with me about stuff and I've been invited to events, barbeques, etc. This past Memorial Day I went to an event barbeque hosted by a Fortune 500 CEO and was surrounded by these so-called elites. The vast majority of these are rich through inheritance. I have no respect for dynastic wealth. I do, however, respect entrepreneurs. The biggest difference between the rich and poor is obviously lifestyle, but little things like borders and laws seem to not apply to them either. I had one very wealthy man tell me that the only reason rich people go to jail is because they "messed with" other rich people that decided to gang up and take them down. I don't know the truth of that, but it's interesting for story. Check both of these links they go into detail on how rich people's lives are different from ours. And, to be clear, I am not rich. People seem to think I am but I am not. I'm a working stiff just like most people.

> http://www.npr.org/2016/10/25/499213698/whats-it-like-to-be-rich-ask-the-people-who-manage-billionaires-money
> http://www.huffingtonpost.com/george-heymont/the-rich-live-are-differe_b_1868050.htm

OTD

https://www.fbi.gov/services/operational-technology

TRANQUILIZER DARTS

Do tranquilizer darts have the instant knockout effect we see in film? Turns out they don't. They're quick, but not instant. A person hit by a tranq dart would have the ability to pull out a gun and shoot the other person before knocking out.

https://www.reddit.com/r/explainlikeimfive/comments/1zzt5a/eli5_do_tranquilizer_darts_really_take_instant/

http://www.scienceclarified.com/Ti-Vi/Tranquilizer.html

SUGAR BABIES

So Lawton at the end has arrangements with women. This is more common than you think. There are dating websites specifically for these types of arrangements. I know two men personally who have arrangements like this. It's become so common that I've actually created a story called *Sugar* by Yishan Li and myself about this specific phenomenon. It's a slice of life book in the vein of *Sunstone*.

https://www.seekingarrangement.com/

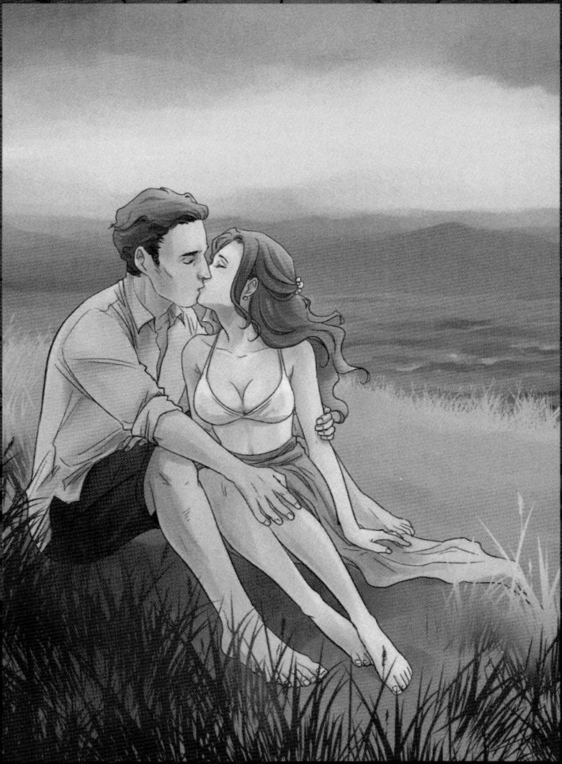

EA-18G Growler is real: http://www.boeing.com/defense/ea-18g-growler/

Scopolamine is real: http://www.businessinsider.com/is-there-such-a-thing-as-truth-serum-2014-10

Radiological inspections: https://www.epa.gov/radiation/radiological-emergency-response

Facial recognition: https://www.theatlantic.com/technology/archive/2015/07/how-good-facial-recognition-technology-government-regulation/397289/

DDoS attack: http://www.digitalattackmap.com/understanding-ddos/

MATT HAWKINS

Twitter: @topcowmatt | http://www.facebook.com/selfloathingnarcissi

A veteran of the initial Image Comics launch, Matt started his career in comic book publishing in 1993 and has been working with Image as a creator, writer and executive for over 20 years. President/COO of Top Cow since 1998, Matt has created and written over 30 new franchises fc Top Cow and Image including *Think Tank*, *The Tithe*, *Necromancer*, *VICE*, *Lady Pendragon*, *Aphrodite IX*, and *Tales of Honor*, as well as handling the company's business affairs.

ATILIO ROJO

http://www.facebook.com/atilio.rojo.52

Atilio Rojo has been writing and drawing erotic comics since 2002. Rojo is best known for his work on *Transformers*, *G.I. Joe*, *Snake Eyes*, *Dungeon and Dragons*, *LOD*, *IXth Generation*, and *Eden's Fall*. He's currently working on *Samaritan: Veritas* (*The Tithe*) for Top Cow Productions.